The Paris Edge

Also by E. Howard Hunt

Undercover: Memoirs of an American Secret Agent

The Berlin Ending

The Hargrave Deception

The Kremlin Conspiracy

The Gaza Intercept

Cozumel

The Dublin Affair

Murder in State

Guadalajara

The Sankov Confession

Evil Time

Body Count

Chinese Red

Mazatlán

Ixtapa

Islamorada

The Paris Edge

E. Howard Hunt

St. Martin's Press
New York

This book is for Nancy Arnold
In memory of Rome

Production Editor: David Stanford Burr
Design by Sara Stemen

LIBRARY OF CONGRESS CATALOGING-IN-PUBLICATION DATA

Hunt, E. Howard (Everette Howard).
    The Paris edge / E. Howard Hunt.
       p. cm.
    "A Thomas Dunne book."
    ISBN 0-312-13138-0
    I. Title.
PS3515.U5425P37   1995
813'.54—dc20   95-14721
                            CIP

First Edition: August 1995

10 9 8 7 6 5 4 3 2 1

After Paris nothing is ever the same.
—BRADLEY MASON

Book One

one

The Ruse

Marking the western edge of metropolitan Paris, the Bois de Boulogne is an immense forest of more than two thousand acres. Along its northeast border runs Boulevard de l'Amiral Bruix whose expensive residences and apartment buildings face the forest's greenery. The zone is one of conspicuous affluence, inhabited by financiers, high government officials, foreign executives, and senior diplomats. One three-story mansion surrounded by a high wall is the residence of the ambassador of Syria. Hafik al-Jamal.

At eight o'clock this fine spring morning a light gray commercial van is parked along the boulevard a hundred feet or so from the mansion's motor entrance. The van's sides are lettered BOULANGERIE CHRISTOPHE; inside are three men. Waiting.

The van has been there less than ten minutes, its crew knowing from surveillance that within a three-minute margin the motor gate will be opened by armed guards, allowing the ambassadorial Rolls-Royce to glide through and turn south toward Porte Dauphine.

According to weekday routine the Rolls is driven by an armed chauffeur. One passenger, an armed guard charged with protecting the other passenger seated beside him, the ambassador's eight-year-old son, Rashid, during the eleven-minute ride to the boy's school: l'École de Saint-Jacques, a venerable gray-faced building by the Invalides

Through the van's tinted glass a man with binoculars focused on the closed gate. Of Corsican extraction, he was a veteran of the

Foreign Legion and had the scars to prove it. Beside him the driver said, "Nothing, René?"

"Nothing yet."

The driver was a short, bull-necked French-Algerian, who had fought De Gaulle's *paras* for the Armée Secrète. Betrayed and court-martialed, he had served five years hard time in military prisons before being cast out among the thousands of other uprooted *pieds-noirs* in metropolitan France. For two years he had been a mercenary soldier in South Africa, a year as a demolitions instructor in Israel, then a Montmartre nightclub bouncer. Over the years he had changed names as he had changed addresses. For the past six months he called himself Raoul, explaining with a thin smile that it was the name of a detested pimp he had fought and killed in a Montmartre alley.

As Raoul he had come under the patronage of the van's third man, a tall, well-built American known as Mace.

"Three minutes," Mace said in a hard voice. "Damn."

"Maybe the kid's sick," René suggested.

"Shouldn't be. Had his tonsils out five weeks ago. Supposed to be healthy."

"With kids," Raoul muttered, "you can never tell."

"They're unpredictable," Mace agreed and lapsed into silence. He had a daughter somewhere, living with her mother and stepfather on some army post in ZI. It was no good to think about them and reassemble, in imagination, the rough shards of his life into a pleasing picture of normal family life. All that was gone beyond recall. He shifted on the seat and felt the 9mm Beretta move against his belly.

"Now," René said quietly. "It's happening."

The heavy iron-shod doors were opening outward, each moved by a guard with a submachine gun over one shoulder. Through the opening came the shiny black Rolls. It turned south and as it passed the van they could see driver, guard, and small passenger. Twin fender flags barred red, white, and black, two green stars across the white. The ambassador's official limo. "Go," Mace ordered, and the van pulled away from curbside.

With two cars separating it from the Rolls the van trailed in desultory traffic until just beyond the Russian Embassy, then the Rolls swung left onto Avenue Henri-Martin and continued east toward the Passy cemetery. Nearing the next intersection the Rolls slowed for a stoplight and a woman came off the curb, hurrying to cross the street. The Rolls driver tried to avoid her, but the car's right fender struck and lifted her partway across the hood, where she lay momentarily then slid down to the street. The Rolls driver got out quickly and knelt beside the woman. The van had braked and all three men were out. Raoul slapped the driver's head with a weighted spring-steel sap, collapsing him beside the prone woman. René jerked open the Rolls' rear door and sprayed pepper gas across the guard's face. Mace opened the other door and tugged out the boy, who was wild-eyed and starting to whimper. "Sorry about this," Mace said, and clamped a chloroform-soaked pad over the boy's nose and mouth. The boy struggled briefly then went limp. Mace gathered him up and carried him into the van. Through the doorway Mace could see René sap the suffering guard, while Raoul ripped out cellular phone wires, and tossed away ignition keys. Then Raoul was behind the van wheel and René on the seat beside him. Mace shut the van's door as it pulled out and around the Rolls to merge with morning traffic.

The boy, Rashid, was lying unconscious on a bedroll, pillow under his head. The woman opened his eyelids and said, "He'll be fine." Then, pulling up her skirt, she removed rolls of heavy padding from hips and thighs and took a seat beside Mace. "How did I look?" she asked.

"Convincing—or they wouldn't have stopped."

"I thought you guys would never come," she complained.

"Oh? From impact to getaway forty-eight seconds," Mace said with a touch of pride. He'd allowed a full minute for the action.

Turning his head, René said, "I hate those Arab bastards. Took a lot of willpower not to kill."

"Kidnapping's one thing, murder's another," Mace replied reprovingly. "The guillotine stays active, and things will be hot enough as it is. Son of an Arab ambassador kidnapped—" He shook his head.

The woman applied makeup with compact and mirror. "Where will you keep him, Mace?"

"C'mon, Yasmi, you know better than to ask. What you don't

know can't be pried out of you. Anyway, you're out of it now. Rest up and I'll see you at the office tomorrow."

"Take care, all of you. I don't want to see your faces on TV tonight."

The van was nearing the Palais de Chaillot. It stopped long enough at the Trocadéro Métro entrance for Yasmi to get out and vanish in the crowd. Then the van continued along the Seine, crossing by the Pont d'Iéna, passing the École Militaire and losing possible pursuers deep in the Left Bank.

Another ten minutes and the van pulled into a scruffy-looking garage whose doors closed behind it. The boy's eyes were open now and they were wide with fear. "Are you Jews?" he asked tremulously. "Israelis?"

"We're friends," Mace told him, "and you're not going to be hurt." Sitting up, Rashid studied his face. "Promise?"

"Promise," he smiled. "In fact, I'll be taking you to someone you haven't seen in a long time."

"Someone?" he asked suspiciously. "What someone?"

"It'll be a surprise. You like surprises, don't you?"

"Sometimes. Like when Papa takes me to the Jardin d'Acclimatation." The children's amusement park in the Bois.

"Then you have to do as I say. Can you follow orders?"

Rashid frowned. "You mean like a soldier?"

Mace nodded. "Silently."

"I understand." The van door opened and they all got out, and into a small white-and-green ambulance standing beside the van. Raoul was pulling plastic letters from the van's sides, then removed the license plates. Within the hour the van would be sprayed black and equipped with new license plates; others would do that.

The boy was still groggy. He lay on one of the litters while Mace sat beside him on a pull-down seat. He was a handsome lad, Mace thought, even better looking than the photos he had seen. Rashid was older now, two years older than his most recent photo. His skin was tawny and his eyes dark brown. Even without the prestige of an ambassador-father he was going to be a killer among the ladies.

As the mini-ambulance backed out of the garage Mace said, "We'll be together for several hours. You've had breakfast?"

"Yes."

"Are you hungry?"

"I can always eat. Like ice cream."

"Ice cream it is."

They had been speaking in French. The boy said something in Arabic and Raoul answered. To Mace Raoul said, "He doesn't want to go back to the residence. I told him not to worry."

Mace nodded agreement. The ambulance reached Boulevard St-Germain and stopped beside an ice-cream vendor. Raoul got out and brought back a pistachio cone. The boy sat up and began eating it delightedly. Two blocks farther on the ambulance stopped again. Raoul climbed back beside the boy while Mace got out. He strolled over to a telephone kiosk and dialed a memorized number. A woman's voice answered. Hesitantly. In English Mace said, "It's done. Everything went down as planned and my young friend is fine. In fact, he seems to be enjoying the change." He stopped while the woman sobbed and felt his own eyes moisten. "Anything on TV?"

"No—no, not yet. Nothing."

"They're figuring how to play it. Maybe nothing will be said publicly, but don't count on it. I won't call again. We'll meet as planned."

"Yes. And—oh, thank you, thank you." Mace broke the connection and returned to the ambulance. For the next hour they drove randomly through the Latin Quarter, finally entering the courtyard of an ancient apartment building through its narrow porte cochere.

Rashid was sitting up now, seemingly at ease with his abductors. He accepted Mace's blindfolding without resistance although he asked, "Where are we going?"

"Where we can relax and rest," Mace replied. "There's still a lot of traveling to do. Trust me."

"I do."

While Mace was guiding the boy up to the second floor the ambulance pulled out of the courtyard. If all went well it would return later.

The apartment was small and rather shabby. The dead air smelled of disuse. The single bedroom had a TV set, another TV in the living room. Mace tuned them to different channels and removed the blindfold. Rashid blinked and looked around. "You live here?"

"Sometimes." Mace locked the hall door and went into the bathroom. From the cabinet he took a bottle of pills and a can of chloroform. When he went back to Rashid the boy was watching a cartoon program. As the wild chase ended Mace tapped Rashid's shoulder. "You're going to have to sleep for a while. Two pills, or the chloroform?"

Rashid's nose wrinkled. "I hate that smell. The pills."

"Coke? Pepsi?"

"Coke," the boy said, and Mace filled a glass from the refrigerator. The boy swallowed the pills without comment and lay back on the bed to watch another cartoon. After a while his eyes closed and Mace checked his breathing: shallow, regular. So far so good. He closed the bedroom door and opened a wall cabinet in the living room. From it he took a police scanner radio and listened to *flic* chatter on the bands. Nothing about the Syrian ambassador or his son. Mace turned down the volume and, half-listening, poured a glass of chilled white wine and sipped while he watched the news channel.

I feel like a damn terrorist, he mused, kidnapping a child, no matter how worthy the cause. Of course, terrorists would have bound and gagged him with tape; he'd be frantic with fear. Instead, he's cooperative even though he can't be sure how all this will end.

Hell, I don't know myself.

In the chair he dozed for an hour, waking when Raoul and René came in with pizza, a big bowl of salad, and a bottle of Sancerre. They ate and drank moodily. Raoul asked, "How's the kid holding up?"

"Peacefully."

"I'll be glad when we make delivery."

René nodded.

Mace said, "Word hasn't gotten out. Yet."

Raoul shrugged.

Mace said, "You don't like the waiting, I don't like the waiting. It had to be a morning snatch because taking him after school would have meant too many witnesses. And his father might have come to collect him."

René grunted. "I don't have a problem with the father. He'd have gone down like the guards."

8

"And we'd have a problem of considerable magnitude, much greater than what we've got." He glanced at the bedroom door, got up and opened it. Rashid was sleeping on his side. Mace muted the TV and closed the door. "So," he said, "we wait."

At dusk Mace roused his men, found Rashid wakeful and blind-folded him again. In the ambulance they listened to the police scanner, heard nothing alarming, but kept it on as the ambulance threaded through choking traffic around the industrial section of Montparnasse. At Porte d'Italie Raoul turned on to the Périphérique, the expressway that circled Paris, heading east then north. Rashid said, "My mouth tastes awful. Have we far to go?"

"Half an hour," Mace took his hand. "Suppose police stop us. What would you do?"

Rashid considered. "What would you want me to do?"

"Agree with whatever I say. Or say nothing."

"Will we be stopped?"

"It's possible."

He twisted off the cap of an Evian bottle and gave it to Rashid. The boy swallowed gratefully. "That's better," he said, then cocked his head to one side. "Will I ever see you again?"

"After tonight? I don't think so. Better for all of us if you forget our faces."

Outside, the sky was nearly dark. Headlights flashed past and tall lightoliers spread their sodium glow along broad stretches of highway. Cars rushed past the ambulance whose speed Raoul carefully kept under the hundred-kmh limit. Then, as they neared the Bagnolet exit Raoul spat *"Merde,"* and began to slow.

Mace crouched facing front and saw a striped barricade manned by two white-helmeted motorcycle cops with white elbow-length gauntlets. To Raoul he said, "Take it easy, just do what they tell you to do." He turned to Rashid, said, "You've got an instant father," and gestured at Raoul. The boy said, "I understand."

Now it was up to the boy. The cops were halting each car briefly, then moving them along. The ambulance crawled, keeping pace with cars ahead, and when one cop held up a gauntleted arm Raoul braked and lowered the window. "What is it, officer?" he asked politely.

Ignoring the question the cop gestured over his partner. "You on an emergency run?"

"Just finished one, heading home now."

"What's in back?"

"A *copain*—and my kid."

From inside Mace opened the rear door. The cop shined his flashlight around the interior, settled on Rashid. The boy blinked and turned from the light, shielding his eyes with one hand.

"Like riding with your dad?"

"When he lets me." The light left Rashid's face. "Okay," the cop said, "close up and get moving."

Conversationally, Raoul said, "Mind if I ask what you're looking for?"

"Yes," the cop replied. "I mind, but what the hell. A man and woman knocked off a jewelry store about five o'clock. We been looking for them the past two hours and it's a crock of shit. Now get the hell outa here." He waved the ambulance on.

As it gathered speed Rashid touched Mace's arm. "How did I do, *copain*?"

"You were perfect."

"Now maybe you'll tell me where we're going, what the surprise is."

Mace breathed deeply. "Le Bourget airport. Your mother is waiting." He put his arms around the boy, who began sobbing while tears of joy coursed down his cheeks.

Raoul turned on his flashers to pass unhindered through the civil aviation gate onto the tarmac. The plane, a long, sleek twin-jet Dassault Falcon was dark as they approached. Raoul turned off all ambulance lights and the jet came alive. The clamshell door unfolded downward until Mace could see a figure in the doorway silhouetted against cabin lights. The woman in slacks and windbreaker came running toward the dark, moving ambulance. "Closer to the plane," Mace ordered. "Block the nose."

Jogging beside the ambulance, the woman wiped tears from her face, and when it stopped she pounded on the door. "He's here?" she begged. "You have my son?"

Mace opened the rear door and stepped out. "He's here," Mace called. "Get in."

Mother and son were hugging and kissing, laughing, crying hysterically. Mace looked at his wristwatch. "Madam, you have what's yours, where is what's mine?"

Her head turned. Dark, swollen eyes, and disheveled hair framed her almond face. Delicate. Very beautiful. He had seen her only twice before. Once in his office when she explained what she wanted done, then at the Relais bar when he named his price.

American by birth, Alaya al-Jamal came from wealthy Scotch-Lebanese parents. Met Hafik when they were students in Lucerne. Rashid born in Damascus . . . Hafik indolent and abusive; administered Assad's terrorist-training program. Refused exit visa for Rashid, expelled wife, and divorced her. Stayed in Damascus until posted to Paris five months ago.

Only a mad fool would divorce Alaya and steal their son, Mace thought, but Hafik had done those things. Now the boy was hers.

"I—I can't thank you enough," she gasped.

"The fee speaks for you."

"Oh—oh, yes. Of course." She kissed Rashid's forehead and stepped down onto the tarmac. Rashid asked, "Can I go with her?"

"In a moment, *copain*." Alaya walked quickly to the jet's doorway and took a briefcase handed to her. Returning, she gave it to Mace. "It's all there—a hundred thousand dollars."

He opened the briefcase, chose a banded deck, and riffled expertly. Fifty hundred-dollar bills. Twenty decks, a hundred large. He closed the briefcase, tossed it into the ambulance. "I've been stiffed before," he explained.

"But I—I wouldn't—not after what you've done . . ." She began sobbing again, clutched Rashid tightly and started away. But her son held back, gave Mace his hand. "Thank you," he said in a small strained voice. "I'll never forget you."

"Try," Mace told him and got into the ambulance as the jet's engines began to whine into life. Raoul called, "Okay to move?"

"Right. And fast."

The ambulance backed off and the jet pivoted around to head for the flight line. He'd positioned the ambulance to block takeoff in case

11

Madam al-Jamal refused payment. But would he have kept the boy? Returned Rashid to his father? I doubt it, he mused, but then I'll never know. And I'm glad of that.

Five thousand each to René, Paul, and Yasmi. Her simulation had been perfect. Professional. And why not? She'd done movie stunt work for years. Until a fractured vertebra warned her to walk away while she could. So she'd studied business law and computers at the University of Paris, answered Mace's ad for skilled, reliable help. Twenty-three young women had applied, but Yasmi outshined them all. Impossible to ignore her language fluency: Arabic, French, English, and Spanish as good as his own. Her mother was Algerian, her father *pied-noir* French. She'd been born in Lyon after Algerian independence, never seen the Algeria her parents so bitterly missed. "I love Paris," she'd told Mace after starting to work for him, "wouldn't dream of living anywhere else." And he'd thought, I love Paris, too, but I'm an outsider, refugee from a different life and glad to be alive.

He passed a money deck to Raoul, another to René. Yasmi would get hers in the morning. Or whenever she came to the office. He hoped the impact hadn't injured her back, bruised flesh, and muscle, but she knew how to protect herself she always claimed.

By prearrangement he left the ambulance at the Place de la République and rode the Métro to the Tuileries. The night was cool and pleasant. Briefcase in hand, he strolled up the Champs-Elysées enjoying the night air, the lights, the constant movement of the city: couples strolling arm in arm, the wafted scents of restaurant kitchens, and the slightly acidic perfume of acacia trees in bud and bloom. In Paris, except for the immigrant quarters, he felt secure as he had never felt in Washington or, say, Managua even after the fighting stopped.

The whores were not out promenading because the city was between seasons. The best of the *poules* were lingering on the Côte d'Azur, in Rio, or B.A. Another few weeks when days and nights were warmer they'd return to service tourist hordes, walk four abreast, arms linked, and clog the boulevard. For now a man could walk unhindered and reflect.

To Alaya al-Jamal he had suggested the pilot file a flight plan to Nice, changing en route to Lisbon. Refuel in Bermuda, then O'Hare.

She'd said she would take Rashid to her family's ranch in Montana. Do you want to know where it is? No, he'd told her, no need for further contact. He hoped their flight would go smoothly.

At Rond Point he stopped at a brasserie for coffee laced with brandy—*fine café*—savored the last drop, and taxied around the Arc de Triomphe and out Avenue de Wagram to the building where he lived. A special key unlocked the side door, another squelched the alarm system before he rode the elevator to the top floor.

Inside, he locked the door and reset the alarm before fatigue hit him. This was the downside of the tension coin, and he fumbled with the safe's combination before getting it right. When it opened he shoved the briefcase inside, then spun the dial, and replaced the panel section. Without undressing, he lay on his bed and felt sleep press down like a heavy blanket. His last thought was that he was now eighty-five thousand dollars richer than he had been that morning when he woke. One more satisfied client.

And tomorrow was another day.

The Girl

Mace gained consciousness aided by a tickling, brushing sensation across his face. He opened his eyes and closed them to avoid the stroking tail of Su-Su, his seal point Siamese. She squatted on his chest, purred, and began making biscuits, her sharp pointed claws penetrating the thin fabric of his shirt. Like roadkill she lay full length on his chest and licked his chin with her raspy tongue. He recognized the delicacy of her tribute but his bladder was full and he had to leave. Gently setting her aside, he received a love bite on his left hand before hurrying to the bathroom.

Unlike many other mornings he wasn't hungover. He splashed cold water on his face and stared at the mirror. His features were fully recognizable: strong nose slightly humped from an old break, rectangular face, solid chin, dark brown eyes, and hair that was beginning to silver here and there. Premature for my age, he thought, which at last count was a mere thirty-five. It irritated him that he had slept without undressing, so he stripped and shaved, showered in hot and cold water, rubbed himself dry, and thought briefly of yesterday's events.

So many things could have gone wrong, he reflected, but none of them had, even to the boy's keeping faith when the cop poked in. If Hafik al-Jamal was going to raise hell he'd have done so by now, but Mace wasn't yet ready to deal with the news of the day.

He got into a bathrobe, stepped into thong slippers and headed for the kitchen. The bracing aroma of coffee tantalized his nostrils—the percolator was timed for eight—and after a fast cup to revitalize nerves, he went down the staircase to the floor below.

From the sales agent Mace had learned that both floors were originally independent of each other. The top floor had been occupied by a banker, his wife, and their children; on the floor below lived his mistress. The arrangement was known to the banker's wife who tolerated it like many French wives of that generation. But when the banker died the widow ousted the mistress and connected both floors with the inner stairway. When Mace took possession he made the top floor his living quarters, the lower floor his office.

His crescent-shaped desk was made of walnut and behind it a matching computer console. There was a leather sofa and functional leather chairs from Brazil. Between his desk and Yasmi's smaller one stood an oval conference table of Chinese cherry, with six handcrafted Chinese chairs.

Yasmi's work space contained computer, laser printer, disk storage, and a cellular phone that was compatible with the one in Mace's BMW. From her console Yasmi could access Interpol files at St-Cloud, and those of the French internal security service, the DST. As a personal challenge she had once accessed the NATO system outside Brussels, though Mace made her desist and wipe the disks. But she had made her point.

He crossed a tufted Moroccan rug of geometric designs and disarmed the alarm system beside the entrance door. The door was steel, paneled in wood veneer, and the hall side bore gilt letters reading:

SECOURS S.A.

PROFESSIONAL SERVICE

B. MASON

Nothing more.

The identification was purposely innocuous. Those who sought his services were usually referrals from law firms or transnational corporations that had heard of him by word of mouth. Secours never advertised and Bradley Mason had no business cards. There were no casual drop-ins, and no corporation or law firm knew the full range of his professional service, though it was generally understood that he was available for unconventional assignments—if the price was right.

Over the five years since Mace had established Secours he had been involved in personal protection, counter-terrorism, hostage recovery (Rashid came to mind), counter-industrial espionage, fugitive return, insurance fraud, counter-narcotics investigation, and the recovery of stolen valuables. Among them a Lautrec painting, an early Matisse, and the seventy-five–carat Imperial Emerald brooch nested in diamonds appraised at three million dollars. As intermediary Mace paid the Italian thieves half a million for its return. He could have identified them to Interpol but preferred to pass knowing that silence established him as a man of trust, a businessman, not a policeman. And from the thieves' underworld information flowed. Yasmi recorded it in the heart of her computer system for possible future use.

The paintings on his office walls were not particularly valuable. When Mace found something he liked in the flea market at Clignancourt or among aspiring artists on the Butte de Montmartre, he added to his office hangings, indifferent to the views of critics for he had only himself to please.

He carried coffee to his desk and leaned back to gaze out over the rooftops of Paris. The view took in the ornamental coping of the Arc de Triomphe and the high relief sculptures depicting Austerlitz. Intervening roofs concealed the archway itself and the eternal flame of remembrance.

He heard a key in the door. It opened inward and Yasmi Tourtellot came in, her appearance much changed from the day before.

Her dark hair was drawn back in a French braid, and her petite figure wore a beige linen suit; a chain of faux gold links circled her waist. She had on lip and eye makeup and her cheeks were lightly roughed. *"Bonjour, M'sieu,"* she said cheerfully, locked the door and walked toward her desk.

Mace returned the greeting. "Coffee's ready."

She unslung a shoulder purse. "Thanks, but I stopped at a brasserie for coffee and croissant. How are you?"

"Fine—more importantly, how are you?"

"A few aches, nothing significant." She sat down and looked at him. "Nothing on TV or radio. Heard anything?"

"Not a word. Good, they're keeping it bottled up. By now Hafik must realize the boy's with his mother. Admitting it publicly would lose him a lot of face."

She nodded. "Just what I was thinking. So, everything came off as planned, *hein?*"

"The mother's happy, I got paid, and by now they should be in the States."

"Where the ambassador can't find them?"

"I'm concerned about that," he admitted. "Her family owns a big ranch in the northwest—where she's taking Rashid. But her onetime husband Hafik has to know about it. If he's desperate to get back his son the ranch is a logical place to look for him."

"You told her that, I suppose."

"I did. She said she couldn't think of any other place to go where Rashid would be safe." He shrugged. "Her problem now—we're out of it."

She turned to the message machine. "Checked this yet?"

"No. Take care of it while I get on some clothing."

Su-Su was sleeping on his bed, one brown paw shielding her eyes from daylight. Before dressing, Mace opened the safe and extracted a banded deck from the briefcase—Yasmi's fee. In the kitchen he microwaved a cinnamon roll and had it with orange juice and coffee. Below, he placed the money on Yasmi's desk. She thanked him and put the deck in her purse. "Three messages," she told him. "One from Madame Angelique, saying she had some thoughts for the weekend and please call. One from the Samuelson law firm, and the third from the embassy."

"Not the Syrian?"

"Surely you jest. Yours. Edward Natsos. Said you've met."

"Briefly, a couple of years ago."

"Wants an appointment today. Shall I call him?"

He looked at his watch. Nine-fifteen. "Tell him to come at eleven."

She nodded. "Samuelson Frères?"

"If it's urgent I'll see Jules at four. If not, tomorrow mid-morning."

"And you'll call Madame . . ."

"Personally." Angelique was one of several lady friends he occasionally saw. A young widow, her husband had been an incidental victim of a terrorist attack on Hermès, where he had been shopping

17

for her birthday present. Guillaume De La Tour left his widow an apartment on Avenue Foch, a house in Passy, an old but productive vineyard near Toulouse, and sizeable bank balances in France and Switzerland. Guillaume's executor had retained Mace to identify and locate the killers, and in the process he had come to know Angelique. As it turned out, two Iranians, an Iraqi, and a Sudanese woman had excecuted the armed attack on one of France's most famous luxury stores, and René had burrowed deep within the Arab community to find the killers in Marseille. Friends of Angelique's husband had done the rest. Four bound, strangled corpses were found in the harbor, and aside from that brief police announcement there had been no further publicity. Nor, as far as Mace knew, any official action.

After feeding Su-Su chopped chicken liver and changing her water Mace taxied to the Place Vendôme, entered a narrow doorway, and climbed a staircase to the second floor. The door bore a polished brass plaque engraved:

BANQUE SUISSE-ALLEMAGNE
SUCCURSALE PARIS

The branch office in no way resembled a conventional bank with teller cages and counters. Its reception room held a leather sofa, two chairs, a coffee table with financial magazines, and a floor lamp. From it clients entered one of two spotless offices, where private business was privately transacted. A corner office, where clients were never permitted, contained computers and fax machines that conveyed funds in and out of France. Forty to fifty million a week, Mace had heard, his transactions being extremely modest in comparison. Yet Herr Schoffman, the branch manager, treated Mace with the same deferential courtesy he might have accorded Onassis in his day.

After Schoffman closed his office door he sat behind his desk and faced the American client. "How may I serve you today?"

Mace opened the briefcase and extracted sixteen banded decks, one deck had been retained for overhead. "Eighty thousand," Mace replied, and wrote his account number on a slip of paper. Schoffman received it without comment, placed the money in a wooden tray, and passed it through a wall slot behind him. "The usual destination?" he asked, "or are you feeling adventurous these days?"

"Far from adventurous," he smiled. "Paying you two percent to safeguard my capital is well worth it. Eventually I'll invest in a farm, a vineyard, a building, an island." He shrugged. "Something tangible."

"And something the Japanese or Arabs haven't already bought. Don't wait too long," he warned.

The wall slot opened and Schoffman handed him the deposit slip. They shook hands, and the manager showed Mace to the door.

Carrying the empty briefcase, Mace walked out to the Faubourg St-Honoré and turned onto Rue Royale past rows of flower stalls to the Madeleine. He took a sidewalk table near the church and enjoyed a *fine café*, surrounded by the mixed perfumes of fresh flowers. Briefly he wondered what business Samuelson had in mind, decided speculating was futile, and thought about the possible weekend with Ange. She was beautiful, charming, sexually compatible, and socially prominent. It was the last attribute he found troubling.

He enjoyed being with her à deux, but weekends at some friend's château where Ange knew everyone and he no one were far from enjoyable. Still, she got great pleasure from partying with upper-class Parisians and enduring those affairs was the price he paid for continuing to see her. Well, he'd find out what she had in mind.

His own background was middle- or lower-middle class, he thought, his father having been a shop foreman at River Rouge until his death. A high school tight end, Mace had been recruited for Penn State, where he played second string for Joe Paterno, kept his scholarship for four years, managed to acquire a reasonable education along with an Infantry ROTC commission. After jump school at Benning he volunteered for Special Forces and qualified as a Green Beret First John. Two months later First Lieutenant Bradley Mason was at a jungle camp in Nicaragua training Contras to fight the Sandinista Army.

He remembered how, as weeks merged into months promised supplies dwindled. Sandinistas controlled road and river routes, and air-dropped cargo too often came down on impenetrable jungle canopy—and stayed there out of reach. Occasionally a chopper landed civilian passengers from Langley to look things over. Once a congressman in starched battle dress arrived, stayed long enough for coffee, and listened uninterestedly to Mace's complaints. Then he, too, vanished.

Even now it pained Mace to recall his young guerrillas hungry, shoeless, and lacking more than a few rounds of ammo per gun. Congress was hostile to funding the ragtag fighters and the media ganged up against them. Finally realizing he couldn't fight Congress, TV pundits, and the Soviet-armed Sandinistas without food and weapons, Mace disbanded his remaining fighters—one hundred twelve survivors out of two hundred originals—sent a final message to Managua headquarters and made his way to the coast. A shrimper carried him to Puerto Barrios, Guatemala, sick with dysentery and riddled with tertian malaria. Barely strong enough to sit upright, Mace rode buses to the capital and reported to the military attaché.

Jesus, he wondered, how did I manage to survive?

The attaché, a light colonel from West Point, issued clothing, ration money, and paid for treatment at a clinic near the embassy. Ten days later, to Mace's shocked surprise, MPs arrested him and flew him in the attaché's plane to Fort Bragg, where he found himself in the stockade, charged with desertion.

Six weeks later he was released, charges dropped, and advised to resign his commission. He'd hoped that was the end of it, but before he could check out of Bragg and start a different life he was subpoenaed by Congressional investigators and flown to Baltimore, quartered at Fort Holabird. Day after day he answered questions about the Contra resistance, supply problems, morale, names of his superiors, contact with a Col. North (none), Air America, chain of command, reasons for his desertion (I didn't desert, I was abandoned: all of us were), realizing soon after interrogations began that he wasn't giving the investigators what they wanted, and the questioning became more hostile. (We can have charges against you reinstated. Fuck you, he'd replied, and the threat was never uttered again.)

Although Holabird detention seemed endless, his dysentery and malaria were treated, and regular army meals brought back weight and muscle tone. When finally told Congress was through with him and he wouldn't be called for public testimony, Mace collected back pay, returned to Bragg, and tried to reach an understanding with his wife. That hadn't worked either, so he hired out on a Biloxi shrimper and earned good money for a year. Fortune definitely changed when they found a sixty-foot sailboat drifting in the Gulf. No crew. Spatters of old dried blood on the deck, and a cabin jammed with plastic bags of pot, two hundred keys of coke. As one of the prize crew Mace stayed aboard the boat while it was towed to Tampa and turned over to Customs, the Coast Guard, and DEA. The skipper hired a lawyer to speed proceedings and when the drug reward was paid and the boat auctioned off Mace's share was nearly twenty thousand dollars. He decided on a long vacation to someplace he'd never been, and having had two years of French at State he chose France and traveled the country for three months before deciding to settle in Paris. At Fouquet's one morning he encountered a hungover buddy from Bragg who was working Post Exchange embezzlement and black marketing and hired Mace as an investigator. Undercover as a stock clerk in the main PX, then located near the Citroën plant, Mace quickly spotted the perps, CID closed in and the job ended. He did a few more jobs for CID, surveillance and reference checking, and finding the work agreeable decided to set himself up in business. His first client was an American lawyer who needed to locate a Will beneficiary. Mace found him and more jobs followed. He did background work against a ring that produced fake American Express cards and passports. Protected visiting VIP's from Raytheon, Xerox, IBM, and Ford. Disabled a would-be assassin trying to shoot a World Bank official, and so his name became known in quarters where it counted.

Natsos, he thought. Ed Natsos. What the hell would he want with me?

Time to get back to the office and find out.

"I can't pay your usual rates," Natsos warned, "so don't start the clock. But you may find interesting what I have to say."

"I'm not hungry," Mace told him, "so speak your piece."

Natsos was a short, swarthy man with thick glasses and a black mustache. At least ten years older than Mace, with a somewhat pock-marked face. He had on pointy-toed Laredo snakeskin boots and a black string tie with a turquoise-and-silver clasp. Deputy chief of the Paris Station, he spoke excellent Greek and no French whatever as far as Mace knew, which was, he reflected, the way government did things. They were seated at the conference table, coffee cups and a thermal supply jug between them. Natsos sipped and set down his Haviland cup. "The MilAtt doesn't like you."

"Why would that be? We've never met."

"Says you have a bad record. Deserted in Nic, couldn't hack military combat."

"That's debatable," Mace said mildly, "but you didn't come here to review history."

Natsos nodded. "True. You ever been in espionage, Mace? Ever want to be a spy?"

"Never."

"But you know the game goes on."

Mace shrugged. "So?"

"After Yeltsin took over he decimated the KGB, turned loose at least twenty thousand trained officers. No salary, no quarters, no retirement benefits. Time bombs, every damn one of them."

"I've heard some went private."

"Too damn many of them. So a lot of Russian ordnance is being sold to Arab states, the Balkans, areas the West has embargoed. That's one part of it. Another aspect of KGB private enterprise is stealing high-tech secrets and selling them to, say, Japan, Taiwan, South Korea."

"Sounds profitable."

He drank more coffee. "Two submarines to Iran; total profit for the sellers. God knows what and how much to Iraq—but that's military, naval goods. Chips, computer design, pharmaceutical formulas, biotech, that's what's really troubling."

"How does it get out?"

"Our transnational corporations operate in Europe and elsewhere. They license foreign subsidiaries or manufacture direct, as in Mexico. Russian ex-agents target a plant, lab, or factory the way they used to go after a foreign embassy like ours. Subvert personnel is the easiest route, but they do very cool entry ops, too. And they penetrate with computers. The leakage—hemorrhage, really—is a multibillion annual loss to the USA. France is a particularly fertile field for theft operations. Anti-U.S. feeling is still strong among scientists and intellectuals. They might balk at selling French trade secrets to the Russians, but U.S. secrets—hell, why not?"

"Sounds like a real problem." Mace poured more coffee, sugared it, and stirred. Natsos said, "Interested?"

"Interesting story. Only, why tell me?"

The embassy man tugged a corner of his mustache. The phone rang softly, Yasmi answered and spoke in a quiet voice. She hung up and wrote a note. Unobtrusively she handed it to Mace.

Jules says it's urgent. I said one o'clock. Mace glanced at her and nodded okay.

Natsos said, "The administration figured what with the Cold War history the Agency had a lot fewer foreign targets. So, budget cuts, pink slips, early retirements. Then the NSC picks us to stop the brain drain." He spread his hands. "No poppa, no momma, no Chiclet gum. We ain't got the resources, Mace."

"What's the pitch?"

"We need help."

Mace grunted. "We?"

"USG. The Agency."

Mace took a deep breath, leaned forward. "In Nicaragua I got a taste of your fellow operators. Big on promises, short on coming through."

"That was a special situation; the Agency had its hands tied."

"Every situation is special. Besides, I've lost a lot of schoolboy enthusiasm. Maybe dysentery drained it out of me. Or seeing barefoot kids with old bolt-action rifles, a handful of cartridges, and empty bellies stand and fight and die. I'm ashamed of how our government encouraged them, then abandoned them." He paused. "Like the Bay of Pigs."

"That was different," Natsos said defensively. "Nikita rattled his saber and frightened Kennedy out of Cuba. They're not comparable."

"I don't agree. But let's cut this short, Ed. For hermetic plant protection you'd need five hundred, a thousand technically trained agents assigned among every foreign subsidiary and licensee. You haven't got them—probably can't afford them anyway. Know what the problem is? It's greed. Our manufacturers get around export controls—weak as they are—by licensing abroad. Get legislation to make them financially responsible for leakage and it'll stop damn soon."

"Politically that's impossible," Natsos said morosely.

"So it's an unsolvable problem—no-win. That's my judgment, no charge."

He eyed Mace. "You won't help?"

"Not even if I were motivated. Be realistic, Ed. Those NSC coneheads sit around a big table and define a problem. They leave it to Langley and the Pentagon to solve it—without the right resources, funds, or personnel. And it's all to be done clandestinely. Well, my time in Nicaragua taught me that clandestinely is the worst possible, least effective way to solve anything. The administration has overt options but not the balls to apply them. You guys are in the middle, twisting in the wind. I've been there so I empathize. Beyond that—" He got up. "Just kill the Russian agents."

"Wet work's specifically proscribed." Natsos rose dejectedly. "The Chief ordered me to ask you, say you needed a friend at the embassy."

"For what, passport renewal?" Mace shook his head. "Couldn't he do better than that? Anyway, I've got a friend at the embassy. Tell him that."

"Yeah? Who?"

"I don't betray friends," Mace said levelly. "Not so long as they produce and keep their mouths shut."

Natsos looked distressed. "You've got a penetration."

"Not ideological, financial."

"I can't tell him that, he'd tear the place apart for your mole. Shit. I said approaching you was useless, but I had to come anyway. That's Peke Parmalee."

"So you carried out orders. Commendable."

"He won't see it that way. Three more years to retirement, Mace. They won't be easy years either. Washington's all fucked up."

Mace smiled thinly. "What else is new?" He showed Natsos to the door and paused at Yasmi's desk. "See if you can reach Angelique." He went to his desk and waited. Yasmi buzzed and Mace picked up his phone. *"Chéri,"* she said warmly, "have you weekend plans?"

"Depends."

"On what?" Worriedly.

"On your proposal. So here's mine. Let's hop over to London, see some shows, wager a few pounds. How about it?"

"Oh, Mace, I'd love it but I'm already committed—wine-tasting weekend at the Armonix château—and I said you'd come."

"And there'll be the usual fifty Parisian high-lifers preening themselves and gossiping about other people I don't know. Or want to," he added.

"Mace—that's inverse snobbery, admit it." Three years at Farmington had given Ange a good command of English.

"Okay, I admit it. But you know I'm uncomfortable in crowds. If the party's important to you, go for it. But include me out."

When she was silent he said, "Anyway, thanks for the invitation. We'll talk soon."

She sighed. "Very well—but I'll miss you."

"And I'll miss you." He hung up frowning. Jostling with the château sybarites would be a form of unarmed combat. Everyone very, very polite, wellborn, well-bred, and totally disconnected from him. Who needs it? Not me.

Yasmi said, "If it's convenient I'll have lunch now, back before Samuelson comes."

"Go ahead. *Bon appétit.*"

"Rosario will be in later." Rosario was Mace's middle-aged housekeeper, half Nicaraguan Indian, half Chinese. Her husband had been killed fighting Sandinistas. She took care of his living quarters and office, did laundry, and cooked meals when asked. A valued employee.

He considered inviting Jessamyn Taylor to London. Jess was a young Second Secretary at the British Embassy who'd been with him in Monaco and Stockholm. She was slim, with long auburn hair and excitingly large breasts. In bed she liked exploring the kinkier aspects of sex: bottom paddling to warm up, acrobatic positions, whipping, and sometimes wrist-ankle restraints for simulated rape. Catering to her tastes, Mace found, distracted him from satisfying his own needs, but they hadn't been together for at least a month . . .

His call reached her as she was leaving her office. "Mace! I've been thinking of you, luv. Still faithful to me?"

"Always. So let's pop over to London for the weekend."

"Oh, what a shame! My mother's here for the week, and I'm all tied up showing her around." He wondered about the ambiguity of *tied up*. "But," she went on, "I'd love to have her meet you. Having a few Embassy people for brunch Sunday midday. Will you come?"

"Umm. Thanks for the thought, but I really want to get out of town. Catch you next week."

"I'll count on it."

Rats! Two down. Maybe he should go alone to London, find a companion there. The gaming clubs attracted a special kind of woman that appealed to him: uncomplicated, attractive, and willing. Not a bad idea. He'd have Yasmi make plane reservations, a room at Brown's for three nights.

He answered the phone. Yasmi's boyfriend, Jean-Paul, a movie bit-player, extra, and occasional stunt man. Young and reasonably good-looking. Mace copied his number and said Yasmi would call after lunch. Jean-Paul sounded slightly hostile. Yasmi had said he was jealous of her employer, suspected a liaison between them. Except for the employee relationship, Mace mused, Yasmi would be a definite possibility. He admired her athletic ability, her courage, and her intelligence, and realized she would be impossible to replace. So, even when sharp-set, as the phrase goes, he had never made overtures, maintaining their relationship as professionally close, personally distant.

He scanned *Le Matin* and spotted a reference to the Syrian Embassy. A man's body, throat cut, had been found in the Seine near the Pont de Sully. Documents on the body identified him as a chaffeur at the Syrian embassy. A Syrian consul claimed the body and was making arrangements to return it to Damascus. Police were searching for the assassin but were believed to be without significant clues.

Mace moistened his lips. Hafik al-Jamal was a tough, unforgiving employer. He could imagine what kind of husband he had been. Refolding the paper, Mace reflected that the op ledger was closed. By murder.

Yasmi returned, chatted briefly with her boyfriend, and answered the door, admitting Jules Samuelson.

Jules was pink-skinned, plump, and balding, the younger of the two brother *avocats*. After brief pleasantries, he got to the point of his visit.

"We have a client, Bernard and I, for whom our combined efforts have been unavailing."

"That's unusual," Mace remarked.

He accepted the compliment. "The client appears to have been deeply involved in the failure of a chain of banks located in such countries as the United Kingdom, Spain, France, Italy, Lebanon, and India." He paused. "Others, too."

"You're referring to the International Financial Trust scandal."

"I am. Something on the order of nine hundred million dollars. A consortium of directors has charged him with embezzlement, bank fraud, and alleged numerous other crimes."

"Is he guilty?"

Jules spread his hands and smiled slightly. "Who is to say? It is a question we never put to a client. Because we are not concerned with guilt or innocence per se."

"Or justice."

"Whatever that may be. The perception changes with venue." He smiled again. "The client's position is that he accepted bad if not criminal advice and is being made scapegoat by the true malefactors. However, the Swiss government is sufficiently persuaded of his guilt to have jailed him pending eventual trial."

Mace swung his chair around so that he could view the top of the Arc, where tourists were walking and taking pictures. Jules said, "Our Swiss correspondents advised us that they have exhausted every legal avenue to his freedom. Because a number of Swiss banks suffered major losses in the overall failure the Swiss government feels obliged to prosecute. You know how the Swiss are where banks and money are concerned."

"Relentless." Mace turned back to the lawyer. "What have you in mind?"

Jules placed his palms on the table and gazed at them. "We recall—Bernard and I—how efficiently you located the German swindler, Burkhardt, and arranged for his imprisonment. Now, we desire the reverse. We want our client freed and out of Switzerland."

Mace considered. "Those Swiss jails are tough to crack, Jules. Cells like dungeons, dedicated guards. No TV, no exercise time, limited visitation, censored mail. And bad food."

"Yes, our client has lost weight. Can Secours be of assistance?"

"I've been contemplating a vacation. The Channel Islands, Tahiti, Acapulco . . ." He let the thought hang in the air.

"If it's a question of money . . ."

"It's always a question of money. It got him where he is, it will take money to get him out—supposing it's possible. I'd have to find specialists, do big-time bribing. If it was Mexico or Argentina I'd say let's try. But the Swiss . . ." He shook his head. "Can't the Swiss lawyers hire a team?"

"I would not dare suggest it—nor have they. It's out of the question."

"Tell me about your client."

"Very well. He is thirty-four, a Spanish national of good background—minor nobility. His wife is Danish by birth, now a citizen of Spain."

"Children?"

Jules's gaze met Mace's briefly. "No."

"You said minor nobility—how minor?"

"Count—*Conde*. His name is Carlos Juan Perez de Montaner. An old, moneyed family."

"But Carlos wanted more money."

Jules shrugged. "Who does not?"

"I've seen the name in some of that unfavorable publicity."

He looked over at Yasmi, hearing the subdued clicking of her computer keys. "I don't know, Jules—this sounds too complicated for me. I'd better pass."

"Name your fee."

"I don't even want to think about it. His money would be better spent hiring another Swiss legal team. Sorry, Jules."

The lawyer rose. "I'll leave for a moment if I may, and return." He crossed the room, opened the door and disappeared in the hallway. To Yasmi, Mace said, "Strange."

"Very."

Presently the door opened and Jules came in followed now by a slim, striking-looking young woman. Her hair was golden blonde, her face so pale it seemed almost translucent. Blue eyes, small straight nose. She was wearing a print jacket dyed in patches of soft pastels over a light gold dress that shimmered as she came toward the table. Her ring finger was circled with a diamond-set gold band. As she stopped, window light burnished her hair red-gold. Her only makeup accented her lips, contrasting their symmetry with the pale texture of her skin.

As Mace rose, Jules said, "*Condesa*, Bradley Mason. Mace, the Condesa de Montaner." Mace stared at her until she extended her hand. "To friends I'm known as Erica. I hope we will be friends, Mister Mason."

My God, he thought, oh my God, and glanced at Jules. Why hadn't the lawyer prepared him for this Nordic beauty?

"I do, too," he managed weakly, "and I'm called Mace."

J ules cleared his throat. "Ah—Mace. I hope you'll excuse the inclusion of my client's wife. But, under the circumstances—" He waved a pudgy hand. The *condesa* regarded Mace with ice blue eyes.

"Jules, your clients are welcome but why bring the *condesa?*"

The lawyer glanced at her embarrassedly. Composedly, she said, "I'll answer if I may."

"Of course. And please be seated."

Jules held her chair, and when she was across from Mace she said, "Even though Jules was dubious you would undertake the assignment I believed there was a chance you would. So, in the interest of time I insisted on coming so we could all discuss the—ah—program more fully. I realize the awkwardness of the situation and apologize for—intruding."

"No problem," Mace responded. "But Jules was right—I don't feel the project is one I can handle."

She leaned forward. "May I ask why not?"

"It's percentages."

Her small nose wrinkled. "Percentages?"

"I won't commit to an assignment unless I feel there's a fair chance of success."

"How fair?"

"Forty percent—no less."

"And how do you estimate my husband's chances for freedom were you to . . . become involved?"

"Realistically—fifteen percent, twenty at best. At enormous expense." He looked at the lawyer. "Jules knows I don't spend money irresponsibly and—"

"How enormous?" she interrupted.

He shrugged. "Roughly, very roughly, not having even sketched a budget, I'd say two million minimum, perhaps three."

"Dollars."

"Dollars." He half-expected that to end it, but she persisted. "Why so much?"

"A helicopter might have to be purchased—a large, cargo-lifting type; that could run a million alone. Another million for related costs, and then my fee." He paused. "But it's all figurative since I won't be involved."

The room was silent until Jules said, "I have an appointment so I'll be leaving. *Condesa?*"

She turned to Mace. "Since I've occupied your time, and I'm famished, perhaps you'd lunch with me."

"Thank you, I accept."

"Seems the least I can do." She rose, Jules beside her. He said, "*Bon appétit,*" bowed and left them. When the door closed she asked, "Have you a favorite place?"

"Quasimodo comes to mind, but there's a business-lunch crowd, waiters do a good deal of bustling, and noise can be a problem. Why don't you choose?"

"Taillevent—if you like it."

"Very much, but—" he glanced at his watch—"at this hour a table could be difficult."

"Perhaps you could call ahead—give my name."

He told Yasmi what to do, excused himself, and went up the staircase. After washing he put on jacket and tie and descended to find the *condesa* smiling. "It's arranged," she told him, "and I have a car below."

They rode in her silver-gray Bentley salon to Rue Lamennais, a ten-minute drive through easy traffic, and when they arrived the maître d' bowed and showed them to a corner banquette set for two. To Mace it was obvious that the *condesa* was favorably known. Her drink was Stoli on the rocks, while Mace ordered Cinzano *au glace.*

She touched her glass to his and said, "Success in whatever you do."

"To your husband's freedom." They drank and ordered. Salads à l'Huile de Noix. Tournedos Rossini for Mace, Sole du Docteur Robine for his hostess. The room was paneled in walnut with tasteful decorations that enhanced the atmosphere of luxury. White linen napery, sterling service, a single pink rose between them. Mace said, "You'll leave Paris now?"

"Haven't decided—and please call me Erica." She smiled. "In Denmark it's spelled with a *k*, elsewhere, a *c*. Erica," she repeated. "And because I hope you'll have me as a client I want you to know about me. That's important, isn't it, to establish mutual trust?"

"It can be," he acknowledged. "Tell me as much or as little as you choose."

"Very well then. My family name is Hanson. From Viborg, where my father was mayor. I'm twenty-seven, flew as a SAS flight attendant—stewardess—until three years ago. Carlos was a passenger when we met. The attraction between us was great, and two months later we married in Madrid. After a year, during which my husband was often away on business, the banking troubles began." She looked away and Mace sipped his drink. "Since then," she continued, "things have become increasingly difficult for us. Culminating in my husband's arrest and imprisonment." She tilted her glass, sipped, and gazed at Mace. "Had he known there was an order for his arrest he would never have gone to Geneva—but he thought he could work things out there, and so he . . . well, you know the situation as it stands."

"I'm very sorry," he said, "for both of you."

"Thank you, Mace. I wish I knew what to do. I'll try anything. Anything at all."

Mace nodded sympathetically, but not wanting to be drawn more deeply into her problem, asked where she was staying in Paris.

"A pied-à-terre on Avenue Friedland. Carlos acquired it before we met so that he could come to Paris, as he frequently did, on short notice without the bother of hotels. Number seventy-eight, sixth floor."

Their salads arrived, crisp and redolent of tangy seasonings. The sommelier recommended a bottle of Château d'Yquem and went off for it. Without finishing her salad, Erica put aside her fork and said musingly, "I've only met a few Montaner relatives, but I believe there are dozens if not scores throughout Spain. Basically, we lived in Madrid, but spent a good deal of time at a large—ranch is the best word—near Toledo. The Montaners breed beef cattle and fighting bulls, have for generations. It's so different from our little Viborg, the Spanish lifestyle, the cuisine—everything. For a long time I was quite dazzled by it all, but I've had to come to earth and try to deal realistically with my husband's captivity." She picked up her fork, toyed with her salad and set down the fork again. "Are you married?"

"Was." He left it at that. He'd asked no questions of her, what he'd learned had been volunteered, and it pained him to recall his failed marriage.

"I'm only permitted to visit Carlos once a week, for half an hour. His letters are read so there's not much point in writing. Our Swiss lawyers see him when he asks, but I don't feel they've been very effective."

"There's a limit on what can be done through any legal system, and the Swiss are particularly hardnosed about financial crimes— alleged, I mean. I suppose the court feels your husband would flee if granted bail."

"Yes, that's been tried. And of course, he *would* flee if he could."

"With so many countries involved in the banking failure, where could he go?"

"Brazil, I suppose." Her lips twisted. "Isn't that the refuge of choice for major criminals?"

"Seems to be. When's your next visit?"

"Next week. I came here two days ago, hoping Jules and Bernard would have a solution to suggest. They named you as the best possible man to take—how shall I put it?—unconventional action. And now that hope is gone."

Mace said nothing.

Her gaze lifted to him. "I understand your reasons, Mace, but I do wish you'd try. Despite the slim chance of success."

He said, "The estimate didn't seem to concern you, Erica. Can you afford it?"

She nodded. "The money's nothing to Carlos while he's behind bars, or to me. He's told me to spend whatever's necessary—and legal bills have been huge."

"I can imagine. The Samuelsons charge plenty, and the Swiss probably charge even more."

"Much more."

After the wine was uncorked, sniffed, and sampled, the sommelier poured their first glasses and left. Erica put down her glass and said quietly, "You haven't asked if Carlos is guilty."

"As Jules pointed out, the Samuelsons don't deal in questions of guilt or innocence. Neither, as a matter of fact, do I."

"Well, Carlos is not guilty of anything—except acting on bad advice. I want you to know that."

"And were he guilty?"

"I'd work just as hard for his freedom."

Spoken like a loyal, courageous wife, he thought, as their entrées arrived. Presently he said, "There was a time—a bad time—when I was charged with a crime I didn't commit."

"But you proved yourself innocent."

"Never had the chance. Congress was involved, other high-visibility targets were found and my charges were dismissed." He shrugged. "There's lingering suspicion in some quarters, one reason I came to France."

"I wondered about that, but didn't ask Jules. After all, expatriates are no novelty in France." After her first bite of sole she exclaimed, "Oh, that is good! And I *am* hungry."

He smiled at her frank enjoyment, and cut into a rare tournedos.

Over coffee she said, "I hate the thought of seeing Carlos without bringing even a glimmer of hope."

"Before you do, you might consult other law firms. Shouldn't be limited to Samuelson connections."

"That's so. And while I'm there would you be willing to consider what else might be done?"

"Like—what?"

"I don't know, Mace. Maybe draw up a plan for others to execute? I'd willingly pay for that."

"It's something I've never done, Erica. I plan for myself and my people—knowing their abilities and limits."

"Would you—consider it?"

Reluctantly he said, "I'll think about considering—no promises from me, no expectations from you."

Her hand extended toward him. "Shake. Isn't that the American way?" He took her hand and felt a thrill just from touching it. After withdrawing her hand she said, "Before meeting you I assumed money would be your uppermost concern. Because it isn't I'm convinced of your integrity. I haven't had that feeling in a long time."

"Secours offers what the word says: help, assistance."

"With certain exceptions."

"There have to be exceptions, Erica, or I'd have been long gone."

"I know," she sighed, "and I can't argue against prudence. Dessert? Anything?"

He shook his head. Erica rose and said, "Let's be going, then. I'm sure you have things to do." As they left the restaurant Mace noticed that no bill had been presented; evidently the Montaners were favored with an open account. When they entered her limousine he handed her the table rose. "Or perhaps I should keep it as a souvenir?"

"But, Mace, we'll meet again. Office for you?"

"Please." She instructed the chauffeur and turned to view the boulevard. After a while she said, "Living alone, having massive responsibilities is something I haven't fully come to terms with. I'm desperately sorry about everything that happened to my husband—is still happening—but none of it was my fault. Had it been I think I could cope better than I'm able to."

"As far as I can tell you've acted responsibly, devotedly. When you married, your husband was already involved in a developing disaster, though I gather he wasn't aware of possible consequences."

"He never discussed anything with me. Now I'm responsible for extricating him from this unbelievable mess, but I resent the burden."

"That's understandable." He paused. "Do you have plans for the evening?"

"No." She shook her head. "None at all."

"Then perhaps we could dine, maybe take in a concert or ballet."

"Sounds wonderful."

"Good. When shall I come by?"

Her features relaxed. "Seven?—no eight o'clock. Shall I send the car?"

He shook his head. "I'll drive."

When the Bentley stopped he got out. Erica held up the rose and said, "Thank you." He watched as the limousine pulled away, then walked toward the building entrance. Abruptly he stopped and looked back. The dark blue Citroën that had tailed them from Taillevent was following again, three cars behind Erica's Bentley. Was it surveilling her movements, he wondered as he entered the building, or his own?

In his office he gave Yasmi the Citroën's license number and asked her to check ownership. "After that," he went on, "I want information on the International Financial Trust failure with particular reference to the involvement of Count Carlos Juan Perez de Montaner."

"Husband of the lady Jules brought in. Prisoner in Geneva."

"Sharp ears."

"Isn't that one of the qualities you pay me for?"

"I wasn't being critical."

"How urgent, Mace?"

"Get what you can today, continue in the morning."

She turned on the computer. "You're taking her case?"

"Haven't decided," he said, and went to his desk to read the opened mail. Across the room computer keys clicked, the monitor screen filled and softly hummed.

Before Mace went upstairs to change he learned the tailing Citroën was registered to Montpelier et Cie., a large investigative agency. Better than Syrians, police, or the DST, he thought as he pulled off his shirt. He wasn't the surveillants' target, Erica was. Should she be told? He decided against it; she had enough to worry her. More than enough. But why was she being watched?

Silently, Su-Su appeared, wrapped her tail around his leg, then hopped up to the side of the wash basin. Sitting there she watched him shave. "I'll be home late," he said conversationally, "so relax and watch TV until then."

Su-Su purred contentedly.

At eight she'd come to the door and joined him in the corridor. Wearing a dark blue dress of watered silk, a short pearl necklace, and a scarf clipped at one shoulder. Her face had more color and her hair was freshly done. From there he'd driven around the Etoile and down the Champs to the Crillon, checking for tails in the rearview mirror. Now in the Bar Grill they were at a rear table having cocktails. She asked if he'd ever visited Denmark, Elsinore, Copenhagen, the Tivoli Gardens. No, it was an anticipated pleasure, he replied. She described the simple, wholesome life she'd known in Viborg, becoming animated as she told of school days, winter sports, an older brother, two sisters, and an uncle whose SAS connection had helped her join the airline.

"Your languages helped, too," he suggested.

"Yes, that was important. English first, and French. I learned Spanish later, in Spain."

"I learned in Central America. Had to."

"How long were you there?"

"Too long," he said, and asked where she wanted to dine.

"Your turn to choose. Anywhere."

So they left by the side entrance and strolled past the embassy and up the Boissy d'Anglas. They crossed the Faubourg St-Honoré, and a little further on, to the left side of the narrow street he stopped before a lighted window lettered in gilt script: CHEZ TANTE MARIE. "It's maybe half a Michelin star," he told her, "but I like it. Came here while I was still a tourist."

"Sounds perfect."

Inside, Mace was greeted warmly by Paul and Virginie, the owners, who showed them to a corner table away from other diners. After ordering, Paul selected their wine, and after sipping Erica said, "I like the quiet atmosphere; even more I like being out for the evening."

"I'm glad you suggested it."

"You had nothing else to do? Truly?"

"Truly."

"Because I'd enjoy myself less if I thought I'd kept you from something you really wanted to do."

"Believe me, there is nothing I'd rather be doing."

During the first course Mace said, "If your husband is the victim of a conspiracy, the conspirators are his enemies, and yours. They'll benefit from his imprisonment, perhaps try to impede legal action that would free him."

"I think that's been done."

"Let's assume so. Do you and he ever talk by telephone?"

"It's not allowed."

"Has he smuggled out letters to you?"

She nodded. "Why?"

"Jailers sometimes enlist a fellow inmate who offers to smuggle letters. The jailers get first look, after which the letter may or may not get through. It's an old device. Enemies can co-opt an inmate to perform the same service."

"I see."

"Which is why communication between you, anything of substance, has to be only by voice when you can't be overheard. Your apartment phone may be bugged, your apartment miked."

Her face was troubled. "You don't mean it?"

"It's best not to make calls you wouldn't want enemies to hear. Or say anything in the apartment."

"But if there are no microphones? . . ."

"The day after a negative sweep one could be installed. Silence is the best defense. The same goes for your Bentley."

"My God," she exclaimed, "those things never occurred to me."

"So be careful."

"I will; I will."

After dinner they returned past the embassy and strolled Avenue Gabriel through the wooded park. In a pavilion a string ensemble was playing. Part of the audience was seated, listening, while others danced nearby. Erica said, "I didn't know about this. Very pleasant, isn't it?"

"Something Parisians can enjoy without spending money. In the

Place du Tertre there's often gypsy music. Ever been there?"

"Only by day."

"Quite different by night—but then Paris opens up after dark, becomes a different city."

"Copenhagen, too."

From time to time he checked for foot surveillants and decided they were unobserved. Near the Palais de l'Elysée they turned back and retraced their path. At the Crillon he reclaimed his BMW and asked, "Where now?"

"Home, I'm afraid. It's after eleven and—well, I got accustomed to earlier hours. Not that this hasn't been a wonderful release for me."

"Then we'll do it again."

At her Friedland building he locked the car and accompanied her to the apartment door. As she unlocked it she said, "Will you come in for a nightcap? Brandy?"

"Unless you're too tired." He didn't want the evening to end so soon. "Besides, I'd like to look around."

"For—what we talked about?"

He nodded and locked the door behind them. There were telephones in kitchen, dinette, living room, and both bedrooms. He opened each receiver for wafer mikes and found none, not having expected to. An organization like Montpelier would have the latest electronic devices. There were a dozen silver-framed photographs and two oil portraits. While checking their backs and frames he noticed a unifying similarity but found nothing resembling transmitter mikes. Erica watched interestedly, and after he examined the table lamps she opened the cellarette and brought out Hine cognac and two demi-snifters. "Are you a purist who insists on warming?"

"No, it's fine as it is."

"I'm terribly grateful for the evening." They sat side by side on a flowered sofa.

"You needn't be. I'd have suggested it but I was afraid you'd think I was taking advantage of the situation."

"And I thought you might think I had ulterior motives." She turned the glass in her hand. "As I did." She looked at him. "My husband—" she began but broke off when he motioned silence. "I

39

started to say he's not even allowed a razor in his cell."

"Standard practice," he remarked, admiring her fast recovery.

She moved against him, turned her head, and lightly kissed his cheek. Her lips were warm and he thought that he had never seen eyes so deeply blue. He placed one hand behind her head and brought her lips to his. For a long time they kissed. Finally she murmured, "If you'd like to stay . . ."

"I want to. More than anything."

In bed her flesh was cool against his. Her body slim, breasts small and firm. Even moist, her channel was surprisingly tight. She moaned at his entrance, he hesitated, not wanting to hurt her, but she clutched his body and pressed him in. Shudderingly, she quickly climaxed, and held him through his own release.

Later in the night she moved atop him and they made love again. Afterward, he kissed her throat, mouth, and face. "I'll try to help," he said quietly.

"Because we made love? You don't need to—"

"Because it may be the right thing to do."

"Oh, Mace," she breathed, "I'd given up hope."

"But only if you'll follow instructions, do everything I tell you to. Nothing more, nothing less. Can you do that?"

She kissed his lips, stroked his loins. "I can, Mace. I will. Yes. Anything you say."

four

The Connection

After a leisurely parting from Erica, Mace reached his living quarters a little before nine. He heard Yasmi come in below as he finished shaving. The intercom buzzed lightly and he answered. Yasmi said, "I have something for you."

"Good. I'm in a receptive mood. Come up."

From a woven shopping bag she drew out a light-colored oval melon that resembled a honeydew. "From my parents," she said, "chilled and ready. Enjoy."

"We'll share."

At the table he cut carefully into the melon to retain the wine that had nourished it. In growing melons Algerians sometimes cut and arranged vines so that they drew moisture from jugs of wine. Giving the flesh a delicate flavor prized by epicures who could afford the specialty.

As they ate, Yasmi said, "There's a tremendous amount of material on the International Financial Trust, much more than you'll probably need. And that's just from yesterday afternoon. So far the Count de Montaner seems a minor player."

"His wife claims he was set up."

"Wouldn't she say that anyway—especially if she wants to engage Secours?"

"I suppose. Anyway, I've made no commitment beyond contemplating what might be done for him."

"Mace, you haven't asked my advice, but if you did—"

"Go on."

"I'd say walk away from this one."

"Premature," he said and swallowed more pink-hued melon.

"Then I should establish a file, right? Keyed how? Montaner? IFT?"

"Uh-uh. For now we'll keep it coded. How about—ah—*Waterloo*?"

"Fine, we haven't used it. *Waterloo*." Her expression was provocative. "A separate crypto for the countess?"

"Unnecessary," he replied, and added coffee to their cups.

"Brown's and British Airways are holding your reservations for Saturday noon. Shall I confirm?"

"Friday's soon enough."

"Today is Thursday, Friday is tomorrow."

"Yes, that's the usual sequence. And, having said that, thanks for the melon, very thoughtful. And thank your parents for me."

"I will."

He left the table, and after showering he buzzed Yasmi's intercom. "Get Jules Samuelson. If he's not in, have him call me."

The lawyer returned the call while Mace was drying off. "Jules, I want you to meet me at Fouquet's. Take a back table, and I'll be there in twenty minutes."

"But Mace—what—?"

"Your office is in the Crédit Commercial, two blocks away; you could use the exercise. I'll have a *fine café*."

He taxied to the café-restaurant and found Jules ordering refreshments. The lawyer blinked and said, "Now, what's this about?"

Seated, Mace leaned forward, "You did me no favor by bringing the countess to my office."

"Oh? I thought the two of you might get on well."

"The point, Jules, is that she's being surveilled. Know that?"

"You're—? Of course not! I would have told you."

"Well, Montpelier's on her case. And by tailing her they've indexed me. Jules, who would retain Montpelier to follow Erica around? Not her husband."

"Hardly. Some party connected to the IFT affair. But why? She's not involved in it."

"But connected because she's her husband's lifeline. Those who want him behind bars would want to know what she's doing to free him. That includes who she sees in Paris. You, Jules, and now me."

He frowned, thumbed the curve of his chin. "She knows?"

"Not from me. So I'm consulting you."

"I see. Do you believe her to be threatened?"

"Not by Montpelier, they don't do strong-arm. But their employer? . . . I'd like to know who hired them."

"I understand. Did you change your mind? Is Secours in the picture?"

Mace shook his head. "I didn't like it yesterday; today even less. The wrong people have gotten my name, and Erica's not even a client. Makes me look sort of slipshod, wouldn't you say? Careless? But I did warn her about phone conversations, letters, a possible bug in her apartment. Quite a place, by the way. You've been there?"

"No. No reason to."

"She told me Carlos owned it for years. Plenty of time to set around photos of his bride, a portrait or two. Reminding him of her when they're apart."

The lawyer's eyes narrowed. "I'm afraid I don't get the point."

Mace smiled wryly. "There's an assortment of framed photos on display, and fairly recent oil portraits—but the subjects are males, rather handsome young chaps, too. Can't all be Spanish relatives."

Jules sighed. "I get your point. Well, you surmised the situation. Apparently Erica married without full awareness of her husband's tastes."

"A bi-guy."

"The Spanish have a descriptive phrase for his consorts: *amigos de la otra banda.*" He cleared his throat, the waiter set down their demi-tasses and cognac. After he went away Jules sipped and said, "I thought you might find it odd that after three years of marriage the couple is childless. That's unusual in Spain where inheritance is ruled by primogeniture. If Carlos dies without male issue his widow would inherit most if not all his Spanish holdings. By now a normal husband of the landed class would have a minimum of two children. But Carlos . . ." He sipped again.

Mace stirred his cup. "She seems entirely dedicated to freeing him."

"I believe she is."

"Strongly urged me to prepare an escape plan to be executed by others."

"Will you?"

Mace shrugged. "It's a confusing situation and I don't like Montpelier's involvement."

"Nor do I." He stretched and leaned back. "In any case she plans to visit Carlos next week."

Mace nodded. "I advised her to be circumspect. Meanwhile, I'm gathering background on her husband's problems. And I suggested she change legal representation in Geneva. Does that bother you?"

"She is, of course, free to proceed in whatever direction she perceives her and Carlos's interests lie. Regrettably, our Swiss correspondents have been ineffectual. Perhaps a change would be for the better."

Mace drank the rest of his laced coffee. "And we both know something more than we did yesterday. By the way, how much is Carlos accused of stealing?"

"Oh, putting it all together, somewhere between fifty and sixty million dollars. But embezzlement remains to be proved. Carlos maintains the IFT losses were caused by bad loans and abysmal business judgment at lower levels."

"Is that a reasonable position?"

"Let's call it serviceable. What concerns me most is the prospect of an endless succession of trials for Carlos in all the venues where he is charged. The most obvious way of avoiding all that would be for him to disappear."

"Erica has plenty of walking-around money—how much is Carlos worth?"

"Hard to say, land values in Spain being highly variable. I doubt if even he could name a figure."

"She didn't shrink from a possible three-million fee. Make an estimate."

He shrugged. "Perhaps eighty million, very little liquidity."

"Meaning holdings would have to be sold to realize cash."

"Yes. But between the time IFT failed and Carlos's arrest he would have had opportunity to divert and sequester personal assets—to avoid impounding."

"Did he?"

"Ethically I can't comment. But our billings have always been promptly paid, that I can tell you."

"It tells me that if Carlos could reach a friendly country—like, oh, Costa Rica—he wouldn't be on welfare."

"Decidedly not." He sipped the last of his coffee. "Are you going to tell the countess she's being followed?"

"She's your client."

"Then I'd say not for the present. But if she becomes aware of surveillance? . . ." His hands spread expressively. "You might want to intervene."

Mace laid money on the table and got up. "Thanks for coming." He left the café and walked to the head of the taxi rank, rode back to his office.

When he saw Yasmi's printer still adding to the reams of paper already in the receptacle, he shook his head. "Take a week to read it."

"It's a formidable database, with a lot of repetition."

"Then let's see what we have."

She turned off the printer and carried the printouts to his desk. He read for an hour, underlining portions, making notes and briefly summarizing significant sections. The International Financial Trust had been organized on a regional geographic basis: Europe, Middle East, Asia, Canada, and the USA combined. Directorships were determined by the size of bankers' regional holdings, and financial information was exchanged among principals whose pooled resources gave the Trust immense financial leverage. It was the sort of loose collusive trust arrangement that had been illegal in the U.S. for more than sixty years. But like the OPEC cartel it had never been challenged by the Department of Justice.

The overall directorate was comprised of French, Spanish, British, German, and Italian participants; Tunisian, Lebanese, Saudi, Kuwaiti, and Egyptian. Hong Kong, Taiwan, South Korea, Thailand,

and Malaya; New York, Chicago, Dallas, Toronto, and Quebec. The principals were named with the financial institutions they headed; however, the reader was warned that reliability of Middle East information could not be guaranteed.

In the year prior to IFT's failure its overall assets were estimated at 3.2 billion dollars. Mace grunted. A billion here, a billion there, and pretty soon you're talking real money.

And real money is what Count Carlos de Montaner was accused of stealing. But how, he wondered, do you prove a negative? As he thought it over he began to view Erica's husband as a Spanish aristocrat who dabbled in international finance without sufficient knowledge and experience to succeed. Prey for sharpsters.

Turning from paperwork he watched the Arc wreathed in mist the cloud-screened sun hadn't yet dispelled, outlines vague in the distance. Like the view of the Montaners and the IFT.

Yasmi let Rosario in, and as she passed him the housekeeper said, *"Buenos días, señor."* *"Buenos días, señora,"* he replied and watched her disappear up the staircase. She possessed, he thought, the Indian willingness to tackle any job, and the Oriental ability to do it right. The one positive asset I got out of Nicaragua, he reflected, and read more of the interminable printouts.

At noon he drove his BMW out of the basement garage and over Avenue Foch, entering the Bois at Porte Dauphine. The road wound through forest past the lake before connecting with Allée de Longchamp. He parked by the Grande Cascade, a pleasant artificial waterfall that dropped into a clear, rippling pool. There at a tree-shaded table he found Erica waiting. Picnic lunch in a wicker basket, wine in a small cooler. They kissed and she said, "You're late, you know."

"Three minutes by my watch. Sorry."

"SAS would be unforgiving."

"SAS is history."

"True. But in some ways I miss it."

He began uncorking the wine, watching her spread a checkered tablecloth, set it with plates and silver from the basket. Today she looked, oh, seventeen, in a loose open-collar denim shirt and matching jeans that accented the curvature of her thighs and loins. Her only ornament was her wedding ring, whose diamonds sparkled like sun-splashed droplets from the falls. Briefly he thought of her husband but couldn't indict himself for making love with her. The invitation had been Erica's. And she was, he reflected, Scandinavian, one of those hardy Northerners whose frank dedication to the pursuit of erotic pleasures exceeded even that of the legendary French. Had she a full-time, all-male lover? he wondered. Even if she'd taken him last night as a fill-in Mace could hardly complain, and no vows had passed between them.

Wine poured, they drank, sitting on opposite sides of the small table. The cascade's splashing covered traffic sounds from the road that bordered the Longchamp racetrack.

For a while they munched chicken breasts without talking. Finally, after a long sip of wine, Erica said, "You're not awfully conversational today."

"You've given me a lot to think about."

"And? . . ."

"I've been learning about IFT, its unusual organization. How was Carlos brought in?"

"Invited, I suppose." She held out her glass. "There was no particular reason he should tell me. Is it important?"

"Probably not. Unless he was selected as a pigeon."

"Pigeon?" Her nose wrinkled.

"Fall guy. Chosen to take the rap."

She placed the breast on her plate. "If you like I can ask him."

"If you think of it."

The ice-blue eyes studied him. "Does that have any connection with getting him out?"

"It may have a different connection—how he got in."

"I see," she said thoughtfully, and picked up her chicken again. "Anyway, this is a perfect day, and a perfect place. You're showing me so much of Paris I never saw before."

"My very great pleasure." He took her hand and kissed it. "Earlier I spoke with Jules. We agreed that because you represent your husband's vital link to the outside world everything you do is of interest to his enemies. That means a degree of danger."

"Danger? How? Why?"

"We feel you're safe as long as Carlos has no apparent prospects of freedom. But if it appeared to—let's say outsiders—that your efforts were succeeding, they might intervene."

"To keep him there. I understand," she nodded, "and it frightens me. Mace, I've come into a situation I can't begin to understand."

"Well, it's complex," he agreed, "and I've wondered if you know whether Carlos managed to get away with IFT money—big money— other directors may be trying to recover. If you tell me I'll never reveal it." He looked at the shimmering surface of the pool. "They only have to *think* he sequestered IFT funds to take the kinds of actions they have. Think it over, you don't have to answer now. Or don't answer at all. I ask because I'm concerned about you."

After a while she said, "Mace, I know you're tactful—and discreet. You saw how his apartment is—decorated, and said nothing, asked no questions. But I knew then that you understood about Carlos."

"Like Alexander the Great. A husband to women, a wife to men."

"But's it's been a very long time since he was a husband to me. That's why, I suppose, I was so eager to make love to you. I'm not— promiscuous."

"Never occurred to me."

"And I haven't always been chaste. I'm who I am, what I am, no apologies."

"I like who you are, what you are."

"And I like everything about you, Mace. That won't change if you decide not to help Carlos. With you I feel alive, secure. I wish it could always be that way. Last night, this morning, meant more to me than you could possibly imagine. Not just the physical thrill of lovemaking, but the holding and touching. Caressing. I'd forgotten how essential it is." A finger stroked the back of his hand. "Would you go to Geneva with me?"

He wondered how to frame the reply. Finally he said, "I can be more useful if there seems to be no connection between us beyond being lovers. If I'm seen with you in Geneva that puts me physically close to Carlos. And from that it could be inferred that I have a professional interest in his situation. We don't gain from that—we lose."

"Well, I'll miss you. You know that."

"There's more. Since it's alleged that Carlos made off with big-time money the losers may reasonably theorize that you know where it is, have access to it while Carlos is behind bars. So stay away from Swiss banks while you're there. Get traveler's checks here, cash them at your Geneva hotel."

Her eyes widened. "You're quite serious."

Peripheral vision had picked up the quiet approach of a car. It was stopped now, on the far side of the cascade pool. A dark blue Citroën sedan no more than fifty yards away. A camera lens glinted as it caught sunlight. Mace left the table and walked quickly toward the Citroën. Nearing it he slapped aside the panel of his jacket and it flared back, exposing the holstered Beretta. His hand gripped it and the car suddenly spurted away, gathering speed. Mace halted and turned back, seeing Erica standing, one hand at her mouth.

He held her in her arms. "You saw what I didn't want to tell you. They're following you—us. This time with a camera." He kissed her forehead, felt her shiver against him. "Yesterday I spotted them when we left Taillevent. At first I thought Carlos hired them to find out who you might be seeing—but later, after I realized he would have no particular interest in extramarital activity, I had to wonder who hired Montpelier to report on you."

"Montpelier? I don't know what—"

"A large investigative firm. You'll be followed in Geneva, too."

"Oh, Mace, *please* go with me."

He shook his head, hating to refuse. "Seeing me here with you is one thing, in Geneva another. But I can have a man go with you. He'll sleep inside your doorway, be at your side everywhere except at the prison. A reliable man, Erica. He'll meet you in Geneva, protect you until you return. Let me do that."

Her shivering had stopped and she stood back. "I'll think about it. But if I hadn't seen what just happened I'd think you were exaggerating things." He filled their glasses, handed her one. "In Paris Montpelier will only watch and report to the client. But I don't know who'll take over in Geneva, so I want you escorted there." She drank unsteadily, spilling drops on the tablecloth. "You just . . . went . . . after . . . them," she said huskily. "Were you going to use your gun?"

"Showing it was enough. Montpelier doesn't hire gunmen."

"How can you know that?"

"Because Henri Troyat, who heads the firm, once made me an employment offer. I could ask him the client's name but he wouldn't tell me, and I doubt that the watchers know. So—" he spread his hands—"you have to get used to being watched. For Carlos's enemies the stakes are very high. They want to know everything you do, everyone you see, eager for any clue to whatever it is they want."

"But how long will I have to live like that?"

"I don't know. But if Carlos can disappear you'll have to go with him."

She bit her lower lip, shook her head. "Not a welcome prospect. I see my responsibility ending when my husband is free. In return I expect a divorce."

"He knows that?"

"He's agreed to it." She managed a tight smile. "Meanwhile, I want to enjoy the illusion of being in love." She looked away. "With you, Mace. Is it a burden?"

"No way." He folded her in his arms, looked up at the sky, felt the fluttering of her heart.

Back in his office Yasmi reported that Henri Troyat wanted to talk with him. "Good. I was thinking of contacting him anyway." And when Troyat came on the line Mace said, "Henri, glad you called; there's a matter that needs to be cleared up."

"Indeed there is." The head of Montpelier was an agreeable former senior officer of the DST, the French FBI. "I want you to know that my people haven't been tailing you. It's your client we've been hired to watch."

"I understand that," Mace replied, "but you're wrong on the relationship, Henri. She's not my client."

"Oh? Whose then?"

"Samuelson Frères. Jules introduced us and we've been, ah, seeing each other. I have to tell you that your watchers are on the clumsy side, Henri. And today—that camera . . . It upset me."

"So I heard." He chuckled. "Did you really pull a gun, Mace?"

"Of course not, just let them see it. Now that I've answered your questions, here's mine: Who's your client?"

There was silence before Troyat replied. "You know I can't tell you."

"It's not her husband, so I'm concerned about your client's intentions."

"Intentions? What do you mean?"

"Bodily harm."

"Mace, nothing of the sort. As far as I could determine my client wants only her contacts, a description of her lifestyle—"

"Which includes me."

"Unavoidably, and I'm sorry about that, but you clarified the relationship, c'est ça."

"Henri, she's going to visit her husband next week. Who do you hand over to in Geneva?"

"No one. If she's surveilled there it's some separate arrangement I know nothing about." He paused. "You feel she's in some danger?"

"I do. Which is why I want to know who hired you, Henri; I need peace of mind."

"So romance can flourish, hein?"

"That's part of it. But if she's harmed or even threatened I'll retaliate. Do your client a favor and put him on notice."

"Sounds like a good idea. All right, Mace, the air's cleared between us, right? I don't meddle in your business, you don't meddle in mine." He cleared his throat. "And my offer stands. You might like working at Montpelier."

"One day I might, Henri. Toute à l'heure."

For the rest of the afternoon Mace diagrammed IFT's interlocking organizational relationships; the final result resembled a web of wires. He pushed the sheet aside and closed his eyes, wondering why he had spent so much time on the effort. To spot villains, I guess, but from the radiating lines no such person had emerged.

Yasmi said good night and went to the door. Bending over, she picked up an envelope and carried it back to Mace. His name was typed on it, and below, the underlined word: Particulier. Private.

He opened the envelope and drew out a single sheet of plain white paper. Also typed was an address and telephone number:

18, Rue Meslay, 2ᵉ
203-51-30

He smiled and silently thanked Henri Troyat for a discreet service that would never be mentioned between them.

So far, nothing he had learned from Erica, Troyat, or Yasmi's comprehensive printouts persuaded him that he should mount an operation to free the Count de Montaner. Nor could he draw up an op plan for others without considerably more information than he had. On a pad he began listing basic questions that needed answers:

Prison location, personnel organization, count's cell location, names of other special prisoners, interior and exterior photographs, press accounts of the prison—especially any breakouts, guard shifts, meal hours, road access, type of cell door, key lock type, wall thickness, prison night routine, wake-up hour, and so on until the page was almost filled. Looking it over, he thought that it represented substantial compliance with Erica's request. And it would show her the difficulties involved in acquiring preliminary information essential to developing an operational plan. Perhaps it would persuade her to hire another legal team to secure bail for Carlos. Posting three or four million dollars in Swiss Francs might bring the courts around and satisfy everyone concerned—except the count's enemies.

And it would be a damn sight easier to get him out of Switzerland when he was no longer behind bars.

In his kitchen he drank coffee and thought about Erica. Tonight she was dining with a visiting cousin of her husband's, one Marisol, taking her to Taillevent or Lapérouse; the cousin to stay overnight in the apartment, leave for Venice in the morning.

After coffee he went down to the street and took a taxi over to the Second Arrondissement. Along Rue Meslay he left it and dialed the number from a corner kiosk. The answering voice was male: "Bureau Inclan."

"You're at number eighteen?"

"Third floor, but we're closing for the day."

"I'm nearby." He broke off and walked back to the numbered

doorway. The door was open so he went up the dark, dusty staircase to the third floor. The office door was half-glass and lettered in flecked black paint:

BUREAU INCLAN

SERVICE MONDIAL

POSTE ET TÉLÉPHONE

FAIRE SUIVRE

CHEQUES ENVAISSERS

TOUT EN CONFIANCE

Shit. The place was an accommodation address that received and forwarded mail and telephone calls, cashed checks, and promised confidentiality. Used by adulterers, receivers of pornographic materials, con men, petty criminals, and others who wanted to mask their whereabouts and names.

This was the front used by Troyat's mysterious client. Here, Montpelier sent reports; through it Montpelier was paid. Without knocking Mace went in.

It was a narrow room, side walls covered with pigeonholes for mail. At the end, a battery of telephones and tape recorders. Across the front of the room a wooden counter, above which he could see the unkempt head of a man. Mace set his hands on the counter and looked down. The man was in a wheelchair; thin, stunted legs ending below his knees. The air held the stench of old food and cigar smoke. The man said, "You just called?"

"I want a price list of your services."

The man leaned forward and reached for a lower shelf. From it he handed up a printed sheet. "Who recommended Inclan?"

"Montpelier does business here."

The man picked at brown-black teeth. "Maybe."

"Good business. Every day."

"That's confidential," the man leered. "Like the sign says."

Mace nodded. "I like a firm that keeps promises, but I need a name." He brought out a sheaf of New Francs and peeled off two fifties. "Confidential, between you and me."

The man grunted, scratched his unshaven chin. "Confidentiality takes more."

Another fifty. The man stared at it, licked scarred lips. "What's your name?" Mace asked.

"Ismael—why?"

"I've got some advice for you, Ismael. Take the money or I'll look for myself."

Ismael shrugged. "You a husband? Lover?"

"That's confidential. Who pays you to handle Montpelier material?"

He snickered as he scooped up the money. "Easy. Same as comes for it."

"Name."

"Messengers. Never seen the same one twice." He tucked the money into a shirt pocket. "That it?"

"How does Montpelier get paid?"

"I mail an envelope. Could be checks in it, I never looked."

"Sound policy," Mace remarked. "How often?"

"About once a week. Account hasn't been open long."

"How long?"

He shrugged. "Month, maybe." He wheeled around, pushed a wall button and ceiling incandescents went out. Above the phone bank the lights stayed on. One of the phones rang, a red light blinked. "Back to business," the man said, and wheeled himself off toward the phone. Nothing more to be gained in this crummy place.

As Mace was going down the dim staircase a man hurrying up brushed him with his briefcase, mumbled something and kept on.

Mace couldn't be positive, but he resembled one of the surveillants in Montpelier's Citroën sedan.

He walked along Rue Meslay looking for a taxi, stopped one, and got in. A long, perplexing day, he reflected. Close it off with a light meal, wine, and the rack.

À demain: Erica

The Warning

Mid-morning. The office.

A smiling Erica was saying, "Spare me from elderly female relations. I'd only met Marisol twice before—at our wedding, then a Madrid dinner party. Mace, you can't imagine how picky and fussy she is. Overflowing with Montaner pride and snobbery. Seven years a widow and still hasn't found a husband despite all her wealth and social position. And the wigs—she travels with a dozen, each separately boxed—in addition to five large suitcases. At Orly she made them crazy with all her demands and complaints. If Alitalia had left late . . . let's say I've had quite enough of her company." She leaned forward to whisper across the desk. "Worst, she deprived me of yours."

He nodded. "As for me, I got to sleep early. Do all traveling Montaners expect to be lodged at your place?"

"If they do they'll be disappointed—I hope the old thing is an exception, but I couldn't turn Marisol away. After all, I hadn't met you then."

"Question. Was visiting Carlos part of Marisol's trip?"

"No."

"Has she ever visited him in prison?"

"No, but I think only immediate family members are allowed to visit prisoners; spouse, children, siblings . . . Why?"

"I guess I think it's strange there seems to be little family interest in his situation. Are the Montaners disgraced by his arrest? Were they ashamed of his . . . lifestyle?"

"It was never mentioned in my presence."

Yasmi came quietly to the desk. "If it's all right I have a few personal things to take care of. Back after lunch?"

Mace nodded, and she went away. When the office door closed behind her Erica said, "She doesn't like me at all."

"Come to see herself as a protective mother-figure."

"That all?"

"Absolutely. Even if I were tempted, there's her boyfriend. Large, muscular, and possessive. A professional stunt man. He could pull me apart like a partridge."

She laughed. One hand moved up and down a long jeweled necklace. "Your assistant doesn't want you involved in Carlos's problem."

"True. It's far away and in another country." He drew out his notepad. "You're going to Geneva on Tuesday, right?"

She nodded.

"Yesterday I drew up a list of preliminary information anyone planning a breakout would need."

She looked down, scanning the items. "I could never possibly find out all these things."

"The man I mentioned, the escort I want to send with you, could get things moving. Not directly, but I think he could enlist helping hands."

"Then he can come with me. I agree."

"I won't expect you back until you've had time to retain other legal advisers. Jules Samuelson and I feel that a concerted effort to have Carlos freed on bail is probably the best present strategy." He paused. "If you have three million dollars available for a breakout, I suggest you add a million and have it ready in cash when new lawyers approach the court."

She thought it over. "It sounds like a logical approach. Whether the money pays for escape or bail it's spent, gone."

"That trouble you?"

She shook her head. "Not in the least. To me it doesn't seem real anyway."

"First, you have to find new lawyers."

"How, Mace?"

"By now Carlos is deep in the prison milieu. Very likely he will have heard of aggressive, successful Swiss lawyers from other prisoners who can't afford them. The clever ones employ all sorts of tactics to free their clients; taking an emergency appeal to a distant judge at night. Finding a physician to certify Carlos's health requires a less restrictive environment—freedom is the bottom line."

Thoughtfully, she said, "And if he were freed on bail?"

"We'd get him out of Switzerland immediately."

"Would I have to go with him?"

"No. But it might be advisable to stay out of sight for a while—at least until you're divorced."

Her expression brightened. "Mace, that's very encouraging."

"But you'll need good legal advice—like the Samuelsons'—concerning what divorce would lose you."

"My title is the least of it. After the initial glamor I became uncomfortable with it. As for Carlos's wealth—of course I want whatever I'm entitled to."

"Jules can determine that, work out a binding arrangement." He gazed across the room. "That would be best done while Carlos is still in prison, dependent on you. You should see Jules this afternoon, get his advice. He'll know whether papers should be drawn up for France, Spain, or Switzerland. Perhaps all, for safety."

She leaned across the desk and kissed him. "Mace, *chéri*, you really give me hope. More than the lawyers."

"That could be because I don't know the obstacles."

"But you think positively. Now I realize that until I met you I'd been getting nowhere. It's been deadly, Mace."

"Now you have things to do."

She nodded. "Let's see: I go with your man to Geneva; he looks for information sources and I ask Carlos about successful criminal lawyers. I hire one, and discharge the present incompetents. Then back here to confer with Jules."

"But see Jules today. Perhaps he'll be able to prepare papers for you to take to Carlos. If not, you'll take them next week. But spend enough time in Geneva to retain new lawyers—let them suggest how much bail to offer the court. They know about such things."

On Yasmi's desk the phone rang. Mace ignored it. Third ring and the message machine cut in. After the chime he heard Jessamyn's voice: Mace, luv, if you're still available for a London weekend, I am, too. Mum took sick and I'm flying her back this afternoon, so I'll be there. Hope you'll come, too. Love you.

The message ended. Erica gave him an arch look. "Competition?"

"Actually, she's a British diplomat."

"Hardly a diplomatic message. The girl's burning for you."

"Erica, I dated her before I met you."

"Then go if you want to. I'll hate you, of course, but you have every right to do as you choose."

"She's a pleasant young person," Mace said, "but hardly in your class. Anyway, I was considering weekend plans for us—if you're free."

Her expression relaxed. "What kind of plans?"

"There's a rather spectacular inn, hotel, country palace—the French word is *auberge*—out by Malmaison. Two-star cuisine, dancing under the stars, and regal rooms with huge, goose-down beds. Auberge de l'Impératrice. The empress's lodge."

"Umm. Well, yes, I think I could fit that into my schedule, because it sounds absolutely heavenly. When can we leave?"

"This time tomorrow. I'll drive."

After lunch at Prunier's they went to the Samuelson office and while Erica consulted the brothers, Mace sat away from the conference table so as not to intrude. She laid it all out for the lawyers, who made notes and spoke to each other in muted voices.

To Erica, Bernard said, "I'm afraid I can't promise the papers before Tuesday, *Condesa*. Your plane leaves when?"

"Eleven in the morning. I'm to see my husband at three."

"Possibly," Jules said, "the papers could follow you by courier. We could send them to our correspondents, or to your hotel."

"I'll be staying at La Résidence, as before."

"Yes, I remember. We will do all that is possible to accomplish in the available time."

"I'm sure you will." She gathered her purse and began to rise but Jules stayed her, saying, "Are you aware of the Montaner-Samuelson connection? How we came to represent your husband, and other family members?"

She shook her head. "No."

"Then I should tell you a story that goes back to the Second World War." Bernard nodded approval.

Jules continued: "As Paris Jews my family—parents, uncles and aunts, cousins, everyone—were subject to arrest by the Gestapo and condemnation to the camps—the death camps about which you know. As Sephardic Jews my family had very old contacts in Spain and Portugal. Under the noses of the Nazis our parents made it to the Spanish border and entered under the protection of the Montaner family. You see, across Europe many decent people helped Jewish refugees keep out of the death camps. Denmark, *Condesa,* your small country, saved tens of thousands of us. And the Swedish humanitarian, Wallenberg—a Christian—saved thousands more. So there is great gratitude in our Jewish communities toward those who spared us from the furnaces. All during the war the Montaner family sustained my parents, provided shelter, food, useful work. And after the war saw to it that my parents returned whole to Paris." He spread his hands. "Where my brother and I were born."

"Jules, I had no idea."

"And in that spirit of gratitude and obligation, neither Bernard nor I could ever undertake any action contrary to the interests of a Montaner. Were your proposal adversarial—against Carlos's interests— we could not advance it. However, should your husband agree to a post-prison divorce we find no impediments to facilitating it. I trust that clarifies the situation."

"It does, and I'm very glad you told me. Thank you."

The brothers stood up. In a deep voice Bernard said, "We wish you well, *Condesa,* and hope your husband can soon be free."

Rising, Erica said, "I'll work for that as long as necessary."

Below on the Champs Mace said, "They seem to forget you're a Montaner."

She shrugged. "Not by blood—and I hope not for long."

"Ethically, they can act where your and your husband's interests are identical, but where they diverge they'll serve Carlos, not you. Jules wouldn't have told you what he did if not anticipating that time would come. I take it as a politic warning."

"So, I'll get other lawyers."

"No shortage of them in Paris," he said as a small beige Peugeot pulled slowly away from the front of Crédit Commercial. "Different car," he remarked, "same gumshoes."

"Oh, Mace, even here."

"Routine, and for them very easy. You're at your apartment, a restaurant, with your lawyers, or me." He smiled. "Unless you have secret destinations."

"Wretch! You know I don't." She took his hand and drew him over to the curb and into her waiting Bentley.

In the morning Mace had René come to Erica's place. She opened the door and invited him to join them at the table for coffee. Hesitantly, cap in hand, the Foreign Legion veteran came in. *"Comtesse,"* said Mace, "my friend and companion, René. *Copain,* La Comtesse de Montaner."

"At your service, Madame *La Comtesse,"* René replied, tucking his cap in his belt before advancing to the table. "The chief has yet to tell me how I may serve you."

Erica filled their coffee cups and sat beside Mace while he explained about Geneva. Protection and information gathering, he said, and gave the Corsican the list he had made.

"I don't expect you to come up with everything in a pair of days, René, but you can look for sources to do the footwork. Or maybe you have reliable contacts there."

"Unless they're jailed, dead, or in flight. What about money?"

"Whatever it takes. The countess will supply you in Geneva. Meanwhile, book yourself on her Tuesday flight, and see to her safety."

They drove out Avenue de la Grand-Armée beyond Porte Maillot, then nine kilometers to a bend in the Seine; pulled into the broad grounds of a sizeable château. Three stories high, the baroque facade rose from two symmetrical wings and was surmounted by a mansard-style roof. In miniature the auberge could have been a wedding cake decoration, the overall effect warm and inviting.

As a porter unloaded their bags Mace said, "The Empress in question was Joséphine, of course."

"And her palace is over there." Erica pointed. "I toured it once.

Versailles in the morning, Malmaison in the afternoon. Then I flew off to Oslo. Or was it Helsinki?" They went in to register—Mace signed for both—and as they walked up the winding carpeted staircase she said, "Were we followed here?"

"As far as the gate. Brown Fiat."

"Will they wait outside? Haunt us?"

"No reason to. Now let's forget the problems of life and live it."

Windows of their high-ceilinged suite overlooked the verdancy of a topiary park. They bathed in a large, old-fashioned tub with gold-washed plumbing, dried each other with immense nubby towels and made love.

Iced champagne and caviar while they dressed for dinner. Dining at a candlelit window table. Coffee and brandy beside the outdoor dance floor. Dancing to the easy rhythms of Les Rocket Boys combo: twin violins, sax-clarinet, base viol, and whispering drums. Pressing against him as they turned, Erica murmured, "This is exquisite, everything. But I feel almost as I did on my first date."

"Well, I'd rather you felt as though you were with an old and trusted friend."

"I do, trusted friend, but you're not old. Anyway, my first date was a dance at the town hall, music by the Viborg marching band." She laughed. "It wasn't great, the dancing, and I was so nervous I almost wet my pants."

"And the boy?"

"Hmm. Olaf . . . Olaf Sörenson. Tall, blond, and clumsy. A career farmer like most Viborgians."

"Was he nice to you?"

"Incredibly polite. . . . I was the mayor's daughter and many eyes were watching. Especially my parents'."

He kissed her forehead. "You're really something, *chérie.*"

"Something?"

"Rich and rare. Never known anyone like you. Never. So I'll always be grateful to Jules."

"I'm just as grateful, believe me." One finger touched his nose, trailed across his lips. "Without you I wouldn't be here, and here is where I want to be. With you."

For daytime amusement and diversion there were walking trails through the park, a putting green, and a cool, clear artificial pool, buffet table al fresco nearby. Mace and Erica enjoyed them all before it was time to leave on Sunday afternoon.

Beside him in the car, Erica looked back at the Auberge and said, wistfully, "For me this has been a heavenly interlude—I hope we'll come back."

"We will," he promised, unsure the promise could be kept.

On Friedland he saw Erica to her door and said he would be back. In his building basement Mace parked the BMW and rode the elevator to his office level. To his surprise the office door was open, light came from inside. Cautiously, he approached, peered in and saw Yasmi sitting in the middle of the floor, a litter of disk files around her. She looked up at him and he saw that her eyes were swollen, expression distraught. "We've been robbed, Mace, where have you been?" She gestured at the disks, her smashed computer. "Poor Rosario—she let them in. They beat her and she's in the hospital." Slowly she got up, looking dazedly around.

He went to her, put his arm around her shoulders. "When did it happen?"

"Yesterday. I needed to tell you, ask if I could call the police."

He walked around surveying damage. "Don't. Tell me about Rosario."

"Black eyes, a broken tooth, concussion . . . She'll recover. Said two men talked their way in, saying they were clients come to meet you."

He glanced up at the two concealed video cameras. Yasmi dried her eyes. "The tapes weren't damaged. I hope they'll show the bastards' faces. The printouts are gone—the robbers weren't street thieves, housebreakers, they came for specific things, Mace, related to IFT and the Montaners." She moved slowly toward her disarranged desk. "The countess was with you, wasn't she?"

"So?"

"She's brought trouble, Mace, just look around."

"Don't make an emotional judgment. When can Rosario go home?"

"Tomorrow, day after. She's terribly ashamed of being so gullible."

"Tell her she shouldn't be. They knew when we'd be away, when she would be here. It's not her fault. Hell, they'd have come in any-way. I want to scan those tapes, Raoul and René, too. They may see a familiar face from the milieu. Meanwhile, you have things to do: Get this place organized again and assess the losses, have the machines repaired, and see to Rosario's needs."

"She has a friend staying with her. She'll call here."

Mace opened his desk drawer, saw it had been searched and his organization diagrams taken. Not the work of Montpelier agents, he knew, so it had to be for someone close to IFT.

Kneeling, Yasmi began restoring disks to their boxes. "Tomorrow I can access the database, replace the printouts."

"Right. Do just what you did before." He phoned Raoul and asked him to come to the office with René.

"Suppose I can't reach him?"

"Come when you can. I want you both here."

"Trouble, chief?"

"Home movies."

He remembered his living quarters, went up quickly, and turned on lights. Kitchen and dinette undisturbed. Bedroom? From the bed Su-Su lifted her head, blinked at him, stretched, and yawned. He stroked her affectionately, and gave her a plate of liver, freshened her water bowl. Remembered Erica.

Her voice sounded sleepy, with an edge of irritation that vanished after he told her what had happened.

"Oh, Mace, I'm so glad—relieved—you weren't there. If you were hurt I couldn't bear it."

"Well, I'm not, but I have things to take care of that can't wait. Yasmi is clearing up debris, and a fellow you've met is coming over. We'll be—a while. I'll call tomorrow."

"As early as you can. I'm accustomed to breakfast with you."

"Another spoiled countess," he said lightly and rang off.

At his desk he reflected that the thieves probably didn't realize the stolen material could be reproduced, but their boss or bosses would. Worse, Carlos's enemies had shifted their attention away from Erica to him. What a rotten ending for a sublime country weekend.

Tired and emotionally upset by the trashing, Yasmi left before René and Raoul arrived after eleven. He gave them coffee and ran

63

the tape from the camera focused on the inside office door. It showed Rosario entering and disappearing as she went upstairs. He fast-forwarded until she came down, listened at the door, and slowly opened it. Two men, one taller than the other, stood there. For a few moments their lips moved, then they shoved her roughly aside and came in. Rosario gesticulated, but the shorter man spun around and knocked her to the floor, kicked her. As she tried crawling away her attacker struck her head with a pistol butt. Rosario lay motionless on the floor. Raoul swore. The men moved deeper into the office, out of camera view.

René said, "Couldn't make out their faces, Mace."

"They come back." He fast-forwarded again, and showed the backs of the men as they left the office. Elapsed time forty-three minutes.

The second surveillance camera was positioned kitty-corner from the first, and its tape showed search and destruction. It also showed the men's faces, and Raoul yelped in recognition. "*Le Poignard!* I'd know that *macreau* anywhere. René?"

He shook his head. "Don't know all your pals."

Mace froze the frame that showed both faces best and encouraged René to study them carefully. After a while René shook his head. "Sorry."

Raoul said, "Get one, get the other. What do you want from them, Chief?"

"Information."

Raoul got up. "Le Poignard hangs out around La Gaieté Bar, St-Denis. If he's not there, money will find him."

Mace gave each a hundred-NF bill. "You know where to take him. Squeeze him for his partner's name, then the identity of whoever sponsored the break-in. If you can collect the partner, soften him up. Keep them separated and call me."

"Could take hours, Chief."

Mace shrugged. "A response can't wait. I don't want their principals thinking I'm a pushover. Fast reaction will impress them."

The men got up, and before they reached the door Mace said, "By the way, harming them is reprisal for what they did to old Rosario, but don't kill them. I want them crawling back to their bosses able to tell what happened."

René smiled evilly. "The line between life and death can become very thin."

"Don't make it invisible," Mace warned, and showed them out. After locking the door and setting the alarm he put fresh tapes in the cameras and secured the other two in his safe.

Midnight.

He went to bed.

At five-twenty the phone rang. René's voice was hard. "You wanted two, we got two." In the background Mace could hear moaning. "Get here soon, Chief. This one may not last the night."

six

The Question

He drove through unlit, nearly deserted streets deep into the
Latin Quarter, and at a little before six, he reached the old
apartment building where Rashid had been held. He closed the
courtyard gates behind the BMW and looked up at the shaded window around whose perimeter there was a leakage of dim light.

Knowing what had taken place behind the window sobered his
thoughts and his mind flashed back to a night by the Río Latigo in
Nicaragua. Violating strict orders, he had gone with six of his guerrillas to a riverbank clearing where five Contra comrades were said
to be held by Sandinista soldiers.

He remembered spotting the campfire through thick jungle
foliage, cautioning his men to approach slowly and quietly despite
the blood-chilling shrieks that pierced the night, the gross, obscene
laughter of the soldiers.

On their bellies they crawled close enough to see five men bound
to tree trunks. One body was decapitated, another's arms were
hacked off, the belly of a third was disemboweled, the fourth Contra—couldn't have been fourteen—had neither nose or ears, his
throat had been raggedly cut. A captain and a corporal were jabbing
the fifth captive with bayonets, withdrawing dripping steel and
thrusting in again. The man was close to death. At each jab his head
moved back and guttural sounds came from his throat.

Mace held up one hand while he counted. Two soldiers asleep
beyond the campfire, four tossing dice in its glow, and the captain
and corporal. Eight uniformed savages.

Prone, Mace sighted his AR-16 and blew off the captain's head, shot the corporal through the throat. Yelling wildly his men surged into the clearing, firing, slashing with machetes until all but two soldiers were dead.

Arango, the Contra unit commander, stopped at each bound, dead Contra and tenderly kissed bare, bloody flesh, weeping unashamedly. When he reached the dying man he kissed his lips, whispered, "Rest with God," and shot him through the head.

Then Arango sat down, covering his face with his hands, sobbing aloud. Bottles of tequila and grappa appeared from a cache of rice and canned rations. When each man had drunk Mace said, "Enough for now. Bury your dead."

Arango looked slowly up, and gestured at the two wounded soldiers. "They did the torture, the killing, they do the burying."

While graves were dug Mace and the Contras ate army rations beside the campfire. If Arango was going to kill the remaining soldiers he would have ordered another two graves dug, seven in all. Right? Mace drank from his canteen.

Finally, after the graves were dug the Contras lowered each body and its severed parts into a grave, and fired salvos to honor their slain comrades. Mace said, "Let's load up rations and liquor and get out of here."

"Not so fast," Arango interjected. "More accounts to settle." He pointed to the two weeping soldiers both with leg wounds, one about sixteen, the other a year or so older. Uniforms stained with blood from their wounds. Mace said, "They come with us; we can trade them for our own men."

Arango spat at the dying fire. "Sandinistas don't trade. And I don't think they can walk the distance." He picked up a machete and walked to the prisoners. Swiftly he slashed off the hand of one, then the other. The soldiers screamed and tried to stem their spouting blood. The sight sickened Mace. As he stood immobilized, Arango brought over four of his men and pointed at the river.

"No!" Mace shouted, but Arango spun around and shoved his pistol into Mace's throat. "Listen, *Teniente Gringo*, this is our affair, not yours. Stay out of it." He took the AR-16 from Mace and backed away. "After what they did to our *compadres* you think they should *live?"* He watched the prisoners being shoved into the water, battered with rifle stocks to force them deeper. "Let the crocodiles decide." He returned Mace's weapon.

One prisoner tried getting back to shore, but shots kept him in the water. In midstream the other soldier shrieked and disappeared. Moments later there was a furious turbulence as a croc whirled and shook the body, then bore it deep. The last soldier lived half a minute longer before he too disappeared in a boil of water.

Arango picked up the severed hands and flung them into the river. His men began removing useful items from the six army corpses: boots foremost, weapons belts, canteens, firearms, grenades, ammo, knives, entrenching tools, money . . . stripping the bodies down to their bloodsoaked uniforms. To carry it all they improvised slings from army blankets, and went back through the jungle as they had come.

So I know something about torture, Mace reflected as he entered the building, and wondered how far Raoul and René had gone.

Inside, they were wearing ski masks and gave Mace one. Raoul said, "Le Poignard is the short one, triangular chin scar. His *mec* is *Le Coquin, Coq* for short." He pointed toward the kitchen. "They didn't talk." Mace pulled on the ski mask and went in, found the man bound to a chair, writhing and moaning. René slapped his face and jerked back his head by the hair. Mace sniffed gasoline and glanced at the counter. A liter bottle was open, beside it a large hypodermic syringe. Seeing Mace's masked face the man bubbled, "No more, no more."

"You beat an old woman, destroyed property, and stole. Who sent you?" Mace turned on a small tape recorder and held it near Le Coq's lips. "Who?"

"A man," he gasped.

"Not a child, eh? Don't fuck with me or you're dead. Who?"

"Guillerain. Louis Guillerain."

"A *relégué* from the Arab Quarter," René supplied. Pimp-thief.

"To do what?" Mace asked. "Precisely."

Breathing heavily, the man swallowed. "Break in, take everything at Secours labeled IFT."

"Why?"

"Guillerain didn't say."

"And paid you—you and Le Poignard. Who does he work for?"

"Anyone, everyone who can pay."

"What did you do with what you stole?"

"Gave it to Guillerain."

Mace cleared his throat. "If I want to talk with Guillerain where would I find him?"

Le Coq shook his head. "Don't know."

Mace stepped back and nodded at Raoul who filled the syringe with white gasoline and pressed the needle to the man's already punctured arm. With a howl Le Coq jerked away.

"Stays with a *poule*," he husked. "Calls herself Fleurette. Rooms over a grocery. Boul' Raspail, by the cemetery."

"What grocery?"

"Le Gasque," he sniffed, and Raoul put aside the syringe.

Mace stepped back, turned off the recorder. His face was wet under the knit mask. He went into the bedroom carrying the hypodermic syringe and the recorder. The captive yelped and scrabbled backward, almost overbalancing the chair. His chin scar was sunken, blue and triangular. Someone's knife had carved out a neat chunk of flesh.

Mace scratched the burglar's bare forearm with the needle and Le Poignard howled. He was a squat, ugly fellow of forty or so with battered lips and a disarranged nose. Powerful arms and shoulders. Mace repeated the questions he'd asked Le Coq and got substantially the same replies. Both burglars had been pretty well demoralized before his arrival.

Turning off the recorder, Mace said to René, "Blindfold them and get them out of here. All their money except Métro fare is for the old woman."

"*D'accord.*"

By the outer door where he couldn't be overheard, Mace said, "It makes a long night, but it's a good time to get at Guillerain. He's an important link as we work back to the source."

His men nodded agreement. "And the *poule* he lives with?"

"Gag and bind but don't hurt her. And don't let her listen." He gave Raoul the recorder. "Leave it with Yasmi." Returned the ski mask and left.

Any investigation but the simplest meant probing, learning, following twists and turns and artificial detours until questions were answered, truth revealed, a name exposed. Mace did not expect even a successful interrogation of Louis Guillerain to identify the burglary's sponsors, but Guillerain's knowledge would advance the inquiry.

As he drove off he reflected that Poignard and Coq had not been treated too badly—certainly not compared to the barbarous torture-deaths inflicted on the Río Latigo Contras. But those had been savage, fanatical times, each side doing what it wanted when opportunity arose. In that cruel civil war Geneva convention did not apply.

Gasoline injections were introduced by the Okhrana in Dzerzhinsky's era and emulated worldwide by Lenin's admirers. Too much gasoline in veins and arteries was lethal; lesser but excruciating amounts induced cooperation. More, and joints were disabled. Eyeballs, breasts, and testicles were not immune to injection.

So I know about torture, saw too much and hate it beyond all things. But tonight I accepted it as a means of defending myself and Erica.

Intimate as they had become he sensed something enigmatic about her, remote. Her freshness was obvious, her candor apparently genuine, but there seemed little depth. Was he overly troubled by her ignorance of Carlos's financial affairs, the IFT involvement that imprisoned her husband, and the nature and identities of his enemies? He had asked directly if Carlos had made off with IFT money, given her the option of silence and she had not responded. No strong point had been made of it, but on reflection it bothered him that she had evaded reply. Especially since she had proposed that he undertake a hazardous illegal operation to free a man of whom he knew next to nothing.

He crossed the Seine at the Pont de la Concorde and rounded the obelisk to gain the Champs-Elysées. Across Paris streetlights were dimming as dawn approached but the high-chiseled thrust of the Luxor obelisk was still warmed by lighting from below. Along the Champs traffic was gathering, mostly commercial vehicles at this early hour: delivery vans from bakeries, butchers, and provision shops; gasoline tankers; newspaper trucks feeding Parisian obsession with print news. Citizens on lawful—or unlawful—business.

Farther along, nightclubs were dark, all but a few movie theaters had closed their doors. Those that ran through the night specialized in Laurel and Hardy, Chaplin, and Jerry Lewis films. How the French could include Lewis in that classic company would always baffle him, but they had and did. Lido closed. Marignan and Fouquet's not yet open for coffee and croissants. White sanitation trucks sprayed and whirlybrushed the curb. Dawn on the Champs-Elysées.

He continued on toward the Arc, awed as always by its majestic design, the inscribed deeds it commemorated, and left the Etoile where it gave onto Avenue Wagram. Wearily, he let himself into his office, careful to disarm the alarm system, reset it when he was inside.

Su-Su was splayed across the end of his bed. She regarded him through one eye and closed it. Master hadn't come home when he should have, had broken routine. The hell with him. Mace pulled off shirt and trousers, fell onto the bed and slept.

The intercom was buzzing like an angry wasp. He rolled over and croaked, "Yes?"

Yasmi. "René's here, says it's urgent or I wouldn't—"

"I'll be down." Prying himself off the bed he looked blearily around, made for the bathroom and immersed his face in cold water. He felt hungover without the pleasure of getting drunk. In bathrobe he went down where René was having coffee. He looked around at Yasmi and René said, "Okay to talk, Chief?"

"Quietly." He took a chair beside René, who said, "Got there too late. Louis was dead, cops carting the corpse away."

"Merde!"

"We hung around. When the area was clear of cops we went up and talked with Guillerain's woman, Fleurette."

"Good move. Yasmi, can I have some coffee?" He eyed René. "Was she talkative?"

"Not at first, she was frightened of us. So we paid her some compliments and some money. Like any whore she responded to both." He sipped from his cup. "Saturday afternoon two men came to see Louis. They gave him two cartons and drove away. From her description they were the ones we questioned." Yasmi set down

71

Mace's coffee and returned to her desk. With her computer down she was at loose ends. "Go on," Mace nodded.

"Well, Fleurette she looked like she knew more. So, more compliments and more money." He chuckled softly. "She helped Louis load his car and they drove off to make delivery. Rear entrance of an office building on Rue Balzac. Left the cartons with the guard—being Saturday and no one in the office."

"Did she know which office?"

"The whole building is occupied by Chakirian S.A. Private bankers. All six floors."

"Good work," Mace told him. "You lads are in for a bonus. What about Guillerain?"

"Fleurette worked the streets until four, came back to her place and found Louis in the store doorway. Throat cut. She called the cops and we got there when they were cleaning up."

"She take it badly?"

"Not when she realized there was money to be made. I told her not to tell anyone what she knew or her own throat could be cut. Forget about this visit, I told her, and flipped a coin with Raoul. He went to bed, I came here." Sitting back he stretched and yawned. Yawned again. "Now we know who paid for the break-in."

"Now I have to find out why."

After paying René, Mace asked Yasmi how long the computer would be down.

"They'll try to get to it today. I told them to bring a replacement and take this one away. Maybe it's repairable, but I'm no expert on computer innards. Anyway," she looked at her watch, "I should have equipment by noon."

"Before you access the IFT database, get background on Chakirian, S.A. Bankers, Rue Balzac." He smiled. "Vartan Chakirian is or was IFT director for France, Spain, Portugal, and Switzerland. Took all night to uncover him but he, or one of his men, ordered our break-in."

"And I thought you were just sleeping off an excess of wine. Well, Mace, *pardonnez-moi*. That's quite a connection, Chakirian."

"Who'd have thought it, *hein*? I need food, coffee, shower and

72

shave, not necessarily in that order, so hold any calls."

"The *comtesse* phoned as I was coming in. I checked upstairs and told her you were sleeping. She asked you to call her. Sounded worried."

Mace nodded and went up to prepare himself for the day.

At ten-thirty he took a call from Ed Natsos. "Mace, friend of yours in town. Thought you'd like to know."

Mace grunted. "I got no friends who can afford traveling to Paris."

"This one can. Colonel North."

"Oliver North?"

"That's the guy. The almost senator."

"Ed, I don't know this guy. I told you before, I tell you again."

"But you were both in that Contra mess."

He took a deep breath and expelled it. "I was in the field, Ed. Whatever North did or did not do for the Contras he did from an air-conditioned office in the White House. I've never been in the White House. Even for the fifty-cent tour. So stop bugging me about Oliver North."

"Don't want to know why he's here?"

"For all I know or care he could be taking over the French Army. North could be one of the ones who got me into deep shit, Ed, but that's history, I'm history. And Sandinistas still run Nicaragua."

"You're right on that," Natsos said sourly and hung up.

Mace shook his head, thinking that three years to retirement might be too long for Natsos to hang on. And Nicaragua still clung to Mace like shit on a shoe.

While technicians were installing a loan computer Mace took a call from Angelique De La Tour. "Mace, *chéri*, I think you would have enjoyed the weekend at Armonix. Truly I do."

"Oh? Persuade me."

She laughed lightly. "Let's see. First, there was the usual amount of heavy drinking among the guests. Four fistfights with two men ending up in the carp pond. Three couples detected in flagrante delicto—one couple in a proper bedroom, another on the lawn, the third on the antique billiard table. None was paired with a mate, needless to say."

"And no way to count the number of undetected illicit couplings. You're right, Ange, it sounds upbeat and amusing. Ah—you weren't—"

"One of the flagrant females? Let's say whatever I did was unobserved. And that does *not* mean I did anything the least outré."

"Glad to hear it. Sign me up for the next Armonix weekend. We'll outrage them all."

"Mace! I hardly expected that reaction. Besides, I only called to report the weekend scene and ask you to lunch. Possible?"

"I wish, but I've got a problem here. Over the weekend the place was burglarized, computer smashed, things stolen, so I'm trying to get things back together, and that means working along with the computer people. Tomorrow?"

"I'm *so* sorry about the burglary. God, who needs it? Tomorrow? Umm. Don't think so. Wednesday?"

"I'll count on it. Long afternoon?"

"But of course."

After hanging up he realized he'd ignored Erica's call. She answered his, but he said no questions. He'd meet her across from Hermès at one o'clock. La Belle Equipe. Perfect.

From the window of an adjacent building Mace was observed leaving by a man with a cellular phone. He buzzed his partner on the street and said, "Moving. Over to you."

"Got it." The street surveillant placed his phone in a small Nike bag, lowered his newspaper, and saw Mace hail a taxi. The street man took the next taxi and followed Mace to the Faubourg St-Honoré. He noticed Mace get out at La Belle Equipe, left his taxi well beyond, walked back to the restaurant, and took a table from which he could watch Mace and the *comtesse*. She was opening a thin, gift-wrapped box bearing the Hermès insigne and they seemed to be enjoying themselves. The man wondered what the box contained. His boss would want to know.

seven

The Interview

But Erica, this is too much. I can only wear one scarf at a time." Four large silk scarves lay folded in the box between them, each printed in a separate distinctive design. Erica smiled provocatively. "Two for wrists, two for ankles—you *do* understand, my love?"

"Well—now I do." He paused. "Your ankles or mine?"

"Ours."

"For leisure wear."

"A little love gift—lest you grow bored with me."

"What an idea."

"Last night you abandoned me."

"Couldn't be helped. I'll make it up to you tonight."

They ordered drinks from the waiter, then luncheon. The restaurant lacked even the vestige of a Michelin star, but it was popular with office workers because service was efficient, and the menu very good. A bar ran the length of one wall. Tables occupied the full reach of the single room. Across the opposite wall, dusty paintings of horse-drawn vehicles. Old leather reins and harnesses hung from ceiling rafters. Erica absorbed the atmosphere and said, "With all the equestrian motif I hope we're not served horseflesh."

"Only in specialty restaurants. But if you've never tasted it, horse-meat is edible. Gamy and chewy but edible."

"You've eaten it!"

"In Nicaragua I ate any protein that moved. Parrots, crocodile, snakes . . ."

"Mace, *please*." Her face had paled. "Let's talk of other things. Was your office greatly damaged?"

"Bad enough. Things can be replaced, information retrieved . . ." He sensed they were being watched. The man in brown suit and stringy tie seemed unable to take his gaze from them. Mace felt a chill. Last night the burglars' middleman had been murdered, probably to silence him, eliminate any trail to the doorstep of Chakirian, S.A. He wondered how long the man had been on him.

Of course, the man didn't have to be a hostile; could be another Montpelier foot soldier, only Troyat's men customarily were better dressed. No point in bracing him, or mentioning him to Erica.

She said, "Preoccupied? Shocked by my gift?"

His hand covered hers. "Hardly. What's against foreplay?" He sighed. "It's the burglary—and my housekeeper."

"Yes. How is she?"

"Better today. Yasmi's visiting. Took her a good lunch, hospital food being what it is."

"So thoughtful. Anything I can do?"

He nodded. "Stay close to me."

"As you let me. Forgotten I'll be in Geneva tomorrow?"

"Regretting it already."

"Shall I telephone?"

He shook his head. "Tell me when you return—and stay as long as necessary to accomplish necessary things. René will stay with you."

Their meals arrived. Mace noted that Brown Suit was spooning from a bowl of soup. Their gazes met and the man lowered his, broke off a chunk of break, and dipped it in the soup. An ex-cop, Mace judged, from the provinces. Surveillants worked in pairs. He wondered where the partner was.

By now Chakirian—or a delegate—would have heard of last night's episode with the two burglars. They could tell how Secours personnel had taken and tortured them—but deny giving information. That might explain Brown Suit's presence. He looked away. Mace asked, "Any word from Jules?"

"He called to say they're working to have the papers ready by plane time. Or they'll send them by courier."

Mace swallowed a bit of medium-rare calf's liver sauteed in

oregano butter. "Faced with reality, how will your husband take it?"

"I—frankly, I don't know. He's always been—unpredictable."

"Meaning he could change his mind about divorce."

"He could," she nodded. "For an upper-class Spanish Catholic it's a grave step."

"Want my advice? Don't fuck Carlos again. I mean ever."

The word startled her. "I've been tested for HIV."

"It can take a long time to show up. Anyway, hiring new lawyers is priority one. If Carlos can't come up with names, René will through contacts. Supply him with whatever money he needs. By nature he's frugal, but some things require laying money around. What he doesn't have to spend he'll hand back."

With a harmonic of envy she said, "You have complete faith in him, don't you?"

"Total. Trust him with my life—and yours. In Geneva he speaks for me. If he makes a polite suggestion, comply, don't argue. Like not crossing a street, dining in your room, staying out of sight."

She swallowed. "You're unnerving me. Will he have a gun?"

"Not on the plane. He'll pick up a piece in Geneva, but that's his business, not yours. His job is to protect you while you do what you have to do in Geneva, return you safely here."

"I'll do as he says." Her fingers stroked the back of his hand.

His mind flashed to René, gasoline, and syringe. The *paras* used the combination in Algeria. So had the Arabs. And the Armée Secrète. The memory shrank his scrotum.

Patrons were waiting for tables, but Mace was disinclined to hurry. Brown Suit was swabbing bread around his soup bowl, getting the last bit of nourishment before his target left. Surveillants don't order full meals.

They shared a cherry tart with heavy cream, and express coffee. Mace paid the relatively small bill, tipped well, and escorted Erica to the street. Behind him, Brown Suit scrabbled to pay up. Mace ignored him, and walked with Erica to the head of the taxi rank. "My place?" she asked.

"Let's. Mine's in disarray."

"I've made some changes."

In the apartment he saw she'd removed the photos and paintings.

He said, "We'll find replacements around the Place du Tertre. Aside from animals painted on dark velvet the Orientals go crazy for, there are some pretty good artists showing there. I've got some favorites whose work you should see. One painter is Vietnamese, looks like your worst nightmare of a villain, but he's creative beyond belief."

She was removing jacket and blouse. He unhooked her bra, kissed the back of her neck with its wispy blonde hairs. He pointed at the Hermès box. "Now?"

"Prefer tonight—when we can take our time. Anticipation will be exciting."

"Just a quickie now?"

"You have an appointment, I don't."

"Medium-quickie then."

By the time he got back to the office a loan computer was in place, Yasmi working it. Hardly looking up she said, "Printout on your desk. Interpol. Interesting."

CHAKIRIAN, Vartan, aka Varti, Victor, the caption read. Of uncertain Mid East origin. Maronite Christian. Banker, stock manipulator, possible clandestine arms merchant. Regional IFT director. Private bank capitalized at US $330 million. Finances international commercial real estate development, office buildings, resort hotels, shipping companies. Suspected of diverting IFT funds. Deals at high levels in French and other European governments. Wife not residing Paris. One son born Tunis 1970. Daughter born Nicosia 1972. Greek Cypriot. Father believed to have supported anti-French rebels in Chad, anti-West revolutionaries in Somalia and Sudan. Thought to have access to ordnance surplus in former USSR and Ukraine. Suspected of sponsoring industrial espionage involving illegal high technology transfers. Employs École Polytechnique graduates. Contributes to broad spectrum of French and Italian political parties. Lives privately at Passy estate, rarely mingles socially. Box at Opera. Major Symphony patron.

The International Financial Trust—the printout continued—of which V. Chakirian is a prominent director was organized as a complex transnational consortium of investment banks/bankers. Its stated philosophy was to apply immense combined resources

toward realizing investment opportunities that less powerful financial institutions had to decline. Regional directors like V. Chakirian
were responsible for identifying and evaluating potentially reward-
ing regional investments, then with consortium consent applying the
necessary funds from the IFT financial pool. Very little of this process
was known to or understood by IFT investors before IFT was forced
to close its doors. Subsequent revelations of international manipula-
tion, fraud, and embezzlement on an unprecedented scale brought
into question the entire concept of IFT. Some government investigators claim IFT was organized as an immense fraud akin to the Ponzi
scheme, and indictments of some individuals have begun. In a cor-
porate sense IFT exists as a shell organization headquartered in
Geneva. However, there is no pay-in, pay-out for investors as before.
IFT lawyers concede that perhaps 78 percent of IFT capital is not
locatable. Whether the fund was illegally distributed to (or plundered by) IFT insiders is a legal/financial question under close study
by fiscal authorities in the countries involved. (Interpol is supplying
data as available). It is anticipated that investigations, indictments,
and prosecutions will continue for a number of years. However,
investors are unlikely to recoup any significant portion of their IFT
investments, if indeed there is any investor recoupment at all.

Within the consortium there is bitter hostility as directors exchange
charges of dishonesty and defalcation. Part of that legal maneuvering
may be merely for public effect. However, in the opinion of this
office massive fiscal crimes were committed, benefiting certain if not
all IFT directors, while defrauding international investors.

Mace looked up from his reading. The printout explained IFT in
terms he could understand. His State degree was in History, a subject
that had been less than useful after college. Now he wished he had
taken banking and finance, but his recollection was that those classes
conflicted with the hours of football practice.

Yasmi's printer was humming smoothly, an endless paper belt
issuing from it. By tomorrow the stolen material would have been
duplicated, and he thought that it held limited value for Chakirian.
Mainly it revealed Secours' interest in IFT. Was that enough to murder Guillerain?

He left his desk and went over to Yasmi's. "*La Comtesse* is leaving for Geneva tomorrow; René goes along to protect her—and acquire information. Meanwhile I'm here, and I think I need something to authorize me to act in her interest—if questioned."

"You mean—like a contract?"

He moved around to the other end of her desk. "More like what lawyers have clients sign, enabling them to take certain actions. Date it today. The countess—full name and title—authorizes me to make inquiries in her behalf, execute contracts in her name, disburse monies, employ individuals, and undertake such other activities as may be necessary in connection with any or all of the foregoing."

He moved back while she finished writing. "Compensation to be the subject of a separate understanding," he concluded.

"Mace, that ought to be included."

"One thing at a time."

"*Bon.* So this is basically a power of attorney. Duration?"

"Open end."

She looked up at him. "Prudent."

"And when that's done, there's something else." He looked back at his desk window. "We're under electronic surveillance of some kind, backing up physical. I spotted the clown who tailed me to La Belle Equipe and watched while we had lunch. Then he tailed me again. Somewhere he's got a partner who vectors him. So I want Bellman et Fils to set up a screen that will detect where signals are coming from, what kind they are. Waterloo's compromised as a key word. We'll change." On her pad he printed *Fornax.* Silently she nodded, burned the paper in a tray.

"Very well. Want the authorization drawn up in proper form by a *notaire?*"

"Why not? From your draft. Three languages."

"Gold seals and red ribbons." She began typing from her notes. Mace thought of the papers Samuelson was readying for Carlos Montaner. Would he sign or balk? "And don't forget Bellman."

Irritably, she stopped typing, phoned the electronics firm. "Mace, they'll send a man today to survey, installation tomorrow."

"Have them check our phones and sweep both floors while they're at it."

He hadn't told her about the night's events, the murder of Guillerain. Better she not know. Safer. If she thought he was taking excessive precautions, *tant pis.*

He heard the phone ring as he started up the staircase. Yasmi answered, listened, and covered the mouthpiece. "Someone from Banque Chakirian."

"Make an appointment, you know the routine." He continued ascending. She buzzed the intercom and he listened to her say, "Mace, perhaps you'd better speak with him."

"With whom? Give me a name."

"Monsieur Victor Chakirian."

"Ah, the noble banker himself." Smiling, he picked up the phone. *"M'sieu* Chakirian? Bradley Mason here. Secours S.A. How can I be of service?"

"By giving me a few minutes of your time, sir."

"Is this a preliminary consultation? Frankly, I'm not able to take on new clients at this time, so—"

Cooly, the oddly accented voice continued. "That also could be discussed. At the moment a vehicle awaits you below. Two capable men are at your door. They will see that you suffer no misadventure en route." The connection broke. Mace looked at the receiver and replaced it. He pulled the holstered Beretta from his belt and laid it on a night table. Then he went down to the office.

Yasmi said, "You're going? I don't like it."

"Off to see the Wizard. Sounds like an interesting fellow. What choice do I have?"

"At least I know where you're going. If you're not back soon—?"

"Feed Su-Su, will you?" He opened the office door and stepped out.

His escorts were dressed in dark suits, black shoes, and black ties. They looked like undertaker's assistants. One had a trim mustache, the other a pointed chin *barbe.* He said, "Turn around, please."

Mace turned and raised his arms while their hands passed over his clothing, checked for an ankle gun. Professionals. Chakirian could afford high-grade help. He lowered his arms, walked between them to the elevator. Nothing was said until they reached curbside, where a silver-gray stretch Mercedes idled. *Moustache* said, "Here, please," and opened a rear door. Mace got in, *Moustache* settled beside him and punched a button. A panel opened, revealing a small liquor bar. "Drink?"

"Early for me, I'll pass." The limousine pulled into traffic and the bar panel closed. Mace said, "Not the best possible way to attract new depositors." *Moustache's* lips twitched but he said nothing.

The chauffeur was in gray uniform and gray billed cap. The bearded escort rode in the front seat beside him. Mace leaned forward and tapped his shoulder. "A little more air, if you will. Germans can't do shit with air-conditioning."

The face half turned. Expressionless. "We're not going far."

"That's a blessing." Mace drew a handkerchief across his forehead for effect. Reaching for it, he'd felt *Moustache* tense beside him. "Is where we're going air-conditioned? Hope so. Of course, a bank that can afford all this wouldn't skimp on comfort." He settled back in his seat, watched the driver turn onto Rue Lord Byron, then left to Balzac. His two escorts could well be the villains who murdered Louis Guillerain. At least Fleurette had lived to tell the tale.

The limo slid into a street-level garage entrance, stopped by an elevator door. *Barbe* got out and opened Mace's door, gestured at the open elevator. Side by side they rode to the top floor and got out. *Moustache* preceded them to a walnut double door. Small gold-leaf letters formed: V. CHAKIRIAN.

"This it?" Mace asked. "Don't leave me now."

Moustache opened the door and Mace stepped into a handsomely furnished reception room. Behind him the escorts closed the door and settled down in leather chairs. Mace noted a video camera scanning from a ceiling corner. Presently the inner door opened and a woman came out. "Mister Mason—if you will." She gestured toward the large office beyond. She was an exotic-looking creature, Mace reflected. Coal-black hair with spit curls; dusky complexion, large dark almond eyes. Nilotic profile. Arabic? Maltese? Full breasts and ample hips gave her the zaftig figure of a belly dancer. "Mister Mason," she said coolly, "Mister Chakirian is waiting."

"Of course he is. And I'm holding things up." He went past her into a large, uncluttered room that had a gleaming marble floor, paneled walls with four or five paintings that looked authentically Impressionist. Corot, Valloton . . . over there a Bazille. A fortune in oil, if legally acquired.

From the end of the room a voice spoke. "You admire my paintings, Mister Mason?"

"Very much. On loan from the Louvre?"

"Purchased by the bank."

"And the bank is you." He walked toward the voice.

It came from a man sitting behind an unusual desk. The horizontal surface was darkly grained marble, supported by stainless steel shafts. On it was a neat stack of paper, a telephone, an intercom. The man's hair was fully white. His face was pallid and unlined. Somewhat hooked nose, thin lips and close-set ears. His dark eyes regarded Mace unblinkingly. He wore a Russian-style white silk blouse gathered at the throat, black loose-fitting trousers, and black leather slippers.

"Do be seated, sir. Your time is valuable as is mine, so let me come to the point." Mace eased onto a black marble bench that faced the desk. "What's on your mind?"

"What is on my mind are two or three concerns. First, why are you looking into my affairs?"

"Am I?"

"Please do not play the innocent. You are probing certain aspects of my business and I must know why, and for whom. Naming your client will perhaps satisfy both questions."

Mace grunted. "Your business seems to be banking. I have no knowledge of it and no reason to—as you say—investigate."

"But you have a client."

"From time to time I take on clients. Occasionally I am retained by the law firm of Samuelson Frères. They are my only active clients at present."

"And their brief to you?"

"They suggested I become involved in the defense of another client."

"Carlos, Count de Montaner."

Mace nodded.

"A former associate of mine. In the International Financial Trust."

"A man in serious difficulties, at present a prisoner. Look, *M'sieu* Chakirian, I've told you more than Samuelson would like. I run a small business that depends on circumspection and confidentiality. Word gets around that Secours talks about its clients and I'm finished." He wanted to sound offended and sincere.

Unimpressed, Chakirian continued: "Whatever is exchanged in this room is confidential between us. As a banker I understand the necessity of reticence. Now, am I to understand that the count is not a client of yours?"

"He is not."

"His wife, the Countess Erica?"

"Same. Samuelson thought I might be willing to assist her efforts to free her husband. I declined."

Chakirian thought it over. "Still, you are in a certain sense involved with her."

"In a certain sense. If you're having us surveilled you know we're attracted to each other, okay? Or maybe your agents don't recognize a love affair. But that has nothing to do with you. It's not your concern."

"Perhaps not. But you compiled a substantial dossier on IFT. That may be my concern."

"Press clippings, open sources."

"Why?"

Tiredly, Mace shook his head. "The IFT scandal put Montaner in prison. I knew little about it. To evaluate Montaner's situation I had to know something about IFT, right? Your name came up among other IFT directors. I had no specific interest in you or your affairs then, I have none now." He stood up. "You don't need to return what was stolen from me, I was going to trash it anyway. I've been frank with you and I don't want any more break-ins, no harrassing the countess. She's not a client, Carlos is not a client, got it?" His voice had risen.

Chakirian shrugged. "I'm seldom mistaken, but I may have been misled about the nature of your interest." He cleared his throat. "I am informed that two low-class burglars were rather badly treated by your employees."

"They beat up an old woman, sent her to the hospital. If I'm to retain credibility reprisal is called for. Always will be."

"You sound impulsive even for an American."

"That's how the West was won," Mace snapped. "You've had all the time I can spare. I've answered all I'm going to answer."

"One final question. How were the burglars identified so rapidly?"

"Elementary, my dear Victor." He pointed at one of the room's ceiling cameras.

Chakirian moved his head slowly from side to side. "Elementary indeed. And since you have not undertaken a client relationship with the Montaners I suggest that our mutual interests would be best served if you did not."

"Why not?"

"To avoid—unpleasantries."

Mace smiled thinly. "I'll decide what clients I serve, where my interests lie."

Chakirian nodded. "That is your prerogative, of course. The suggestion is made for purely practical reasons."

"As was my reply."

Chakirian sighed softly. "Very well, sir. I believe we understand each other. On your way out Mademoiselle Mansour will write you a draft covering damages to your office and employee, and the time you've granted me."

"No. That would ease your conscience while affronting mine." He turned and walked the length of the room, pulled open the door and bore through the reception room into the corridor. His escorts got up rapidly and scurried after him. *Barbe*'s coat panel flared back exposing a holstered pistol. Mace jerked it out, chambered a shell and stepped back. To *Moustache* he said, "I'll take yours, *mec.* Two fingers." With a growl *Moustache* handed over his piece. Mace said, "I don't need you to find my way home, so you stay here, okay? Read a magazine, have a drink. And don't come around again. That's important advice—in fact it's a warning. I've smoked more villains than you can count on both hands. Fucking with me adds two more. Got it?" Adrenaline rush heated his blood, suffused his brain.

Barbe spat, *"Cochon! Sale cochon!"*

Mace feinted, slashed the pistol muzzle across his face. *Barbe* howled and clawed at torn flesh, broken teeth. "That's for the old

85

woman," Mace snarled. *Moustache* stared at him stonily. Mace shoved the pistol against his throat. "No comment? You'll address me respectfully or take the consequences." He glanced down at *Barbe* who was on his knees, pressing a reddening handkerchief to his face, and moaning.

Mace pushed the call button and backed into the open car. On the way down he pocketed *Moustache's* piece—H&K 9mm, black matte finish. No shell in the chamber. Careless.

Slumped behind the wheel the chauffeur was smoking, listening to radio news. Mace opened the door, got in beside him. The chauffeur stared in astonishment, peered beyond Mace at the empty elevator. "Where—where are they?"

"Ask when you see them. Now, back to my place." He jabbed the pistol into his ribs. "*Avec célérité.*"

The chauffeur laid rubber as he backed out of the garage. They were three blocks away when the car's cellular phone chimed. Mace ripped it out, tore wires from the electronic base, tossed the handset into the backseat. "I'm not taking calls," he said, and on impulse turned far enough to open the liquor panel. From it he pulled out a bottle of cognac. Hennesey Gold. He uncorked it with his teeth and drank. Swallowed. Drank again. "Have some," he said, and spilled liquor across the chauffeur's lap. The man yelped.

"Shut up!" Mace ordered, "or you'll get it in the eyes."

"It burns," he whimpered.

"It won't rot your cock," Mace snapped, "and worse things could happen." He splashed more cognac down the front of the gray uniform. "I ought to shoot out your tires and leave you to the traffic *flics*—but this is your lucky day."

He recorked the cognac, took it with him when he left the limo at his building. So much adrenaline flooded his veins he hardly felt the alcohol. He was reasonably even with Victor Chakirian, and his thugs were on notice. Chakirian was not aware he knew Guillerain was dead, so the two burglars had denied revealing their go-between's name. They were streetwise enough for that. And from Chakirian's well-dressed thugs he had two pistols he hadn't had before. Overall, a worthwhile hour.

In his office he told Yasmi there had been a low-key conversation with the banker. "I'm so glad, Mace, I was getting worried. Bellman came and will set up in the morning." She gathered her purse to leave. "The document's on your desk. Spanish, French, and German. Notary ribbons and seals. Very impressive." She glanced at the bottle in his hand. "What's that?"

"Bank freebie."

"How odd. I'll visit Rosario on my way home."

"Give her my affection," he said, and went up to shower and dress for dinner with Erica.

The Watcher

With her *femme de ménage* Erica had prepared a light repast: truffled pâté, endive salad, broiled mushroom caps, and pistachio ice. When she brought coffee to the table Mace produced the authorizations, and poured cognac while she read. Looking up, she asked, "What's the purpose?"

"A little protection for me. Object?"

"No—I don't think so." Her face brightened. "Does it mean you've really decided to help Carlos?"

"I'm helping him now. Let's see what develops in Geneva."

"Where do I sign?"

"There, and the other copies." He watched her sign, and countersigned below her signature. Capping her pen she said, "Isn't it time I began paying you?"

"After Geneva." He folded the documents and stuck them in his jacket. "Did you ever have any dealings with Victor Chakirian?"

"The banker?"

"There's only one. More significantly, an IFT director. Did you?"

Slowly she nodded. "About two years ago Carlos took me to his Passy estate, we had lunch and they talked privately while I wandered around the garden."

"Do you know what they talked about?"

"Whatever it was upset Carlos. As we drove away he cursed Chakirian but didn't say why."

"Is it likely Chakirian brought Carlos into IFT?"

"Possible, I suppose, but . . ."

"Chakirian sent hoods to take me to his office. Victor was keenly interested in whether you and Carlos were clients of mine. I told him no. He advised me to keep it that way. I told him I'd make decisions for myself."

She sighed. "Sounds like you, even though it's probably unwise—even dangerous—to offend him."

"He offended *me*. And the old conspirator admitted having my place burglarized. Had the effrontery to offer to pay damages."

"Mace—you refused, of course. Let me pay—my responsibility."

"Forget it. Trip plans perfected?"

She nodded.

"You'll see René on the flight, but don't recognize him. He'll join you at the hotel. La Résidence, right?"

"Route de Florissant."

"Bail money?"

"I'll transfer it when new lawyers tell me." She touched his hand. "I so wish we'd be together. And I desperately hope Carlos can leave prison—legally."

"The best exit by far. If there's time you may want to consider telling him of Chakirian's activities. Just think about it. Don't want Carlos more depressed than he is."

She left the table and brought back champagne from the fridge. Two tulip glasses opaque with frost. He uncorked the Moët & Chandon and partly filled them. "To your very good health, Madame."

"And to yours, *mon coeur*."

Their glasses touched. "Success in everything."

"And now—playtime."

Black candles, black silk sheets and pillowcases. Hermès scarves tied to the bed's four posts. Erica spread-eagled, face down, naked but for a square of iced silk across her rump.

Each time he whipped the silk she moaned and writhed, thrust her pelvis hard against the pillow below. Her golden hair flared out across the black silk, her wrists fought their restraints. Her throat sounds were inarticulate until she ordered, hoarsely, "More. Harder."

He pulled off the protective square and drenched it in ice water, replaced it across her reddened bottom. Switched harder. Soon she was gasping, gulping for air, vomiting obscenities as passion rose. Her body arched, she gurgled, "Now. Oh, Now. *Now*, damn you! *Do it!*"

More than ready, Mace knelt between her thighs and took her. Erica spasmed almost at once, he needed only a heartbeat longer, then lay atop her pulsing body until their breathing slowed.

Turning her face, she looked back. "Oh, Mace, that was wonderful. *Wonderful!*" She licked her lips. "Champagne?"

He untied the scarves and nestled her in his arms while they drank. "How's your bottom?"

"Glowing," she smiled lazily, and groped him. "You have talent, Mace. Or have you been told?"

"It's been mentioned," he admitted, remembering Jessamyn's fondness for the lash.

She held up the switch, touched it to his nose. One end was no thicker than a finger, tapering to a fine point. Polished russet-colored wood slightly over a yard long. "An antique," she told him, "from a very old *maison de tolérance.* I found it at the Marché aux Puces, a little corner shop specializing in—the unusual."

"And had to have it."

"Think of all the lords and ladies, the courtiers and courtesans who had their bottoms warmed with this." She drew its smooth length between her fingers. "Just seeing it made me tingle."

"And of course everyone needs discipline," he said wryly.

"Even you, love. Ready?"

"After champagne."

As she tied his wrists and ankles her expression grew serious. Her eyes glinted coldly in the candlelight. The first slash came without warning. He yelped, sucked in breath. "Hey, don't forget the silk."

"Oh, no, I want to see those beautiful buns light up." With the fine end she beat a half-painful, half-stimulating tattoo across his unprotected buttocks. Moved to the other side of the bed and repeated it. Mace gritted his teeth, felt arousal from the switching. Her eyes were mere slits. She licked her lips lasciviously and got onto the bed, straddling his shoulders as she switched right and left. Her crotch ground into his flesh. Pain diminished, suffused into a warm exciting glow. Dropping the switch she slapped his cheeks with both hands, guttural sounds issuing from her throat. His back was wet from her flowing notch. He couldn't see her face, only the back of her bobbing head, but he could visualize the intensity of her expression as she slapped even harder. Pain dissolved, his whole being seemed focused under her punishing blows. "No more," he husked, "enough is enough."

"*I'll* tell you when you've had enough, prisoner!" Then came a string of obscenities. He was a pervert, a pedophile, an addict of unspeakable things. He required punishment, discipline to purge his criminal tastes. Her body moved agitatedly, her voice raised hysterically as she cursed and raved. Finally—from exhaustion, he thought later—she untied his right wrist and ankle, made him roll over, and mounted him. Tears coursed down her reddened face. She punished her breasts as she rode him to climax. Then, sobbing, she collapsed limply along the length of his body.

He held her close to him as her breathing slowed. Finally, she half-rose, wiped her face and stared at him. "God," she murmured, "I lost control."

"Close enough."

"I'm sorry if I hurt you." She kissed his cheeks, his lips; he tasted the salt of her tears.

"Thought that was the idea."

"No, just the excitement." She rolled aside. Her flesh glistened with perspiration. The flickering black candles created an occult setting.

He studied her face, relaxed now, from the erotic frenzy that had seized it. Black magic. Unsanctioned things. Unhallowed. *Le baiser noir.* Depraved. Their hands clasped. Silently they lay together immersed in separate thoughts.

She was the first to leave. Brought back another chilled bottle. He thumbed off the cork and drenched them with the spouting fizz. Laughing, she spread the cool liquid across his body, lay beside him while he wetted hers before they drank.

"I love you," she whispered. "You know that, don't you?"

"Do you?"

"More than anything—anyone. Ever." She breathed deeply. "I

think all my life I searched for someone like you—never found him until now." Her finger traced his lips. "Is it a problem, Mace?"

"Not a problem, a complication."

"Because I'm married?"

"That's part of it."

"But I won't be married much longer."

"Then we'll explore our feelings. Even if Carlos hasn't been much of a husband I feel—*restricted*, for want of a better word."

"But I *need* you, married or not. You'll be with me, won't you? Promise?"

"When you need me I'll be here for you."

"I'm crazy about you," she said flatly. "You seem indifferent to money, but I'll have tons of it, more than we can ever spend. If necessary I'll buy you."

"Sorry, not for sale."

Her face nestled into his shoulder. "I never belonged to anyone before. No one. Certainly not Carlos. But I was faithful to him . . . until you."

He lifted the bottle to his lips, drained the last few drops. "Anymore?"

"You want to get me drunk and seduce me. Admit it."

"Admitted." She padded off to the kitchen and brought back champagne and fresh, chilled glasses. Presently she said, "This place was only a temporary convenience, you know. I'm uncomfortable here because of what Carlos and his lovers . . ." She looked away at the candles. "After Geneva I'll find something more—suitable. You'll help me look, won't you?"

"Of course."

"It will be ours, no old ghosts. New. A fresh start, dear. Something I badly need."

"Well, it's something you deserve." One of the candles guttered out. Now in the near dark her face was paler than ever. He marveled at its smooth translucence, kissed her nose and forehead. "I'll miss you," he said quietly, "but don't phone or write. If you need to, send a fax. It's more secure."

She nodded. "I hadn't thought of that so I may. To remind you I'm alive."

He grunted and turned her over. Kissed her inflamed derriere with special attention to the darkest stripes. The wet silk had protected her flesh from cuts, though telltale abrasions would linger. "You're exciting me," she murmured.

"No more flagellation."

She shook her head. "I'll feel it for days—and think of you." One hand grasped the antique whip and moved it away. Suppressing laughter she said, "There was a time in Victorian England when it was a crime for anyone but a coachman to possess a buggy whip. Isn't that droll?"

"Tells a lot about Victorian hypocrisy." And her knowledge of curiosa revealed a lot about her. She was an experienced flagellatrix, and he wondered who had initiated her. Was it how she and Carlos got off? His subconscious flashed a silly couplet:

Erica's her name
Bondage is her game

She left the bed and returned with a bottle of scented oil. Under her tender massage some of the smarting left his flesh. Then he oiled and rubbed her body, concentrating on her loins until she shivered with delight. Her arms clasped his neck as she drew him onto her body and they made love that was fully satisfying though less exuberant than before. Silently, the other candle flickered out.

When he woke, morning light outlined the room's heavy window drapes. He heard Erica in the bath, and joined her there, soaping oil from each other's bodies, embracing without passion because the night had been one thing, the day another.

They shared coffee and croissants before he left, reviewed her Geneva priorities, and kissed good-bye. Mace took the back way out and found an early taxi home.

He stored the trilingual authorizations in his safe and went down to open the office for the electronic technician. The young man wheeled in a number of black boxes and said, "*M'sieu*, before setting up scanners I should sweep walls and check your phones."

"You know your business, go ahead." He went upstairs and drew coffee from the percolator, shaved, and dressed for the day. The technician brought up two of his equipment boxes and set one on the dinette table. From it he assembled a microwave screen and plugged it into what looked like a shortwave radio of many dials. After orienting the parabola toward the near window he switched on the unit that included a slow-moving recording tape. He covered the other window the same way, and when the machine was activated he said, "Anything coming through the windows will be picked up and recorded." To the table he added what looked to Mace like a large oblong cellular phone, extended the metal antenna. "Continuous scanning will pick up any radio or telephone transmissions within a block. There is another scanner on your desk. Two parabolic microphones cover your office walls. If a signal is penetrating it will be registered." He closed the empty equipment boxes and moved them out of the way.

Mace looked at his watch. "Let's test. I'll go down and look for a taxi. If I'm seen that should trigger transmissions."

"I was going to suggest it."

Mace left the building, stood by the curb waving at taxis that had passengers. He walked to the end of the block and repeated the performance. After five minutes he appeared to give up in disgust and went back into the building. When he entered the office the technician was smiling. He pointed at the scanner. "Listen." He rewound the recording tape, set it on Play.

A breathy voice said, *"Moving. Looking for a taxi. See him?"*

"Not . . . yet. Now I do. I'll follow."

"Careful, don't let him see you."

"I know my business."

Silence except for an electronic whisper. Then, *"He's walking away. Taxis aren't stopping.* Merde, *he's coming back."* Finally, *"Into the building again. Out of sight. Over to you."*

"Resume position."

The recorder went off. The technician said, "Now we'll locate the spotter. He's not in this building so he's probably in the adjoining one, facing Wagram. The parabolic will give me azimuth, next we need the floor he's watching from. So I'll go down ahead of you and activate the scanner. You come looking for a taxi and he'll transmit."

Mace nodded, and the tech left with his detector gear. A few minutes later Mace crossed the sidewalk and stood at the curb. Two taxis slowed but Mace shook his head and they drew away. He walked to the intersection and went around the corner. Then came back. The tech was sitting on a bench, apparently talking into a cellular phone, but Mace knew he was using the antenna as a direction finder. Mace passed behind the tech and walked farther along the block. As he started back he saw that the tech was gone.

Yasmi was in the office, but not the tech. She surveyed the array of electronic gear and asked, "Any results?"

"There's a spotter in the adjoining building. He directs a man on the street. Or men."

"Chakirian's?"

"Don't know, but I intend to find out."

She settled into her desk chair and turned on her console. "Did the *condesa* leave?"

"Guess so."

"With René?"

"That was the arrangement."

"When will they return?"

"When they've accomplished all they can. How's Rosario?"

"Much improved. She might even come in today. I said it was too soon, but you know how dedicated she is." She paused. "Raoul had some money for her but I think we should add to it, don't you?"

"A month's salary wouldn't be too much. Plus the hospital bill. Whatever she needs."

Yasmi tapped a finger on the desktop. "The *condesa* has so much money—she ought to pay."

"Offered to," Mace said as the tech came in. He nodded at Yasmi and said, "Fourth floor apartment. Name on the door is Valére Fabricant. I could hear the spotter talking from the hall."

"As simple as that," Mace said wonderingly. "More than one man?"

"I heard only one." The tech gestured at his equipment. "Is there anything else?"

At his desk Mace wrote out Erica's address and apartment number and gave it to the tech. "By evening this place will be vacant. I want it swept, phones checked. If it's clean, put in mikes and phone bugs, voice-activated recorder." He handed over Erica's door key. "Make a copy and get it back to me."

The tech nodded, pocketed the key. Mace got up. "I have the owner's authorization to install protective devices."

"You want the take monitored?"

"I'll do it myself."

"Very well. Ah—what about the spotter?"

"Leave him to me."

It took the tech half an hour to dismantle and pack his gear. Yasmi paid him, and after he left said, "I'm surprised you're monitoring *La Comtesse.*"

"That's incidental. I want to know if her place is entered while she's away, and by whom. Now, we're going next door."

"We are? Why?"

He stuck the H&K pistol in his belt. "Tell you on the way."

It was one of the oldest buildings on the block. Porte cochere entrance into a courtyard paved with worn cobblestone. To the right the concierge's office quarters. No concierge visible through dirty panes. They walked to the staircase and climbed to the fourth floor. As the tech said, the front right-hand apartment door was labeled VALÉRE FABRICANT. They approached quietly, listened outside the door. No sound from inside. Yasmi looked at Mace. Nodding, he drew out his pistol.

She knocked on the door, Mace slightly away from her. Knocked again. No sound inside. Yasmi took a deep breath and cooed, *"Chéri,* I'm waiting."

"Hein?" From inside. "Who's that?"

"You know . . . don't pretend. Now let me in."

Footsteps approached the door. A bolt drew back, a chain rattled, the door opened. Mace could glimpse a man's features, he needed a shave. For a few moments he stared at Yasmi before saying, "I don't know you, what do you want?"

"You," Mace rasped as Yasmi stepped aside. Pistol in hand, he backed the man into the room. Yasmi followed and locked the door. Then she patted him down, found no weapons. She took the cellular phone from his hand and put it aside. "Valére Fabricant? I think not."

The man licked his lips. "I haven't got much money. Take it, don't hurt me."

"On the floor," Mace ordered. "Face down. Speak when you're spoken to." He looked around the room.

Set back from the window, and pointing down at the street was a large telescope mounted on a tripod. There was a slow-moving reel-to-reel tape recorder jacked to a receiver. Typical observation post. He handed the pistol to Yasmi and went through the other rooms. A single bedroom, twin beds, one unmade, slept in. Kitchen sink with dirty dishes and cups. Greasy skillet on gas range. Soiled plates on table. Empty wine bottles in trash can. Stained, rusted bathtub, shaving gear in basin. Dirty towels on floor. Closets empty.

Mace returned to the spotter, set his foot on the small of his back. "Been here a while," he said conversationally. "What's the story?"

"Live here," the man said hoarsely.

"You and the pigs." Mace stepped on the man's back, heard him groan. "Take it easy," Mace told him. "You're doing a job—they don't pay you to get hurt—right?"

"I got nothing to say."

"Turn over." Yasmi went through his pockets, pulled out a billfold, handed it to Mace. A *carte d'identité* showed the man's photo and name; Georges Sully Casenove. Mace dropped the few bills on the floor. "How long have you been spotting?"

"Week."

"Target?"

The man squirmed, said nothing. Mace toed him over on his face, stood on the base of his spine. "I don't want to hurt you but I will if you don't talk. So think about this. I can finish your job here and now, bust your equipment and mark your face. Or you can tell me all you know and keep the job. Who's the target?"

"You—or a man who looks like you."

"Next question: who hired you?"

"Don't know."

"Not good enough." Mace set his shoe on the man's cheek. "Try again."

"Wait—phone call. Man told me what to do. I got here, there was money on the table. I set things up, been here since."

"How do you report?"

"By telephone." He breathed deeply. "Calls are on tape. Go ahead, listen. No names."

"Just yours, Georges. And the street man—who's he?"

"Charles. Charles Vigny. I—I hired him. We were police together."

"I believe it. All right, get up and let's hear some calls."

Slowly Georges Casenove got up, shook himself, and went to the reel recorder. While tape rewound Mace said, "No other target, just a man who looks like me?"

Surlily, the man nodded.

"Woman?"

"Time to time there's a woman with him."

"Identified?"

He stopped the tape, clicked it to Play. "Listen."

"Georges, how's it going? Any action?"

"Not much. Guy comes and goes. Routine."

"Nothing special?"

"Charles follows, reports. He eats with a woman, well-dressed."

"Name?"

"Don't know."

"Keep watching."

Mace turned off the recorder. Georges said, "It's like that. I never seen him."

Mace nodded thoughtfully. "We'll leave now. Keep doing what you're doing, say nothing about visitors, not even to Charles, and the job goes on. How long is up to you." With Yasmi he left the apartment, heard the door lock behind them. As they started down the stairs Yasmi said, "What is it, Mace?"

He shrugged. "Not much there." But he had heard the voice before.

nine

Night Work

Rosario was tidying his living quarters when Mace returned. He gave her a warm *abrazo* and told her how sorry he was for her injuries. She dabbed moist eyes and said it was all her fault, she shouldn't have been so easily deceived, begged his pardon. But she brightened when he told her the assailants had been found and punished, and said it would always be her pleasure to serve him in whatever ways she could.

For lunch she prepared a mushroom omelette lightly flavored with amaretto, and served with fresh bread and cheese. Her black eye and blue cheekbone were obvious, and Mace noticed that when she walked she shifted weight from a bruised leg. While he ate she went slowly down to the office and began cleaning it.

At two o'clock he took a call from Albert Boulet, Franco-American distributor of American films. "Mace, I hope you're not too busy to handle a sort of bodyguard-type job for a few days."

"Depends. What's 'sort of' mean?"

"Well, this guy's an adult but doesn't act it. Big Hollywood director-producer. In tomorrow through Saturday, seeing distributors, studios, flacking his own pics."

"Why does he need protection?"

"Loves parties, nose candy, underage girls. We don't want problems while he's here. Get the picture?"

"Only too well."

"Let him autograph but not fondle or snort. Ah—the money's there. How much?"

"Who's the adult delinquent?"

"Laurance—you've heard of him."

"Oh, yes." An ugly little man with a penchant for attacking waiters and parking valets. Made fortunes from conspiracy films that laid the world's ills at America's doorstep. Laurance. The name gave off bad vibes. "Albert, I'd like to accommodate you but right now I'm shorthanded, and your man sounds like he requires round-the-clock attention."

"Unfortunately so. Mace, I'm in a spot."

"All right. What I can do is recommend a larger agency, very reputable. Montpelier."

"Heard of it. English-speakers?"

"Anyone Montpelier puts beside your man will speak better English than he does. I seem to remember Laurance having a fourth-grade education he never improved on."

Boulet laughed in a strained way. "Brags about it, too. All right, Mace, how do I connect with the agency?"

"I'll have the boss call you. Henri Troyat, formerly a DST heavyweight—one of the honest ones."

"Thanks, Mace, we'll talk later. Incidentally, this promises to be a summer filled with visiting beauties from Beverly Hills—and they'll all need protection. Interested?"

"Professionally, yes. Where can Henri reach you?" He wrote down Boulet's number and had Yasmi call Montpelier. To Troyat, Mace explained Boulet's requirements, said the film distributor paid promptly, and relayed his contact number. Troyat said, "We can handle it, Mace, and I appreciate the referral. I owe you."

"You paid in advance," Mace demurred, thinking of Ismail Inclan, "we're even."

"Well, we'll lunch soon. Thanks again."

After hanging up Mace considered calling back and mentioning the Valére Fabricant surveillants, but he was convinced they weren't Troyat's men and there was nothing to be gained from letting Henri know how complicated his life had lately become.

By now Erica and René should be active in Geneva. Erica visiting her husband, while René worked the streets for useful contacts. His dominating hope was that new Swiss lawyers plus massive bail would extract Carlos from prison; the alternative was dubious at best.

Yasmi answered the phone, spoke briefly, and said to Mace, "*Avocat* Samuelson—Bernard." The elder brother rarely called, so Mace was surprised by direct contact. "Yes, Bernard, what can I do for you?"

"Are you free to undertake a small commission this evening?"

"I suppose so. What's its nature?"

"Basically, it's meeting a man and escorting him to—ah, I'll send details by fax." He cleared his throat. "A remote cousin in The Hague sends merchandise here from time to time. Normally the courier is accompanied by a—ah—protector. Unfortunately, the customary escort is ill, and while there is no concern about in-flight robbery my relative sensibly wants his representative protected until delivery is accomplished."

"Of course. I've done it before." A Samuelson relative was sending diamonds to a Paris store or dealer. The courier would fly alone from Holland and be escorted from airport to destination. Mace admired Bernard's indirection. "Fax me," he said, "and if it looks feasible I'll handle it."

"Thank you so much, Mace. Ah—Jules sent documents to Geneva by commercial courier. She should have them before visiting her husband."

"She'll be grateful."

Within ten minutes Mace was reading contact details. KLM Flight 301, arriving Roissy Charles de Gaulle 2300 hours. Jan Fendler, the courier, described as five feet six, full black beard, wearing black clothing and black hat. Aluminum attaché case cuffed to his left wrist. Value of contents: approximately two million dollars.

Mace was to contact Fendler as he left Customs and escort him to the Place Vendôme, where an employee of Joailler Cayol would receive the courier. End of assignment.

"That's a lot of diamonds even for Cayol," Yasmi remarked. "Shall I call Raoul?"

He nodded. "We'll use his car."

But after a quarter hour's trying Yasmi reported Raoul away from Paris, visiting relatives in the Auvergne. "Damn," Mace growled, "I'd counted on him when I agreed."

"Mace—" she left her desk and approached him—"may I make a suggestion?"

"By all means."

"Jean-Paul. No, don't refuse until I explain. I know there's suspicion on his part and a certain antagonism on yours, but Jean-Paul is strong as a horse, he's a stunt driver, top physical condition, and fearless."

"Can he handle a gun?"

"Trick shooting is part of what he does for action films. And he was an infantry sergeant in Mogadishu. Right now Pauli's not working and could use the money. That makes him surly and I suffer."

"But you recommend him."

"Take him on a trial basis. If you got to know each other even a little you'd find you can work together. If you're satisfied with him he can fill in when René or Raoul aren't available. And I'd appreciate it."

"Very well," he sighed, "have him here at nine—he's got a car?"

She shrugged. "An old Peugeot."

"It won't attract attention. Tell him he'll drive and I don't want any bullshit. He takes orders, executes them promptly and fully or he's history. Tell him."

"I will," she nodded, "and thank you."

"If he's got a piece, bring it. If not, I'll supply one."

"I suppose it's necessary," she said musingly, "with all those diamonds . . ."

"Secours guarantees delivery."

Jean-Paul arrived at nine wearing tight jeans and an even tighter denim jacket. Two inches taller than Mace, and from the waist up bulked like an oil drum. From an underarm spring holster he released a semiautomatic pistol and placed it on the table. 9mm Tokarev, barrel bluing worn. "Yasmi said I should bring it."

"Now put it away. Car gassed?"

"Yes, *Patron*."

"What else did Yasmi tell you?"

"I should take your orders and execute them. Fast."

Mace had never really looked at Yasmi's boyfriend before. Now he saw a rectangular face with blunt chin. Brown hair wiry enough to fracture a comb. Ruddy complexion, a boxer's cheekbone scars. No wonder Yasmi had a restricted social life; the big stud scared off competition.

Mace asked, "Did Yasmi mention tonight's pay?"

"No, *Patron*—just that you're fair and will pay what the job is worth."

"Correction, Pauli, I'll pay what you're worth to me. *D'accord?*"

His feet shuffled and he looked down at them. This was a big country boy, maybe twenty eight, without psychological blocks or a lot of mental burdens and Mace found himself willing to give the yokel a fair trial. As Yasmi said, it would be good to have a standby man, and in a way Jean-Paul was already part of the Secours family.

Jean-Paul's ancient Peugeot was a four-door sedan model whose original gray paint hardly showed among patches of rust, red primer, and other colors. Four noisy cylinders tugged it northward on autoroute A 1, and after a while Mace grew accustomed to cars flashing past at double the Peugeot's speed. Well, they'd started out with time to spare, so unless Jan Fendler's flight arrived well ahead of schedule the diamond courier would be met without delay.

"Pauli, tell me again what you're to do."

"Yes, *Patron*. I let you off at the Customs exit and drive slowly around until you appear with another man. I pick you both up and leave the airport quickly. You and the man will sit behind me." He hesitated.

"And?"

"Oh, yes. I am to be alert to any following vehicles."

"And if it appears we are being followed? . . ."

"I notify you and follow orders."

"*Bon.* Our Paris destination?"

"Place Vendôme, *Patron.* Joallier Cayol."

"Precisely." Mace settled back in the uncomfortable seat and watched the radiance of the huge airport light up the distant sky.

By now, he thought, Erica would be asleep in her hotel suite, the meeting with her husband accomplished. But with what results? he wondered. And what had René been able to produce? Nothing, probably, until tomorrow or the day after, but Mace was confident that René would come up with reliable facts and figures.

Jean-Paul steered the Peugeot into the Arrivals lane and slowed to join the chain of slowly moving cars. Mace reached under his coat and pulled the Beretta from where his belt held it against his spine. He jacked a shell into the chamber, thumbed on the safety, and slid the pistol into his trouser pocket. Jean-Paul noticed the shift but said nothing. Mace said, "It's eleven-ten. I don't expect him out of Customs until after eleven-thirty. Park if you want, have a stretch and be at Customs then." He got out of the car and Jean-Paul pulled back into traffic. According to the Arrivals display KLM 301 from Amsterdam had arrived on schedule. Even now the courier could be displaying his gems to Customs officials for bonded entry. Cayol was responsible for duties and taxes.

Lounging near the exit doorway, Mace watched cars come and go, picking up passengers, many with bulky bundles from buying expeditions abroad. Jean-Paul's Peugeot passed and slowly merged with departing traffic. Mace shifted position and narrowly watched the gate.

At eleven forty-two a singleton came out: short, thin, black, loose-fitting suit and black stovepipe hat. Thick granny glasses, full black beard. Thin metal case pressed to his left side. Halting, he peered around, saw Mace approaching, and seemed to start. Mace nodded, stopped before him and said, "If you're Fendler I'm Mason. Your escort."

"Oh, oh, yes. Well, I'm glad you're here," he said in arrhythmic, oddly accented words. "Your car—it is here?"

"My car, it is nearby. But before leaving we'll go back inside."

"Go—? But why?"

"So you can show me what you've got."

His pinched face frowned. "But that is—"

"Irregular? Look, I'm substituting. I need to know what I'm guarding." He took Fendler's right arm and guided him into a passageway that ran beside the Customs area. At door 12-C he stopped and knocked. Presently the door was opened by a young airport security corporal in a neatly pressed blue-gray shirt with shoulder loops. Mace said, "Secours, S.A. I'll need ten minutes."

The security man checked a clipboard list and nodded. "Take half an hour if you want; not much on tonight." He went out and Mace entered with the courier, locked the door behind them. He gestured at a lighted counter. "Open it there."

Fendler gulped. "But—but I have no instructions to do so."

"You have mine. Open it. I'll check against the manifest."

Hesitantly, the courier approached the counter. "This should only be done at Cayol."

"They're welcome to—after me."

Fendler removed his hat, fingered the inside rim and withdrew a key. He laid the attaché case on the counter and unlocked it, still cuffed to his left wrist. Mace opened the lid and found the interior velvet-lined over foam rubber. On the center lay a dark blue velvet bag closed by drawstring. Beneath it the folded manifest. Mace opened the bag and spilled a glitter of diamonds onto the velvet lining.

According to the manifest there should be seventy-seven cut and polished gems of assorted weight, water, and value. He formed seven piles of ten stones, and counted out the final seven. "Count checks," he said, and returned the diamonds to their bag, closed the case and locked it with Fendler's key. The courier replaced the key in his hat rim. "Can we go now?"

They left the security room and went out to the curb. Within three minutes Jean-Paul pulled over and opened the rear door. Fendler got in first, then Mace, who looked around for possible surveillants before telling Jean-Paul to move it.

The highway was well lighted, and they crossed the Périphérique and entered the city by Avenue St-Denis. Streetlights were dim and infrequent. Fendler had the attaché case on his lap, his lips moved as though intoning a prayer. Mace asked, "Do this often?"

"Twice before, never to Paris."

"Relax," Mace told him, "we'll be there in fifteen, twenty minutes." Fendler closed his eyes, seemed to grip the case harder.

As they moved into a particularly dim section a black car emerged from an intersection, and tailgated. After a bumper to bumper jolt Jean-Paul said, *"Patron?"*

"Evade." He pushed Fendler down, got out his pistol and looked back as the pursuing car drew parallel. Abruptly, Jean-Paul braked, and when the other vehicle shot by, he whirled the wheel hard left spinning the Peugeot around so that it faced the opposite direction. Fendler whimpered, "I think I'm going to be sick."

"Take it easy," Mace snapped, and saw the other car turn fast and accelerate after them. "Shake them," he told Jean-Paul, who turned into the next alley and sped ahead. The alley gave out onto a broader street, where the other car's greater speed pulled it ahead of the Peugeot. As before, Jean-Paul braked, but now from the other vehicle came flashes of automatic weapon fire. The windshield splintered, Jean-Paul cursed, brushed glass fragments from his face and accelerated in a twisting pattern that overtook the other car. Mace could see the face of the shooter who seemed baffled by the Peugeot's closeness. Mace fired at him, but not before he got off another short burst into the Peugeot. His head sank downward and disappeared.

Then Mace saw Jean-Paul do an amazing thing. Steering with his right hand he slammed into the other car, bearing it toward the curb. Simultaneously, his left hand flipped out the Tokarev, and fired across his chest at the other driver. The man's head exploded spattering glass with blood and debris. Jean-Paul braked as the other vehicle mounted the curb and crashed into the face of a building. Then the Peugeot moved ahead and followed the street to the next intersection. They were turning into it when behind them the crashed car exploded. As they took an evasive course away from principal streets and avenues they could hear secondary explosions reverberating through the night, each one more distantly. Even a half-blind cop would notice the car's shot-out windows, the bullet-pocked side, and Mace had no handy explanations. Remembering the courier, he said, "Jan, it's over, we're safe now," and pulled him up by the shoulder. Only Jan didn't stay upright, he slumped forward again without a sound. Mace put away his pistol and with both hands pulled the courier erect. Streetlight flashed on a pallid face, chest wetness. The aluminum case was slick with blood. Mace pressed

Fendler's carotid. No pulse, nothing. He leaned forward and tapped Jean-Paul's shoulder. "You okay?"

"Yes, *Patron*."

Mace sighed. "Our man didn't make it." He saw Jean-Paul shrug. "Shall I dump him?"

"No, Secours guarantees delivery."

They found Joailler Cayol in the Place Vendôme a few doors from the Ritz, drove down the narrowest of alleys to the jeweler's delivery entrance. "Wait here," Mace said, and walked around to the store's front entrance. Through barred glass he saw a dim inside light, rang the bell, and waited.

The man who peered out at him was wearing a powder blue smoking jacket, gates-ajar collar, and foulard cravat. Mace said, "I have a delivery for Cayol. From Amsterdam. Come to the delivery entrance." He walked back to the Peugeot, and with Jean-Paul hoisted out the courier and hauled him upright to the entrance. The attaché case dangled from his wrist.

When the door opened, they pushed inward and the receiver closed the door behind them. As he started to mouth questions, Mace said, "Hijackers killed Fendler. Your diamonds are in his case."

The jeweler backed away, fingers scrabbling at trembling lips. "But—but, you can't just *leave* him here."

"Secours guarantees delivery, not disposal. And you have more influence at the prefecture than I do." He pulled off Fendler's hat, got out the key and gave it to the jeweler. "Check the merchandise and receipt for it."

Daintily, the jeweler opened the aluminum case and withdrew its velvet bag. Mace followed him to a worktable already lighted.

Instead of counting the stones, he placed them on an electronic scale, noted the karat total and nodded. He signed a copy of the manifest and noted the time: twelve forty-one. Already Wednesday morning, Mace thought groggily, and pocketed the receipt.

The jeweler placed the diamond bag in a small safe and spun the dial. Turning back, he said, "What of the hijackers, *M'sieu?*"

"Dead."

"Perhaps it's better that way."

Mace smiled thinly. Better for whom? he thought, but said, "They can't tell who tipped off the delivery, arranged the hijack."

"Certainly nobody at Cayol," he said primly.

"Perhaps not—that's not my business. But in The Hague questions should be asked. Like why the usual escort couldn't come with Fendler. That sort of absence is always—suspicious. Ah—where do you want the unfortunate?"

The jeweler glanced at the corpse, still supported by Jean-Paul's loglike arms. Briefly, he closed his eyes before saying, "I suppose one place is as good as another . . . no, the lavatory, *hein?*" He led the way and Jean-Paul propped the dead man on the toilet seat. The case still handcuffed to the limp wrist gave an absurd touch to the mise-en-scène. As they walked back through the shop Mace said, "If you'll take some advice, simply tell police you heard noise at this door, opened it, and found Fendler's body. You have no idea who shot him or when, and cannot understand why the diamonds were not stolen. That's enough to say, *M'sieu*—is it Cayol?"

"Yes, I am Cayol." He hesitated before asking, "But will the police believe me?"

"Why shouldn't they? You're a person of substance, not a footpad. And if they don't entirely believe you, why should you care? You're not going to be charged."

He nodded slowly. "That is so."

"Then phone the prefecture, give us a quarter hour to leave."

"Of course." He sucked in a deep breath, squared his shoulders. "Let me say that I applaud your discretion in all this. Whoever engaged you is to be congratulated." He paused. "I suppose there will be an extra charge for the—ah, amenities."

"There will," Mace replied, and with Jean-Paul trailing went out to his car. Eight bullet holes punctured the car's off-side. The windshield was gone, and the rear window shattered by the automatic gunner. "This machine ought to be put out of its misery, Pauli."

"As you say, *Patron.*" He touched the roof tenderly. "It has taken me many kilometers, good and bad."

"Everything comes to an end," Mace remarked. "Before dawn get rid of it so it can't be traced to you. Find a replacement, and I'll pay for it."

"*Patron,* that is truly magnificent of you," he said emotionally.

"And that was pretty damn magnificent the way you steered and shot left-handed at the same time. I don't think I ever saw a cross-chest like that before."

"A movie trick," Jean-Paul said dismissively. "Shall I drive you home?"

"No way—I don't want to see this wreck again. But come to the office tomorrow."

"Yes, *Patron.*" He swallowed. "Yasmi said that if I—" He swallowed again. "Are you satisfied with my performance tonight?"

"Five-star, Pauli, five-star. You've earned a place in my heart—and Secours'." He grasped the man's large hand and shook it before walking away.

On the Rue de Rivoli across from the Louvre, he found a taxi, woke the driver, and headed home. He was tired from the furious chase, the shootout, and depressed by Fendler's death. Poor little man, he thought; it wasn't the road to Samarra but Death found him anyway. Adrenaline that had heated and charged his blood was draining away. He could barely keep his eyes open. Sometime, not tomorrow, but within a few days, he might try to deduce where the deadly leak occurred, who was responsible. He owed that to Jan Fendler, as well as to himself.

After paying the driver Mace trudged to his building door. High above, a crescent moon hung over Paris. Mist shrouded the crest of the Arc de Triomphe. Low clouds obscured the Eiffel Tower. Nearby, the glow of sidewalk lightoliers turned acacia leaves into shimmering golden coins. Everything peaceful, everything as it should be.

While he fumbled with the alarm key he thought of Erica, safe in bed at her hotel, and was glad she was there and not nearby to ask questions about the night's events. Only Bernard Samuelson had a right to the full story, and that was something to accomplish before noon. In addition to a substantially increased fee for gunfighting, Samuelson or his Amsterdam cousins were going to buy Jean-Paul another car.

ten

The Seduction

Yasmi interrupted his breakfast. "Mace, I have to know what went on last night. Jean-Paul wouldn't tell me anything. Not a word."

"As it should be. Have coffee and I'll tell you about it. And I have to say your man was spectacular. That he keeps tight lips is a bonus."

"I don't want coffee; I want information. Please."

So he told her all that had happened from the time of Jean-Paul's arrival. Her face paled as he described the car chase, the shooting, the unnoticed death of the courier. Huskily she said, "You killed two men."

"One each. After they got one of us. And I'm very glad Pauli was at the wheel. Splendid suggestion, Yasmi. Bill Samuelson at twice the usual rate and add whatever the Peugeot was worth." He finished his coffee. "Double that. You two should have wheels that won't break down when you're out of an evening."

The phone rang and she went down to answer it. Presently via intercom she reported Bernard Samuelson on the phone. "Say I'm in the shower and suggest he come here—if he wants to consult. Have our bill ready when he arrives."

He finished dressing, scanned *Le Matin,* and caught a short inside paragraph describing a fiery car crash near St-Denis. Residents in the vicinity spoke of hearing a speeding car just before an explosive crash. The two victims were unidentified but police expected to throw light on the case after vehicle ownership was established. No details were immediately available.

Yasmi answered the door and Bernard Samuelson came in. The elder brother was pink-faced and portly, his large head framed with well-trimmed white hair. Without preliminaries he sat across the conference table from Mace and snapped, "What happened last night?"

Mace produced the Cayol-receipted manifest and pushed it across to the lawyer. "Delivery made."

Samuelson thumped the receipt impatiently. "I know that, Cayol phoned The Hague early this morning. What I'm being asked with urgency is where is the courier? What happened to Jan Fendler?"

Mace eyed him before replying. "Tell me who leaked the plan, set us up for hijack, and I'll tell you about Fendler." His voice raised, "Yasmi, I'm retaining Bernard as my attorney." He handed Samuelson a ten-franc note. "What's that for?" the lawyer asked.

"Establishes client confidentiality. I can now speak of dirty deeds without fear of revelation. Right?"

The lawyer nodded. "Go ahead, Mace. Where is Jan Fendler?"

"Probably in the morgue. Took an unlucky hit from hijackers who wanted his gems." He pointed at the newspaper report. "Tells half the story." Then, before Samuelson could interrupt with questions Mace related the night's events as he had earlier to Yasmi.

When he finished, Samuelson slowly shook his head. "Poor Jan. Never found his niche in life, and now he's gone."

"Happens."

"Well, I must notify his father, and make burial arrangements." He sighed. "What a tragedy for the family." His gaze lifted. "Is there any way it could have been avoided?"

"Not after the shooting started. Bernard, listen to me. It was a surprise attack, an ambush. The shooter used a machine gun. My driver and I were unbelievably lucky to survive. When Jan's family starts looking for someone to blame—as they will—tell them to look among their associates and employees. Until the leaker is found they better hold back on sending gems from Holland."

"I don't suppose you would care to undertake the investigation?"

"No. I don't speak Dutch, and if I fingered a suspect it could be suggested I was trying to divert suspicion from myself. I'm out of it, Bernard. I'm sorry Jan was killed, but it could have as easily been me. Yasmi?"

She brought over an envelope and placed it before the lawyer. He opened it and scanned the billing. "Seems high," he remarked. "I'll see what my relatives have to say."

"That wouldn't please me, Bernard. You hired me. Pay the bill and settle with your relatives. Now, you have things to do, and so do I." The lawyer rose. "I'll send over a draft in full."

"I'll appreciate it." He showed Samuelson to the door and heard the fax machine start clattering.

"It's from La Comtesse," Yasmi said, and handed Mace the message.

Recommended law firm is Schreiber, Wollancz & LeFevre. Initial discussion today. Miss you. Erica.

Progress, he thought; one priority accomplished. Had Carlos signed the divorce agreement? Would he? Yasmi interrupted his thoughts, saying, "Jean-Paul will be here shortly, said you asked him to come."

"I did. If he wants dollars, pay him five hundred. And you should go car-shopping with him."

"I've found some possibilities in the classifieds."

"Four-door," Mace specified, "big enough so he can fit in comfortably. I'll be back later."

From his office he taxied to Erica's building and entered the apartment by the rear service door. He went directly to the closet where the Bellman tech had installed monitor equipment.

Last night after one o'clock two men had moved around the apartment. The motion sensor registered their movements for forty minutes, while the tape recorder carried their muted voices as they discussed planting microphones. One was installed in the living room chandelier, the other in the bedroom night lamp. Mace confirmed visually and reset the electronic monitors. Then he returned to his office.

Yasmi was gone but there was a blinking red light on his message machine. Angelique De La Tour. "Mace, dear, don't think we settled on luncheon time, so would one o'clock suit you? If I don't hear from you I'll assume it does."

He turned off the machine, rebuking himself for having overlooked their luncheon date. Well, gunfighting could do that, but he was back on track now and looking forward to being with her. How foresighted to remind him, but there was an implication of prior forgetfulness that made him uneasy.

While changing, Mace thought about the nocturnal intruders in Erica's place. They had picked a time when she was away from Paris, and his earlier suspicions that the apartment was targeted were now borne out. On her return she should find another place, as planned.

He was preparing to leave when the door buzzer sounded. "Who is it?" he called, and heard, "Message from Samuelson Frères."

Cautiously, he opened the door and saw an office messenger. The young man opened his pouch and handed Mace an envelope addressed to Secours S.A. Mace thanked him and locked the door before opening the envelope. It contained a copy of his bill and a bank draft for the full amount. He laid it on Yasmi's desk for depositing, set the security alarm and drove to Ange's place on Avenue Foch.

Champagne cocktails, Haviland china, Swedish crystal, salad, and grilled salmon. Ange in green silk harem pants, matching bra and jacket. That was before.

Now they lay drowsily side by side, Mace musing that this was the first time he had been truly relaxed since the gunfight. It hardly troubled him that he was making love to Angelique, not Erica. She was in another country, and today had been planned before he met her. The infidelity was easy to justify, and Erica would never know.

Ange turned and, eyes still closed, kissed him deeply. They made love again, and when Mace left at four she was already asleep.

Yasmi greeted him cheerfully, saying they'd found a Pontiac with only sixty thousand kilometers on the dial, and made a deposit pending inspection by a mechanic friend of Jean-Paul's. "Also," she said, "I deposited Samuelson's draft and paid Jean-Paul. He's very grateful, Mace."

"So am I. But for him I'd probably be cold in the morgue with Fendler. Anything else from Geneva?"

She shook her head. "But there was a call from Forbes Paxton. He wants to come in today, if that's possible."

"Forbes—?" Had he heard that name before? "British? American?"

"I'm sure he's American. Shall I call him?"

"Yes, I'm curious." Forbes Paxton. The name was unusual enough to be remembered even without a face to tack on to it.

When Paxton came on the line Mace said, "Your name isn't familiar—have we met?"

"Yes—under circumstances we'll go into if I can have—oh, half an hour of your time."

"Where are you?"

"Eighth Arrondissement. I'll be there by five." The line went dead.

To Yasmi Mace said, "Stay around until I determine if he's friend or foe. From the accent he's American."

"So he could be either."

"That's a cynical remark."

"Not if you think it through."

He shrugged. Why argue?

"Did you have a pleasant afternoon?" she asked with a knowing smile.

"Very agreeable. This unsolicited visitor may want coffee."

"Or cognac."

"Be generous, we can afford it."

Forbes Paxton was tall and thin, with gray-streaked hair and matching mustache. His face was weathered, nose narrow and somewhat hooked. Teeth glinting with porcelain perfection. He was ten feet into the office before Mace recognized him.

"Well, Colonel," Mace said, "it's a long way from Guatemala City." He eyed the former military attaché who had fed and clothed him, then turned him in.

"Is at that," Paxton replied, with a lupine grin. "May I have a chair?"

Mace pointed to a space on his desk. "Visualize this sign: BE SEATED, BE BRIEF, BE GONE."

"Pentagon crap," the visitor remarked as he eased his lean frame into the chair. "You're looking well, Captain."

"Better than when I crawled out of the bush." His eyes narrowed. "You had a different name then."

"Many of us did while we were supporting anti-Sandinista activity. But Paxton it is, and I expect you'd like to kick the shit out of me."

"Kneecapping would do it, but you're safe here." He signaled Yasmi she could go. "Unless you're packing iron."

Paxton spread his hands. "In the City of Light? Come, come, Captain."

Mace grunted. "I don't worship titles of rank, not company grade. You were a light colonel then—"

"Yeah, squeaked a grade more, and did my tombstone tour as Assistant MilAtt here in Paris." His lips twisted. "That made me miss Desert Storm, the combat assignment that would have handed me a star, no questions asked." He twisted his gold class ring.

"Well, you had *beaucoup* good life," Mace remarked, "so it wasn't a total loss." He looked at his watch. "What's on your mind?"

"Care if I smoke?"

"Yes."

Paxton shrugged. "During my years in Paris—in and out of the embassy—your name surfaced now and then. You come off as the quintessential expatriate who did well in a foreign land. Reputation for honesty, integrity, and accomplishment." His lips pursed, made a sucking sound. "Enviable."

Mace said nothing.

"Someone like myself," he continued, "occasionally needs to turn to someone like you for—information. Occasionally action."

"In what context?" Mace inquired.

"Well, I made contacts before retirement, enough to set myself up informally as a consultant."

"In what area?"

Paxton leaned forward. "Military procurement."

"The French don't buy ordnance from us anymore—we can't even give the stuff to them."

"True. But Paris is a big center for arms deals. At any time there are dozens of little men running around looking for—ah, special items. To use in their homeland—or someone else's."

"You're talking Stinger missiles and so on."

"And so on," Paxton agreed. "Illegal to ship from the U.S. except to favored allies of the moment. But not illegal to send them from country B to country C."

"At least difficult to prosecute."

Paxton nodded. "You'd be amazed at the worldwide demand among pugnacious small countries and, ah, special interest groups for proscribed ordnance."

"I'm not amazed by it—everyone knows it's going on—I'm just worried those Arab mothers will level the Eiffel Tour for practice. Because this building, Colonel, is in a direct transit line from the Tower."

"More likely they'd Scud the embassy." He cleared his throat. "Not an altogether bad idea."

"Can't disagree."

"Yeah, all those feather merchants and faultfinders . . ." He shook his head morosely. Mace said, "Ed Natsos is still holding on there and he's getting to be a pain in the ass."

"Yeah? How so?"

"Needling me about Nicaragua, the Contras."

"Tried it with me but I came down hard. Last I heard he'd been sent to Berlitz language school to get him out of the way."

"What language?"

"French. So he could make himself reasonably useful at the station." Paxton laughed deprecatingly. "Two years immersion while drawing full pay and allowances. A while back he hit me up for a job after retirement. Laughable. An empty suit whose only qualification is speaking French." He thumbed the point of his chin. "But Berlitz did a hell of a job, his French is even better than mine."

"But you didn't hire him."

"Look, I may have stayed too long in the hot countries but I'm not crazy. Fuck Natsos and all the spooks like him. Don't let him bother you, not worth it."

"Good advice. Well, Colonel, good of you to stop by."

Paxton nodded. "I wanted to get square with you, Mace. Believe me, all I did was by the book: took care of you and reported you in. Routine. Headquarters sent the MPs, not me."

"Bad times for everyone," Mace acknowledged. "It's history. So, you're into military procurement. I assume it's profitable."

"Does a bee make honey? Plenty profitable. But now and then I need a front man, someone trustworthy to go in and lay on arrange-

116

ments while I stay in the back room. Not Ed Natsos."

"And why would you stay in the back room?"

"Let's say to avoid the appearance of any conflict of interest. To keep my face fresh for the next buyer. The kind of work you do, living here, speaking the language, you've got an edge. The Paris edge. If you'll work with me from time to time I see you making an astonishing amount of money."

"Interesting," Mace replied. "I'm listening."

"For several months I've picked up rumors that seemed incredible at first, but on analysis are less so. Has to do with some sort of anonymous consortium with endless money that's doing two things: buying up Russian and Ukranian arms, ordnance and warplanes, and—get this—taking over an entire country to use as a warehouse and sales depot. That strike you as wild?"

"Maybe, but probably feasible. Alive, old Basil Zaharoff, the original Merchant of Death, would be in it up to his neck. It's the sort of fantastic operation his mind would create."

"You're right, Brad. At first I thought the Saudis were prime suspects, then I considered Iran, Syria, and Libya. But there's too much hatred and suspicion among those countries for them to work together overtly or covertly. Pakistan? Hasn't got the bucks." He looked at Mace. "Anything like this cross your scope?"

"Can't say it has."

"Well, there's enough talk going round that something like it is going on, though possibly not in the rumored form. Meanwhile, I have merchandise to locate, sales to make."

"Before a monopoly freezes you out."

Paxton nodded. "My Russian contacts are pretty closemouthed, but maybe they'll drop something soon."

Mace got up and brought over the coffee and cognac tray from Yasmi's desk. Opening the thermal jug he said, "After five."

"And I'm ready." Paxton poured cognac for himself, another for Mace. "Forget the coffee." He drank and smacked his lips. "Sources tell me you're squiring a gorgeous young countess around town. Client?"

Mace shrugged.

"I checked with the embassy, Mace. The count is in prison suspected of embezzling megabucks from that banking group, International Financial Trust. I also hear that a lot of people want the count to stay in prison until he coughs up what he stole."

"Could be."

"And the wife is none too eager to see him out and running. Anything to that?"

"Anything I may know of their situation comes under the heading of client confidentiality. But why would the embassy be interested in the Montaners?"

"Because some pretty heavy U.S. citizens were taken to the cleaners when IFT bellied up. I mean mega-millions. And they're pressuring our embassies in Paris, Rome, Zurich, and Madrid. Sort of an international treasure hunt." He smiled. "Countess ever talk about it?"

"I can't say."

"Okay, okay, shouldn't have asked," he said hastily. "The husband isn't thought of as the most macho fellow in Europe, so if you're into hand-holding, who cares?"

"Anything else, Colonel?"

"I'll leave my card." He drained his glass and produced a business card from his billfold. "It's me and my message machine. Holds down overhead, and I have yet to find a Frenchman, or woman, I'd trust working for me. What secrets I have I want to keep secret."

Mace rose with him and Paxton turned to leave. "So, how do we stand?"

"I guess you'll call me if you need me."

"Could be soon." He went out, Mace locked the door, and carried the drink tray up to his kitchen where he swallowed another shot of cognac. What a strange visitation, he thought, with more behind it than Forbes Paxton chose to reveal. The colonel's talk of a super-rich consortium cornering the arms trade suggested a possible connection to the IFT; then it could be nothing at all, just rumor. But Paxton had brought up IFT and the Montaners, and Mace wondered who reported his liaison with Erica to the retired colonel. Well, as long as they appeared together in public people would draw their own conclusions. Nothing to be done about that.

At six he turned on a TV news channel and saw live coverage of a mob scene around the Hotel Georges Cinq entrance. According to the anchorman the American film director Laurance had spat on a group of autograph seekers and fought with one who resented it and struck back. Bodyguards hustled Laurance away from the mob, and Mace was cheered by the sight of his bloodied face. Unbloodied, the face was gnarled like a leprechaun's, and surmounted by tightly curled brown hair. Of small stature, the pugnacious director resembled a malign gnome. Troyat's men were earning their pay, and then some.

Still, he reflected, Laurance's conduct wasn't as outrageous as that of the famed American actress, beloved of millions for her motherly type portrayals, who, a few years ago—drunk or zonked on drugs—had perched on her hotel room balcony and mooned an assemblage of admirers before defecating on them. The Interior Ministry had expelled her forthwith, and the Foreign Ministry sent a severe note of complaint to the Embassy. Since that episode, Albert Boulet once confided to Mace, it had been impossible to book her films into France. Insulted, the French understood how to react.

Dusk was spreading across Paris; between now and nightfall was his favorite time of day. No Erica for cocktails and dinner this evening, she was far away working for her husband's freedom. Paxton's suggestion that she was less than eager for his release irritated Mace until he dismissed it as tabloid-type gossip attachable to anyone of wealth or prominence. He wondered what the tabloids would do with Laurance's despicable outburst. The Interior Ministry wasn't going to expel him; spit was less offensive than shit.

What troubled him, as he sipped another cognac, was Forbes Paxton's sudden appearance out of nowhere; the reasons given were unconvincing, so Paxton was on some sort of fishing expedition. If not for himself, then for whom? Mace had no fear of Paxton, viewed him as a post-service hustler working Europe rather than the D.C. Beltway, and hoped he would see him no more.

Feeling at loose ends, Mace phoned Jessamyn Taylor. She'd left the British Embassy, and her apartment phone rang repeatedly before she answered. "Mace, I really rather expected a response to my invitation," she said severely.

"Hell, Jess, you were in London, how was I to reach you?"

"Oh. I didn't leave my number?"

"Definitely not—and me all pining and horny. Let's have dinner and take in some jazz."

"Oh, Mace, what a heavenly idea, but I've just done my hair and it takes hours to dry and look decent. Can't possibly tonight, thanks anyway, luv. Will you call tomorrow? I do want to see you. Honestly I do."

And I want to see that pink-and-alabaster body doing what it does best, he said silently. "Right, I'll call."

So he Métroed over to the Left Bank and walked to Le Jazz Caveau on the Boul' Miche', where he ordered house wine along with an edible hamburger and good fries. The below-street room had boulder walls and heavy, smoke-stained rafters. Old round tables with Coke chairs, and a raised platform for the musicians.

Of the night's three jazz combos, one was Swedish, the second Rumanian, and the main draw hailed from Kansas City, or so the sign said. Anyway, it was by far the best of the three. Tenor man had heard a lot of Plas Johnson solos, cornet paid homage to Bobby Hackett, and the piano echoed figures originated by Teddy Wilson a couple of centuries ago. Still, he hadn't wanted bebop Birdland stuff and was more than contented with KC nostalgia, an astral improvement over the Auberge's Les Rocket Boys' offerings.

The crowd was composed of university students—this being their quarter—and the Parisian equivalent of young Manhattan Yuppies. Mace liked their enthusiastic response to number after number, felt easy and comfortable among them. Hell, he wasn't all that much older, he told himself, and as though in answer to his thought he saw a black-haired young thing leave a five-girl table and walk over to his. She wore a tight black bandeau and thigh-gripping black spandex shorts. Glistening neutral lipstick, darkened eyes, and rouged cheeks. Not a *poule*, a student trying to look like one. *"Américain?"* she asked pleasantly.

"Australian," he smiled. "Like in *Crocodile Dundee.*"

"I'm Monique," she said as her small figure slid into the chair beside him. "I'm a university student."

"I guessed that," he told her. "Drink?"

"If you don't mind." A toss of her head swirled hair behind her shoulders. "I love *le jazz*, but being with females all evening can get boring."

"So you thought you'd chat with me." He signaled the waiter who took her order for wine-and-seltzer.

She nodded. "You live in Paris? Work here?"

"Both."

"Married?"

He shook his head. "You?"

"Oh, no, and perhaps never. I don't want to *belong* to anyone."

"I know the feeling," he remarked. "Enjoy life while you can. What are you studying?"

"Classical Archaeology. I hope to work in Athens next year—or Central America."

The waiter brought her a tall glass and she sipped through a straw. She looked too young to be drinking anything alcoholic at all, he thought, then remembered that wine not milk was served to the young in many French working-class households. Accounting for a depressing number of juvenile alcoholics. She got out a packet of Gauloises and handed him a lighter. As he held the flame for her cigarette she asked, "You don't smoke?"

"Cigars."

"Never . . . pot?"

"On occasion."

"I have some," she confided, and exhaled smoke to one side. "From Tunis. Strong and very pure. I don't like to use it alone."

"I shouldn't think you'd lack company."

"I'm—selective." She smiled.

The Swedish combo struck up a danceable slow tune. Monique took his hand and drew him erect. They danced with both arms around each other, and presently he felt her pelvis pressing and rotating below his. "What do I call you? she asked huskily.

"Dundee. Rhymes with *cher ami.*"

She laughed. "And whose 'dear friend' are you, Dundee?"

"Yours. *Pour le moment.* We live from day to day, don't we?"

"Hour to hour. I detest wasting time." Her head tilted back so she could whisper in his ear. "Dundee, I have a place we could share some Tunis leaf. It's very near."

"Let's check it out." He paid the bill and they left amid heavy applause for the Swedes.

As they climbed up to the sidewalk she took his hand and walked ahead. Then she backed against the wall and pulled him against her. On tiptoe she kissed him open-mouthed, tongue probing his. "*Capote?*" she whispered.

"No." He didn't carry condoms.

"Don't worry, I do." She hugged him tightly, her arms around his.

Then Mace felt a gun barrel bore into his spine.

eleven

The Cemetery

Robbery, Mace thought, then a rough voice growled, "Don't try anything. Move back and let the girl go."

He looked down at her face and saw an arrogant, triumphant smile. "Sorry, Dundee, some other time."

Her arms still circled him. *"Merde,"* he said disgustedly and took a half step back before spinning her around and shoving her into the gunman. Monique yelped as the pistol jammed her back. Mace pushed her aside, grabbed the pistol, and twisted it from the other's hand. Then he kicked the man's crotch. As the erstwhile gunman snapped forward grabbing his crotch, Mace kneed his face and chopped the back of his neck before he fell. Gun in hand, Mace turned to the girl staring unbelievingly at the fallen man. "You were very smooth," he told her, "very professional. Now it's explanation time."

"I don't know anything," she said tautly.

A car was parked at the curb, lights on. "His?"

She shrugged. He showed her the pistol. "Grab his belt and drag him." Mace held the gun on her, and pulled with his free hand. Together they hauled the man to the car. Mace opened the rear door and shoved him in. The man was gasping with pain, his face a bloody mess.

"I'm going," she said hoarsely. "Try to stop me and I'll scream."

"Try to leave and I'll put a bullet in your ass. Get behind the wheel."

Briefly, she hesitated. Mace snapped, "Now!" and saw her open the door and get in. He rounded the car and got in beside her. "Drive."

"But—where?" Her face was ashen.

"That nearby place you mentioned—with the pot stash."

"I was lying."

"Then the *commissariat*. Rue Jean-Bart. Let's go."

"*Cochon!*"

"*Cochonne*," he replied, and gripped her neck firmly, thumb closing her carotid. She tried clawing his fingers away but lost consciousness. He removed his hand and went through the clutch purse on her lap. The *carte d'identité* gave her name as Monique Rachèle Denoize, student, age twenty-one. He put the ID card back as she came awake. Blinking, she looked at him, fear frosting her eyes.

"Ready to cooperate, Monique?"

She started the engine and steered from the curb. Mace half turned so he could watch damaged man and driver. "Little piglet," he said to her, "what's your partner's name?"

"Aron—he's not a partner, I only met him tonight."

"And you went in to the Caveau looking for me."

Silent, she bit her lip. Her eyelids welled over, mascara blotched her cheeks.

"Was he to rob me or take me away?"

"He—he didn't say."

"So, we have to ask him, don't we? Have you a police record?"

"No!"

"If you don't want one you'll be helpful, understand?"

She nodded, turned the car onto Rue Soufflot and stopped at the curb short of the church. She pointed at a building doorway. "I'll take the keys," Mace said.

Surlily, she handed them over. Mace said, "We're going to waltz Aron into your pad, understand? Any surprises and I start shooting. You go first."

Between them, on the sidewalk, Aron tried to hold back, but Mace stuck the pistol barrel in his mouth and resistance collapsed. Partly holding Aron, Monique got out her door key, then they went up to the third floor, Aron groaning at every step. Partway down the hall she opened a door and switched on an inner light. Mace pushed

Aron inside and closed the door behind them.

It was a typical student apartment. Books everywhere, soiled clothing on the floor, magazines scattered here and there, unmade bed. He shoved Aron into the bathroom, said, "Clean yourself up," and locked the door. Then he turned to Monique. "Strip."

"*What?*"

"Strip," he repeated. "Do it or I will." He twirled the pistol around his trigger finger. When it stopped it was pointing at her. Slowly she undid the bandeau, freeing lemon-size breasts. Her body was trembling. "All the way," he ordered, and she began peeling down the Spandex shorts. "Shoes, too?" she sneered.

"Suit yourself. Where's the pot?"

After stepping out of high-heeled shoes she padded to a kitchen cupboard and brought out a brown paper bag, a packet of cigarette papers. "Roll them," he told her. "Both of us need a jolt."

As she worked at the counter he admired her smooth, tight flanks, the dimpled love-holds. Unsurprisingly, she was a natural brunette, *motte* well trimmed. He could hear Aron running bathroom water. The blood would wash away, but do little for his smashed nose and lips.

She brought over two joints and a lighter. He stuck one between his lips and she lighted it, then hers. Simultaneously, they inhaled. The smoke hit his lungs like a thorax punch; he hadn't had pot as good as this since Nicaragua. "*Jésus!*" he gasped. "Tunisia?"

"As I said." She drew again, let smoke drift from her mouth and nostrils. Her pupils were constricting. Mace toked again, removed the pistol magazine, and laid it down with the pistol. She giggled. "You're unarmed, Dundee."

"Necks can be broken."

Her face sobered. "Would you hurt me?"

"If necessary." He studied the glowing joint in his fingers. Time was slowing down. "Aron's your pimp?"

"No!" she flared, "I'm not a whore."

"But doing a whore's work. Keep smoking."

Reluctantly, she inhaled again, repeated it when he gestured.

"This shit is too good to share with Aron," he remarked, cupped the joint and pretended to inhale. "Besides, it'll be a while before he

125

can enjoy a smoke. How much did he pay you?"

"Fifty francs." Mace opened her purse, inverted it on her desk, saw a fifty-franc note. And three condoms. "Three Merry Widows," he said. "That's what we called them when I was a kid. Came in a round aluminum box." He saw her hands move up and down her body as though stripping off water. Her small nipples were pink and visibly enlarged. "Smoke," he told her. "Grab a piece of Dreamland."

"So you can fuck me?"

"Your invitation, *chérie.*"

"I—I didn't mean it."

"Too late now." He moved behind her, drew her against him and cupped her breasts. Her body shivered. "I said, Smoke."

Defiantly, she sucked in deeply, held a long time and expelled with a gasp. Her body ceased trembling. She pressed back against him. He stroked her cheeks, fingered the tight divide until she quivered. Unbidden, she inhaled again, turned her head and exhaled lightly against his cheek. "Smooth," she breathed, "so fucking smooth."

From the bathroom Aron yelled, *"Let me out!"*

"Shut up," Mace called back, "or the first thing through that door will be a bullet. Then five more." He hugged Monique tightly. "You were surprised when I took him, *bébé.* Who did the two of you think you were setting up?"

"He—he didn't say. Described you. Told me what to do."

"Lot of trouble for a street robbery, *hein?*"

"I think so. He was going to take you with him."

"And you?"

"Drive."

"Well, you did, and here we are. Any suggestions?"

In reply, she toked again, turned to him, and began fondling his crotch. "Let's do it," she breathed, went to the bed and lay back, feet on the floor.

He felt under the pillow, touched metal, dug out a kitchen knife. Wordlessly, she watched as he flipped it at the far wall. It clattered down behind her desk out of sight.

Closing her eyes, she spread her thighs. He stroked her crotch and fingered her clit, large and hard as a pencil eraser; she murmured pleasurably. Mace said, "Finish the joint, all of it."

She toked greedily, and when the smoldering paper reached her nails, he gave her his and told her to finish it, too.

When the roach dropped from her fingers he put it in an ashtray and opened her closed eyes. The pupils were dilated but the receptors were numbed. Monique was out. Totally zonked.

Mace picked up the pistol—an old Llama—and stuck it under his belt. Then he pulled the sheet over her body.

Opening the bathroom door, he saw Aron on the toilet seat, hands covering his face. "Time to go, *mec*. On your feet."

Slowly, the injured man got up. His eyes were bloodshot, nose bent, lips swollen and scabbed. Aron shuffled out of the bathroom, blinked at the brighter light, and glanced at the sheeted figure on the bed. "You killed her," he said dully. "No one was supposed to get hurt." A sob choked his throat. He looked away from the bed and went haltingly to the door. "You're going to kill me," he said despairingly, "like you did her."

"Down the stairs and into your car." Mace followed Aron, who grasped the handrail and went slowly down to the street. "You drive," he told Aron. "Take me to your leader."

"I—I can't—he'll kill me."

"Not if I kill you first. Start the engine."

Like a robot Aron turned the key and steered away from the curb, his smashed nose making snuffling sounds. Wordlessly, he drove through the Left Bank toward the Invalides, turning onto Rue de Varenne and stopping short of Rue du Bac at the Italian Embassy. Guards flanked the ornate entrance gate, no casuals admitted. "Who hired you, Aron?"

"The commercial counselor, Giulio Forasteri."

"To bring me here?"

"After taking you I was to telephone for further instructions."

"Drive to a kiosk, phone him for those instructions."

Aron thought it over, reached a decision when Mace prodded his ribs with the Llama. Along Rue du Bac Aron stopped at a kiosk where they both got out. Mace listening beside him, Aron dialed a number, waited. Six rings before a man's voice said, *"Pronto?"*

"It's Aron," he said in a muffled voice. "What do I do with him?"

"Bring him to the embassy, I'll tell the guards to let you in."
Mace replaced the receiver. "You heard the man. Ten minutes and
we go."

The man who came down the embassy steps wore a pleated evening
shirt, no tie, and striped tuxedo trousers. His patent leather shoes
glinted in the courtyard's soft light. Long hair complctely white,
facial skin surgically taut across his cheekbones, and thin, curving
nose. Mace withdrew the Llama magazine and pressed the pistol into
Aron's hand. "Cover me," he said quietly, "or I'll break your neck."
Obediently, Aron pointed the pistol at Mace's ribs.

The man came to Aron's side of the car, placed his hands on the
window sill and peered in, then drew back. "Your face—Holy
Mother—what happened?"

"What does it look like what happened?" Aron said bitterly. "This
son of a whore didn't want to come." His left hand touched swollen
lips.

"Well, he's here." He glanced around at the embassy's facade.
"Took you long enough, Aron. Too late to go in, have to talk here."
He opened the rear door and slid in as Mace regained the Llama and
homed the magazine. He pointed the pistol at the white-haired man,
who stared at it in sick astonishment. *"Bonjour,* Counselor," Mace
welcomed him, and to Aron, "Take us to the Cimetière des Batig-
nolles. Quiet there and the dead don't listen. Drive."

Forasteri grabbed at the door handle until Mace said, "Be tranquil,
Counselor, or I'll destroy that pretty face."

Aron turned the car around and headed through the gate. One of
the guards saluted. Mace laughed. Shakily, Forasteri said, "What are
you going to do with me?"

"Depends, Counselor. You wanted to talk, this is your opportunity."

In a strained voice he said, "I'll pay you to let me go."

"Money doesn't resolve everything. Your profession tells you that.
You wanted information, so do I. Who put you up to this—or was it
your idea?"

The counselor's lips tightened, he said nothing. Mace said, "Aron,
you're driving too slow, let's move, *hein?"* He smiled at the passen-

ger. "There I was, enjoying an hour of jazz, and Aron pulls a gun on me. This gun." He pointed it at Forasteri's face. "What's it all about, Giulio? Ambassador motivate you?"

"No," he said sullenly.

"Why pick me? What am I supposed to know that you don't?"

The pale face looked away. "You can believe this or not—I'm only the middleman."

"So, who's your principal?"

Slowly he shook his head. "Telling would destroy my position."

"Tell me now or there'll be an unburied body in the cemetery."

Forasteri shuddered, closed his eyes. Mace asked, "Is it worth your life?"

Forasteri breathed deeply, opened his eyes, averted them from the gun barrel. Aron cried, "Tell him, for God's sake. Talk or he'll kill us both!"

"That's right," Mace said, "so let's hear some truth."

Pulling his thin figure together the diplomat said, "Pascal Covici."

"Never heard of him," Mace lied. "Tell me about him."

Forasteri licked his lips. "A very powerful banker, financier. A man of great influence in Italy."

"Why would a big man like him be interested in me? And why do his bidding?"

"I worked for him until he placed me in the diplomatic service."

"And still do?"

Forasteri shrugged. "There is little money in diplomacy and few rewards. *Signor* Covici has always been generous with me."

"Congratulations. But you haven't answered the main question. What's his interest in me?"

"It—it has to do with the IFT."

"The what?"

"International Financial Trust. Pascal suspects that you are assisting persons who stole large sums of money from the Trust. He desires to know the extent of your assistance and where the money is."

Mace saw the high wall surrounding the old cemetery. "Drive in," he told Aron, "all the way." And to Forasteri, "Covici is in Italy?" The car entered between vine-hung stone posterns. The cemetery was dark except for moonlight on old crypts and gravestones.

"No," the Commercial Counselor said quickly, "we—he, that is, has a Paris office. And he is in Paris now."

"Where is Covici's office?"

"Malesherbes, number forty-nine." The car was winding slowly into the far reaches of the cemetery. Mace said, "Stop and turn off the engine, give me the key." When the car stopped he ordered them out, and prodded them to the darkside of a weather-worn stone crypt. They stood side by side until the counselor dropped to his knees and began praying. Ignoring his mumbling, Mace asked, "Where does Covici stay in Paris?"

"An apartment—" he began, and broke down. Wringing his hands he looked up pleadingly. "Go on," Mace ordered. "An apartment—where?"

"Avenue Hoche—near Parc Monceau. Number one thirty-eight, penthouse." He began to sob. Looking down, Aron spat on him. "Try to be a man, Giulio," he said with contempt, and Mace said, "Stand up."

Slowly, Forasteri rose, leaned against the crypt for support. "Now," said Mace, "I'm going to tell you something. First, I don't know anything about this IFT or the thieves. Second, I think I'm the victim of mistaken identity. Who do you think I am? What's my name?"

Forasteri and Aron stared at each other. Weakly, Forasteri said, "Bradley Mason."

"Never heard of him." He fished Forbes Paxton's card from his pocket, handed it to the Italian, who held it close to his eyes. "Paxton? You're not Mason?"

"Never was. You went to a lot of trouble to abduct the wrong man. Caused me a world of trouble." He pointed the gun at Aron.

Suddenly Forasteri shrilled, "You idiot! Bringing all this to my door—I'll have your balls for this."

"Take it easy," Mace snapped. "I can't kill you for a mistake, so here's what you do. Counselor, tell Covici Aron produced the wrong man and you wasted the night finding out. Now, where can I find this Mason?"

"He has an office on Wagram," Forasteri said in a stronger voice. "Operates the Secours agency."

"Well, as one American to another I'm going to tell him about tonight, warn him to be watchful, suggest he carry a weapon, and shoot anyone who gets in his way. You can tell that to Covici or not, up to you." He gestured them away from the crypt. "You two in the front seat." He returned the ignition key to Aron. "Drop me at the Clichy Métro. Aron, you ought to go to a clinic for repairs, let the counselor pay."

Wiping wet cheeks on his starched shirtcuff, Forasteri got in beside Aron. Mace settled back in the rear seat and closed the door. The car wound back through the cemetery, neither man uttering a word. At the Métro station the car stopped and Mace got out. "Aron," he said, "bear in mind your fingerprints and blood are in the girl's bathroom, not mine."

In a shocked voice Forasteri exclaimed, "Is this true?"

Aron glared at him.

"Mistakes happen," Mace said calmly, "but repetition sours. You understand my meaning?"

They nodded.

"Good night, girls." Mace watched the car pull away.

He entered the Métro and rode the line to the Etoile. There was only one other passenger in the car, a harmless old drunk who smelled of onions.

Mace walked through the cool, quiet night to his building, and made notes of his findings before going to bed. He remembered Pascal Covici's name from the Fornax printouts, but had attached no particular significance to the Italian banker. Now he realized Covici was an active enemy of the Montaners—and himself.

An enemy he didn't need.

twelve

The Morgue

In the morning Mace left his building by the back way intending to check on the surveillance in the adjoining building. But he saw two men at the service entrance of the adjacent building loading the rear of a battered Toyota pickup. One was Georges Casenove, the other, brown-suited Charles Vigny, his street partner.

From the doorway Mace watched until their surveillance equipment was loaded and the pickup chugged away. Job ended, they'd cleared out, and he wondered why. Perhaps it had to do with last night's misadventures, but he rejected that thought, there being no connection apparent between Giulio Forasteri and the surveillants. Moreover, thanks to Forbes Paxton's revelations of Ed Natsos's unsuspected French facility, Mace had confirmed the voice of Casenove's employer as belonging to Natsos. But why was Natsos having him watched and tailed? A Station job, or Ed's personal initiative? A third possibility was that Natsos, like Forasteri, was accommodating an unidentified sponsor who had money to spend. Paxton had described Natsos as seeking private employment, and setting up a simple surveillance operation would be an easy way of ingratiating himself with a potential employer. No point in bracing Ed for answers, he told himself; in any case the surveillance had ceased—at least from the Fabricant observation post.

From his garage he drove his BMW toward Boulevard Malesherbes, reflecting that he had probably done Paxton no favor by giving Forasteri his business card. Should I warn him? he asked himself, or let it go? And decided that Pascal Covici was unlikely to harm Paxton, or himself. Besides, if Aron was the best talent Forasteri could field, no one was going to get hurt.

Driving slowly along Boulevard Malesherbes, he scanned the facade of number 49. It appeared to be a conventional elderly building housing apartments, offices, or both. By now its owner would have learned of the failed mission from Forasteri, and Mace wondered how far Covici would pursue his interest in Bradley Mason. For that, fresh troops would be needed.

From there he drove on toward Parc Monceau and found 138 Avenue Hoche to be a dazzling, new eight-story building with no trace of Parisian influence in its architecture. Part of the penthouse seemed to be set back, perhaps for an urban garden or starlight entertaining. And this was only a pied-à-terre for Pascal Covici, a trifling refuge away from Rome for the onetime IFT director.

The IFT was at the root of all his recent problems, Mace mused, as he idled past Covici's hideaway, with Erica the one positive gain for his side. And that plus was not to be taken lightly. Soon, on her and René's return from Geneva, he would have a better perspective on the Montaners' situation and future prospects. So far, almost everything he knew of Carlos's difficulties came from Erica—except for the persistent theme that Carlos had embezzled uncounted millions from the Trust. Either that was true—accounting for the involvement of Chakirian and Covici—or they themselves had deceived their partners by looting consortium funds and blaming Carlos. Perhaps the Montaners' new Swiss legal team could sort fact from fiction and begin extracting Carlos from his predicament. As for Erica she denied knowing whether her husband was guilty or innocent of the charge. He was in jail and she saw it as her wifely duty to free him. To Mace that was both understandable and laudable. Still, he wanted to see Carlos Montaner and appraise the husband of the woman with whom he was becoming so deeply involved. If they were to have a shared future he knew it could not begin until Carlos was no longer a factor.

When he got back to his office he found Yasmi at her desk, fists clenched, eyes swollen. At first he thought Jean-Paul was responsible until, wordlessly, she thrust a fax sheet at him, began crying and blotting her eyes with a handkerchief. "From your girlfriend," she managed between sobs, and turned away. As he read the message he felt his stomach turn to ice.

René murdered. Need you.
Please come. Erica.

"Her fault," Yasmi said bitterly. "René could always take care of himself. Has to be her fault."

"We don't know that," he found himself saying, "but I'm going to find out."

She took a series of deep breaths and went back to her desk. "You're booked on the one o'clock Swissair flight to Geneva."

He nodded. "Better tell Raoul, I may need him there."

"If I can find him."

"Find him." He went upstairs to pack a carry-on for the trip.

The weapon Mace took with him was an Ares Folding Machine Gun, designed by a Frenchman named Warin. Folded, the 9mm automatic measured 10" x 3" x 1.4" and weighed slightly more than five pounds with a twenty-round box magazine. Mace had had it fitted with a black leather case and false antenna to enhance its resemblance to a portable radio. So few FMGs had ever been made that Mace felt Swiss Customs would not be looking for one, and estimated his chances of carrying it through as six out of ten. By coincidence that had become ironic, the weapon had been acquired through an underground contact of René's. Now it could become an instrument of reprisal.

He had not alerted Erica to his coming even though she would be vulnerable to danger until he arrived. Had René taken a bullet intended for her? Met death in an alley brawl? It was maddening to know nothing beyond the bare fact that his friend was dead.

Mace had never thought of Geneva, city of watches and fine jewelry, as a dangerous place. One walked its night streets without fear or hindrance, and aside from a handful of terrorist incidents over the past decade—most aimed at international organizations or oil cartel ministers—Geneva was known as a quiet haven for the law-abiding. Unlike Bonn, Rome, and Madrid. Or Paris, he reflected, which drew lawless animals like raw meat.

So, René was dead. The onetime Foreign Legionnaire, who had survived a score of bloody skirmishes, found death not on a battle-field but in a city dedicated to world peace. More irony for you, he thought, and ordered a second iced vodka from the roly-poly Swiss flight attendant.

The chill Stoli set his teeth on edge, but he sipped enjoyably, feel-ing that he needed alcohol to dilute the adrenaline in his blood. Didn't want to appear edgy as he went through Customs.

Presently, the plane began descending over Lake Geneva, high, snow-topped Alps in the distance, until it touched down at Cointrin airport. Off to one side of the landing runway lay the French border, a proximity he found conveniently European.

The Customs inspector was a buxom female well past her prime, bored and indifferent to a tourist whose sole baggage was a canvas carry-on. She chalked it, yawned, and wished Mace a pleasant stay in Geneva.

From Cointrin he taxied into the city via Route Meyrin, across Mont-Blanc bridge, where lake and the Rhône River joined, into the old section of a very old city.

Another ten minutes of narrow, mostly cobbled streets, and the taxi pulled up at the hotel. La Résidence, he saw, had escaped any brush with modernity. It looked old, settled, and comfortable, more German in appearance than French. Of five to six stories, it had a pri-vate park and tennis courts, neatly trimmed shrubbery, and a flower garden. The sort of place sought by cosmopolitan travelers seeking privacy and traditional fine service. A young *chausseur* came out for baggage, but Mace slung his bag over a shoulder, tipped the boy, and asked to be taken to Erica's suite. Outside the double door he called her name, said, "It's Mace," and in a few moments heard the bolt slide open.

Face taut, she cried, "Oh, darling, thank God you're here!" and half collapsed in his arms. He closed and locked the door behind them, slid off his bag, and held and kissed her until she drew slightly away to touch his face. "It's been terrible—poor René. I'm so very sorry."

He drew her to the sitting room sofa, poured cognac for both and made her drink. "What happened?"

"I—I just don't know." She drank again, stared at the glass as though in shock.

"Tell me." He took her hand in his, calming her. "When did it happen?"

"It—it was last night." She closed her eyes and shivered. "As before, we ate here together, and about ten o'clock René said he had to meet someone and would be back in an hour or so." Her hand trembled as she put the glass to her lips. "Before leaving he told me to keep the door bolted and only open it for him. Mace, *he never came back.*" Her hands knotted into small fists. He kissed her cheek and said, "Go on. Who found him? When?"

"Sometime—it must have been four or five o'clock, before dawn— the concierge phoned, said my companion had been found in an alley a few blocks away by a hotel cook coming to work."

"Did you have to identify him?"

She shook her head. "I was spared that. The police were courteous. They came while I was having coffee, showed me René's *carte d'identité* and asked me to confirm his identity." Tears welled in her eyes. "He was so thoughtful and protective . . . and because of me he—he's dead." Her face burrowed into Mace's shoulder.

"We don't know that, so don't believe it. Was he robbed?"

"No money in his billfold, just the *carte.* And yesterday I'd given him four thousand Swiss francs he needed to buy information. When he left he had it with him."

"So either he bought it or was ripped off by the seller—or his killer." He held her tightly. "What killed him?"

"It was—Mace, he was stabbed, throat cut. How horrible!"

"Murder is always horrible." He added cognac to their glasses. "Did the police question you about him? What he was doing here?"

"I said he was my bodyguard—they know about Carlos and seemed to understand. There were no more questions."

"So what needs to be established," he said musingly, "is whether he was killed because of his connection to you, or if it was robbery unconnected to you." He paused. "Or me." He got up from the sofa. "René Gabriel Gomard. Where is he now?"

"The morgue—police headquarters."

"Did you say you were his employer?"

She nodded. Mace opened his bag, took out an envelope and extracted the French-language authorization she had signed in Paris. "This will be useful," he told her. "I'll be gone no more than an hour. If there are complications I'll call. But above all, stay here, let no one in."

"But you've only just arrived," she protested.

"I owe this to his widow," he said firmly, took her door key and left the suite.

Police headquarters was an old, stern-faced building rising from the intersection of Avenue Sainte Clotilde and Boulevard Carl Vogt. Inside at the information desk Mace asked to see the morgue-keeper and was shown to a staircase that led underground to the cold precincts of the city morgue. After showing his authorization document, Mace was allowed to enter.

René's body had been autopsied, blood drained away leaving his flesh ash-gray. The medical assistant turned over the body to show six stab wounds from neck to kidney level. His throat had been cleanly slashed—the immediate cause of death—and sutured after autopsy. The assistant asked, "Is there anything else, *M'sieu?*"

"I want to make arrangements to fly him back to Paris."

"I can supply the name of a funeral service that specializes in international shipments." He slid the steel cradle back into the vault and closed the door. Then at his desk he wrote out name, address, and phone number of the service, and asked, "He was a friend?"

"A good friend," Mace said somberly. "Trustworthy, reliable—" He broke off, remembering he had so characterized René to Erica only a few days ago. "One of a kind. A man of standards and integrity. I'll miss him." He left the room's deathly chill and emerged above into a world of sunlight and motion.

Service Funéraire Pichon took Mace's instructions with quiet efficiency, photocopied the French authorization, had him sign a mortuary release, and said the transfer could be made the following morning. While the bill was being prepared Mace used their telephone to call Yasmi. He asked her to help René's widow and suggested Jean-Paul be useful as well. The funeral director supplied the flight number of the cargo plane, after which Yasmi asked, "Do you know anything more? Why he was killed?"

"Apparently it was robbery," he told her to avoid details. "I'll know more in a day or so. Tell you when I return."

"Mace—when are you coming?"

"A few days, no more. Take care of things." He broke the connection, took the bill—a large one—and said he would make payment at the hotel. A Pichon assistant drove Mace to La Résidence and waited while Erica signed traveler's checks that Mace gave the driver. Then they were alone.

"I don't know what I'd do without you," she said quietly. "Always you know just what to do."

"Not always, far from it. Just now and then. I'm going to shower and change, and then I want to hear about Carlos and the lawyers."

As he half anticipated she joined him in the large tiled shower room where they soaped each other's bodies, kissed, and embraced until overcome with excitement they made love amid rising steam.

"Well," she said, sitting up and brushing back her streaming hair, "I've never done *that* before."

"Old Japanese custom," he said, "I think."

"Whatever the custom it's made a new woman of me. I needed you, darling, God, how I needed you. Now I think I can go on, do what needs to be done. Until you got here I was paralyzed, too frightened to move—but that's over." She touched his lips. "I can even smile. See?"

"I see and I like." He kissed her and smacked her rump. "Back to reality, *chérie*, we've got work to do."

"I'll call the lawyers now."

The firm of Schreiber, Wollancz & LeFevre occupied the top two floors of an old building on the Quai Gustave Ador, a short distance from the American Consulate General. In late afternoon Mace and Erica were received by Hugo Schreiber in a large conference room whose windows afforded a broad view of the lake. Schreiber was around fifty, with a trim Vandyke beard, starched wing collar, and thinly knotted tie. His nose was a network of florid capillaries, a condition Mace laid to genetics rather than strong drink.

"*M'sieu* Mason," Schreiber began, "you are here in the capacity of adviser to *La Comtesse?*"

He nodded. "And authorized to act in her behalf."

"Very good." He folded his hands. "So we have a clear understanding among us. Comtesse, you have discharged your former attorneys?"

"I have. The files should have reached you today."

He shrugged. "And indeed they may have. However, logging them in requires meticulous attention, so perhaps we can proceed de novo."

Erica leaned forward and placed her arms on the table. "The purpose of my retaining you is to secure the release of my husband, Count Carlos de Montaner. I am prepared to put up bail in almost any amount to guarantee his presence for trial."

Mace said, "In the event there *is* a trial."

"Precisely," Schreiber noted. "Without benefit of your files, I must ask if this route has been attempted before?"

Erica shrugged. "I'm not sure but the files should tell you. And in addition to whatever bail may be required I'm quite prepared to cover any additional costs."

"Such as, Madame?"

"That's your province, *Maître,* is it not?"

He allowed a small smile to lift the corners of his lips. "Indeed. Again, for the purpose of complete understanding. Now, I understand you have seen your husband recently?"

"I visited him Tuesday afternoon. It was he who recommended your firm."

"And—to put this as delicately as possible—what is the state of your marital relationship?"

"We're separated, *Maître,* that's obvious."

"Beyond physical separation?"

"Divorce is contemplated, if that's what you mean."

"That is my meaning," he agreed. "Has the matter proceeded beyond mutual contemplation?"

She sighed. "I didn't come to discuss our domestic situation, but, yes, there are documents concerning our present and future relationships."

"Documents?"

"Prepared by my French lawyers. I left them with my husband who will sign them, or not, as he chooses."

Schreiber tented his hands, pressing fingertips tightly together. For a while he said nothing, then stroked his beard and said, "I perceive the very distant possibility of a conflict of interest, Madame *La Comtesse.*"

"In what way, *Maître?*"

"Suppose, for the sake of argument, you and your husband have a falling out, as it were—that he declines to sign the documents you describe. Who am I then to represent?"

"My husband, of course," she said smoothly. "The possibility of divorce has no bearing on your securing his freedom."

Schreiber glanced at Mace. "Very good. I simply wanted your assurance."

"Now that you have it," Mace said, "how soon can we expect action on your part? I don't mean results, *Maître*, I mean getting the damn wheels moving? The count has been imprisoned far too long."

"I understand your desire for haste," the lawyer said evenly, "but our Swiss system is not designed to accommodate it. I suspect that numerous avenues, approaches, will have to be tried, each one confidentially if not secretly—you understand my meaning?"

"I think I do," Mace replied. "The question remains—how soon?"

"Very soon, I believe."

Mace leaned forward. "For months the countess has been put off with tomorrows, she didn't come here for more of the same. You've been paid a healthy retainer; how soon will you get moving?"

He looked away. "Why, tomorrow I can begin drawing up a plan."

Mace grunted. "Tell you what, *Maître*, draw up your plan today, start acting on it tomorrow. We'll be in Geneva long enough for progress reports."

"Of course I will have to consult my partners . . . "

Erica said, "You didn't have to consult your partners when you accepted my retainer. For a hundred thousand dollars, *Maître*—let us be very clear—I expect action, not impediments. Now, if you feel the case is beyond your firm's capacity to resolve in my husband's favor, then you may return the retainer and I will find other counsel."

"Please, Madame, be tranquil. If any firm can accomplish your goal it is this one. We have enjoyed notable success within the criminal justice system, and I have no present reason to believe that in this instance we will fail."

Erica smiled slightly. "That is very reassuring."

"Although—" he held up one hand—"there are influential interests who would oppose your husband's release."

"Were they to learn of it," Mace remarked. "Which is why the countess and I expect your work to be accomplished prudently, circumspectly, and if necessary, in the dark of the moon." He smiled. "So we all have a clear understanding. Right, Countess?"

Erica nodded. "Quite so. Are we in complete agreement, *Maître* Schrieber?"

"I feel that we are. And permit me to express my sympathy for the loss of your valued employee."

"Kind of you," Erica said expressionlessly, to which Mace added, "He was my longtime friend. One hardly expects street violence in Geneva, but—" he shrugged and left the thought unfinished.

As Schreiber rose he said, "One final question, Madame: in the event of your husband's release, what are your and his intentions?"

Mace said, "The countess has begun looking for a comfortable lakeside villa where they will stay pending further developments."

Schreiber smiled. "I was going to suggest it. It could assist the court to reach a favorable decision by eliminating thought of flight to avoid prosecution."

Stiffly, Erica said, "My husband belongs to an old and very proud family, *M'sieu*. He would never dishonor it by fleeing justice." She paused. "Wherever that justice may be."

"Thank you, Madame *La Comtesse*, for your reassurance. If my firm or I can be of assistance in securing an appropriate villa, you have only to let me know."

Erica rose, extended her hand. Schreiber bent over it, then said, "You are staying at La Résidence?"

"For the present," she said smoothly, "and I anticipate seeing you tomorrow."

"*À demain*, then," Schreiber echoed, and saw them to the outside corridor.

In the elevator Erica said, "Do you think he really believes Carlos will stay to be tried?"

"Let him believe what he wants to believe. That verbal dance was simply to satisfy the code of ethics. He may look like a stuffed shirt but he's a man of the world. Knows he can't be held responsible for what Carlos does after he's freed." Mace smiled. "I think things are looking up for your husband, don't you?"

She nodded. "For the first time in months I'm beginning to feel a bit optimistic. You pushed Schreiber, made him commit to early action. Without you, I'd have left empty-handed."

"Maybe. But you're a once-in-a-lifetime client. Millions to spend and his firm will get a chunk of it. That's powerful motivation for even a slow-moving Swiss lawyer. Yes, I think there'll be action, and Schreiber seems crafty enough to pull it off."

They walked along the quai toward the tall water plume of the Jet d'Eau, wavering in early evening breeze from the lake. Soon colored lights would illuminate and make it visible from almost every part of the city. Geneva's trademark, he thought, as the Eiffel symbolizes Paris.

She took his hand, pressed it. "Suppose Carlos won't sign our agreement?"

"Then he'll have to be shown where his best interests lie. Try to get me in to see him tomorrow."

"Tomorrow? But—"

"Try."

Book Two

thirteen

The Meeting

Through the hotel concierge Mace hired a chauffeured limousine for Erica and saw her off for a morning meeting with *Maître* Schreiber. Afterward she was to visit realtors specializing in lakeside rental villas. As he watched the black Mercedes pull away Mace thought of René, remembering that his friend's coffin would reach Paris that day. Any children of René's would be grown, he reflected, so there was only the widow to compensate—and Erica had enough money to do so generously.

In the suite he drank more breakfast coffee, and felt that he was grappling ineffectively with forces that knew much more about him—and Erica—than he did about them.

Why had René been murdered? Chance street robbery or planned assassination? Had René paid an informant only to be killed by the same man? Or had contact never been made? To Mace it seemed unlikely that he would ever learn the truth, and he was a reluctant believer in coincidence.

He slipped off the Ares's leather disguise case, unfolded the machine gun with a single snap, thumbed up the recessed bolt, and fanned the room with the barrel. Then he folded the weapon and restored it as before.

The telephone rang. Mace answered and heard Yasmi's voice: "I'm calling from the airport to report the shipment arrived. Jean-Paul is with me, and Raoul is available." She paused. "Do you want him with you?"

"Not now, but I want him to be where you can reach him if I need him."

"I'll make sure he does. Oh—your friend with the funny-looking reptile boots wants an appointment. I told him you were out of town and would get back to him when you returned." That would be Ed Natsos, paymaster of the two-man surveillance team. Possibly wanting to explain his involvement, probably not. In any case the guy was untrustworthy. Two years' French immersion, Mace thought, what a waste of government money. Unless the course was a way to get Natsos out of the Station, away from serious ops. That could be worth a good deal to Peke Parmalee, the Chief of Station.

"Thanks for calling," Mace said, and broke the connection. He poured coffee and sugared it. COS Peter Parmalee had gained his nickname during a tour of duty in Peking when George Bush was the diplomatic liaison officer. As the story went, Parmalee had been so surrounded and monitored by Chinese security agents that he had accomplished nothing in two year's time. No informants recruited, no moles, no agents-in-place; just an abiding familiarity with Chinese cuisine—and the derogatory nickname. Not a bad guy, though, Mace thought, and wondered how much Peke knew about his deputy's after-hours activities. All? Nothing?

The phone rang. Answering, Mace heard the voice of *Maître* Hugo Schreiber. "At Madame's request I have agreed to document you as a 'legal associate' of this office. That will authorize you to visit her husband."

"Excellent."

"Ah—how soon do you plan to see him?"

"As soon as possible, *Maître*."

"Then I will send over the document. Meanwhile, the countess will be visiting various relocation sites, as we discussed."

Mace thanked him and hung up. This lawyer was at least able to accomplish simple tasks; how he performed with major issues remained to be seen. But he'd made an encouraging start.

As Mace dressed, he reflected that he might gain much or little from a face-to-face with Count Carlos de Montaner. The least he expected was an evaluation of the man's character. Was he mega million embezzler, as charged, or hapless scapegoat? Mace doubted the

146

question could be resolved in one meeting, but indications could surface leading to eventual conclusions.

But, should he be concerned over Carlos's guilt or innocence? The lawyers were not, hadn't been; they'd defend him either way. Just as Erica was working in her husband's behalf, unquestioningly. True, her efforts put her husband under a degree of obligation to follow through with their divorce agreement but Mace suspected that Carlos would do what he thought best for himself despite prior commitments.

Half an hour after Schreiber's call the authorizing document arrived, and Mace took a taxi out the Lausanne highway to the cantonal prison. The old, four-story building looked as though it might have served as a fortress a century ago. Narrow barred windows, massive gate, and a side entrance door through which Mace entered. Inside, two uniformed guards behind a counter, both armed with semiautomatic machine pistols that resembled Uzis. Mace produced Schreiber's authorization and requested an interview with Carlos de Montaner. Then waited while one of the guards phoned the prison governor and repeated Mace's request. Waited ten minutes more while the governor phoned Schreiber to verify Mace's identity. Finally, one of the guards unlocked a metal-encased door into the prison courtyard and escorted Mace to the cell block. Inside, after being searched for contraband, Mace was shown into a small visiting room that held a bolted-down table and two metal chairs. The stone walls were bare; illumination came from a ceiling lamp recessed behind heavy wire mesh. At the end of the room a mirror was set into the wall. A one-way mirror, Mace realized, through which prisoner and visitor could be observed and videotaped. He assumed a microphone was part of the overhead lamp assembly. In the U.S. eavesdropping on a prisoner's legal conversations was illegal—but this was Switzerland.

Hearing a key rattle a door lock, Mace turned and saw the door open wide enough for a man to enter.

The man was about five-seven in height. Of slim build, he wore shapeless blue denim jacket and trousers, old carpet slippers, and no socks. Prison-short black hair, and thick black eyebrows that made his sallow complexion seem almost bleached. His features were more delicate than in newspaper photos Mace had seen, making him a handsome man of thirty-five or so—or an attractive woman. The man clutched a large accordion envelope bound with string, and when the door behind him was closed and locked he stared at Mace. "I don't know you," he said breathily.

"You will. Have a seat, Count."

Almost warily the Spaniard sat down, set his envelope on the scarred tabletop. "You brought cigarettes?"

"No."

"Erica said she'd get me some. Promised." His voice was plaintive. "Who are you?"

Mace slid Schreiber's document across the table. The count gazed at it before drawing it close enough to read. The effort took what seemed a long time. Then he shoved the document back to Mace. "What does it mean?"

"Your wife, the countess, hired me in Paris as a sort of bodyguard. I sent a man here with her but he was murdered. So I came."

His eyebrows drew together. "Bodyguard? Murder? Why would Erica need a bodyguard?"

"She's been surveilled ever since she got to Paris. I identified two sponsors: Chakirian and Covici. Didn't she tell you?"

He shrugged. "I suppose she didn't want to worry me. And we had other things to discuss." His gaze strayed to the brown file. "You work for the new lawyers, then."

"The firm you recommended." Mace sat forward. "Are you in danger here? Ever been attacked?"

The count shook his head. "I'm in a cell isolated from other prisoners. I even eat alone." He breathed deeply. "I wish I could have a good meal sometime."

"You will—after you're free."

His expression lightened. "That's all I think of. But, when?"

"Too soon to guess. Meanwhile, you have to guard your health."

"Erica said she'd be looking for a villa where we can stay—if I'm freed on bail." He paused. "Is she?"

"She is."

That seemed to please him. "You haven't asked if I stole IFT funds."

"I'm not going to because it has no bearing on getting you out of here. Besides, we're watched and listened to." He gestured at the one-way mirror. The count untied the string and opened the envelope. "You came for the papers?"

"No, but I'll take them if you like."

With the edge of his hand the count straightened a multipage document. The first page was headed with the name Samuelson Frères. "I've made some changes. My wife wants too much. Tell her that."

Mace said nothing.

"She wants me dead, Mason. She'd like nothing better."

"That's nonsense. She's doing everything possible to free you. She's gotten a new legal team you have confidence in—would she do that if she wanted you dead?"

"Window dressing, acting the loyal, faithful wife." He eyed Mace. "*Is* she faithful?"

"Ask her," Mace said irritably. "I don't know your domestic arrangements, don't want to. What I think is you've been alone too long, too much time to think of too many things. It's obvious your enemies want you in prison but I don't think they want you dead."

"Oh? Then what do they want?"

"I assume they want to recover any sequestered funds and they'll try to keep you here under pressure until they do. After that you become expendable."

His eyes narrowed. "How do I know you're not working for Varti or Pascal?"

"Good question. The answer is I haven't asked if you're guilty as alleged, or where the funds are located. Count, I was retained originally by the Samuelsons, and I've learned of their long relationship with your family. Considering their debt to the Montaners it's not likely they would hire someone unreliable, or dangerous to you."

Slowly he nodded. "Why didn't my wife tell me about you?"

"The last time you saw her I was in Paris, no thought of coming here. My man's murder changed that."

The count shifted in his chair. "Why was he murdered?"

"Not known. He was buying information the night he was killed."

"What kind of information?"

"The kind that could have been beneficial to you."

149

In a strained voice he said, "Then Varti or Pascal had him killed."

"A serviceable theory lacking proof."

"And I wouldn't put it past Erica to have had him murdered." He touched the Samuelson document. "If I sign this I'll be of no further use to her. She'll have a divorce and most of my property and money."

"Worse things could happen," Mace replied. "By now you should have figured out the alternative. Once she has everything she becomes the target, you'll be left alone and probably freed. That's a big improvement over your current situation."

"I can't contemplate that kind of future, I'd rather be dead."

"Your many friends will miss you." Mace got up and folded the thick document into his pocket.

The count stared up resentfully. "You're a cold, cynical bastard. For all I know my wife hired you to kill me."

"I'm not in the murder business," Mace snapped.

"She'll get around to it," the count said with a smirk. "You'll see. Erica has winning ways. Men do her bidding."

"As they've done yours," Mace retorted. "I'll see you get cigarettes. Think less about death and more about freedom." He went to the door, rapped loudly, and in a few moments the door opened. His last glimpse of the prisoner showed him at the table, head bowed, hands meshed over his envelope.

The count, Mace mused, as he left the prison, was stubborn, resolute, and devious. And he had conjured up a fantastic vision of his wife. But as Mace knew, prolonged isolation could do that to a man. Any man.

Back in the hotel suite Mace went over the changes the count had made in Samuelson's divorce agreement. As he anticipated, the count wanted the divorce postponed until after he was freed. In place of the proposed fifty-fifty property division the count was willing to concede ten percent of his cash and holdings to Erica. That would still be a lot, Mace reflected, but far from what the Samuelsons believed Erica might be entitled to. Realistically, what the count had done was establish a negotiating position using bluff and bravado though knowing that his wife held most of the cards and possibly the keys to his release. She also had access to several million dollars for her husband's bail, and probably a great deal more. So Mace wondered how Erica would react to her husband's downsizing her proposal.

The door buzzer sounded and Mace got up to answer it, assuming a waiter had come for their breakfast cart. Instead, he saw a short, wiry man who was shabbily dressed and carrying a worn briefcase. He stared in surprise at Mace before saying, "René? I need to see René."

"Come in, I'm René's employer," Mace told him, and after hesitating the man came in. "Where's René?" he asked.

"If you have something for him you can leave it with me."

"No, I can't do that. I'll come again." He turned to leave.

"What's your name?"

"Gabriel."

"I have bad news for you, Gabriel. René's dead."

"*No!* How?"

"Knifed in an alley two nights ago. After paying you."

Gabriel's face paled. "Who killed him?"

"We don't know. But tell me, after meeting with you where was René going?"

"Here, I suppose." He looked around the suite. "He didn't say."

"Was he meeting someone else?"

Gabriel shook his head. "If he was he didn't tell me." His gaze lowered to the briefcase in his hand. "Where was he killed?"

"Nearby. I'll miss him, believe me. Now, René gave you four thousand francs for information on the cantonal prison, so whatever you have, I'll take."

Gabriel went to the table, opened the briefcase, and drew out a sheaf of papers and photographs. "Nearly everything is here. I couldn't get names for some of the new guards."

"Maybe someone you talked to decided to rob René, followed him after he left you."

Gabriel shrugged. "It's possible."

"How many people did you—consult?"

"Three—all men I trust."

"Give me a number where I can reach you if I need to."

On a hotel note pad he wrote a telephone number and the name:

Gabriel Bonaventura. "My wife can always reach me," he said, and closed the empty briefcase. "I'm sorry about René, we were in the Legion together. Tell me if you find out who killed him." Mace nodded and watched him go, thinking that he would do the job himself, not leave it to the former Legionnaire.

He spread out Gabriel's delivery on the table, examined the photos first. Some, taken from the ground, showed different sides of the prison. One, taken from the air, revealed the prison layout, another aerial view included access roads. He scanned written answers to questions he'd posed, and read newspaper clippings some of whose photos included the interior and exterior of prison cells. There was an account of a 1963 breakout by two prisoners who had tunneled under the wall only to be recaptured a few days later. The then state-of-the-art alarm system hadn't detected the breakout because the escapees took the underground route and their cell door remained closed. Interesting, Mace mused, and wondered if the system had been updated over the past thirty years. No other prison breaks appeared in the clippings. Well, tunneling was not an option for the count.

The prison organization chart had been photocopied from the original as had the prison's twenty-four-hour routine. It detailed shift changes and prisoner activity: meals, exercise, confinement. Lights out at 9:00 P.M., a skeleton guard force remaining through the night.

Mace studied a view of the prison's west side. An X marked Carlos's fourth-floor cell with its single barred window. Shouldn't be too hard to get him out of there, Mace thought, if all else failed.

He began packing his few belongings, having decided there was nothing more he could accomplish in Geneva, and heard Erica come in. After a greeting kiss she asked about her husband.

"He sent back the agreement," Mace told her, "with changes," and gestured at the table where the document lay. Erica frowned as she read, then turned to Mace. "What do I do now?"

"Take it to Samuelson."

"But Carlos is being so unfair," she complained. "And after he'd agreed to divorce. When he's free he'll never go through with it."

Mace nodded. "I'm sure that's crossed his mind. And you shouldn't be surprised when I say Carlos doesn't have a high opinion of you. Even warned me against your manipulations."

"Oh? And what do you think?" Nervously she opened and closed her purse.

"I think he's resentful and embittered. Can't strike at his former partners so he takes it out on you. Anyway, this is just the beginning of negotiations and you'll both compromise before it's over. But let the Samuelsons advise you, they're skilled in these things." He paused. "How many villas did you see?"

"Three, one more attractive than the others. Not that we'll be living in any of them for long."

"Well, pay a deposit on one and keep Schreiber informed."

"Today?"

"Why not? Nothing more we can do here and I want to get back to Paris."

"I suppose you're right." Her gaze shifted to Gabriel's sheaf of papers. "What's this?"

"I had a surprise visitor. He brought what René paid for."

She touched the papers. "Is this what you wanted? Is it enough?"

"Probably," he replied, "but only as a last resort."

"Do you want to tell me your plan?"

"Premature. Give Schreiber time to work things out."

"But how long?"

"I'd say a month. By which time you and Carlos should have reached agreement. Now, get back to the realtor, see Schreiber, and I'll get plane tickets. We'll have lunch and fly back to Paris, okay?"

"Okay," she smiled, and left to pack her bags.

Mace phoned the concierge for two seats to Paris and chose a four o'clock Air France flight. Her limo could take them to the airport from the restaurant, and they'd be in Paris while it was still light.

They had lunch in a quiet café near the Rhône's east bank and decided to stroll through the small park that lay between the restaurant and the Quai du Seujet. They were halfway through the park when Mace heard the crunch of tires on gravel, and turned to see a car approaching from behind. Its seeming stealth alarmed him so he squeezed Erica's hand, and said, "If the car stops, start running."

"Mace, you—?"

153

"Don't look around, just do as I say." One hand began unsnapping the Ares's cover. He heard the car stop and said, *"Go!"*

Abruptly Erica began running toward a stand of trees. Mace whirled around and saw two men spill out of the car and run after her. Mace unlimbered the Ares, cocked, and fired a burst just ahead of the pursuing man. Halting, they peered back at Mace and one drew a pistol. Mace fired two shots at his feet and called, "Drop the gun, get in the car." Erica was nowhere to be seen. The car's driver floored the pedal and steered at Mace, who stepped aside and fired two shots into the radiator. The radiator hissed and the car sped past trailing steam. Heads down, the two men jogged toward it. Mace covered them until they reached the wounded vehicle whose engine gave off clanking sounds. He watched them get in and drive noisily off, saw Erica emerge from behind a tree. As she came toward him Mace folded the Ares and replaced its cover.

"My God," she said shakily, "what was all that?"

"They weren't autograph hounds," he said drily as she clung to him. "Someone wants you out of the game. Or me."

"I'm glad you didn't kill anyone," she breathed.

"Glad I didn't have to, we'd be up to our eyes in cops. Let's leave Geneva while we can." Taking her arm he led her along the Quai to where her limo waited.

The Air France flight left promptly at four, and by six they were going through French Customs at Orly. In the taxi Mace asked her to stay with him, her place having been miked.

"You're sure?"

"Positive. I put in detection equipment. Anyway, you're getting out of that apartment."

She nodded. "Tomorrow I'll find a new place and move." She paused. "After seeing Bernard."

"Right."

"But suppose he says Carlos's proposal is reasonable?"

"Accept his advice, or get another lawyer. But you can't back down on divorce timing."

"Never intended to."

"Put a little pressure on your husband—don't visit him next week. Give him time to think things over, realize he's dependent on you."

She nodded thoughtfully. "I'll welcome the respite. It's never easy being with Carlos, hearing his complaints. He hasn't appreciated what I've been trying to do for him."

The taxi drew up at Mace's building and they got out. Mace carried their bags to the entrance door and unlocked it.

Upstairs he poured drinks and they relaxed in his office. "The only living room I have," he remarked, and kissed her gently.

"I can't stop thinking about René. Do you think he was killed by the men who came after me in the park?"

"Could be a connection. Obviously someone knew where you stay in Geneva, knew René would be heading there that night, and followed us today from the hotel to the café. I should have been alert for surveillance."

"Nevertheless you were with me when I needed you." Her finger tapped the side of her glass. "Who sent those men—have you any idea?"

He drank deeply before replying. "I know of two IFT directors who want Carlos where he is: Victor Chakirian and Pascal Covici, both utterly ruthless. They want the money Carlos is accused of embezzling. Or they have the money and are harassing your husband and you to convince other directors that Carlos is the guilty one." He drank again. "Or only one of them has the missing money."

"Wouldn't Carlos know?"

"He'd know whether he took the money."

"He says he didn't."

Mace grunted. "What would you expect him to say? He's not going to confide in a wife he dislikes and doesn't trust."

She sighed. "What do you think?"

"He has guilty knowledge. And the directors probably think you know far more than you do."

"Mace, if I knew where that money is I'd return it, all of it. No amount of money is worth this feeling of being hunted like an animal."

"I agree," he said and got up to freshen their drinks. "Still," he continued when he came back, "it would be nice to have some of it if Carlos continues to stonewall. I don't want to see you end up with nothing."

"I had nothing when I met him."

"So what? You're entitled to certain things now and he knows it. Maybe his game plan is to get out of prison without divorcing you and without turning over any of his wealth."

"Could he do that?"

"That prison hasn't seen an escape in thirty years. Carlos couldn't manage it without help—your help."

"Your plan."

He shrugged. "What's the rush? Let Schreiber try every angle. Me, I wouldn't lift a finger for Carlos until he gives you everything you want." He touched her cheek, pressed her lips. "Did Schreiber have anything to report?"

"Oh, he said he was working on the case, devoting most of his time to it. And he said it was best that I not know details, names. He seemed very cautious about everything."

"I like a closemouthed lawyer but I also like results. As I said, he's entitled to a month's time, maybe more. Be patient."

"I will." She breathed deeply. "I wasn't emotionally prepared for all I've gone through. Having my husband in prison was bad enough, but being followed, eavesdropped on would be too much if it weren't for you."

"Well, you don't need to go back to Geneva for a while. Spend time with the Samuelsons working out something acceptable. Maybe visit your folks in Viborg—how long since you've seen them?"

"Months—too long. Yes, I like the idea, but I'll miss you."

"I'll miss you, too. Are you hungry?"

"Mainly I'm tired."

"Then we'll eat in. I think I can put together a fondue."

"Whatever there is."

"Last time I looked there was cheese and wine and bread."

So while she showered and got into a bathrobe he made their fondue, and afterward they went to bed, too tired to make love but lying close together until sleep quickly came.

When he woke, sunlight washed the room and there was a note on her pillow. She had gone to the apartment to start the *femme de ménage* packing. After that she was going to Samuelson's office, then look for another apartment. Will call about lunch.

He needed, he thought, a few hours to get back to the real world. Last night he'd noticed the light on his message machine but hadn't taken messages, suspecting that Angelique or Jessamyn's voice would be heard by Erica. And he remembered Yasmi saying that Ed Natsos wanted to see him. Well, he could do without Ed, and the ladies could wait until after coffee.

When he played back the message machine both ladies said they missed him and wanted him to call. Was it time to break off with them? In fairness he probably should. Still, if Erica went to Viborg . . .

Yasmi unlocked the outer door and came in. "Well," she said, "it's good to see you," and gave him a sisterly hug. "Did you learn anything in Geneva?"

"About René? No."

"Letting the police do the investigating?"

"Have you a better idea?"

She shook her head. "Countess still there?"

"She came back with me last night." He looked at his watch. "After the embassy opens tell Natsos to come in at ten, no, nine-thirty."

"You're actually seeing that snake?"

"He's harmless. And I'm curious what's on his mind."

"Nothing good, Mace, you can bet on that. She answered the telephone, listened, and covered the receiver. "Forbes Paxton. Will you take it?"

He went to the desk extension and greeted the retired colonel, who said, "Listen, Mace, I think you've gotten me into trouble."

"How so?"

"Two days ago I was roughed up by a pair of thugs. I tried to explain that I wasn't their man, but they produced my business card and kept on beating me."

"Sorry about that. But how am I involved?"

"Mace, the only card I've given out recently was the one I left with you. How do you explain that?"

"I can't. But, you've passed out other cards, how can you tell one card from another?"

"Do you still have my card?"

157

"Doubt it. Our practice is to put card info on a disk and discard the original. Saves space. Ah—how badly were you beaten?"

"Well, I've got a black eye, bruises, and sore kidneys. I apologize for suspecting you. Okay?"

"Okay."

"We'll lunch soon—when I'm presentable."

"Look forward to it," he lied. "Call any time."

"I will, Mace, and I still think we can do business."

"Always willing to listen." He broke the connection thinking that the attack on Paxton was sponsored by Pascal Covici via Giulio Forasteri. Better Paxton than me, he told himself, and went upstairs to dress for the day.

Promptly at nine-thirty Ed Natsos came in.

fourteen

The Snatch

The deputy station chief wore a hangdog look, and Mace did not extend a welcoming hand. "Have a seat," he said coldly. "How's the surveillance business these days?"

Natsos grimaced. "I want to explain about that, Mace—it was nothing personal." Slowly he sat down across the desk from Mace, not meeting his gaze.

"Nothing personal? How else would you describe it?"

"Well—I set up the OP as a favor," he said uncomfortably. "I told the guy you'd probably detect it but he said go ahead anyway."

"And you did this favor for—who?"

"The commercial attaché."

"The *embassy's* commercial attaché?"

"You got it."

"Terrific," Mace grunted. "There used to be a ban on surveilling U.S. citizens abroad. Ever hear of it?"

"Yeah, and that's why the legal attaché wouldn't touch it. So the commercial guy came to me."

"And you hired two mooks and rented the hall. Peke Parmalee know about it?"

"Well, not actually. Peke was down in Marseille at the time—I was acting chief."

"And you didn't bother to tell Peke when he got back. So tell me what possible interest the commercial guy has in me and my movements."

"You're not going to like this, Mace—"

"So far I don't like any of it."

"Has to do with the IFT banking scandal. The attaché—his name is Plotkin, Norman Plotkin—showed me a circular from the Department of Commerce. They want all information on IFT people and their contacts. Worldwide."

Mace scratched his chin. "So, why target me?"

"You know the answer—the *condesa* and her husband, the former IFT director jailed in Geneva. You're working for them, ipso facto you're involved."

"Oh? Suppose I told you I'm *not* working for them?"

"I'd say you ought to refresh your memory. You went off to Geneva and came back with the countess—right? Looks like circumstantial evidence."

"Maybe I'm just fucking her while the count's confined."

Natsos managed a weak smile. "You'd be crazy not to. She's gorgeous."

"So they say. Now, whatever relationship the countess and I have is private, okay? She's the client of a law firm with which I do occasional business—that's how we met. As for Geneva, one of my employees was killed there. I made arrangements to have his body brought back to Paris, and I came back last night."

"With the countess."

"The Air France passenger list confirms it. Ed, you can tell Pritikin—or whatever his name is—anything I've told you. Get him off your back, and you stay off mine. Any more mooks pry into my personal life and they're likely to regret it. Understood?"

Natsos nodded.

"Say it."

"I understand."

"Incidentally, I was amazed by your command of French."

"Two years, Mace, but it'll be a big help in post-retirement employment."

"Didn't impress Forbes Paxton," Mace remarked.

Ed's eyes widened. "Screw him, he's not the only employer around, and he owed me. I tipped him to the Stinger missile market. You know the deal?"

Mace shook his head. "Not sure I want to."

"It's legit, Mace. The Agency's promoting a program to buy back Stingers we supplied the mujahideen during the Afghan war. According to estimates as many as three hundred were left over and we can pay up to two hundred grand for each one."

"In Afghanistan."

"Not necessarily. The FBI hasn't said so, but Stingers were recovered from the ragheads who blew up the World Trade Center. The administration is worried about Stingers in the wrong hands. If you could come up with a couple there'd be a nice finder's fee for you."

"Sounds more like Paxton's line of work."

Natsos got up. "I told you as a favor—to sort of make up for that half-assed surveillance."

"Anything else?"

Natsos shrugged. "How do we stand?"

"As before."

After the door closed behind Natsos, Yasmi came over. "He's unbelievable," she said. "Why would he bring up Stinger missiles?"

Mace shook his head. "Ed probably sees a profit for himself. Say Paxton locates one and tells Ed it's available for a hundred grand. Ed tells the Agency he can buy it for two hundred grand, and he and Paxton split the difference—fifty grand each."

"And Natsos was trying to interest you."

"Ed's letting avarice take charge of his life. Bad things could happen to him."

He told her about the surprise delivery by Gabriel Bonaventura and the kidnap attempt in the park. "Other than that," he said wryly, "it was a quiet time in Geneva."

"But who could have sent the kidnappers?"

"I wish I knew."

"They could be connected to René's murder."

He nodded soberly.

"And it's all connected to the count and countess. I wish her husband were out of that prison, then maybe they'd go away."

"They will. In the meantime, don't fret about it." He handed her the sheaf of material René had paid for. "For the safe," he told her. Yasmi took it and went away. He had no intention of mounting a breakout op for Carlos de Montaner. If *Maître* Schreiber failed and

161

Erica still wanted her husband freed, the most he would do would be to outline a skyhook snatch and tell her to find a team of mercenaries to bring it off. He had made no commitment to do more.

Phoning Angelique, he told her he'd been out of the country and was tied up with business for at least a week. "Mace, you're becoming so elusive," she said with a touch of asperity, "or are you telling me something I'm not bright enough to grasp?"

"Not at all. I have a very demanding client but I'll call as soon as I can," he promised.

"I've missed you, dear. Life isn't interesting when you're not around."

"I feel the same, *mon amour*," he lied, and hung up.

According to the British Embassy, Jessamyn Taylor was escorting a female MP on a fact-finding tour of Clermont-Ferrand and other industrial centers for the next several days. Mace left his name and turned to other things.

At noon he joined Erica at Prunier for iced oysters, Coquilles St-Jacques, and a carafe of house *blanc*. After a sip of wine Erica said, "Jules feels Carlos is being unreasonable, so he's preparing a counter proposal that gives me forty percent."

"And the divorce?"

"He agrees with you, dear. Carlos is obligated to go through with it as he said he would, and the sooner the better. He's sending Carlos a letter saying so." She sighed deeply. "I barely had time to see two apartments. One is on St-Germain, the other on Rue Caumartin between the Opera and the Madeleine. One's vacant, the other furnished, and to lease it I have to buy the furnishings."

"Well, you have nothing of your own here; if you like it, why not?"

"They're not the sort of things I'd buy if I were furnishing the place, but I don't expect visitors—just you, really. I can look further, but there isn't a lot to choose from. If I take it I can move in today. Should I?"

"Sounds right," he said. "Can I help?"

"My driver and Simone can manage, and we'll stay there tonight."

They rode to his building in her Bentley, and she continued on to the rental agent's office.

After late dinner in her new apartment, Mace poured cognac and

Erica said, "If Schreiber is able to free Carlos on bail what's the next step? We haven't discussed it—probably until now it's seemed too illusory."

"Good point. Both of you ought to stay at the villa for a few days, long enough to let the releasing judge feel Carlos will stay in Switzerland for trial. More than a few days would give the opposition time to appeal his release, so there has to be a fast move." He sipped from his glass. "The French border is just by the airport and there's a tunnel under the runways that surfaces at the French checkpoint. You'll have a limousine and driver. With Carlos hidden in the trunk, take the airport tunnel and tell the French border guards you're going to the Divonne casino for an evening's gambling—if they even ask. Once at the casino, distract the driver long enough to get Carlos out. The two of you merge with the casino crowd, then Carlos takes a taxi to the bus station and a bus to Lyons, the nearest city with a sizeable airport. Does he have a passport?"

"The Swiss Judicial Police took it when they arrested him. That's a problem, isn't it?"

"Not necessarily. With one he could fly directly to Costa Rica but he can get a new one in Madrid and go wherever he wants."

"Why Costa Rica?"

"Like Brazil it's a refuge for fugitives, no extradition for fiscal crimes."

She thought it over. "It's ingenious—but suppose he's kidnapped and brought back to Switzerland?"

"He'll have to guard against it. Besides, you'll be divorced, no further responsibility for him. From Divonne he's on his own."

"And I'll be free. Dear, it's a marvelous plan. It sounds so simple. But after Carlos leaves the casino what should I do?"

"Spend time and money at the tables. Stay overnight at the casino hotel and return to Geneva next day. Then fly out as soon as you can, no baggage."

"Where should I go?"

"If I wanted to shake off pursuers I'd fly to Paris and buy a ticket to St. Petersburg—"

"Russia?"

"Right. Take the Hermitage tour and ride the hydrofoil to Helsinki.

Fly to Oslo, then Stockholm. You're an experienced traveler, you know how best to reach Denmark. By boat?"

She nodded. "At home I'll be safe. But why shouldn't I stay here, in Paris?"

"After Carlos vanishes, the opposition will focus on you. Why make it easy for them?"

She nodded understanding. "It will be like living underground."

"I told you that."

"Oh, I remember," she said with a short, mirthless laugh, "but it all seemed so unlikely I didn't really think it through." She touched his arm. "Will we see each other?"

"When it's safe to arrange." He smiled. "Maybe I'll vanish, too."

"That would be wonderful. We'll go to Greece, buy our own island," she said enthusiastically.

"And abandon everything you'll have in Spain?"

"Oh, we'll go there, too, but I won't expect Carlos's relatives to be very friendly."

"No."

"So we'll avoid them, lead our own lives."

"And hope Carlos stays away."

"Very important. In Spain he has influence that could hurt us."

"But not in the States. Would you mind living there?" He was thinking of Alaya al-Jamal's remote Montana ranch.

"Not if you'd like it, dear."

"Or Canada."

"Definite possibility." Her finger traced the line of his jaw. "How do you feel about children?"

He thought of his daughter, and shrugged.

"Not soon but two or three years away we should start a family."

"Absolutely. Now, let's go to bed and practice."

She took his hand and led him to the bedroom where they had never made love before.

In the morning he left Erica sleeping and went down to the street. He was walking along Rue Caumartin in the direction of a bakery, thinking of fresh-baked croissants for their breakfast when he sensed a car pulling to the curb behind him. Mace glanced around and saw three men pile out of a black limousine and start running toward him. Weaponless, he sprinted away from them until a shot and a shouted order made him stop. Quickly they surrounded him and shoved him roughly into the rear of their limousine. As the car sped from the curb the man riding beside the chauffeur turned and Mace saw the grinning face of Syrian Ambassador Hafik al-Jamal.

fifteen

The Brotherhood

For a few moments they stared at each other before the Syrian spoke. "You took my son so I am taking you."

"Don't know what you're talking about. Let me out of here."

A knife blade flashed before his eyes as something dug painfully into his ribs. "I do not," the ambassador said, "propose to waste time on you. My wife—my former wife—paid you one hundred thousand dollars to kidnap my son; the money was hers, the boy was not. Where is he?"

Mace's throat and mouth were desert-dry. How had Hafik traced him? "I—I don't know," he husked.

"Perhaps not. But before you lie further I will tell you that I found you through the carelessness of my former wife." He held up a leather-bound calendar booklet. "The particulars are here. Your name, telephone, and fee. Now, where is Rashid?"

"She didn't tell me where they were going and I didn't ask." Again his ribs were jabbed and he grunted in pain.

"I don't believe you, *M'sieu*, but enough questions for now. In a little while you will beg to tell me all you know. Everything." He turned from Mace and spoke in Arabic to the chauffeur.

"Listen," Mace said, "there was a plane waiting. She and the boy left in it."

"A plane?" The ambassador faced Mace again. "Your idea?"

"No."

"Then Alaya has more imagination than I thought. What kind of plane?"

"A jet, small one."

"Be specific."

"It was dark at the airfield, I paid no attention to the aircraft."

"She must have chartered it," the ambassador said musingly. "Which airfield?"

"Orly," Mace lied. At Le Bourget there would be a record of the Dassault's ownership and destination. With that, al-Jamal could trace it to O'Hare and conclude she had gone on to Montana.

The limousine had been heading in the general direction of the Syrian Embassy, but now it crossed the Seine and Mace suspected their destination as the Arab Quarter. There he could be disposed of without trace.

There were men on either side of him. A quick move and he might reach the door, hurtle onto the street. Turning again, the ambassador spoke to the guards. One bound Mace's wrists in front of him with nylon cord.

A few minutes more and the limousine swung into a garage. Before it stopped the door closed behind them. Hafik al-Jamal got out and the guards shoved Mace onto a packed dirt floor. A guard pulled off his shoes and socks as Mace heard chains rattle above him. The other guard lowered the hoist's metal hook, set it between his wrists and pulled Mace off his feet. Hafik al-Jamal watched with a gloating smile.

Mace was lifted a yard off the floor, the cord cutting deeply into his wrists. He yelled in pain and the ambassador said, "I credit you with being an intelligent man, M'sieu Mason. You now realize that I can do with you as I choose. I can cut off your testicles or cripple your feet. Is it worth suffering to shield Alaya from me? I have no desire to harm her, I want only my son." One of the guards grabbed Mace's ankles and pulled downward, making the wrist cords cut even more deeply into his flesh. Mace shrieked again and darkness began clouding his eyes. The Ambassador smirked and continued: "The court awarded me sole custody of Rashid—did you know that?"

A Syrian court, Mace thought, and saw the guard hand Hafik al-Jamal a length of spring steel that the ambassador fingered before slashing it against the soles of Mace's feet. Mace shrieked at the new attack and swung his body like a pendulum as he drew up his legs. He rammed them into Hafik's face and saw the ambassador topple backward with a loud yell. Guards siezed Mace's legs and bore downward. Their combined weight shot indescribable pain from his wrists through his body. His vision dulled, but he saw Hafik whip out a knife and stumble toward him, hatred contorting his features.

Suddenly there was noise behind him. The garage doors swung open and Mace heard shouts, the sounds of shooting. One of the guards dropped, the other began shooting at the invaders but a burst of automatic fire doubled him over before he fell. Just before Mace fainted he saw Hafik al-Jamal scrambling toward the far end of the garage. Darkness closed in. He felt no more pain, heard nothing.

Consciousness brought back pain. Groaning, he rolled over, found his wrists free. Mace blinked, looked up and saw five armed men. One was wearing a suit of pearl-gray silk. From his hand dangled a short-barreled shooter, Ingram or Mac-10, Mace thought, as slowly his brain resumed functioning. The man stopped beside him. "How do you feel?" he asked softly.

"Alive," Mace croaked. He licked his lips, swallowed and sat up. The man's face was smooth and slightly olive in color. His eyes were as gray as his suit. His coal black hair was laid close to his skull. Aquiline nose and thin, nearly bloodless lips. Mace began massaging his numbed wrists to restore circulation. "Who are you?"

"Your rescuers, *M'sieu* Mason."

"Police?"

The lips twisted into a mirthless, half-smile. "Hardly. By profession I am a banker." He gestured, and one of the men brought over Mace's shoes. Mace tried to grasp one but his fingers weren't functioning. "Later," he said as the man stood erect and handed his weapon to a companion. Another gave Mace a silver flask and said, "Drink." Using both hands Mace sucked on the flask, tasting vodka. The liquor warmed his throat and belly. The man who called himself a banker said, "Why was al-Jamal torturing you?" One hand with two heavy gold rings adjusted the knot of his silk tie.

Mace drank again. The vodka was doing more for him than a plasma transfusion. After swallowing, he said, "I helped his wife regain their son. Hafik wanted to know where they were."

"Did you tell him?"

"No."

"Do you know where they are?"

"I have a general idea." Unsteadily, he got up, wavered until one of the men steadied him from behind. "Where's the ambassador?"

The banker gestured at the far end of the garage. In the dimness sprawled the body of Hafik al-Jamal. "He declined to surrender, thinking diplomatic immunity would save him." He laughed shortly. "So, you were questioned about a domestic dispute, nothing more?"

Mace held up his hands, showing the deep red abrasions that circled his wrists. "It was enough."

The man nodded. "My interest in you is entirely different," he said evenly, "so I could not have you killed before you satisfied my curiosity." He paused. "Are you feeling better?"

"A lot better," Mace acknowledged. He glanced around and saw the bodies of the two Syrian guards. "I think," the banker said, "that before we leave an arrangement should be made to satisfy the police." He spoke to his men in a language unfamiliar to Mace. Two of them left the garage while the other two carried back the body of Hafik al-Jamal. They bound his wrists with the cords from Mace's wrists, and hoisted the body as Mace had been hoisted. There was a bullet hole in Hafik's throat, a small bloodstain by his heart. The men who had left the garage brought in the body of the limousine chauffeur. They dropped it near Hafik's dangling feet. To Mace the banker said, "What do you think?"

"Political murders. Disloyal guards killed Hafik and apparently killed the chauffeur and each other."

"Not a complete setting," the banker said, "but I think it will do. Can you get on your shoes?"

Mace sat down and forced swollen feet into his shoes, wincing from pain in his wrists. The banker watched him and said, "Arabs still use the *bastinado*; I thought it was out of fashion, but then al-Jamal was a professional terrorist. He won't torture you again, *M'sieu* Mason."

"So I see." He began taking painful steps toward the garage doors. "I've never met a banker who could handle a gun. Who are you?"

Walking slowly beside him the man said, "Without answering directly I'll say that you have had dealings with an incompetent associate of mine."

"Paris is full of incompetent associates."

"True. This one has a position at a certain embassy. Surely you can—"

"Forasteri! So you're Pascal Covici." He grunted. "I suspected one day we'd meet, and the meeting couldn't have been better timed."

When they were out of the garage the doors were closed. They passed the Syrian limousine to a silver-gray stretch Mercedes.

Covici helped Mace into the backseat. Two men faced them on jump seats, and the other two got in front. The Mercedes backed out of the fenced enclosure into a narrow, cobbled alley. Covici said, "I've gone to some trouble to secure you, and I prefer my effort not go unrewarded. You understand?"

Mace nodded. "You want to know what I know about the Montaners. And where the money is. That's what Chakirian asked me."

"I was not aware the two of you had met. Did you satisfy his curiosity?"

Mace shook his head.

"I know that you and the Countess are involved in a love affair and that you recently visited Carlos in prison."

"That's so. The Montaners' Paris law firm introduced me to the countess, thinking I might be able to relieve some of the burdens associated with her husband's imprisonment."

"Such as?"

"Counseling her."

"To what extent?"

"Actually, I've been able to do very little. I don't know if the Count took IFT funds, which I suppose is your principal interest. Consequently, I have no idea where those funds are."

Covici sighed. "If you are truthful I see that I could have avoided the morning's—ah, violence, without losing essential information."

"So it seems."

They were crossing the Seine, heading into the heart of Paris. Pascal Covici said, "So you will understand that I am a serious person but not interested in personal gain, I will tell you that I represent certain interests in Italy, Sicily, and Corsica that have lost great amounts of money through the IFT failure. These interests want it restored."

"I acknowledge the confidence," Mace replied. "You were chosen to invest their money in IFT?"

Covici nodded. "Consequently they look to me to recover it. Not a comfortable position, *M'sieu* Mason. My hope was that you could extricate me from it."

Mace shrugged.

"How much does the countess know?"

"About embezzlement? She knows that her husband has been charged and imprisoned because of it. Her belief is that he is innocent of those charges. She feels a responsibility to work toward his vindication and freedom."

"And when you saw Carlos what did you discuss?"

"It had to do with a divorce agreement and property settlement drawn up by their Paris lawyers. Carlos rejected the proposal and returned the papers to me. Unsigned. Yesterday the countess referred the matter back to the lawyers. Presumably they are preparing a counter-proposal."

"And nowhere in this property settlement was there any mention of what could be construed as IFT funds?"

"The settlement concerned Montaner holdings in Spain."

"Which does not exclude the possibility that Carlos has concealed the funds in such a way that only he has access to them."

"I suppose not—if he embezzled them."

"You seem persuaded that he did not."

"It could go either way. He's guilty, or being made a scapegoat for the sins of others."

Covici grunted. "You take a sympathetic view of the count."

"Not necessarily. I consider him an amateur in the field of high finance, a man whose grasp may have exceeded his reach."

"The *fagoli* was avaricious—and ambitious. Qualities that resemble chemicals producing poison when combined." He shook his head. "A poor choice for a directorship in IFT."

"There must be other suspects."

Covici nodded. "With Carlos in prison the guilty ones may feel confident enough to make an indiscreet move."

171

"Such as?"

"One that can be recognized if and when it occurs."

"Perhaps something as bold as gaining control of a country."

Covici's eyes narrowed. "That would be a strong indication. I haven't thought along those lines before. How did the idea occur to you?"

"Talk among arms merchants, dealers in illegal ordnance—surplus from the old USSR."

"You mean missiles?"

"And aircraft. The entire range of weapons." He chafed his wrists. They were feeling better. Most of the numbness had left his fingers. "Even a very small country would do."

Covici stared at him for a while before saying only, "Grandiose."

"If there's anything to it."

"The theory may open an entirely new line of inquiry. If it does, M'sieu Mason, I may request your cooperation."

Mace said nothing. Covici was gazing out of the tinted window at the Tuileries. Moments later, he said, "Where do you want to go? Rue Caumartin, where you were kidnapped?"

"Fine," Mace said. "I was on my way for breakfast croissants, but it's late for breakfast now."

"Somewhat," Covici agreed. "Tell the lady not to attach too much importance to your injuries. Tell her also that she has nothing to fear from me." He eyed Mace. "Nor do you, assuming you have been honest with me."

"I'll tell her," Mace said as the Mercedes drew up in front of Erica's apartment building. "And I appreciate what you did for me."

Covici waved a hand dismissively as Mace got out. Behind him the Mercedes moved quietly away and Mace faced the doorway. He grimaced as he tried to decide how much of the morning's events to tell Erica and how much to hold back. Then gritted his teeth as he limped painfully toward the doorway.

An hour later he was still soaking his feet in ice water while Erica changed the bread-and-milk poultices around his wrists. Her eyes and voice were filled with solicitude as she said, "How incredibly fortunate that the police came when they did."

"I imagine neighbors heard me yelling and reported it."

Her eyes welled as she bent over to kiss his forehead. "You were so brave."

"It's over. History. I don't want to talk about it again—relive it."

"Of course—I understand completely." She dried her eyes. "When I woke and you were gone—no note or anything—I began to think you'd left me forever." She smiled wanly. "I couldn't bear the thought of staying alone in Paris so I went ahead and bought a ticket to Copenhagen. But now that you're here—"

"No, don't change your plans. Go ahead, visit your family. You need a change of scene, something to get your mind off Carlos."

The telephone rang in another room and she left the kitchen to answer it. Mace looked at the soles of his feet—still red-striped from Hafik's blows. *Bastinado,* Covici had said, a word only dimly familiar to Mace, and he reflected that Pascal Covici was the first member of The Brotherhood he had ever met. Not a street thug but an educated man, and something of a dandy, who could become a powerful, resourceful adversary.

Erica's return interrupted his thoughts. "Bernard," she told him, "wants me to look over the counter-proposal and sign before sending it to Carlos."

"And tell Bernard you won't be seeing Carlos for a while, you'll be visiting your neglected family. He and your husband can deal directly with each other. And you ought to phone *Maître* Schreiber from time to time—keep him aware of your continuing interest. He may need you on short notice to transfer bail funds."

"Yes—of course. And you'll be here?"

"As usual."

She came over and undid the poultice cloths around his wrists. "I hope they're not as painful as they look."

"Improving rapidly, and my feet don't need more soaking."

She brought over a kitchen towel and dried his feet. "I love taking care of you. Now I'll go out and bring back our lunch—unless you want me to stay."

"Great idea, suddenly I'm very hungry."

After she left he drank a shot of cognac and recalled Covici's restorative vodka. Then he found himself wondering how Covici happened to be around when the Syrians took him. Doubtless Covici was having him surveilled, the surveillant tailed the limo to the garage, and Covici gathered his raiders to intervene.

For which I'm very grateful, he mused, though it would only have frightened Erica to learn that the Sicilian Mafia and the Corsican Union were trying to regain their missing IFT funds. A total of sixty-million dollars missing, Jules had estimated, of which The Brotherhood had probably lost a few million. But the overall loss could be much greater, say a billion, but only the embezzler really knew. And Jules had suggested Carlos's personal worth at around eighty million. Would a man with that much risk his life for sixty more? I wouldn't, he thought, but I'm not Carlos de Montaner.

Erica brought back plates of sautéed chicken livers on rice with crisp asparagus and chunks of·fresh bread. After lunch she wound his wrists with gauze and tape and told him she'd noticed a physician's plaque down the street and asked if he would see him. Mace shook his head. "No infection and I heal fast," he assured her, "but a nap would get me back to normal."

While Mace slept Erica went out, telling him later that she signed Bernard's revision, which called for prompt divorce and a forty-sixty property division. The papers would reach Carlos in a day or two.

Yasmi was still in the office when Mace arrived, so he described the morning's events as she listened in near disbelief. "Oh, Mace," she exclaimed as he finished, "I'm so sorry! But how in the world did the ambassador identify you?"

"Alaya left her calendar book behind and the Syrians found it." He shrugged. "If Covici's banditti hadn't been watching me I'd be dead. So I owe him."

"You do," she agreed, "but no one can be that lucky all the time. Did you tell the countess everything?"

"Not everything," he admitted, "just enough to explain my bruises. Any calls for me? Any business come in?"

She shook her head. "I wish the countess would pay for your services—something, anything, Mace."

"She's leaving Paris for a while, visiting her family."

"Then with all respect I suggest you mention payment before she goes."

"I'll think about it," he replied, and went up to his living quarters. There he took off his shoes and lay down beside Su-Su, who licked his hand in welcome. She sniffed his wrist bandages, stretched, yawned and got off the bed. Bedroom slippers eased his feet as Mace fed his pet. He heard Yasmi leave the office and went down to lock the door from inside.

The six o'clock news reported the murders of the Syrian ambassador and three embassy employees, whose bodies had been found in a garage near Ivry, Thirteenth Arrondissement. Unidentified police sources speculated that bad blood among the Syrians provoked a gunfight resulting in the deaths of all four. The chain hoist was shown without the ambassador's body. The police and public prosecutor were pursuing the case actively. The anchorwoman announced a yacht explosion off Antibes and Mace turned off the set, wondering if his name would surface during the investigation.

Erica called to ask how he was feeling. "Well enough to take you to the airport tomorrow."

"Are you sure?" she asked worriedly. "Your poor wrists . . . "

"Healing nicely," he assured her, "and by tomorrow I won't be limping."

"If you're sure . . . I'll come by about ten. Love you."

In the morning Mace took his Ares out to Erica's waiting Bentley and rode with her to De Gaulle airport, alert to possible tailing vehicles. But he spotted none, and escorted Erica to the SAS flight gate, where they said good-bye.

Back in his office Yasmi reported a call from a woman named Selina Mansour. "She said you might remember her."

"Mansour . . . Chakirian's confidential secretary. What does she want?"

"Didn't say, Mace, just that she wants you to call her."

"Guess I'd better," he said and went to his desk.

"Mister Mason," she said in soft syllables, "I'm calling for Mr. Chakirian. There is a business matter that might interest you. Can we discuss it?"

"I suppose so. I'm available this afternoon."

"Mister Chakirian is preparing to leave Paris and instructed me to

175

represent him. Could you come to my place after, say six? We can discuss his proposal in relaxed surroundings."

"Would I be safe?"

She laughed amusedly. "I guarantee it. Avenue Victor Hugo one-three-seven, fifth floor."

"I'll be there."

sixteen

The Proposal

Selina Mansour greeted Mace in a loose black silk blouse and matching slacks. Black Persian slippers decorated with seed pearls, necklace of heavy gold links, massive gold ring on her left hand.

"Thank you for coming," she said as she closed the door and gestured at a low marble table around which were positioned colorful ottomans. Thick white carpeting, white leather sofas. Ceiling fans turned lazily, moving a slight musky scent through the air. "Drink?" she asked.

"Vodka on the rocks. You?"

"Raki is my preference." She moved sinuously to a white cellarette by the wall. Mace sat on an ottoman and watched her prepare their drinks, noticing her full bosom and Rubenesque hips. She was a woman, he reflected, in the full ripeness of feminine sexuality, and wondered what use Chakirian made of it. Glancing around he said, "Your employer pays well."

"He does," she said bringing over their drinks. "One of the perks of working for a wealthy employer." After handing Mace his glass she arranged herself on an ottoman facing him, crossing her legs Arab style. "Your health," she said, lifting her glass.

"And yours." They drank together. The raki in her crystal glass had a slightly golden color. "I would have sent the limousine for you but Victor had it at Le Bourget," she said apologetically.

"Just as well. I don't have great memories of the limo."

She smiled. "I suppose not. Still, you taught those men a lesson

177

they'll not soon forget. I'm sure not one of them wants ever to see you again."

"Feeling's mutual." The taste of vodka reminded him of Covici's silver flask. He felt at ease in his surroundings, in the presence of this exotic woman. How old was she? he wondered; late thirties? Early forties? Her somewhat dusky skin was unlined, her throat firm, unwrinkled. As she bent forward he again noticed the fullness of her bosom and sensed a latent eroticism in the atmosphere. "I silently applauded the way you dealt with those thugs, and even Mister Chakirian was impressed. That you declined payment for damages to your property impressed him as well." Her tongue dipped into the raki, lazily stirred the surface.

"I doubt he's easily impressed," Mace suggested.

"Not by ordinary things. He appreciates honesty and resourceful-ness." She paused. "Shall we get down to business?"

"At your convenience—I'm at loose ends this evening."

"Very well, we can dispose of it rather quickly." She sipped more raki, recrossed her legs. "Would you be willing to conduct an inves-tigation for Mister Chakirian?"

"Possibly. What sort of investigation?"

"It concerns a person who wants to do business with Mister Chakirian."

"Banking business?"

"Not entirely, though money is certainly involved. A discreet investigation. Mister Chakirian does not want the person aware of it."

"Perhaps if you'd—"

"Name him? Of course. He goes by the name of Frederic Lanoix, but in actuality his name is Yuri Chesnikov—Russian."

"What does your employer want to know about Chesnikov?"

"His reputation. Whether he is trustworthy."

Mace laughed shortly. "Trustworthiness often depends on the issue involved. In finance Mister Chakirian would be a better judge than I. Is Chesnikov in Paris?"

"Part of the time. He has an office in Monte Carlo as well." One finger traced moisture beneath her chin. "Are you comfortable, Mister Mason? It seems warm in here." She glanced up at the fans. "Do remove your jacket if you care to."

Mace pulled off his jacket revealing the Beretta holster on his belt. Selina Mansour said, "Apparently you did not believe my guarantee."

"Better to have a weapon and not need it than need one and be without—no reflections on present company." He drank more vodka.

"I understand," she nodded, "and I take you for a man customarily prepared for—anything. Ah—are you more comfortable now?"

"I am."

"I really should have air-conditioning here, but the French are hopeless about it. Even a few window units here and there." She stood and took his almost empty glass. "May I freshen it?"

"By all means."

At the cellarette she refilled both glasses, added ice to his. Before seating herself she touched her glass to his. "May you travel many miles without danger, and sire many sons."

"I like the first part of it. An Arab toast?"

She nodded. "I was born in Lebanon but I have lived in many places. Cyprus, Malta, the Emirates. My family was Christian and I attended American University in Beirut. Before that once-lovely city was destroyed," she added with a touch of bitterness, then drank deeply from her glass.

"Tell me more about this Russian," he said.

"We believe that he was an officer in the Soviet Army, or perhaps their security service, the KGB. He wants Mister Chakirian to finance a large purchase of weapons from Ukraine."

Mace drank again. "I don't know much about your employer but I understand he's not unfamiliar with the arms trade."

"That is true. So he is cautious about business with a person of uncertain reliability. Is this of interest to you—and will you please call me Selina?"

"If you'll call me Mace."

She dipped a finger in her glass and moistened his lips. "Perhaps you'll like raki."

He licked the trace from his lips. "Challenging," he remarked. "I suspect it's an acquired taste, like retsina."

"Oh, that dreadful resin drink! In Athens one must pretend to like it, or be ostracised."

The flavor of raki persisted in his mouth. It was pungent, like raw pulque, the Central American cactus liquor he had drunk in Nicaragua when nothing else was available. He sipped vodka to rinse away the raki. "Were I to investigate Chesnikov I would have to go to Monte Carlo. Or send someone."

She shrugged. "That would be up to you. Then you're interested, Mace?"

While Erica was away he might as well earn some money—even if it came from Chakirian. "I'll have to check other commitments."

"Of course—we did not expect an immediate reply."

Her legs shifted again, as though to distance her loins from a source of heat. "May I offer you some caviar? Pâté de foie gras?"

"Sounds delectable." He followed her into a small, modern kitchen. From the refrigerator she took out a jar of Beluga and a tin of pâté, asked him to open them. While he was doing that she arranged thin crackers on a tray, then scooped caviar onto a crystal saucer. Mace transferred the block of pâté to a plate, and Selina added small silver spoons and knives to the tray. Mace carried it to the marble table and as she sat beside him she said, "Not knowing if you would be available I let the cook off for the evening. And I don't really want to dine out." She heaped caviar on a cracker. "Do you?"

"No," he said, and let her slide the cracker into his mouth. The caviar was cold and delicious. He followed it with a drink of vodka. "Excellent," he said appreciatively, put a small slice of pâté on a cracker and placed it in her mouth. "Umm," she said, closing her eyes. "Delicious. I should indulge myself more often."

"You should," he agreed. "Especially when alone. Selina, satisfy my curiosity—does Victor come here?"

At first she frowned, then smiled. "In other circumstances I would regard that as an impudent question, Mace, but I'll tell you that my employer came here once—to view the furnishings and decorations, never since. Does that answer you?"

He nodded, helped himself to more caviar. Their glasses were nearly empty so he refilled them at the cellarette. "I seem to be making myself at home," he remarked. "Mind?"

"Not at all. Victor's absence allows me to relax for the first time in—oh, weeks. And I like being with someone I admire and trust."

"Sure you can trust me?"

She twirled the glass between her fingers. "Most men who see me are really interested in my supposed influence with Victor."

"Supposed?"

"Trusting me doesn't mean he accepts my advice." She looked away. "Victor has many good qualities, but he's as chauvinistic as an Arab. Makes his own decisions."

So far, he thought, she's let me know that Chakirian is not her lover, and we're alone here. For the night. He felt a stir of desire. Wordlessly he ate a slice of pâté and downed more vodka. The liquor was hitting him, and he wondered at her capacity for raki. "Being a talented woman in an Arab world can't be easy," he suggested.

"It's very difficult, Mace, but as an American you have no negative notions about female ability."

"None at all." He gave her more caviar. After swallowing she drank raki and licked her lips. "This could be habit-forming," she remarked, "and I'm very much at ease with you. When Victor suggested I see you I'll admit I was apprehensive. I knew that you were a man of strength and integrity but I also thought you could be—difficult."

"Oh? In what way?"

"Scornful, dismissive." Her gaze met his. "I know better now, but it was necessary to see and talk with you." Her hands spread. "You're a very attractive man, Mace."

"I hardly need tell you how attractive you are."

"Thank you. Would you like some music?"

"If you would."

"I have a Connick medley." She got up and walked unsteadily to a stereo cabinet below a painting. As she returned, throbbing music drifted through the room. Lowering herself beside him she laughed shortly. "The raki seems to be affecting me. I've drunk far more than I usually do." Slowly she licked her lips.

"Are you all right?" Mace asked.

181

"Yes—quite. Though I'm feeling uncomfortably warm." A finger touched light perspiration on her forehead. "So if you'll excuse me a few moments . . . "

"Of course."

She glided away carrying her drink and Mace watched her go. Raki, he mused, was the standard Middle Eastern drink, and he wondered where this intriguing female had acquired a taste for it. He found himself wanting to know more about her even if business came to nothing. As he looked around he noticed several large expressionist paintings on the walls, their bright slashing colors contrasting with the overall white decor.

When his hostess returned she was wearing a gauzy gown whose plunging V revealed flesh to her thorax. The gown reached down to her bare feet and Mace saw that her toenails were colored lavender matching the hue of her gown.

"Feeling more comfortable?" Mace asked as she seated herself beside him.

"Much more comfortable."

Through the translucent gown Mace could glimpse dark nipples no longer hidden by the discarded bra. She fingered a fold of material. "Do you like the color?"

"Yes, it goes well with your complexion." Her thighs parted, revealing a patch of dark wool beneath the translucent material. He thought of inviting her to dinner but that would mean her dressing again and he liked seeing her the way she was.

Idly, she touched one bandaged wrist. "I won't ask about this."

"No."

"Hurt?"

"Not now." His tongue was thick and not from liquor alone. He put an arm around her shoulder. "If you don't feel well I'll leave."

"Oh, no, don't do that, Mace. I shouldn't have mentioned the raki." She looked up at him, and he saw the depth of her dark, kohl-rimmed eyes. "But we're being honest with each other, aren't we?"

"Entirely." He kissed her forehead.

She murmured, "When I said I found you attractive, I meant as a woman finds a man attractive." Her face lifted so that her lips were only a few inches from his. "Need I say more?"

182

He pressed his lips to her open mouth and her tongue became a serpent mating with his. Through the flimsy fabric her breasts pressed against him. He peeled the gown from her shoulders and caressed her breasts with hands and mouth. Despite their fullness they were firm to his touch. Selina moaned and arched her back to give him full access to her breasts. Presently he opened her gown and stroked the darkness between her loins. She shuddered and her thighs parted for him, but he drew her off the ottoman and onto the white carpet.

Even before he was completely naked she reached up and pulled him kneeling beside her. Hungrily her mouth enveloped his tumid shaft and a misty delirium suffused his brain. Looking down at her hollowed cheeks, gazing at her voluptuous body, he felt himself in an erotic paradise. Then her head drew back and she said hoarsely, "Don't spend yet, I want to go with you."

Obediently, he knelt between her splayed thighs and entered her hot, moist matrix, matching thrust with thrust until she cried out and clutched him convulsively. "Now! Come now, Mace!" Almost frantically her pelvic thrusting quickened and brought him off, clutching him close while her spasms came.

Afraid he would collapse atop her Mace rolled aside and kissed her lips. Her body shivered, her eyes stayed closed as though to preserve some private fantasy of her own. Then languidly, she opened her eyes. "Magical," she murmured, "so complete. God, how I wanted you." She turned to nestle against him. "Must be why I was perspiring—did you notice?"

"Seemed possible," he admitted, "but I hardly dared hope."

"So I put on the gown to—encourage you."

"I wasn't entirely sure of your intentions."

"Now you are. Does it bother you?"

"It bothers me that we spent time eating and drinking when we could have been making love." He kissed her again, felt a warm lassitude spread through his body.

"Can you stay the night?"

"Try putting me out." They got up and went slowly into her bedroom. Like her living room it was completely white except for gold outlining the furnishings. The sheets were cool, Selina's body warm against him. Sated, depleted, he slept.

* * *

Before dawn he left Salina sleeping and drove back to his own place. During the night they had renewed their lovemaking, and Mace felt the need of restorative sleep. He went to bed and woke to sunlight and the smell of coffee perking. He could hear Yasmi below at her machines.

As he sipped coffee he felt a twinge of conscience. Only a few hours after Erica left Paris he was fucking a black-haired houri with a fabulous figure. He considered the circumstances and concluded that as a bachelor he was entitled to take pleasure as it came. And he had never vowed celibacy to Erica. A flimsy rationale, he mused, but it's not as though I'd made the first move. Selina set things in motion by half-exposing herself and dulling my conscience with liquor. Her plan, he thought, must have been to determine if she liked me. If not, nothing would have transpired. Alternatively, she was resolved to fuck me and subliminally I realized she was in heat, so I responded to her witchery. A very smooth seduction, he reflected, fashioned with the care of experience.

But was everything as it seemed? he asked himself. Was the proposed investigation only a pretext to get me to her apartment? If so, what was the purpose? Even if photographed by hidden cameras I'm not vulnerable to sexual blackmail. Still, they had come together with unusual ease, as though the encounter was choreographed.

Objectively, Selina was Chakirian's trusted confidante—perhaps his mistress, for Mace did not entirely believe her disavowal. He could have told her to seduce me for reasons of his own, some covert motive I can't define. Maybe he's impotent, a voyeur who gets his kicks watching replays of Selina's conquests. There are men like that, a lot of them. Only, why me?

Until I can find out if and why Chakirian set me up I ought to accept the evening at face value: a natural consequence of two mutually attracted adults in a setting conducive to sex.

That settled, Mace finished his coffee and went down to his office where Yasmi said, "You slept late, boss. What did Mademoiselle Mansour want?"

He told her about the proposed investigation of Yuri Chesnikov aka Frederic Lanoix. Offices in Paris and Monte Carlo.

"Did you accept?"

"Not yet. A preliminary inquiry is in order. See if you can get Ed Natsos on the phone."

When the embassy officer came on the line he sounded grumpy. "What's up, Mace?"

"A trade-off. Meet me at the Rond Point brasserie and I'll buy you a *fine café*. Half an hour?"

"If it's important."

"Don't quibble, Ed, you still owe me. See you there." He hung up, and said to Yasmi, "If we take the investigation you could do the Monte Carlo part of it. With Jean-Paul."

"Oh, we'd love it."

"Drive down to the Côte d'Azur and mix business with pleasure."

"Mace, that's the best idea I've heard all year. So I hope you take the job."

"Nothing's settled so don't start packing."

"No—but I can hope."

He got to the brasserie ahead of Natsos, took a table and ordered two *fines cafés*. He was sipping his when Natsos arrived. Sitting across the table, Natsos looked at his wristwatch and said, "I'm pressed for time so let's make this fast. What's on your mind?"

"A simple matter. Run these names through your computer." He handed Natsos a card with both names on it. "Ever hear of them?"

"Sure. They're the same guy. What's your interest?"

"Character reference. I want your printout."

"I can't do that for a civilian, against regulations."

"Look at it this way. Administration policy encourages the Agency to cooperate with American businessmen abroad. I'm an American businessman abroad."

Natsos dropped the card in a jacket pocket and sipped his demitasse. "The guy's an arms dealer, but you probably know that."

"Had dealings with him?"

"To this extent: He was informed of our Stinger buyback program. Lanoix and twenty other locals."

"Any response?"

"Lanoix said he'd look around, listen to trade talk and get back to me. Nothing yet." He eyed Mace. "What's your interest"

"Maybe the same as yours. What was his army rank as Chesnikov?"

"Light colonel, artillery specialist until he was demobbed. Figured there was money to be made in the capitalist world and settled here."

"Is he big or little?"

"Medium, I'd say, but looking for the ultimate weapons deal, one that would set him up so he could really retire." He drank from his cup and stared at it. "Aren't we all?" he said bitterly.

Mace shrugged. "Can I have the printout today?"

"I guess," he said resignedly, "but tell me how you got on to him."

"Through a mutual acquaintance. What's Lanoix's reputation for honesty?"

"So-so. Small deals, okay. But if it's major, watch your ass."

"I intend to." Mace replied, "and I appreciate your cooperation."

Natsos drained his cup, glanced at his watch and stood up. "I'll drop the stuff off on my way home." He walked away and Mace lingered over the last of his drink. Then he taxied back to his office.

Yasmi was holding the telephone when he went in. "Mademoiselle Mansour," she told him and Mace took the call at his desk. "Good morning, Mace," Selina said in a cool, professional voice. "Can we talk?"

Yasmi had put down her phone. "Yes," he said, "go ahead."

Throatily she said, "Last night—I loved every minute of it."

"So did I."

"I anticipate a reprise—is that possible?"

"It is."

"Now, Mister Chakirian phoned to ask me what you decided. I told him you were checking commitments and would let me know."

"Impatient cuss, isn't he? I thought there was no rush."

"So he said, but he often changes his mind."

"Where is he?"

"Geneva—meeting with IFT directors. He'll be back in a few days so I want to take advantage of his absence." She paused. "I thought I'd leave early today. Will that suit you?"

"Certainly will."

"Then I'll have my cook prepare dinner so we won't have to go out." He heard her sigh. "Until I see you I'll be thinking of you—and last night." Her lips made a soft sucking sound.

"Jesus," Mace exclaimed, "don't *do* that!" and heard light laughter before she whispered, "If you think I'm insatiable you're right. So don't disappoint me." She broke the connection.

From the far side of the room Yasmi had glanced around, disapproval on her face. She picked up her purse and went off to lunch with Jean-Paul.

So Chakirian was in Geneva with the IFT gang, sans Carlos de Montaner. Mace wondered if they had gotten wind of Carlos's new lawyers and Schreiber's efforts. If so they would do whatever might be necessary to keep him behind bars. It was the first time Selina had mentioned IFT and her information disturbed him.

Victor Chakirian could hire any of a hundred Paris investigators to check on Frederic Lanoix; why had he chosen Brad Mason? Unless there was a reason involving IFT. That was a logical inference, and perhaps he could learn more from Selina while in the lists of love. It was worth trying.

Until Yasmi returned Mace typed a summary of all he had learned from Ed Natsos about Lanoix/Chesnikov, and told Yasmi to enter it in the computer.

"Then you're going ahead?"

"What Ed Natsos leaves with you could determine it. So please wait for him."

"Of course. You won't be here, then?"

"I'll be explaining to Mademoiselle Mansour the difficulties and complications of a character investigation—to justify our bill."

"Of course," she said with a knowing smile. "Just make it a big one."

He went out to lunch at a neighborhood café and afterward stopped at a liquor shop for wine, raki, and vodka. The proprietor's wife arranged the bottles in a raffia basket, which Mace took back to the office. At three Selina phoned, asking him to come at four. That gave him time to shave, shower, and change clothes before taking a taxi to 137 Avenue Victor Hugo, the building he had left ten hours before.

seventeen

The Whip

As before, Selina met him at her door, but this time it was a different Selina who greeted him.

In place of last evening's pants suit she was wearing tall black patent leather boots with spike heels and a one-piece black lace chemise tightly fitted from split crotch to breast cups open for her protruding nipples. Black lipstick and eyebrows completed the outré ensemble—except for the riding crop dangling at her wrist.

Mace gawked at the transformed Selina, saw a glint in her eyes. "Lock the door," she ordered, and when he had slipped both bolts she stood, legs apart and sneered, "Don't you know how to greet a lady?"

"I—" he began, but she cut him off contemptuously and handed him the crop. "Here, fool," she snapped, turned and bent over to present voluptuous buttocks. "Strike," she demanded. "Strike hard or get out."

Mace licked his lips and the crop whistled through the air. It struck her rump with a loud fleshy report, she cried out, and yelled, "Again. Harder!"

The second blow staggered her forward, checked by the back of a chair. Mace could see the swelling red stripes and fingered the crop expectantly. Instead, she stood erect and turned to him. "You'll do, lover."

He stepped toward her. "More?"

One hand lifted. "Enough for now." Rubbing her backside she eyed him lustfully. "You've learned what I want from a strong man."

Her arms circled his neck as she pressed black lips to his. "Like it? Excite you?"

"Yes," he admitted. "What now?"

Even her fingernails were black, he noticed as she peeled off his jacket, undid his belt, and dropped his trousers. His fingers parted the divided crotch, entered the tangle of crinkly bush. "God," she moaned, "oh, God," and dropped to her knees. In seconds she was worshipping the rod. Dazed, Mace watched until his knees were too weak for standing. Roughly he pushed her on her back. Both boot-encased legs shot upward and he found his way between her naked thighs. Savagely they thrust at each other, but not for long, spending together with little cries and heavy breathing. Her heels drummed on his back just before her final spasm ended.

For a while they said nothing. Slowly Mace disentangled himself and moved aside. "Well," he managed, "that was different."

"You were surprised?"

"Almost into shock."

"But you recovered fast, lover. I wanted you to be surprised, see how you reacted."

"And—?"

"You were perfect." She rolled over on her stomach. "I bought the accessories for your—shall I say excitement? Truthfully, for my excitement, too. Now, massage my sore behind. Gently."

He kneaded and stroked her tender bottom, kissed the angry stripes and she murmured contentedly. After a while she said, "I debated confronting you later or when you arrived. Decided to clear our heads so we wouldn't be thinking about sex during cocktails and dinner."

"Do this often?" he asked idly.

"No, damn you! I *said* I bought these things for you, Mace, you alone. I'm not addicted to the whip, if that's what you mean."

"Meant nothing," he replied, "just curious," and saw anger on her face.

"But you loved it, didn't you?" she challenged. "Am I as exciting as your blonde countess?"

"Now, now, let's not discuss personalities." He peeled down her breast cups and picked up the riding crop. Touched each dark nipple with it. "Don't provoke me, Selina," he said sternly, "or I could lose control."

Her body shivered against him. "Oh, Mace, I'm sorry. I don't ever want to anger you." Her hand roved his loins. "Forgive me?"

"Sure. And now it's cocktail time." He helped her up and watched her rearrange her disheveled costume, thinking that despite differences in age, complexion, and national origin, Selina and Erica had one thing in common—a taste for the lash. Selina sat on an ottoman, legs apart, while Mace made drinks at the cellarette. After they toasted each other he remembered the raffia basket and brought it in from the hall. After unwrapping each bottle she said, "How thoughtful of you, darling. How very dear. I'm not accustomed to thoughtful gifts so yours is very special." Her finger moistened each swollen nipple with raki. She shivered and smiled.

"Now," he said, seated before her, "I've learned a little about Lanoix/Chesnikov," and summarized Natsos's information. "By tomorrow I may have more."

She clapped her hands. "Then you'll do the full investigation?"

"Not necessarily. Just reciprocating for—" he spread his hands— "all this."

"As if that were necessary. Mace, you're out of order, very much so. For that you ought to be punished," she said slyly.

"Possibly—later on." She was still playing the dominatrix when for him the game was over.

"Then let's take our drinks to the Jacuzzi," she suggested, and stood up. "We can play there, too."

Immersed in warm flowing water, Mace felt revived. Selina adjusted jets to play gently over her buttocks, then shifted one to her crotch. Leaning back, she closed her eyes and breathed deeply, her breasts lifting above water level as she became aroused. Presently she moved over to sit astride his thighs, and soon they were making love again.

Her fervor, he thought, was that of a woman starved for sexual release. And it occurred to him that Chakirian might require whipping for his pleasure, not hers.

After leaving the Jacuzzi they showered and Selina soaped black makeup from her face. He was glad she was out of her garish costume.

Selina dried and rebandaged his wrists, saying, "I'm still not going to ask about this."

"Admirable restraint. Some day if you're still interested I'll tell all—though it's not a pretty story."

After drying themselves Selina handed him a new Hermès bathrobe and drew on one of rose-pink silk. She was, he thought, changeable as a chameleon. One minute the Whore of Babylon, next a semi-demure housewife. The role changes fascinated him; nothing dull about Selina. She'd brought excitement into his life.

The cook had prepared a crown roast of lamb with artichokes and small rissole potatoes. Salad and pistachio ice. His Bordeaux added savor to the meal.

"In Geneva," Mace said over cognac, "I suppose your boss is lamenting his IFT losses with the other directors. Or former directors."

"Victor?" She shook her head. "He lost very little, not like some of the others. He was too smart for that." She smiled proudly. "He pulled out before the crash became public."

"Then he's smarter than I thought. Much smarter than, say, Count Carlos de Montaner."

"Oh, him. He was nothing. A fool, maybe, nothing more."

Mace sipped more cognac. "I wonder how much disappeared overall. I've heard estimates that run from fifty mil to over a billion."

She shrugged. "I doubt it will ever be known, but I'd guess the larger figure. Only my guess, and I suppose the directors don't want the public to know."

"Or the prosecutors. Now only the lawyers will profit from the scandal. Vultures devouring whatever's dead."

She nodded agreement. "Let's go to the living room and listen to music."

Side by side on a sofa they heard the plaintive voice of Natalie Cole, drank raki and vodka until inhibitions dissolved. Then they made love, Selina kneeling on the sofa, rump upraised, crimson stripes clearly visible.

Later they stood at the window, looking out at the skyline of Paris, the golden haze above. "It's so lovely," Selina murmured, "that I don't ever want to leave Paris." She kissed his cheek. "Do you?"

"Only if forcibly ejected." Lightly he patted her rump and led her off to bed.

During the night movement woke him. They were lying together spoon fashion and her buttocks were bucking against him. Her passage felt tighter than before, and Mace realized that she had maneuvered him into the road less traveled. As his pleasure grew, Mace grasped her hips and brought them off together. Panting, they lay as they were while passion gradually subsided. *"Le baiser noir,"* she murmured. The dark kiss. "Do you like it?"

"Always have."

"Thought you might have scruples so I took advantage of you." Twisting her upper body, she kissed his lips. "Were you surprised when you found that—?"

"A little," he admitted, "but not for long."

She pressed back against his loins. "You accommodate my whims, you're a perfect lover."

So, another mode was added to their sexual repertoire, he thought sleepily, and he shouldn't have been surprised, buggery being endemic across the Middle East. An age-old practice having to do with birth control, avoidance of venereal disease, and personal choice.

When he woke she was dressing for work, black boots and lace chemise placed neatly in her closet. He wondered when the mood to don them would possess her again. "How do you feel?" he asked.

"Wonderful. Fulfilled. Shall I call you today?"

"Let's have dinner together," he suggested. "Dine out."

"Then come by around six. I'll leave a key for you in case I'm delayed at the office." She bent over to kiss him. "Until then, *chéri.*"

Her modestly dressed figure seemed to undulate as she walked away. What a marvelous female, he thought, turned over and slept until mid-morning.

* * *

In his office he reviewed the printout supplied by Ed Natsos, who had blacked out the classification stamp. The subject was CHESNIKOV, Yuri Stoyanovich aka LANOIX, Frederic André DOB 11/8/44 Plevinko, Ukraine, USSR. As the son of a military hero killed in the Great Patriotic War Yuri was admitted to Frunze Military Academy as a student of battlefield ordnance. After graduation he was not assigned to an artillery regiment, but to the Institute of Foreign Languages, the prep school for KBG and GRU—military intelligence—spies, where he became fluent in French, English, and Spanish. His postings followed: New Delhi, Buenos Aires, Goa, Algiers, Ottawa, finally to Afghanistan as a troop morale officer charged with preventing disaffections, desertions, and punishing cowardice before the enemy. In short an executioner with broad powers at the front. Demobilized 1992, emigrated abroad. Since then actively engaged with fellow officers, who stayed behind, in plundering stockpiles of weaponry and selling them abroad. Paris office at Champs-Elysées 149-*bis;* Monaco, Rue Royale 47. Probably unmarried, no known issue.

A final notation stated that Subject at one time supplied arms to rebel organizations in El Salvador, Nicaragua, Guatemala, and Peru, and employed intermediaries to develop sales to Iraq, Iran, Syria, and Somalia.

Mace shoved the printout aside. A very busy guy, he reflected, and very dirty. Not a fellow I'd want to do business with, but Chakirian observes no moral or ethical constraints.

To Yasmi he said, "Transfer this printout to a special disk, cross-reference to Chakirian."

She picked up the printout and scanned it. "Shall I pack for Monaco?"

"Not yet. The guy looks plenty ruthless; an executioner in Afghanistan. He could be dangerous to your health and I don't want to lose you over the son of a bitch. Or Jean-Paul. Good help is hard to find."

"Thanks, boss," she said drily, and started away.

"Better prepare a Secours report form leaving out Chakirian's name."

She nodded. "Forgot to tell you the countess called, wants to hear from you."

He felt a twinge of conscience over his infidelity. He'd been enjoying a dark-eyed enchantress, with hardly a thought to his Danish blonde. For his sins of commission and omission he should be whipped. Stoutly whipped. Meanwhile . . . "Get *Maître* Hugo Schreiber on the line—Geneva."

She dialed from her desk and a few moments later buzzed Mace who picked up the phone. "Mason here, *Maître*," he said. "The IFT directors are meeting in Geneva."

"Yes, there was a notice in the paper."

"Occurs to me it could affect our client's prospects. Negatively."

"I see." The line hummed vacantly until Schreiber spoke again. "I've heard nothing about such a possibility but I appreciate your alerting me."

"Otherwise, any progress?"

"It is slow, as I said at the outset. Incidentally, the countess called earlier and I told her what I have said to you."

"Are you optimistic?"

"I must be. A lawyer cannot allow himself to be otherwise. Again, I appreciate your call."

Mace replaced the receiver and drummed fingers on the desktop while he considered what to say to Erica. Finally he told Yasmi to call Viborg. When Erica came on the line he said, "I've missed you, honey, are you having a good time with your family?"

"Very good, *chéri*. I really must come here more often. How have you been?"

"Working," he said vaguely, "making a franc here and there."

"I've phoned the past two nights but no answer. I thought perhaps you were seeing friends—female friends." How prescient she was, he thought, and said, "Not a chance, dear. I phoned Schreiber to let him know the IFT directors are meeting in Geneva. I thought it might be bad news for Carlos, but he doesn't agree."

"Mace, you're seldom wrong about anything. Should I go there? Should you?"

"To do—what? Schreiber will let us know if anything's to be done."

"Yes," she said slowly, "of course."

"Seeing a lot of old friends?"

"Those still in Viborg, and I don't let them call me countess because I won't be one much longer. Dear, I do hope Carlos commits to divorce. I suspect he's being difficult just to aggravate me."

"You're probably right."

"And the weather is wonderful here just now. We'll come here next spring. You'll see."

"I look forward to it," he told her, "and I'll be glad to see you again."

"Miss you," she said and rang off.

Mace breathed a sigh of relief. Things were under control in Denmark. Turning to look out over the city, Mace reflected that his affair with Selina was a short-term thing, ending when Chakirian or Erica returned. But Erica was a long-term investment, eventual marriage a possibility. Meanwhile he had no intention of depriving himself of Selina's company. They were compatible, companionable, and she was enjoyably unpredictable in their relationship. In his experience she was unique.

At six he rang her doorbell, waited, and rang again, thinking she might be in the shower or changing. After another three unanswered rings he let himself in with the key she had left for him that morning.

The apartment was silent. He turned on ceiling fans and went to the cellarette. There he made drinks for both of them, and strolled around while he sipped iced vodka. Their bed had been made, he noticed, and the kitchen was meticulously clean. Alone in a woman's apartment he always felt himself alien, an intruder among her most intimate things, and the feeling returned again. He was approaching the cellarette when he heard a key in the door lock and saw Selina come in. "Mace," she called, "I'm glad you came in, sorry I was delayed." She came to him, took her drink and kissed him lingeringly. "How was your day?"

"Good. You?"

"Busy." She opened her jacket and laid it on a chair, pulled off her blouse. "Victor pays well but he can be very demanding." She stepped out of her shoes. "There, that feels better. Now I must change for dinner. We are going out, aren't we?"

"Where would you like?"

"Here, undo my bra." He freed her breasts, kissed them. "Umm," she murmured. "What were you saying?"

"Your restaurant choice."

"Oh, anyplace with you." She paused. "Périgourdine, Place St-Michel?"

"Good choice."

"But there's no hurry, is there?" She picked up shoes and clothing, walked toward the bedroom. "None at all," he replied, and watched her undress, noticing the sway of heavy breasts as she bent over to pull off pantyhose. He drank to moisten his dry throat, finished his drink while she soaped her body, visible through the shower's glass door. He helped dry her glistening body and when that was done she pressed against him and said throatily, "I need you. Take off your clothes."

So they made love on the edge of her bed, hastily, urgently, and after she dressed they had another drink and took a taxi across the Pont Neuf, past the Palais de Justice to the restaurant.

It was early enough that they had a choice of tables and after ordering, Mace let the sommelier select their wine. During dinner Selina said, "It's good to make love before dinner so we can enjoy it without distraction. Don't you agree?"

"I do," he said and felt her hand stroke his leg under the tablecloth. "And I'll have a report for Chakirian tomorrow."

"So soon? I thought you'd have to go to Monte Carlo." She leaned forward interestedly.

"In view of what I learned it wasn't necessary—or wise."

"Tell me."

"Chesnikov is fifty, a former Army Intelligence officer, and a life-taker. In Afghanistan he was a regimental executioner. Since then he's been selling weapons to undesirable people."

"I see." She paused. "Is he honest, trustworthy?"

"Let Chakirian decide."

"What's your judgment?"

"I'd avoid him—but I don't know what he and Victor have in mind." He sipped from his wineglass. "I'd guess Chesnikov wants your boss to finance a big-time deal—missiles, say, even nuclear warheads. If a deal like that goes through it would make a lot of people very unhappy. The offended parties would take reprisals. The Israelis, for one."

"Against Victor."

"And Chesnikov."

She considered his words. "That's very alarming. I wonder how Victor will react."

"Not my problem, or yours." The sommelier refilled their glasses and drifted away. When he was out of earshot, she took Mace's hand and held it. "For a long time I've wanted someone to help me. Someone thoroughly honest and reliable. An intelligent, resourceful man able to handle himself in difficult situations."

"As a bodyguard?"

She shook her head. "As a partner."

"I don't understand."

"You will." She glanced away, then her gaze met his. "You're thirty-five, divorced, one child. You conceived Secours and gained an enviable reputation for honesty and discretion. Last year Secours earned just under three hundred thousand francs, a portion of which you invested at Banque Suisse-Allemagne. You are neither poor nor wealthy and I doubt that you intend to keep working the rest of your life."

"I have a dream or two," he admitted, "when I have enough money to realize them."

"So do I, Mace."

"You know a good deal about me. Did you have me investigated?"

"Banks exchange information. Chakirian's is no exception. After I first saw you that day at the office and learned how you put down Victor's thugs I made it my business to inquire about you. Discreetly, of course."

"Does Victor know?"

She shook her head. "But when he wanted information on Chesnikov I suggested hiring you. That gave me opportunity to be with you and form my own opinion. And I found you extremely attractive."

"It was mutual—you know that."

She nodded, squeezed his hand. "Suppose you had a chance to gain an immense fortune with very little risk. Would that interest you?"

"Without knowing more I'd be plenty interested. Okay, you've been considering me as a partner—in what?"

"Acquiring the funds embezzled from IFT. Eight hundred million dollars."

He swallowed. "You're serious? You know where it is? How?"

"Victor stole it."

eighteen

The Intruder

It was computer theft, Selina told him, transferring funds from IFT to investments that were no more than bank account names. On the surface the investments appeared sound to other directors, but when accountants investigated, the money was gone. "In some ways," she said, "Victor is a genius. He began stealing just after IFT books had been audited and approved; he had a year to operate before the next accounting and he took full advantage of it."

"But didn't the Trust maintain internal financial controls?" he asked in puzzlement. "How could it happen?"

"I'm not familiar with whatever safeguards the Trust established, but it's obvious they weren't effective." She paused. "Knowing Victor as I do, I feel he could have sought out two or three key officials and bribed them to ignore what was going on." She shrugged. "Having served their purpose, I don't doubt that Victor could have had them murdered to prevent their ever talking. There was even public speculation over the disappearance of some IFT employees, but it was brief and died away." She breathed deeply. "You understand how Victor manipulates and operates?"

"I'm beginning to. But I don't understand why the directors allowed themselves to be bamboozled—did none of them ever check a balance sheet or analyze how their investments were doing?"

She smiled. "Probably not. Men at that level—Arab sheiks, Middle Eastern political leaders, military figures, and corrupt dictators— lack the knowledge to understand sophisticated financial strategies. In some cases they have neither time nor interest to keep careful watch on the funds they supplied the Trust. I say *interest* because those men—some at least—control incalculable fortunes. They depend on advisers, perhaps as financially illiterate as they are, to invest and manage prudently."

Mace nodded. "Making a circle of ignoramuses, blind leading blind."

"And Victor was shrewd enough to detect the vulnerabilities. I don't know what actually caused the failure of IFT, and the public may never know, but I suspect it was some final straw that broke the camel's back."

Mace considered her words. "So how did you learn all you have? Victor confided in you? Boasted of his killing?"

"No, Mace, I found out on my own. You see, when Victor began staying late in the office alone I began wondering why. On various pretexts I stayed after hours and heard his computer running. Then I came in early morning after morning, checked his console and finally found a disk he'd neglected to remove. Before he arrived I ran the disk and discovered it contained three transactions withdrawing funds from IFT and transferring them to different-named accounts. By computer I checked those names and found they were only shells. Then I realized what Victor had been doing." She drank deeply from her glass.

"And he framed Carlos de Montaner."

"He needed a scapegoat and the count was perfect for the role. Over time Victor transferred fourteen million dollars into two Montaner accounts and after the IFT investigation began, the count couldn't explain it. He was a landowner, after all, not a finance expert. Perhaps he thought the deposits were the lucky result of computer error. His mistake was in not asking questions, not revealing the anonymous deposits to his fellow IFT directors. Instead, he stayed silent—Victor counted on that, knowing the count's financial naïveté—and in effect the count became an accomplice. After he was charged and jailed he must have realized what had happened, though he couldn't know who was behind it. And the evidence against him was fourteen unexplained millions in his two accounts." She breathed deeply, breasts lifting under the fabric of her dress. "Are you going to tell the countess?"

He thought it over. "I don't know. But when I became involved in her husband's situation I realized that if Carlos wasn't guilty, his imprisonment was useful to those who were."

"How deeply are you involved?"

"I want him out of prison, one way or another."

"Because of his wife?"

"It's what she wants." He drained his wineglass, watched other diners arriving. "With all you know about Victor's embezzlement why do you need a partner—even want one?"

"I don't have the access passwords. Without them Victor's accounts are invulnerable."

"He probably keeps them hidden in his office."

She shook her head. "He's hidden them in his brain, that would be his way. Trust nothing, trust no one."

"And with them?"

"We could empty his accounts, transfer the money to our own. And expose Victor Chakirian."

"Those aren't the words of a grateful employee," he said wryly. "Why do you want to bring him down?"

"Because," she said quietly, "I am the illegitimate daughter of Victor Chakirian."

Mace stared at her, beginning to understand as Selina went on. "My mother was a dancer, an artiste if you will, famous throughout the Middle East, by birth Egyptian. Chakirian made her his mistress, gave her money, jewels, treated her like a queen—then I was born. He changed after that, became indifferent, then brutal, until she fled to the protection of friends in Beirut. After a while he wanted her back but she refused. So he harassed her—rather his men did blackened her name as a whore who had dishonored him." Her lips curled. "She took her own life—my mother whose only wrong was to bear his child. Me. Do you wonder I've lived my life looking for revenge?"

"No."

Her lips trembled. "I've never told anyone before."

"Why does he employ you?"

She shrugged. "Perhaps it's his way of making up for the way he treated my mother. Well, it isn't, and I'm not a grateful employee, even though he pays me enormously well. He values my intelligence, my work, and we're civil to each other, nothing more." She grasped her purse from the table. "Mace, I want to leave now, go home."

He summoned the waiter, paid, and they went out to a taxi just emptied of riders. On the way to her apartment she was silent, tears in her eyes. Her hand gripped his arm tightly as though she needed something reassuring to cling to.

As he unlocked her door she murmured, "You can't know how I've longed to tell the truth—to someone who would understand, and care."

"I do," he told her gently, locked the door behind them, and followed her into the bedroom. They undressed in darkness, she pulled back the covers and lay quietly beside him, her flesh chill against his body's warmth. Mace stroked her hair, kissed her cheek, and found her hands tightly clenched. Gently he opened them and kissed her fingers. She began to cry, turned on her side and buried her face in his chest. When sobs diminished she wiped away tears and said, "Could I have a drink, Mace? I really need one."

At the cellarette he poured tumblers of raki and vodka and took them to the bed. She gulped quickly, exhaled, and said, "I'll be all right now. It's not often I'm emotional, and I could feel it coming on at our table. I didn't want to embarrass you."

"You managed very well." He swallowed half the vodka and held her hand.

Her face lifted and even in the darkness he could see traces of tears in her eyes. "There is one other thing, Mace, perhaps the most important—at least to me." She breathed deeply as though preparing herself for an ordeal. "When I was twelve Chakirian had me taken from my foster family to his estate on a Greek island. He had tutors for me, a speedboat, riding horses—everything a young girl could want, except friends her own age. And when I was fourteen he came into my room one night and raped me." Her body stiffened beside him. "Nothing gentle, Mace, he forced me, ignoring my shock and pain.

"He was an animal—no, worse than an animal. Even they have more regard for their mates." She paused and he could hear her deep breathing. "At that time my father was physically strong and highly sexed though to see him now it's hard to believe. I was his prisoner, physically, sexually his slave. On his travels he had other women, but on the island he had me. I was his resident cunt, trained to his desires, and I sometimes wondered if when he was fucking me he pretended he was fucking my mother. I don't know. But my hatred grew until when I was seventeen I told him I would find a way to kill him unless he left me alone."

"Did he?"

"He was frightened enough to release me, let me go to Beirut and the university. I lived with my foster family again, my mother's old friends. In that semi-Arab society there was very little dating as it's known in the West, so I had no boyfriends. I didn't miss them because I knew there would be a sexual overture at some point, and I shrank from the idea. After university I found work on Cyprus as a translator-interpreter, and my employer—a gentle middle-aged widower—became my lover. For me he opened a new vista of sexuality, and after he remarried I began normal encounters with men I carefully selected."

"As you selected me."

"You could say so—does it matter?"

"What's important is, we're together."

"And I love being with you, making love with you because it's more than just fucking, understand."

"I feel the same way," he acknowledged. "You never married?"

"I couldn't. Victor's shadow was always there, and I knew he would somehow manage to interfere, destroy the marriage. He regarded me as a defector, one who'd defied him and fled. To see me happy was unthinkable to him. At least that's what I believe."

"Horrible but logical." He shook his head in disgust. "I thought you and Victor might have a relationship, but I had no idea he was your father."

"Mace, I lied when I said he was here only once. The truth is he comes almost every month. He pleads with me to whip him and I do—cruelly. Sometimes he gets a limp erection, occasionally an orgasm, and I get an outlet for my hatred. But I never let him touch me." Her voice trailed away. "Finally, Mace, he pays for the encounter. A thousand francs. Does that make me a whore? I don't

203

think so. He didn't pay for raping me, for using me those years so I take the money by way of diminishing him, letting him understand that the great Victor Chakirian is so unattractive he has to pay for pleasure." As her face turned her expression beseeched his understanding. "Have I destroyed everything between us?"

"No. I admire you even more."

She moved close to him, extending her body the length of his. "It's not as if I was the instigator, I was the victim. Victor Chakirian's victim—as my mother was." Sudden sobs racked her throat. When the spasm passed she whispered, "Hold me, please hold me close. I want your arms around me." At first her body quivered then relaxed and he felt it absorbing his warmth. After a while she began moving sinuously against him, hips and loins undulating, exciting him.

He kissed her open mouth, drew her body over his, and silently they began making love. She gasped in climax but without words as she clung, shuddering, to him and covered his face with kisses. Then, with a sigh, her body went limp and he felt only the slowing rhythm of her heart.

Later—it seemed only minutes later—he woke and noticed the bedside clock showed after two. At first he heard only her shallow breathing, then came the sound that must have wakened him. Alert, he sat up, listening. There it was again—a metallic scratching on the hall's entrance door. He recognized the sounds for what they were— lock-picking tools raking the door lock.

Naked, he slid off the bed and pulled the Beretta from the holster on his trouser belt. Selina stirred, lay motionless again, and Mace drew on his shorts. Barefoot, he tiptoed over the thick carpeting and out of the bedroom, closing the door behind him. He lay down against a sofa, listening. The sounds persisted until he heard a bolt slide free.

He thumbed off the pistol's safety, heard the second lock attacked, and wondered if the intruders were burglars, or assassins on a deadly mission.

In ten minutes the lock failed to yield and Mace heard a nearly inaudible curse, then soft footsteps moving away.

When he thought the hall was empty he carried a chair to the door and angled it under the inside knob. Then he relocked the opened one and went back to the bedroom, leaving its door open as before. Selina still slept undisturbed, half turned on her back, one breast exposed by the sheet.

Fully awake, bloodstream churning with adrenaline, Mace sat on the edge of the bed and waited. Two twenty-eight by the clock. At two fifty-one he heard scraping sounds that seemed to come from outside the window. When they became louder he got up and opened the night table drawer to take out Selina's riding crop. Then he moved against the wall near the window. Briefly a light beam slashed the panes, and as he peered sideways he saw a dark figure rappelling downward on a taut line. Outside movement halted, and presently he heard the window creak as something pried it upward. When the window was half open two legs came across the sill followed by the upper body of a man whose feet now rested on the bedroom floor. The intruder was in black, and a black ski mask concealed his features as he flashed his flashlight around the room. Mace watched him release the spring shackle and draw a knife from its belt sheath. Knife in hand, the man took two steps toward the bed and Mace struck.

He slashed the crop across the man's throat, smashing the hyoid bone like eggshell. An agonized muffled screech tore from the ruined throat as the man fell forward, clawing at his neck. Mace stepped on the throat to speed suffocation as Selina woke with a startled cry. She sat up, sheet clutched to her neck, and began repeating, "Oh, God, oh, God, oh, God," her voice shrill with shock.

"It's over," he interrupted, "no danger now," and took his foot from the masked man's neck as the body stopped twitching. Mace set aside crop and pistol, and leaned through the window to look upward. No comrade there, just dangling line. Breeze stirred it against the building's wall. He left the window and took Selina in his arms until her convulsive breathing eased. "A burglar," he told her. "Tried the door but one of the locks held. So I waited." When she was still he went to the corpse and peeled back the mask, lighted features with the flash still attached by lanyard to the waist. "Never seen him," he said, "have you?"

"No," she said quickly, "never have," then she saw the fallen knife blade glint as Mace moved the light. He heard her sudden gasp. "A burglar?" she asked in a thin, rising pitch. "A burglar with a knife?" "Pistol, too." Mace shined the light on a black fabric holster that showed the weapon's knurled grip. "Get drinks," he told her. "Big glasses, while I figure things out."

Slowly, rigid as an automaton, she left the bed and walked stiffly away. In a few moments the clink of glasses sounded exaggeratedly loud in the stillness. He switched off the flashlight and wiped it clean of fingerprints. Then through the window he looked upward and grasped the nylon line. The upper end was firmly secured, no chance of shaking it loose, so he held the line a yard from the steel shackle, and twirled it like a vertical lasso before flinging it upward. The line flew over the cornice and disappeared. If the police found it, *tant pis*. The essential thing was to eliminate anything that might indicate Selina's window as the target.

Kneeling, he went through the dead man's pockets, found only a dozen francs—enough for Métro fare and a shot of grappa. No identity *carnet*, no name labels in clothing. Rubber-soled *tabi* on his feet. A pro. Before pulling off the mask Mace had half expected the face of *Barbe* or *Moustache* but this brigand was unknown. The police would identify his body soon enough. Cat burglar; death by misadventure.

Mace raised the window fully before shouldering the corpse. Peripherally he saw Selina in the doorway, a glass in each hand. Halting, she watched horror-struck as Mace lowered the corpse to the window ledge before shoving it outward into space. Quickly he drew down the window and tried locking it, but the little thumblock had been broken on entry. From five stories down the thudding impact reached the bedroom. Selina gasped and closed her eyes. Mace took his glass from her and said harshly, "Drink." He lifted his glass and nudged hers. "Drink, dammit, then drink again." Hesitantly she drank, then with closed eyes repeated it as Mace drained his glass. He drew her to bedside and made her down all the raki. Then he had her lie back, and drew up the covers to warm her against shock. He got in bed beside her, nerves still supercharged.

After a while she turned against him to whisper, "You killed for me, *mon amour*."

"For both of us."

"If only he had been Victor."

"I thought you wanted the secrets in his brain."

"Also his death. Who else would have sent that *burglar* but Victor Chakirian?"

"Why would he?" Mace objected. "What would his motive be?"

"Insane jealousy. If he's having me watched he must know we've become lovers—an insult he couldn't stand. He'd strike back at you." She clasped his hand, sighed deeply. "I'm drained, dreadfully tired." Her body turned away and presently her breathing shallowed in sleep.

Just after dawn harsh, grating police claxons roused them, the sounds lifting from the alley below. They held each other until finally the vehicles drove off, and they went back to sleep undisturbed.

Later, when he woke, she was gone. A note by the kitchen percolator read: *Do I have a partner or not?* Signed with a single *S*.

How, he asked himself, should he reply?

Book Three

nineteen

The Safe House

Three days later Chakirian returned from Geneva. That afternoon Selina phoned to tell Mace her employer/father was satisfied with Secours' Lanoix/Chesnikov report. "So send me the bill and make it a lot. I write the checks, after all."

"Is he going to do business with Yuri?"

"If so, he didn't tell me; some things he's closemouthed about."

"I can think of a few," Mace remarked. "Are you free tonight?"

"Afraid not. Hate to disappoint you, but the man wants an encounter—you know what I mean."

"Only too well." He thought of Chakirian submitting to a fearful, vengeful beating. What would hurt him even more would be the disappearance of his plundered funds. "Can we get together tomorrow?"

"I'm sure we can. I'll be there at six unless something comes up."

"There" was the small studio apartment Mace had rented in a *maison de rendezvous* on Courcelles conveniently near their apartments. Anticipating Chakirian's return, Mace found a safe house so he and Selina could meet clandestinely and discuss plans, away from any watchers. And make love.

The house business was providing secluded haven for persons desiring privacy in their affairs and did not require luxurious surroundings. Mace's studio was skimpily furnished; a few chairs, sofa, bed, telephone, and running water. For his purposes it was enough.

Although he had given tacit agreement to Selina's proposal he managed to avoid complete commitment. Stealing Chakirian's computer disks containing details of his secret accounts was comparatively simple. The difficult part was getting Chakirian to cough up passwords that would tap the disks' information. For that, he assumed, Selina had torture in mind, but Mace had reservations. The thing about torture was that you had to follow through. After interrogation Chakirian could not be permitted to live and Mace was not prepared to take part in murder. Even though he was reasonably sure Chakirian had ordered the masked intruder to kill them both. To be certain of Chakirian's complicity Mace would have to know his motive, and so far that was lacking.

He and Erica spoke daily but he thought it unwise to mention Carlos's innocence over the phone. She was enjoying her family visit, had ordered a new kitchen for her parents, bought them a Saab station wagon, and gone shopping in Copenhagen. Mace encouraged her to stay until Maître Schreiber offered news of encouraging developments. Much as he wanted to be with Erica, Mace understood that he and Selina were in the grip of strong sexual attraction, and Erica's return would limit their indulgence.

Next morning he had Yasmi bill Chakirian for eleven thousand francs: *Attention Mlle Mansour.*

"By courier?"

He nodded. "And send a case of Jim Beam to Ed Natsos's house, he'll appreciate it. Ah—no card. Don't want him fired for corrupt practices."

She shook her head. "What Puritans you *amis* are, so hypocritical."

"Makes us fascinating to foreign folk—and irresistible."

"Incomprehensible."

At mid-morning, Montaner problems weighing on his mind, Mace paid a visit to Jules Samuelson and asked if the count had agreed to Erica's counter-proposal. Jules shrugged. "Who knows? No response whatever. Perhaps he's giving it deep consideration."

"Or being recalcitrant to annoy Erica."

"Equally possible." He looked at his watch. "You could have asked by telephone."

"There's more and it's confidential."

The lawyer's eyebrows lifted. "So?"

"A source tells me Carlos was not the embezzler."

"A reliable source?"

"I think so."

He rubbed the curve of his chin. "Can the count's innocence be proved?"

"In time. The source also revealed that the guilty party wired fourteen million dollars to two of Carlos's bank accounts in Madrid."

"The amount is known. Who made the transfer?"

"I'm not able to say. When I can that should prove the count's innocence."

"Most interesting," Jules remarked. "Have you informed his Geneva lawyers?"

"Not yet. I wanted to tell Erica first."

"I see. Meanwhile, the scion of the Montaner line languishes in prison, innocent of wrongdoing."

"Happens. And let's not forget that Carlos could have avoided trouble if he'd questioned those unexpected deposits."

"He maintains he did not know of their existence."

"Not credible."

Jules shrugged. "Now that you know what you know, what position do you take?"

"It affronts me to see an innocent man behind bars."

"So you've become his advocate."

"I want his enemies brought to justice."

"Laudable," he nodded. "All of us in the profession want justice done, but the occasions are rare indeed."

"Someone has to break the stalemate, Jules. Maybe *Maître* Schreiber can accomplish it. If he can't . . ."

"You're well informed, you have a grip on things. Perhaps a solution will occur to you."

"Possibly." He got up. "We'll stay in touch."

At the office Yasmi waved a blue bank draft and said, "La Mansour paid by return courier. We should have more clients like Chakirian."

"And the booze for Natsos?"

"En route to his house in Neuilly. Anonymous gift. I'll deposit this draft at lunchtime."

213

"Go now if you want, take off."

After she left, Mace sat at his desk and considered a call to Erica, decided to place it later. He was living on different levels, he mused: one level involved Erica, Carlos, and his incarceration; another starred Selina, her mesmerizing sexuality, and craving for the millions stolen by her incestuous father. Finally there was the normal work of Secours to which he had been paying little attention since Erica came into his life. Events were leading him; at some point he'd lost both the sense and the reality of being in control, and it disturbed him.

He was waiting for Schreiber to suborn a Swiss judge. He was waiting for Erica's divorce, and waiting for Selina to advance a concrete plan for acquiring Chakirian's loot, and his feeling of impatience grew. He placed a call to Viborg, spoke with Erica's mother, who said Erica was spending the day with friends and was expected back for dinner. Could she take a message? Mace said no, thanks, and rang off. After feeding Su-Su he ate a cheese sandwich and drank a bottle of beer. Then he watched TV news and slept until late afternoon.

On his way to the new safe house he bought vodka, raki, and a bottle of Chardonnay. Inside the flat he sipped iced vodka and waited for Selina's arrival.

She came in a little after six, kissed him deeply, and kicked off her shoes. They made love on a noisy bed, and in the aftermath she said, "Last night I thought Victor might die, the way he was panting and gasping he could have been having a heart attack."

"Take it easy on him," he warned, "or you'll have a corpse on your hands and no information."

"I thought of that, but he demands more and more whipping. It's as though he's impervious to pain."

And so not a good subject for torture, Mace thought, but said, "Keep the smelling salts handy."

She moved against him. "I know where Victor hides the IFT disks." Her fingers trailed his thigh. "Can you open a safe?"

"If I can't I know people who can. In his office?"

"Set in the floor under his desk."

The safe combination might be vulnerable to a suction mike

hooked to an amplifier but if not the door would have to be drilled or blown. "Assuming we can go in at night I can try opening the safe without damaging it. We take out his disks and substitute others."

"Wonderful!" she exclaimed, "then all that remains is getting the passwords."

"All? You make it sound simple. Why would he tell us?"

Breath whispered in her nostrils. "You must know ways to make him."

He thrust out his bandaged wrists. "Like this, Selina?"

Her face turned away. "It wouldn't bother me to watch."

"And after that?"

She swallowed. "I haven't thought that far ahead."

"Well you better," he told her, "because he'd hunt us down wherever we were." He turned her face to his. "Think about it, Selina."

"Aren't there truth drugs?"

"They take time, specific dosage. They're dangerous."

"All right." Her body relaxed against him. "We'll think of something."

"Is there a night-alarm system?"

"Yes, but I know how to disconnect it."

"Special security in Victor's office? Motion or thermal sensors?"

"No."

"I've seen video scanners."

She nodded. "They can be shut off."

"How often does Victor go into that safe?"

"Very seldom, maybe twice a month."

"Takes out the disks?"

"I doubt it—why would he?"

Mace frowned. "I'd like an interval between the time we take his disks and he discovers the substitution. You'll be his prime suspect, maybe the only one."

From above came the sounds of bedlegs pounding into the floor, the squeaking of bedsprings, and they listened smiling. "Love in the afternoon," Mace remarked.

"*Cinq à sept,* the French tradition. *Chéri,* I do hope we're not so noisy."

The rhythmic pounding accelerated to a crescendo, then ended. "I hope they're satisfied. What were we talking about?"

"Chakirian holding me responsible. Killing me."

"Yeah. Don't want you rich and dead." He turned over and sat up. "Let's think it through. Danger comes only when Victor finds his disks missing. Can you duplicate them?"

"Why, yes . . . But—even with duplicates I'd need the passwords to run a printout."

"Ah, yes, the magic words. Well, let's make dupes as the first step, get the passwords later." He paused. "When can you get me in to try his safe?"

"Tomorrow night?"

"How long will duplicating take?"

"It depends on the number of disks. Perhaps hours."

"It's too risky to stay that long in the office."

"Yes, but you have computers in your office, modems. We could duplicate there. Afterward I'll replace the disks in his safe."

"All right. Tomorrow night."

The next day Mace went to an electronic specialty shop and bought miniature earphones, a sensitive cup microphone, an amplifier smaller than a Walkman, wire, and alligator clips. At a camera store he bought a Polaroid and film, a box of latex surgical gloves from a pharmacy.

Before Yasmi left for the day he had her link their computers, and waited for Selina's call.

twenty

The List

A t eleven that night Selina unlocked the building's garage entrance, locked it from inside, and guided Mace to the inner staircase. On the office floor she unlocked the hall door, went into her office, and turned on the light. Next, she unlocked the door to Chakirian's dark office, switched off the video scanners, and said, "The safe is under his desk, just pull the rug aside." Mace heard her close the door behind him as he walked to the desk. She would stay in her office apparently working, in case a building guard looked in.

On hands and knees under the desk, Mace drew aside the rug exposing the steel face of the sunken safe, turned on his mini-flash and gripped it between his teeth. The combination dial pointer was on eleven; he noted it on a pad and lay face down. From his pockets he took out the sound equipment and assembled it, licked the cup mike for vacuum sealing, and pressed it on the safe beside the dial. Then he drew on latex gloves and slowly began turning the dial to the right listening to the tumblers until through the earphones he heard a click on twenty-three. On his pad he noted R 23, and turned the dial slowly to the left. At forty-seven a second click. He noted it, and turned right again, hearing a click at thirty-three.

Sucking in a deep breath, Mace rolled on his back and took the flash from his mouth. His forehead was slick with perspiration, as were his hands inside the tight latex. Was it a three-way combination dial, or was there a fourth number?

Before touching the dial again he shined his light around the safe door looking for trap wires, saw nothing in the dark, narrow fissures.

Okay. He wiped his forehead on his coat sleeve, licked his lips and moved the dial left until he heard a click. Now he had the combination: 23-47-33-52. He zeroed the dial, grasped the recessed handle and lifted. The door came up.

Before touching contents Mace used the Polaroid to photograph the interior, and while the print was drying he shined his light inside.

He was reaching for the disk box when he heard voices in Selina's office, hers and a man's. Mace turned off his light, closed the safe door and drew the rug across it. He crawled behind a sofa and lay there, pulse racing, while the office door opened and overhead lights came on. Apparently the guard merely glanced around without entering, for after a few moments the lights went off and the door was closed and locked. Mace stayed where he was, perspiration dripping from his face, until he heard Selina's voice singing, "Don't Cry for Me, Argentina," the all clear signal. He mopped his face again and crawled back to the safe.

When he lifted out the disk box he exposed a piece of paper with four printed words: *Egmont, Vartan, Nicosia,* and . . . *Selina.* The box contained four disks so those could be the key words. Not trusting memory completely, Chakirian had left the passwords in a place as secure as the disks themselves. Mace left the list where it was and reclosed the safe. He straightened the rug, collected his equipment and turned on the video scanners before leaving the office.

He looked in through Selina's doorway and gave her the thumbs-up sign. Quickly she left her desk and joined him. "God, but I was nervous," she breathed, "especially when the guard came in without warning." Shakily she took his arm. "You got everything?"

"Everything. Let's go."

They got into his car, parked at the far end of the alley, and Mace pulled off his latex gloves before starting the engine. His hands were slick with perspiration as he steered into Rue du Balzac. Ten minutes more and they were in his office—ready to begin.

Mace gave Selina the disk box and duplication began.

To relieve tension he poured drinks, and after the first disk was copied he started the second. Selina asked what else was in the safe.

"Some bundles of currency—dollars and Swiss Francs—and a small-caliber pistol."

"And the combination?" He copied it from his notepad. "After you've replaced the disks, leave the dial set at eleven." He handed her the Polaroid print. "This is how Victor will expect to see the contents."

"*Chéri*, you think of everything. Now we have only to get the passwords."

"I'll keep the dupes in my safe until they're needed."

She glanced at the humming computers. "We have time, and I want you very much."

So they made love in his bedroom, and when they came down they copied the other two disks.

Mace reboxed Chakirian's disks and drove Selina back to the garage entrance. He saw her unlock it, enter, and close the door. Then he drove back to his garage and went up to his office. He set the duplicate disks in his safe and locked it, hoping Selina would not be seen so late in her office. He assumed she would notice the password list at the bottom of the safe. Failure to tell him would reveal the extent of her honesty and he would act accordingly.

The operation had gone off smoothly, and finding the passwords was unanticipated good luck. Assuming they were valid, Chakirian's plunder was accessible to him, but unless Victor confessed, Carlos de Montaner's problems lacked solution. And short of forcing Chakirian to sign a confession Mace could think of no way to extract one. So, he reasoned, it came down to getting Carlos out of prison while still presumed guilty. Maybe Schreiber could do it; the alternative was a breakout op dangerous to everyone involved. Only when Carlos was free could he be told Chakirian was the embezzler. Then let the count prove it if he craved vindication.

Egmont, Vartan, Nicosia, Selina—silently he repeated the key words. Sired by Vartan, Selina had been born in Nicosia. Like most amateurs at concealment Chakirian had selected familiar keys easy to recall. *Egmont* evoked a symphony, a musical opus of some kind, perhaps Chakirian's favorite . . . He yawned, drained by stress, and answered the ringing phone. Selina spoke one word: "*Accompli.*"

"*Merci.*" He broke the connection. The disks were back in the safe, all was well. The knowledge relaxed him as he sought sleep on the bed where only an hour ago he had made love with Selina.

From now on their safe house meetings would be infrequent, arrivals and departures more circumspect than ever to avoid detection. If Selina was right, Chakirian had dispatched the masked killer out of jealousy. What would he do if he found himself robbed of his stolen fortune? Unimaginable things.

In mid-morning Mace received a prospective client, a round-faced, middle-aged importer of Portuguese lace who wrung his hands and half-sobbed as he confessed to a brief, indiscreet affair with a much younger female he'd encountered at a hotel reception. "Now her husband or boyfriend—I don't know which—threatens to tell my wife," he choked.

"What proof does he have?"

"Pictures," he said distractedly, and pulled an envelope from his pocket. He covered his face with his hands and blubbered while Mace scanned four color prints. Each showed the man's face and naked body positioned for *minette* and *soixante-neuf*. Mace returned the photos to their envelope and laid it on the desk.

"How much does he want, this boyfriend?"

"Fifty thousand francs—New Francs," he said shakily.

"Can you pay it?"

"Yes, but I'm afraid that would be only the beginning."

"You're right about that. Blackmail doesn't end until the victim is bankrupt or dead." He looked out of the window at the familiar view of the Arc de Triomphe. "The female's face had been blacked out so they're probably in it together. She finds a victim and the man takes compromising pictures. It's a rotten racket." He turned back to Lucien Broussard. "What do you want me to do.?"

"Get back the pictures, the negatives." He pulled out a flimsy handkerchief and mopped his cheeks.

"Who suggested Secours to you?'

"Albert Boulet. Call him if you will." He leaned forward, eyes reddened from weeping. "Can you help me, M'*sieu* Mason?"

"Probably." Poor bastard, another victim of the age-old badger game. "Do you know the man's name?"

"Jacques Dehorne," he said.

"Probably not his true name. The woman?"

Broussard swallowed. "Madeleine—Madeleine Derec she said."
He cleared his throat. "Jacques is very big, he frightens me."

Mace nodded understandingly. "Have you a phone number? Some way to contact them?"

"He—Jacques, that is—told me to call Madeleine's number when I was ready to pay. He gave me until tomorrow. Then he—"

"Surprise him, call this afternoon, arrange a meeting."

The plump face relaxed. "And you'll—take care of things?"

Mace picked up Broussard's business card. "Get fifty thousand francs together and I'll have two men with you when you telephone Jacques. They'll be at the rendezvous when you arrive. All you have to do is give Jacques the envelope, and while Jacques is counting they'll move in."

Broussard's face brightened, seemed to glow with relief. He wiped perspiration from his upper lip and said, "Suppose Jacques actually gives me the negatives?"

"They'll make him regret his crimes. But I'm positive you won't get the negatives in exchange. My men will do that."

His face sobered. "And—Madeleine?"

"She won't be around, that would show complicity. Anyway, she'll keep playing the game, no way to stop her."

Broussard shifted uneasily in his chair. Almost pleadingly he asked, "Are you *sure* Madeleine is in the plot?"

"I'm sure," Mace said curtly. "Secours' fee will be ten thousand francs, half now, half when you have the negatives. Agreeable?"

"Yes," he replied. "Seems high but I'd pay almost anything to escape this dreadful fear." He got out his checkbook. "Secours S.A.?"

Mace nodded and watched his new client make out the draft in purple ink. He laid it on the desk and reached for the photo envelope but Mace drew it away. "Pending full payment," he said, and placed it in his desk drawer. "It's eleven now, my men will be with you in two hours, if that's convenient."

Broussard got up. "Very. My employees will be off at lunch." He gave Mace a warm, moist hand. "Thank you, *M'sieu*." He swallowed. "Shall I tell Boulet?"

"Not unless he asks."

Yasmi left her desk and opened the door for Broussard. After the door closed Mace said, "I have a job for Raoul and Jean-Paul," and told her what it was. She took Broussard's card and asked, "What's their pay?"

"Thousand each." He gave her the bank draft to deposit. "I want them here in an hour. If by any chance I'm away I want you to brief them. Have them at Broussard's office by one."

A few minutes later Yasmi answered the phone and buzzed Mace. *"La Comtesse, M'sieu,"* she said, and then he heard Erica's excited voice: "Dearest, did you hear from Jules or Bernard?"

"No."

"Jules just phoned. Carlos sent him the papers—all signed. Mace, I can get divorced in Switzerland! Do you think I should go there now? Have Schreiber's office begin proceedings?"

"Come here first, I have things to tell you."

"Not even a hint?" she coaxed.

"Too private for the telephone."

"I see." Her voice suggested some of her enthusiasm had drained away. "Since you tell me to I'll fly in today, be there by evening— we'll dine together."

"Can't wait to see you. Call when you get in."

He phoned Jules Samuelson for confirmation and the lawyer agreed that a Swiss divorce would take less time than a French one. "Though neither venue," he said judiciously, "is comparable to the speed and convenience of your state of Nevada."

"They're Europeans," Mace said, "so the divorce should be European."

"I agree. She wants to go to Geneva today."

"She's coming here."

"Oh? May I ask why?"

"Because I suggested it. I want to tell her what I told you last time we met."

"Then I'll give her the executed documents."

"Good. She'll need them in Geneva."

Still, he mused as he replaced the receiver, Carlos could always renege at the last minute so nothing was certain. His thoughts turned from the Montaners to Selina. All morning he had been hoping she would call, tell him she'd found the passwords, but so far no call. To

Mace it seemed unlikely she hadn't seen the password paper in Victor's safe, though that was possible. Clever as she was, Mace thought, she could be weighing chances he hadn't noticed the password list. Now that she had access to Chakirian's safe she could drain his secret accounts at a time of her choosing, unaided. No partner required.

How much would he care? he asked himself. The eight hundred million always seemed intangible, illusive as a rainbow's pot of gold. He had no need of half, even a tenth share. A hundred thousand would more than compensate him for his night's work. Let Selina take the rest as reparation for childhood suffering at her father's hands: rape, degradation, isolation. Death of her mother. A frightful legacy to endure.

Raoul and Jean-Paul arrived within minutes of each other and listened quietly to Mace's briefing. Then Raoul asked how badly the blackmailer should be beaten. "Up to you," Mace replied, and Raoul drew from his pocket a spring-steel sap lead-weighted at one end. "This should do it."

"No shooting," Mace warned. "Show a piece to impress Jacques but don't pull the trigger. What's important is getting the photo negatives." He opened Broussard's envelope and handed them the color prints. Both men smiled and Raoul said admiringly, "The *poule* has a good figure." He returned the prints. "Will she be there for the payoff?"

"She's too smart to show herself to Broussard, too experienced." Jean-Paul looked at his watch. "Anything else, boss?"

Mace shook his head. "Any questions?"

"We'll handle it," Raoul said as they got up. "The Secours way—no loose ends."

On their way out Yasmi kissed her lover and watched him leave. Turning to Mace she said, "I'll worry about him, you know."

"A bread-and-butter job," Mace replied. "No danger at all."

But next day Mace learned that Broussard's appraisal of Jacques as large and scary had been accurate. When Jean-Paul lunged at him Jacques disabled the apprentice with a kick in the balls. He pulled a gun on Raoul, who broke his wrist with the sap before pounding the lead-weighted steel on the big blackmailer's skull while client Broussard clutched his payoff envelope and watched in horror. In the end, a groaning, subdued Jacques handed over negatives with a dozen prints and Raoul sapped his kneecap as a parting reminder.

As the day wore on Mace grew less optimistic about contact from Selina. No phone call, no message by courier, nothing. *Rien du tout.* Gloomily he felt she had unwittingly revealed intent to defraud him. She wanted the whole enchilada, nothing less.

So he was glad to hear Erica's voice when she called from the airport. She needed time to freshen up while her cook prepared their dinner. Could he come at seven? He could.

He arrived at her new apartment with iced champagne. They embraced lengthily before Erica drew him inside. "Now, what was so private you couldn't tell me by phone?"

"First we drink to your return." He popped the cork and filled glasses in the kitchen, where a roast was warming in the oven. After sipping, he kissed her, and said, "Fellow's on the dock waiting for ship passengers to disembark. His girlfriend's at the rail calling, 'E.F., E.F.' He yells back, 'F.F., F.F.,' and a man standing beside him asks, 'What's E.F. and F.F. anyway?' "

"Eat first or fuck first, mind your own business."

Erica laughed. "Mace, how coarse," but her eyes twinkled. "Me, I'd rather eat first."

"Your house, your choice."

"Now I'm dying to hear your news."

When they were seated on a sofa he said, "Good news and bad. The good news is I've acquired information from a source that convinces me Carlos didn't steal IFT funds, he was framed."

"Why, Mace, that's wonderful—you're absolutely convinced?"

"I am."

"I didn't think my husband would do it, that he was even capable of doing it, and I was right." She nibbled his ear. "The source—will he clear Carlos? Who is he?"

"That's the bad news, honey, I can't tell you."

"Can't—?" She drew back. "Why not?"

"I promised confidentiality until certain things take place. When the real embezzler can be exposed."

"The real—? Tell me his name," she demanded.

He shook his head. "Sorry, Erica, you have to trust me on that one, too. For your protection, and mine. If he learns that others have uncovered his secret he'll kill to save himself. But I'll tell you this: The IFT directors have never disclosed the actual amount of money that disappeared because it was many times the figure they made public. And my source told me that fourteen million were deposited in Carlos's bank accounts by the embezzler. You never told me."

Somewhat stiffly she said, "I must have supposed you knew. Why should I withhold it?"

"I don't know."

"What isn't fair is withholding names from me, important names, Mace."

"I've told you I'll reveal them when I feel it's safe. While you get your divorce we'll keep working for your husband's freedom."

She turned to him. "You really want him freed."

"He's innocent. Only don't tell Carlos what I've just told you; it would make his life intolerable."

"Wouldn't think of it. But I want to know why you're suddenly hostile to me?"

He shrugged. "I think I expected a more positive reaction to what I felt was extraordinary news. Instead you fire questions at me after I've told you all I can—and I don't like it."

"And I don't like being treated as a child."

Mace set aside his glass and got up. "Listen to me: I didn't press my services on you, you came to me, remember? Begged for my help. Maybe I shouldn't have gotten into Montaner problems, but I did. So far, helping you has cost a good friend his life. If I don't remind you of that constantly, it's because we can't remedy what's past. And on top of that—if you'll pardon me—I've taken not a franc from you, it's been freebie time in Paris."

"What do you want? I'll pay you now."

"I don't want your damn money, I thought we were beyond that."

"Because we sleep together?" she challenged.

"Whatever. Anyway, I'm out of the Montaner mess." He strode to the door and wrenched it open before she caught up with him. "Mace, darling, I can't believe we're quarreling—don't go. I'm sorry,

I should have appreciated you more . . ." A hand pressed her fore-head distractedly. "This separation . . . I stayed away too long, I know that now. Don't go, please, we'll put this behind us, get back to where we were . . ." She tugged his shoulders until he turned and they were face-to-face and her voice lowered. "I won't ask more questions, I promise. There are things I don't need to know, should-n't know." Her voice trailed away as her body moved into his. "Don't leave me. I love you, I need you. I don't want to quarrel any-more."

He looked into the cool depths of her eyes, felt her loins press his, move excitingly. "Neither do I," he said and took her in his arms. Openmouthed, she kissed him, seeking with her tongue. "F.F." she whispered, "If you want to."

"I do."

And they did—while the forgotten roast shriveled in the oven.

In the morning he watched from the bed as she dried shower droplets from her white, perfect body; watched her dress, and while she packed for Geneva he took a shower and shaved. As he pulled on clothing she brought him a cup of black coffee. "I'll see Jules before going to the airport—my flight is just before noon."

He tied shoelaces. "Where will you stay? Not La Résidence."

"Hotel du Rhône. I'll see *Maître* Schreiber this afternoon, ask him to begin divorce proceedings."

"Find out if he's been able to accomplish anything positive. Like locating a sympathetic, avaricious judge."

"Of course. Shall I try to visit Carlos?"

"Only to take him cigarettes."

"I'll ask Schreiber's advice."

After a parting embrace, she said, "Last night was especially won-derful. Perhaps we should quarrel more often, reconciliation is so exciting."

"Quarrels no, scarves yes." He kissed her again and left for his office.

There he fed his Siamese, made coffee, and sipped it at his desk until he felt an impulse to touch base with Pascal Covici.

When The Brotherhood's front man answered Mace's call he said,

"Only yesterday I was thinking we ought to get together soon. How are you feeling?"

"Up to speed again." He glanced at the still-red abrasions circling his wrists. "Are you free now?"

"I'll make time. Your place or mine?"

twenty-one

The Trap

Covici's Avenue Hoche apartment was decorated and furnished in middle-class Italian style. Thick rugs in dark designs covered most of the travertine flooring. Furniture heavy dark oak with anti-macassars; yellow walls, niches for painted statues of the Virgin, Jesus, and several presumed saints. A large ornate wood crucifix hung from the wall behind Covici's varnished oak desk.

A manservant had admitted Mace and now Covici came toward him, hand extended. "I thought we could talk here away from undesirable observers. You don't want to be noticed with a notorious figure, and I prefer not being seen with a well-known American investigator." He smiled. "Coffee?"

Mace nodded, and sat across the low coffee table from his host, who said, "Tomorrow I'm leaving for a few days in Florence and Palermo, perhaps Sardinia depending on business. What can I do for you?"

The manservant brought demitasses on a small silver tray, added sugar to Mace's coffee, and withdrew. "Appreciate the offer," Mace replied, "but I have information that might interest you. You alone."

Covici nodded. "It will go no farther than this room."

Mace sipped and lowered his cup. "What were your IFT losses? Less than five million? More?"

Covici considered before replying. "In confidence, it was slightly under five."

"You were at the Geneva directors' meeting?"

"For a day, I had pressing business elsewhere."

"I suppose nothing significant was discussed?"

"Not in my hearing. The Trust is dissolved except for continuing legal actions. We meet periodically as required by law." He leaned back and folded his arms. "Your information?"

"In the course of—well, I'd rather not say—anyway, I received information from a source of great reliability concerning funds embezzled from the Trust."

Covici's thin black eyebrows lifted. "Go on."

"My source—which I can't identify to you—told me that IFT's overall loss was around eight hundred million dollars, a figure never publicly revealed. Is that true?"

"Your source has excellent information."

"That helps confirm my source's credibility." He sipped from his demitasse and went on. "The source described a plot in which one individual cleverly embezzled the funds and framed Count Carlos de Montaner—by transferring fourteen million to his Madrid accounts. Without the count's knowledge."

"So Carlos claimed when he was charged. The assumption was he made the transfer himself."

"And appeared guilty because he retained the fourteen million."

"Exactly. Now, who did the embezzling and where is the money?"

"I'm not prepared to identify the embezzler until the crime can be proved. As to the funds, they were secreted in accounts around the world. However, I have the possibility of access to them."

"By forcing the embezzler?"

"By working quietly, out thinking him."

"If successful, you would return the eight-hundred million to IFT?"

"I haven't decided that point. But if I were able to refund your five million, wouldn't that satisfy your interest?"

"Except for envy," Covici smiled. "And when, my friend, is all this to take place?"

"Soon, I hope, but I can't predict. Then, at some point Montaner has to be absolved of guilt. Accomplishing that may prove more difficult than recovering the stolen funds."

"You care for his wife that deeply?"

"An innocent man is in prison—it offends my sense of justice."

"Mine as well," Covici replied, "So, if I can assist your effort you have only to let me know." He got up. "I have a place on the Costa Smeralda at Punta di Volpe—you know Sardinia?"

Mace shook his head.

"A strange island, Sardinia, which happens to be my place of birth. It is a land where the word for *shepherd* is also the word for *bandit*. In any case, I invite you to use my place whenever convenient. Bring one or more companions. There are servants, or if you prefer privacy, none. And my plane will take you there."

"Tempting," Mace said, "and I'm grateful for the invitation." He stood up and stretched.

"I mean it sincerely. And I will hope for further word from you."

"When things come together," Mace promised, and left the apartment.

As he walked to the corner taxi rank, Mace reflected that he had given Covici hope that The Brotherhood's funds might be replaced—a favor in partial repayment for Covici's rescue though neither had mentioned the incident. Beyond that they had been able to converse in relaxed surroundings and assess each other somewhat more thoroughly than before. The invitation to enjoy Covici's Punta di Volpe place—probably a modern palazzo—showed that Covici respected him, and the way was open to further dealings if either party desired.

In the taxi Mace pondered enlisting Covici's aid in clearing Carlos de Montaner through Chakirian, then disposing of Victor. The rationale being that Chakirian had defrauded The Brotherhood and must pay the traditional price.

Let Covici do the wet work, he decided. It was the only way he could think of to keep his and Selina's hands free of blood.

In his office Yasmi announced, "Two deliveries by messenger: Broussard's draft for five thousand, and this envelope marked *Particulier*, which I didn't open." He took it from her and handed her the envelope of Broussard's sample prints. "For the shredder," he said, and opened the private envelope at his desk.

Handwritten, the small folded sheet read: *Must see you. At six if possible.* The signature was her characteristic *S*.

He shredded the message, feeling better about Selina. He had not decided how to deal with her presumed duplicity, so if she were to tell him of the password list they could continue as before—trustingly.

Covici was a new element in their conspiracy but Mace felt it was premature to tell Selina in what ways The Brotherhood's man could be useful. Time enough after Chakirian's secret accounts were emptied and the funds transferred to their own.

For lunch Rosario prepared a steak sandwich and an endive salad, which Mace enjoyed with a glass of Beaujolais. He was considering siesta when the office doorbell rang. Yasmi was off consoling Jean-Paul so Mace opened the door and saw Erica's gray-uniformed chauffeur. After touching his cap visor the chauffeur said, "M'sieu Mason, I have this from Madame *La Comtesse*," and handed him an envelope. Mace thanked him and closed the door.

Inside the envelope was a message from Erica. *A down payment for everything you've done. Love.* And her signature. Included was a draft on the Banque Transatlantique for twenty-thousand dollars. For a few moments he stared at it, embarrassed that he had mentioned payment last night, and thinking he would have billed less. Still, he mused, it's nice to have services appreciated, and rewarded, and decided to have it cashed by Herr Schotfman at the Banque Suisse-Allemagne where he had an account. Mace took half the proceeds in green dollars, the other half in Swiss francs, and when he returned he indulged in a siesta and slept undisturbed until five.

Although Selina had her own key to the safe house door he left it unlocked for her. When she arrived, cheeks flushed and out of breath, he kissed her and gave her a glass of raki. She swallowed, fanned her face and stepped out of her shoes. "So warm on the street—and I ran for a bus."

"You took a bus?" He couldn't imagine it.

"To avoid anyone following. Help me with this blouse—I'm so hot."

He unbuttoned the back and she pulled it off, unhooked her brassiere, and shed her skirt exposing a snug black lace bikini bottom. She sank onto the sofa, drank, and looked up. "I'm so glad you

231

came, dear. I was afraid you might have other plans."

He sat down beside her, the old sofa creaking under his weight. "Like what?"

"A business appointment—or some other woman," she teased.

"Not likely."

"There's your countess, for one."

"She's not even in France. Now, why are we here?"

Her face sobered. "Frederic Lanoix came in this morning."

"Yuri Chesnikov."

"Yes. He and Victor talked for more than an hour. I managed to hear some of it."

"Go on." He stroked her thigh, moist like her face with perspiration.

"They talked about an island, an island that is also a country—no, I didn't hear the name," she added, anticipating his question. Other snatches had to do with getting control of the island—the country."

"Why?"

"I heard the word *dépôt* or *dépôts* I'm not sure which." She frowned. "Mean anything to you?"

"It could." His mind flashed back to what Natsos had told him. "Chesnikov wants Victor to put up capital to gain control of the country."

"I heard no mention of money, but why else would Chesnikov come to Victor? What would they do with the country?"

"Turn it into a huge storehouse for arms, ordnance of all kinds. Bring in weapons from Russia, Ukraine, Czechoslovakia, and sell them to outlaw countries in the Middle East, Africa, Central America. Profits could be immense. For Victor a risk worth taking. Chesnikov has the supplier contacts already. With Victor's capital he could control the country."

"And that capital would come from his secret accounts."

Mace nodded.

"So we have to take it first."

"We need the passwords."

Selina emptied her glass, set it aside. "When I replaced the disks in Victor's safe I was too nervous to see what else was there and the light was poor. Last night I thought it over and decided that since I knew the combination I could open the safe and satisfy my curiosity. I thought there might be something concerning my mother—a marriage license, for instance, or a photograph of her, old letters . . ." She took in a deep breath and her breasts lifted tantalizingly. "So this morning I went in early knowing Victor was at his house in Passy, and opened the safe. This time I was less nervous, the light was good, and under the disk box—Mace, I found the passwords!"

"No! Incredible! But why would he leave them there?"

"Just what I asked myself, because it seemed too good to be true. Then I remembered his memory slips, which he has to be aware of, and decided he didn't dare trust his memory." She shrugged. "Besides, his health is declining and I think he's had a minor stroke or two. He's not a young man, Mace, and nearly impotent." She paused before saying, "Of course he could have left the passwords some other place, but I think he believed the disks were securely hidden, so why not place the passwords with them?"

"Makes sense. What are they?" The final test.

"Four. *Egmont, Vartan, Nicosia,* and *Selina.* Dear, we have them now, can use them anytime."

"I feel like a fool not noticing the words. But you found them. How clever of you."

"But I was looking for something else, so I wasn't all that clever."

"Think how much trouble that saves us."

"Yes, it's almost as though he gave us a blank check. But if he finances Chesnikov—and I think he will—there'll be that much less for us."

"So we have to get there first. Only we're not ready, our accounts aren't established, and that will take time. Travel, too. My God, eight hundred million . . . We can't possibly set up eight hundred accounts for a million each—or even four hundred at two million. It's not possible." He wondered how much Schoffman's bank would be willing to absorb. "There isn't time."

"We start in Paris," she suggested, "using foreign banks established here. But I shouldn't be away from the office more than a day at a time or Victor will wonder why. But you can cover Europe in a week: Zurich, Bern, Geneva; Rome and Florence; Madrid. Then Panama, the Bahamas, Cayman Islands, Mexico City." She paused to think. "Buenos Aires, Caracas, Montevideo, Santiago," she added. "If I go to every international bank in Paris will you do the rest?"

"There's no alternative." He kissed her cheek. "And Victor will still suspect you."

"That's a chance I have to take." Her thighs parted, invited his hand between them. "We can do it, Mace, all of it. You know we can." She pressed his face to her moist breasts and presently they were grappling on the bed, slick bodies intertwined like Greek wrestlers until Mace feigned weakness and let her mount him in the dominant position she loved so well.

Afterward, they lay side by side and heard telltale sounds from the ceiling and floor above. Smiling, Selina remarked, "They should live together, have a nice quiet bed of their own."

"Still, furtive sex is exciting, don't you think?"

"I do." She glanced up as the floor-pounding accelerated to a crescendo, then stopped.

"Which reminds me," he said, "There's a way of neutralizing Chakirian I should have thought of before."

She rose on one elbow and trailed a finger through the perspiration on his chest. "What is it?"

He told her about Lucien Broussard and the blackmail attempt, then asked, "Where do your encounters with Victor take place? Bedroom?"

"Living room, too, depending on his mood. You mean—?"

He nodded. "Two videocams can cover all the action, one in each room. A tape could save your life."

"I like the idea," she said musingly, "but my face would show." She shook her head. "I wouldn't want that."

"Wear a mask, the fantasy kind you buy at costume stores. That black chemise, your boots. Make it bizarre, erotic, outrageous. Victor will love it."

"But the cameras? . . ."

"I can have them installed tomorrow, concealed, he'll never know."

"But Victor may not come for weeks," she objected.

"So play your role. Call him tomorrow, tell him he needs more punishment, more discipline, be the stern dominatrix he craves. That you demand the encounter should excite him, the sick bastard will be slavering by nightfall. And while the cameras run, beat the shit out of him."

"All right, I'll call him from outside at noon, tell him his mistress expects him—" she paused "and other things."

"Good, I'll draw a floor plan for the technician, and he'll leave you a note telling you how to start the cameras. After Victor leaves, play the tape to make sure it shows what we want."

"You'll see it with me?"

"No, I wouldn't like that. Next day leave the tape here and I'll make copies, keep them in my safe until needed."

"Yes," she said thoughtfully, "I can do it—only what if he's suspicious?"

"Why should he be? The two of you have been encountering for months. Why should tomorrow night be any different?"

"Just one thing—suppose he sees a camera?"

"He won't, but in the unlikely event he does, tell him it's for security, you've heard burglars trying to get in and you've been frightened. If one comes while you're away the tape will help police arrest him."

"Oh, Mace, you have an answer for everything—and a good one. I'll be really excited knowing he's being filmed doing things no man would want revealed."

"The threat, should we need one, is giving the tape to a porno house for showing on the Paris circuit."

She laughed. "Imagine watching a blue movie and seeing someone you recognize. For Victor even the thought of exposure would be intolerable. Yes, I think it's worth trying."

"Happens I have a friend, a film distributor, who could pass the tape around for maximum exposure." Albert Boulet would love it, he thought. "We might even be paid."

"Please, no. Then tomorrow I'll get the mask, and perhaps a few other items, call Victor."

"And the tech will do his dirty work."

"In a good cause. My protection." She stretched out atop him, kissed, and licked his face, moved downward to his groin and soon they were making love again. While the upstairs lovers began a noisy coupling that made the ceiling reverberate like a jungle drum.

In the morning Mace called the Bellman shop and asked for the young technician who had serviced his office before. The tech came at ten and listened to Mace explain what was needed.

"I've done it before," he said, "divorce cases for lawyers. How long will you need the installation?"

"Probably only tonight." He diagrammed the apartment and said, "One camera here, the other there. You know best where to hide them."

The tech nodded. "Above eye level but not too high since you want faces recorded. I'll use nonreflective lenses to reduce the chance of discovery." He paused. "Lately I've been using voice-activation. Saves tape and the camera doesn't have to be switched on and off. Lawyers prefer it when neither party knows they're being surveilled."

"Do it. And leave a note in the apartment before you go." He handed over keys to both door locks. "How long will it take?"

"Around two hours."

"Just be out by five."

He looked at his watch. "I'll be gone by two."

Later, Mace went to the Banque Suisse-Allemagne and met with Herr Schoffman.

"It's possible," Mace said, "I may have to relocate large sums of money for a client, millions of dollars transferred to numbered accounts."

The banker tented his fingers. "How many millions?"

"Five or six hundred, perhaps more. How much could your bank handle?"

"How long would the funds be with the bank?"

"Hard to say. Weeks at least, perhaps months."

Schoffman smiled. "Without inquiring, I suspect your client is Arab. Before and after the Gulf War we received similar deposits from oil-rich Arabs, some members of royal families. Your deposits—would they be in the form of cash?"

Mace shook his head. "Electronic transfer from other accounts."

"Approximately how many accounts?"

"I don't know. My client represents a group with worldwide interests. What are the formalities, the procedure?"

"Quite simple, really." He gave Mace a brochure from his desk drawer. "This explains it in six languages, including Arabic. A client receives a secret number from the bank, and our bank's electronic code. His computer can then effect transfer from a previous account to our numbered account. And the client can work from any part of the world that has a long-distance telephone system."

"I see. And your accounts remain secret, invulnerable."

"Except in cases of fraud as established by competent legal authorities. Or if drug money is involved. Even that has to be shown prior to disclosure. Aside from those exceptions—" he spread his hands— "we guarantee total secrecy."

"So you could accommodate—how much?"

"Up to a billion dollars."

Mace whistled. "My client will be glad to hear that."

"One question. When can the bank anticipate the transfers?"

"I'd say within a month." He got up and shook the banker's hand. "You've been most helpful, thank you." He took the brochure with him as he left.

A little after noon Selina phoned. "I made the call and he's thrilled."

"Everything will be in place by two. After that it's show time for you."

"Actually I'm looking forward to it."

"Top all previous encounters, hold nothing back, be merciless. Your life may depend on it."

"I won't fail."

twenty-two

The Theft

Selina's call woke him early next morning. "Everything happened as planned. We were in both rooms so I have two cassettes to leave you."

"You reviewed them?"

"Yes, and it was unpleasant. But the mask helped me pretend I was seeing two perverted people, not me. God—I was afraid he'd have a heart attack, but he only fainted." He could hear her heavy breathing. "Afterward he was humbly grateful, paid me double to show it." She paused before continuing. "I don't want you to see those tapes, Mace. And if he ever sees one—well, he'd rather die than have anyone else watch his degradation."

He thought that would be all but she went on: "He licked my boots, my—backside . . . the old man was ecstatic. Mace, I won't go through that again. Ever."

"Won't have to. The tapes are all we need. Yesterday I saw one bank, today I'll try Zurich, and if there's time, Bern. Tomorrow, Rome, maybe Florence, and so on. I want to get back in less than a week."

"Meanwhile, I'll work Paris."

"You know how it's done?"

"I've done it for some of his clients. Mace, I'll miss you."

"And I'll miss you. Payday when I get back."

Though it was early, Mace made breakfast, dressed, and sent a fax message to Erica in Geneva. It told her he would be traveling for a week and out of touch; he'd call when she returned.

Meanwhile, he thought, *Maître* Schreiber might come up with positive results. And if Carlos were freed they would go to the lakeside villa and follow the departure plan from there.

He called Swissair for reservations, then telephoned Bellman. The technician answered and Mace told him his equipment could be recovered anytime. "After that, put keys in an envelope and leave them at my office."

"The results were satisfactory?"

"Excellent. Service appreciated."

He packed then and put Erica's payment in a fabric money belt worn under his clothing. Before leaving, he wrote a note to Yasmi saying he'd be away for a week; she could close the office or come in to check mail and messages. Have Rosario take care of Su-Su while he was gone.

His flight reached Zurich at one o'clock. Mace opened accounts at three banks with deposits of five hundred dollars each before banking hours were over, carefully recording account numbers and bank codes. From Zurich he rode an electric train to Bern and stayed at the station hotel overnight. In the morning he established accounts at two banks and flew to Rome where he made arrangements at another three. He took the overnight Rapide to Florence and opened an account at a single bank in the morning. Then on to Berlin and Stockholm. He avoided Madrid where Carlos's accounts had been bared with scant formality. Lisbon was his final stop—two accounts there—before flying back to Paris at night.

Tired from travel, his biosystem disarranged, Mace slept twelve hours before rising and returning to business. Overall, he had established thirteen accounts, investing nearly seven thousand dollars in the trip, money he expected to be returned a thousandfold.

Those thirteen accounts plus whatever Selina had been able to establish would absorb a good percentage of Chakirian's loot. Schoffman's bank would handle the balance.

Now they were ready to rob Chakirian.

His desk was cluttered with messages. Among them a fax from Erica telling him that Schreiber's firm had filed a divorce petition, and

Maître Schreiber anticipated success in the other matter within a few days. Encouraging news, he thought, and sent a return fax acknowledging hers and saying he hoped all would go well.

He phoned Selina before she left her apartment suggesting they meet at noon—implying lunch if anyone was listening. She replied, "Yes, I understand," and nothing more.

While traveling, Mace had decided to set up their computer operation in the safe house for security and to avoid interruption. For that he bought a Bull computer/word processor, printout paper, and accessories, and took it by taxi to the safe house. After unpacking and making the necessary connections he stopped at the Banque Suisse-Allemagne and opened a numbered account with Herr Schoffman. In his office he added the account number to his growing list, and removed the duplicate disks from his safe, taking them to the safe house at noon.

Selina came in shortly afterward, hugged and kissed him and said, "I haven't much time, dear, so let me show you what I accomplished." Her dress was light blue silk with pleated skirt.

From her purse she drew a list of eight banks that were Paris branches of foreign institutions, their bank codes and her account numbers. "Aren't you pleased with me?"

"Thrilled. That makes twenty-two accounts and I'm pretty sure they'll be enough." He gestured at the new computer. "I can begin this afternoon, or wait until you return."

"No reason to wait, dear, I'll come as soon as I can. By the way, Lanoix has been attentive to me. We lunched once, then dinner and ballet. He wants to go to bed with me but I refused. He'll probably try again."

As she bent over to examine the computer Mace asked, "Does Victor know he's interested?"

"He encouraged me to see Frederic or I wouldn't have."

From behind his hands molded her breasts. Selina murmured and sighed, finally saying, "It has to be fast, dear." She pulled up her skirt and they made love on the sofa. Afterward she kissed him, rearranged her dress, and hurried out. Mace rested before activating the computer and inserting the first disk. After trying others Nicosia

240

turned out to be the access password and he watched the monitor as the printer began responding.

After the first disk emptied, printout paper piled on the floor, Mace turned off the computer and went out to a nearby rotisserie for chicken and a mug of beer. While eating he thought about Chesnikov and Selina and wondered why the former GRU officer had focused on her. Was he thinking of recruiting her to spy on Chakirian, or was his approach stimulated by her attractiveness? Without question, an aura of sexuality surrounded Selina, but even in Paris it was considered bad form to seduce a partner's secretary. Chesnikov, though, would be as indifferent to societal norms as he had been in Afghanistan to taking human life. Even so, Mace mused, he would be alert to further moves by the Russian on Selina, and suggest she avoid him.

After lunch Mace returned to the safe house and inserted a disk that accessed to Vartian, and scanned the lengthy printout from the first. It detailed dozens of numbered bank accounts around the world with their access codes, and he thought glumly that it would take days to drain them all. He needed an account number from Covici in order to replace The Brotherhood's losses, so he phoned Covici's office and told the Sard what he wanted.

"That is welcome news," Covici responded, and in a few moments supplied the number. "It relates to my bank," he added, "so I will know when the transfer is made. My gratitude will endure."

At four o'clock Mace accessed disk number three—to Egmont—and went out to buy another carton of continuous paper sheets. By the time Selina arrived after six the job was completed. It elated her to see the stack of printouts, she hugged him and said, "I can't believe it's all in our hands—but it is. Oh, chéri, when shall we begin?"

"Tomorrow, when banks open. Now I need a drink. You?"

"Please."

While he poured raki and iced his vodka he noticed her go into the bedroom, and when he carried drinks there she was naked in the shower. He joined her with their glasses; alternately they drank and soaped each other's bodies until their glasses were empty. Then they relaxed on the bed, lying spoon fashion while he entered her *par der-rière.*

After Selina left for her own apartment Mace boxed the duplicate disks and returned to his. He put them in his safe, and while drinking a nightcap thought about Yuri Chesnikov aka Frederic Lanoix. He viewed Chesnikov's move on Selina as a probable attempt to penetrate Chakirian's inner core for business reasons; seducing Selina combined pleasure with business. The Russian had to be as smart as he was dangerous, and Mace wanted to neutralize him at minimum, eliminate him as a player if possible. Reviewing Chesnikov's vulnerabilities, Mace fell asleep.

In the morning, while making breakfast for himself, Mace realized that overnight his subconscious had assembled elements of a possible plan. So when Yasmi arrived he told her he wanted Raoul and Jean-Paul to commence surveilling Lanoix.

"May I ask why?"

"I've learned that he and Chakirian are going into a major arms deal that could stir up big trouble in a lot of places. Without Chakirian's financing Lanoix can't bring it off. Without Lanoix's contacts and know-how Chakirian is out. So get the *copains* here and I'll brief them."

He was eager to tap into Chakirian's accounts but felt pressed to attend to Chesnikov. By telephone Yasmi confirmed that the Russian was in Paris, not Monte Carlo, and when the men arrived she gave them his office and apartment addresses.

"Start surveilling today," Mace told them. "If he meets anybody one of you break off and tail him or her; get a description and address, if possible a name. But keep on Lanoix, he's the target. I want to know where he goes, who he sees. Tomorrow night you'll grab him."

"And—?" Raoul inquired.

"This may be the hard part. I want him roughed up by two Afghanis. As lieutenant colonel Yuri Chesnikov he executed Afghanis as well as Russian soldiers, that's their motivation. I want him photographed with the Afghanis—one of you will do that—letting him hear you say how pleased Monsier Chakirian will be. That's very important. Let them take money from his billfold, I want everything else. Now—" he paused—"can you find two Afghanis before tomorrow night?"

Raoul said, "In the Arab quarter there's an Islamic Center. I can try there."

"I'm counting on you," he said and gave them five hundred francs for expenses. After they left he typed a caption for the expected Polaroid photo: *Paris arms dealer Frederic Lanoix assaulted by vengeful Afghanis. As Lt. Colonel Yuri Chesnikov in Afghanistan "Lanoix" was a notorious torturer and executioner of mujahideen and Russian soldiers.*

He wanted to add more but decided the information was sufficient to discredit Chesnikov in France.

That done, he left for the safe house and began the laborious process of emptying Chakirian's accounts in order of their printout appearance. Working at the computer he transferred two million dollars from a Chakirian Bern account to his new account in Panama. Next, a Zurich account whose contents went to Schoffman's bank. From a second Zurich account, Mace transferred four million directly to Pascal Covici's bank, then sent a fifth million from Bonn.

At one he shut down the computer and had lunch at the brasserie. Then he went to his office and checked messages.

A fax from Erica informed him that her husband's early release was anticipated. Could he come and help him get oriented?

By which, he realized, she wanted him there to orchestrate Carlos's escape to France. His reply fax told her he was too committed in Paris and felt she was able to manage details without him. Then Mace went back to the safe house, transferring more than eighty million by the time Selina arrived.

"Seems impossible," she said in an awed voice, "that suddenly we're unbelievably wealthy. Do you feel it, too?"

He shook his head. "It seems like an exercise in numbers rather than real money. When I have some of it in my hands I'll know it's real."

"I understand." She slipped out of her shoes and dress. "This morning Chesnikov came in. Even before seeing Victor he asked me for lunch, then dinner. I said I had previous engagements, so he asked me for lunch tomorrow. Shall I go?"

"Not if you can avoid it, and dinner is definitely out. But he won't bother you much longer."

"Why, Mace? Do you know something I don't?"

"I suspect he'll be traveling soon. Maybe to his Monte Carlo office." He wondered if Raoul had been able to recruit the Afghanis, if the boys were on Chesnikov's tail.

"Since banks are closed why don't we go out for dinner?"

"If you'll settle for an out-of-the-way place where we're not likely to be noticed."

In the morning he received an early call from Raoul, who told him Lanoix had a late-afternoon visitor, whom Jean-Paul tailed from Lanoix's office to the American Embassy.

"Description?"

"Short, dark-skinned, mustache. Mexican tie."

"What kind of tie is that?"

"Jean-Paul said it looked like a shoelace. And cowboy boots."

Ed Natsos. "What else?"

"Our man dined alone at Le Boeuf then went to his apartment. When his lights went out we broke off."

"Any recruits?"

"They're ready for tonight. Bad-looking types. When I supplied the officer's name they said they'd kill him, no charge."

"Restrain them," Mace ordered, "that's not part of the script."

"I understand, boss. And I'll be sure to mention that other name you gave us."

"Very important. I'll expect photos in the morning."

As he taxied to the safe house Mace thought about Natsos. He could have been seeing Chesnikov about Stinger buyback or working some nonofficial deal. Either way, Mace was confident Chesnikov would not be around much longer, leaving Ed minus one contact.

At midday Selina visited him long enough to check on progress which, Mace told her, amounted to twelve million more withdrawn, and redeposited in their accounts.

"Poor *bébé*," she consoled, "you're having to do it all. So I'll tell

Victor I need the day off for shopping and beauty salon."

"I don't mind, really. Besides, it won't be a good day to be away from the office. I want you there to monitor developments."

"Oh? Is something going to happen?"

"I hope so."

"You won't tell me?"

"Tomorrow night."

By the end of the banking day Mace transferred nearly seventy million. Despite the hours worked he still hadn't managed to spread four hundred million among their accounts, and tomorrow was Friday, the day before banks closed. Depending on Geneva developments he might go there over the weekend to update the situation and spend time with Erica. The idea appealed to him. He was beginning to tire of Selina's aggressive sexuality and a few days' separation would break what had become routine and be good for both of them. Besides, he mused, with Montaner problems nearing resolution he needed to focus on a future shared with Erica, if there was to be one.

At his office he returned a call from Pascal Covici, who said, "I'm grateful for the gift. I did not expect it so soon. What can I do to repay you?"

Mace thought before replying. "Friendship is without price," he said, "though I may have a favor to ask sometime in the future."

"Have no doubt I will be fully receptive. As I said before you have only to ask."

After he replaced the receiver Yasmi said, "Jean-Paul is glad to be working for you and I'm glad he is. We're talking of marriage again."

Mace nodded. "I expect he'll be working late tonight."

"Yes, he told me." She hesitated. "Will it be dangerous?"

"Shouldn't be. Before you leave get me a reservation to Geneva, Saturday morning. Return Monday morning." Then he sent a fax to Erica giving her his arrival information, but wondered if she was already installed in her villa awaiting her husband's release.

He telephoned Albert Boulet, and said, "Albert, you must have pretty good press contacts."

"I do."

"Suppose I passed you a nugget—captioned photo—could you get it published?"

"If it has news value. Where do you want it to appear? *Figaro? L'Aurore? Le Monde? France-Soir* has the largest circulation."

"Well, I'll leave that to your judgment after you've seen the material. I'll have it at your office in the morning."

"I'll do what I can, Mace. Ah—appreciate what you did for our friend Broussard. He was like a man spared the guillotine."

Mace chuckled. "A satisfied client is the best recommendation."

That night he met Selina at La Mediterranée, a seafood restaurant on the Left Bank, and while they were enjoying bouillabaisse he told her he was going to Geneva for the weekend. Frowning, she said, "To see your countess, I suppose."

"She's a client, as is her husband."

"Surely you have enough money to stop working forever."

"Establishing Secours wasn't easy, Selina. Maybe I'll sell it some day but meanwhile I have an obligation to my clients."

"Moral? Ethical?"

"Both. And we don't discuss other affairs past or present."

"True," she sighed, "but I still don't like it. I'm jealous of every woman you see."

The waiter boned and divided a poached Iceland salmon, served vegetables, and refilled their wineglasses. After a while Selina asked what he was going to do with his wealth.

"I want a boat," he told her, "a couple of nice houses, maybe a ranch in the U.S. or Canada . . . You?"

"Jewels, a yacht, a place in Saint-Tro' . . . travel. I'll think of other things as time goes on. And I want to take care of my foster family in Beirut."

"I should establish a trust fund for my daughter, independent of her mother and stepfather. Scholarships for my university . . ."

"We'll see each other, won't we? From time to time?"

"Of course we will." He lifted her hand and kissed it. "Meanwhile, I have to protect you from Victor."

"With the tapes, you mean."

"That's one weapon, but his fury might exceed the fear of exposure. I have some ideas but nothing solid. Until I have a foolproof plan you need to be alert to any change in his demeanor. Be very careful."

"I will—partner."

twenty-three

The Reunion

He was wakened early by Jean-Paul, who entered with Yasmi's key. Mace trudged down to the office and took to his desk the envelope Jean-Paul delivered. It contained four Polaroid flash photographs taken at night: Three figures before a brick wall. Two wore Afghan robes and large turbans, faces concealed by cloth. Between them they supported the sagging body of a man in Western clothing. His shirt was spattered with blood, one eye was swollen shut, hair wildly disarranged. Jean-Paul said, "Is this what you wanted?"

"Excellent." The other photos were taken from slightly different angles but the scene was the same. "Give you any trouble?" Mace asked. He sat in his chair and rubbed sleep from his eyes.

"Not much. We were four in my car. We tailed him from his restaurant and the two ragheads were out of the car and on him before he knew what was happening. Raoul taped his mouth, and when he kept struggling, sapped him. That kept him quiet the rest of the way." He cleared his throat. "The ragheads kicked and beat him unconscious." From his pocket he took an ostrich-skin wallet and set it on the desk. "They kept the francs and Raoul paid them a hundred each."

"Happy Afghanis?"

"They hadn't seen that much money in months. They want more work, anything. Anytime."

"*Bon.* Did Lanoix see your faces?"

"No, wore handkerchiefs."

"And did Lanoix hear Chakirian mentioned?"

248

"When Raoul said, '*M'sieu* Chakirian will be pleased,' his head snapped up and he swore. Yes, he heard the name."

"All right." Mace took the typed caption from his desk and slid it into the envelope with the photos. He addressed it to Albert Boulet and told Jean-Paul to deliver it after nine. "Only to Boulet, he's expecting it."

Jean-Paul nodded. "Anything else, boss?"

"Make delivery and get some rest."

They shook hands and Jean-Paul left.

Mace made coffee, fed Su-Su, and returned to his desk where he opened the gold-trimmed wallet and examined its contents. There were business cards from three houses of joy in St-Denis, an ornate laminated card in Cyrillic and French identifying Yuri Chesnikov as a member of the Red Army Artillery Association, a safe-deposit box key, three credit cards, an international driving *triptyque,* and a miniature address book. Turning the pages, Mace found entries for Chakirian, Selina Mansour, and E. Natsos with an embassy phone extension. The phone numbers of several restaurants were listed, and those of two florists and a dry cleaner. Other names were meaningless to Mace. He restored the litter to the wallet and locked it in his safe, again wondering how close Natsos and Chesnikov were. Well, he thought, after today Chesnikov may find France no longer to his taste.

Before he left for the safe house he took a call from Boulet, who said, "An interesting package. Check the afternoon papers."

"Thanks, I will."

Through the morning hours he continued transfers and shortly after noon Selina came in, face flushed as she exclaimed, "Chesnikov came and there was a terrible argument with Victor! He forced his way in just after Victor arrived and I didn't even try to keep him out. They were shouting at each other and Chesnikov threatened to kill Victor. Mace, he was wearing bandages, limping, and his face was so bruised and swollen one eye was shut."

"Did he kill Victor? Harm him?"

"I called guards and they dragged him out but not before he'd managed to choke Victor. He was coughing and massaging his throat when I went in."

"What provoked the dispute?"

"When Victor could talk he was furious. Apparently Chesnikov was mugged last night and blamed Victor."

"Do you think Victor was responsible?"

She shook her head. "He was outraged Chesnikov should blame him for a vulgar street assault." Her expression became sly. "Want to know what I think? I think you had him attacked, somehow let him believe Victor ordered it."

"Why would Victor harm a potential partner?"

"That's a mystery. Anyway, there's no partnership now or ever." She blotted perspiration from her forehead. "You knew something would happen this morning, that's why you wanted me there. Admit it."

Mace smiled. "Could be coincidence."

"A very small chance. Now Victor won't tap his secret accounts to finance Chesnikov—that should give us more time." She looked at the printouts with which Mace was working. "How much longer, dear?"

"Three or four days next week. That should do it all."

"All," she echoed. "I think of all that money and I still can't believe it's mine—and yours."

"After next week you ought to disappear. Don't ask Victor for vacation time, don't do anything to suggest you're leaving, just go."

"But, where?"

"There's time to think about it, but not much. Anything you leave behind you can replace, that's what money is for."

"I could hide in Beirut," she suggested halfheartedly.

"He found you there before. Forget Beirut. As soon as you're safely away from Paris I'll work on Chakirian. If I'm successful you won't have to worry about him finding you."

"Mace"—she touched his hand—"will you join me?"

"In time," he replied. "Now I'm going to tell you something I've done, and why." He saw her glance at her watch. "A banker I know handles Brotherhood money, launders it, makes investments for them. He invested five million in IFT—"

"The Brotherhood? What is it?"

"A criminal organization combining Italian and Sicilian mafia and the Union Corse. I didn't want The Brotherhood pursuing us so I replaced their lost investment. The banker can be useful to me, to us, when needed. The money came from my account, so it's no loss to you."

"Five—million? What banker?"

Ignoring the question he said, "The Brotherhood would pursue their stolen money more relentlessly than a hundred Chakirians. They have contacts, resources he couldn't possibly match. Returning their funds is the best insurance I could think of. It's one thing to neutralize Victor, but impossible to appease The Brotherhood, so I eliminated the threat."

After a long pause she said, "I believe you did right, Mace." Again she looked at her wristwatch. "I must go. At six I'll let you know if anything else happens at the office."

They kissed, and she was gone.

After the close of banking hours Mace slept in the safe house and though it seemed only minutes had passed he woke to find Selina beside him, her body warm against his. She reached over and showed him a copy of *France-Soir* folded to a captioned photograph. "Dear," she murmured, "isn't it remarkable how a photographer was there when Chesnikov was beaten?"

"Remarkable," he sleepily agreed.

"When Victor saw this he left the office, more confused than ever. Then Chesnikov phoned, insane with rage, yelling he was going to kill Victor." She put the paper aside.

"You told Victor?"

"I called him at home. Now he's deathly afraid of the Russian."

"He should be—knowing Chesnikov's talent for killing." Turning over, he kissed her lips. "Problems have a way of resolving themselves if one is patient."

"So I've found. And to know Victor is afraid for his life excites me." He felt her hand burrow between his loins. "Before dinner?" he asked.

"What better time?"

251

* * *

Geneva.

Mace reached Cointrin airport before noon and phoned the Hôtel du Rhône for Erica. The *comtesse* left yesterday, the concierge told him. "Is she in Geneva?" Mace asked.

"I cannot say."

"Thank you." He was about to hang up when the concierge said, "Wait, please, *ne coupez pas.*" He paused. *"La Comtesse* hired a private car with chauffeur, one I arranged at her request. Not seeing either since they departed, I assume car, chauffeur, and *comtesse* are, if not in the city, perhaps in the environs."

"That's helpful," Mace replied, "and thank you."

From the public phone he dialed the office of *Maître* Schreiber, and after a brief wait heard the lawyer's voice. "Where are you, *M'sieu* Mason?"

"At the airport. Where's Erica."

"At her villa since yesterday. Is she expecting you?"

"I'm not sure if she got my message. Where is the villa?"

"Perhaps a fifteen-minute drive from Cointrin, on the other side of the lake. Tell your taxi driver to take you to Vésenaz. Just beyond the town there is a road that goes toward the lake. He should ask anyone for the Château du Cerf."

"Vésenaz, Château du Cerf," Mace repeated, and thanked him for the information. Then before he could hang up the lawyer said, "This might not be a propitious time to visit—if you understand my meaning?"

"It concerns her husband?"

"It does."

"No reason for me to back away," Mace said, "I'm practically a member of the family."

"As you wish, *M'sieu,*" the lawyer said archly, and rang off.

So, wheels had turned, money had changed hands, and prison gates were soon to open for Count Carlos Juan Perez de Montaner. Lucky lad, Mace thought, picked up his suitcase, and headed for the taxi stand.

From the airport the taxi drove around the southern reach of the city to avoid traffic, then picked up the main lakeside route to the

252

northeast. Road signs listed Vésenaz and Douvaine ahead at fourteen and forty-three kilometers. Gradually the land rose, and when they were at a police kiosk in town the driver paused to ask directions.

From the highway a narrow, well-graded road wound past meadows and copses of silver birch toward a château surmounting a grassy rise. As Swiss châteaux went it was of medium size, with clean architectural lines and no archers' towers or crenelated ramparts. Mace noticed a beige-topped black Rolls salon parked in front of the wide entrance steps. A gray-uniformed chauffeur was polishing a rear fender. He heard the taxi, peered at it, and went into the arched entrance. While Mace was paying his driver a maid came out and politely inquired what it was he wanted. "To see *La Comtesse*," he told her, "and you may say a friend from Paris is here."

The maid curtsied and hurried up the steps. Mace carried his suitcase into the entrance, and set it down. In a few moments Erica came running down the hall. "Mace," she called, "darling," and came into his arms. "What a wonderful surprise!"

"Then you didn't get my fax—I sent it to the hotel."

"And I left yesterday." Her expression was chagrined. "But after telling me you couldn't come, you came anyway. I'm thrilled."

The chauffeur picked up Mace's suitcase and carried it down the hall while they kissed lengthily. Then they walked side by side, Mace saying, "Have I come at a delicate moment? A bad time?"

"Well—why do you ask?"

"Schreiber's suggestion."

Her expression grew into a smile. "Then you know."

"Not until you tell me."

"I'm expecting Carlos tonight!"

"That's wonderful." He kissed her. "How big was the bribe?"

"Schreiber said half a million Swiss francs."

"And bail?"

"Two million francs."

As they reached a broad staircase Mace said, "I hope Carlos will appreciate all you've done for his freedom, but I won't be surprised if he does not. Is someone bringing him here?"

"*Maître* Schreiber. He said it would be late to avoid anyone noticing, especially the press."

They reached the balconied second floor and approached a series of bedrooms. Her large master suite occupied a corner. Erica opened the next door and said, "Carlos will sleep here. You're next beyond."

"It will be strange being with you but not being with you."

"You will be, dear—it's a short walk between rooms. We'll be together, I promise."

As they entered his assigned bedroom, he said, "Everything will seem strange to Carlos for a few days. I have to get him to focus on leaving Switzerland as we planned. So you're right not to rub his nose in our relationship."

"I'm sure he suspects we're lovers."

"So am I."

She closed and locked the door, they undressed and made love on the big four-poster eiderdown bed. While they were showering she said, "How shall we spend the rest of the time we're alone?"

"However you like."

"Schreiber said he would phone as they left the prison."

"Good. I'd rather not be surprised by a husband with a bad attitude."

She pinched his rump. "Were you ever?"

"Once, but not a husband, a father."

"I insist you tell me."

They began drying each other before he said, "It was a close call. There was this art professor at college. His wife was screwing some of the faculty, and their daughter—a first-year student—blonde like you—was sexually precocious. She preferred athletes and fraternity men, and one night in the libe she passed me a note suggesting I call on her next afternoon while her father was teaching. I went to her house, saw her mother's car was gone, and went in. Penny met me at the door and said she couldn't wait. She pulled up her skirt, I dropped my pants, and we got on the alcove sofa. Well—wouldn't you know—just when we were getting it on the front door opened and in trots her father. Talk about heart failure."

"He *saw* you?"

"He was pissed off about something and never glanced at the

254

254

alcove, just headed for his studio and slammed the door. Jesus, what a fright!"

Erica was laughing. "What did you do?"

"We got the hell out of there and sneaked into the next door church. It was empty, so we found paradise on a pew."

"How sacreligious. I suppose you never saw her again?"

"Wrong. Couple afternoons a week we got it on in the church; no foreplay, no tenderness, just primal lust." He slapped her rump. "And that's what made me what I am today."

"Ouch, you hurt! Made you cautious or lustful?"

"You tell me."

"You're certainly not cautious, *mon amour*, so try to be tonight." She rubbed her behind and showed Mace his palm print. "You haven't said what else we should do together."

"Let's drive along the lake, I don't know this side of it."

The chauffeur drove them nearly to Hermance and stopped at a rustic inn from whose patio there was a fine view of lake and Alps. They were served thick hot chocolate and delicate sandwiches, and as he gazed at her flawless face Mace thought that he was probably very much in love.

Late that evening they were driven to the Hotel Richemond and dined in its spacious grill. Then they returned to the Château du Cerf and played backgammon and gin rummy before an open fire. After his third cognac Mace said, "After you leave Carlos in Divonne you'll return here."

She nodded. "Next day."

"I have to make Carlos understand that while he's a fugitive I'll be working to prove his innocence."

"Do you think that's possible?"

"I do. But not until the guilty man's guilt can be established."

She looked toward the fire. "I thought you might feel you'd done enough."

"I made a commitment."

She fingered her glass. "Will it take money?"

"I have more than enough." Eventually he would tell her he was wealthier than any of the Montaners, but that was for later on.

They resumed play and at eleven o'clock Erica yawned and said, "I don't think I can stay awake much longer. I want him to come so we can all get to bed."

"Go ahead, I'll meet him and wake you. Coffee will help."

He went into the old-fashioned kitchen with her, lighted the gas range, and watched her boil water that she poured through a coffee strainer into a ceramic pot. "All for you, dear. I'm for bed."

She took a full brandy snifter with her and disappeared up the staircase. He heard her door open and close, found a Paris fashion magazine, and scanned slinky photos of white-faced anorexic mannequins until his eyes closed and he drowsed in the chair.

A ringing phone startled him awake. The phone rang again and he located it on a shadowed table. *"Oui?"*

"We're leaving now." Voice of *Maître* Schreiber. "Forty minutes we'll be there."

"We're waiting." He replaced the receiver and stood for a moment gazing at the fire's few glowing coals. Away from the fireplace the huge sitting room was dark, empty. He could barely make out colors on the backgammon board.

In the kitchen he warmed the coffee pot, drank a cup with sugar, then another. Fatigue peeled away and he turned on hall and sitting room lights for Carlos. He opened the double entrance doors and went out on the marble steps. For a while he stood in the stillness, experiencing the visual illusion of a crescent moon racing across a bed of dirty clouds, then brought his thoughts back to the present.

Meeting Erica had set him on a strange journey into a labyrinth, driven far more by desire for her than for her husband's freedom. Yet tonight, at this old Swiss estate, roads converged, a pattern complex as a kaleidoscope's would shift and rearrange. He was part of a sort-of triangle, the kind on which tabloids thrived, and he hoped that Carlos, disoriented and bitter as he might be, could find it in himself to play the *caballero*. Still, the pride of a humiliated Spanish aristocrat could drive the husband impulsively and imprudently in directions harmful to the interests of them all.

I shouldn't have come, he thought suddenly, but having come I should not have stayed. The inevitable confrontation between husband and wife ought to take place without a third party, her lover. But it's too late now.

Turning, he looked up and saw a dim light in the corner bedroom, obscured by drawn blinds. Erica's bedroom, where she slept alone.

He looked at his watch. Thirty minutes since Schreiber's call. He went back inside and poured a brandy. Today with Erica he had enjoyed tranquil hours but now a situation partly of his own making was coming to a head. How he handled himself could determine the outcome.

Through the open entrance filtered the sound of a distant car. As he listened, he realized it was nearing; the car bringing Carlos de Montaner. Mace gulped more brandy and squared his shoulders. Gravel spun under tires as the car braked at the entrance. He heard a door open and slam shut. Ascending shoes scraped slowly on the steps as the car drove away. Feet shuffled along the hall. Stopped. Mace turned to the arrival.

Pale-faced, shoulders hunched, wearing prison pants and a shapeless jacket, Carlos de Montaner clenched his hands into fists, took a step forward. "You had to be here," he sneered, "I knew you would." His voice rose, coarsened. *"Damn you, where is my wife?"*

twenty-four

The Understanding

Mace pointed at the staircase. "Upstairs, corner bedroom. Sleeping."

"Couldn't even greet me, her husband," Carlos rasped. "Left it to you."

Mace restrained himself. "She's stressed-out," he said evenly. "Too much tension for too long—working to get you free. Weeks of it, Carlos, months of waiting."

"But she had you, didn't she?" he challenged. "Fucking my wife *por delante y por detrás*, you *hijo de puta.*"

Mace sucked in a deep breath. "Listen, sonny, you're the luckiest man I know. It was your wife who got you out, your wife who paid and bribed and set things up. Not you. Because of her you're here. You're not much of a man and far from a *caballero* but try to see things as they are. Go to your wife, wake her, talk with her. Calm down, be reasonable."

Mace filled a cognac glass and offered it to Carlos whose gaze flickered from it to Mace, to the glass again while his hands opened and closed. Finally he reached for the glass and drained it in one long swallow. He coughed, shivered, and said in a lower voice, "I want you out of here, Mason."

"After we've talked. This isn't your final destination."

"No? Where are you sending me? I've already seen Hell."

Mace glanced upward. "Erica will tell you the plan."

Carlos looked around. "I like it here, this is what I was used to before—" He broke off, looked down at his hands. "Why should I leave?'

"Because your enemies want you in prison. They'll work to revoke the judge's release order. You can't stay in Switzerland. Now wake Erica and talk with her. If it's within you, show some gratitude." Mace went to the fireplace, stirred the coals with a poker, and laid on three logs. When he looked around, Carlos was climbing the staircase.

Mace sat in an overstuffed leather chair, sipped cognac, and watched the logs slowly begin to burn. From upstairs, silence. Suspense made him edgy. He sipped more cognac. Suddenly he heard Carlos yelling, then Erica screamed. Mace shot upright, set down his glass as he heard running feet. Erica was coming down the staircase, Carlos pursuing her. "Mace," she called, "don't let him—"

Then her husband caught her shoulder, struck her face, and pushed her down three steps to the floor. Carlos stood over her, pale face contorted with anger. "Bitch!" he shouted. *"Puta!"* Then Mace pushed him away. "Hit *me*," he challenged. "Hit me, *caballero*," and when Carlos did nothing, slapped his face. Carlos staggered back. *"Maricón,"* Mace snarled and shoved him to the floor. As Carlos lay there, covering his cheek, Mace drew Erica to her feet. "I thought it might come to this, so go to your room, stay there." She gripped the bannister and began pulling herself up the steps. Even in the dim light Mace could see the bruise on her face. He turned back to Carlos de Montaner. "On your feet, *puto*," he ordered, and kicked him until Carlos scrambled upright.

"If you were even half a man," Mace said in a steely voice, "I'd break your back—but you're pathetic, a woman-beater, a piece of shit."

The Spaniard's face was deathly pale but for the mark of Mace's palm. His mouth opened as though to speak, then closed. Mace grasped his arm and thrust him into the sitting room, shoved him into a chair. Carlos looked up, eyes wild with hate.

Mace folded his arms and gazed back until Carlos looked down at his trembling hands. "Now, man-lover," Mace rasped, "you'll listen to me. Touch Erica again and I'll kill you. Understand?"

259

Slowly Carlos nodded.

"In prison men have time to think, too much time. You thought the wrong thoughts and now you're a danger to yourself, your wife, and me. But that's not how it's going to be."

Carlos's eyes closed. Tears welled, began rolling down his cheeks. "We're going to get you into France. From there you go wherever you like. Do you understand that?"

Carlos nodded, wiped wet cheeks on his sleeve, and swallowed. "Why are you doing this—for Erica?"

"I'm doing it because I found out you didn't steal IFT money, you're innocent of that."

He sat forward. "You believe that?"

"I know it. Proving it is harder than getting you out of prison, but soon I think I'll have proof. Until then you're a fugitive on the run."

"Convenient for you—and Erica. And I'm giving her a divorce."

"You married her under false pretenses, didn't admit to your homosexuality. That's annulment grounds in any church, so don't claim generosity. It isn't in you." Mace went to the fire, poked logs until they flamed. "In that visiting room where every word is overhead, every visit taped, it wasn't possible to let you know the plan. Well, it worked, the first part, and you're free. Erica was to tell you the rest but you began beating her." He set the poker down. "It would be easy to have you back in prison before dawn, easier for me to just walk away, let you contrive your own escape but that would haunt me. Not now, later, and I have this compulsion to finish what I start. The sooner you're in France the better for us all. That clear?"

Carlos swallowed again. "If you say so." He looked at the cognac decanter. "Can I have a drink?"

Mace refilled his glass, handed it to him. "Presently we'll call Erica here and you'll apologize, beg forgiveness, express some gratitude even though you don't feel it. Is that also clear?"

Carlos lowered his glass. Dully he said, "In prison there were men like you, guards even—hard men without mercy. You don't know what it's like being a prisoner, stripped of everything, just a number . . ." He began to sob and Mace waited until the jag passed.

"As you've begun to learn it's a hard world, Carlos, very little comes for free. What happened to you is largely your own fault. You should have reported that fourteen million in your accounts, disclaimed it. But you kept quiet never thinking you were being set up, framed for the fiscal crime of the century. That was stupidity and you're paying for it. Unless I can prove you weren't the embezzler you'll be a fugitive the rest of your life. Fix that point in your mind. To you nothing else should matter."

Slowly Carlos nodded, drank more cognac.

"You need clothing but stores won't open until Monday.

"This is—what day?"

"Early Sunday morning."

He looked at his prison garb. Mace said, "My clothing won't fit you. Monday Erica will take you into Geneva to buy a decent outfit you can travel in. Now, are you ready for Erica?"

He breathed deeply. "Call her."

From the bottom of the staircase Mace called her name, waited while she appeared and began taking the stairs, slowly, uncertainly. He walked beside her to the sitting room and said, "Carlos and I have been talking. We've cleared away some misunderstandings— isn't that so, Carlos?"

The Spaniard nodded.

"So, we're ready to go on from here, isn't that right?"

Carlos left the chair and dropped to his knees before Erica. "I'm very sorry for what I did and I beg your forgiveness. Now that I know all you did for me I'm very grateful. Will you forgive me?"

Erica glanced at Mace in surprise and when he nodded she said, "I forgive you." Absently, one hand touched the facial bruise.

"Now tell Carlos the plan." He turned and walked toward the staircase. Erica called, "Shouldn't you stay?"

"Too tired," he replied, and went slowly up the staircase to his bedroom, leaving the hall door open. For a while he listened for raised voices, then sleep washed over him in a giant wave.

He was wakened by movement on the bed. Erica. Windows showed the first gray streaks of dawn. Clinging to him, she murmured, "You were wonderful. I think everything will be all right now." She turned on her side to face him. "He cried a lot, and that was hard to see, but I believe he's remorseful."

"He had a lot to be remorseful about." He felt the parting of her loins. "He'll get a final pep talk from me. Subject: Absolute cooperation."

Her stiffened nipples bore into his chest. "He's afraid of you so he respects you. He'll do whatever you say."

Her golden fleece was damply warm as he parted it. She shuddered and held his body close. "And you?" he managed before the fever rose, "what about you?"

"Obedient always—because I love you."

The fever flared, burst into consuming flame.

During late breakfast Carlos appeared chastened, even humble. Among them there was restrained conversation until Carlos said, "What about money—I'll need money to get away, survive."

Mace bit into a croissant. "Tomorrow," he said after swallowing, "when you're in Geneva for clothing Erica should establish a bank account for you, a number account you can draw on from anywhere in the world. Half a million should cover you for a while." He looked at Erica.

"Of course," she said, "it's Carlos's money, after all."

"Sixty percent," Carlos said wryly, "so be aware of your own interests." He looked across the table at Mace. "Have you been properly paid?"

"The *Señora* saw to that," Mace replied stiffly, and finished the rest of his pastry. "The Rolls' trunk will be hot and uncomfortable so you might want to put in some pillows before tomorrow night. Silence is imperative at all times until Erica lets you out at the Casino."

Erica's forehead wrinkled. "But you'll be with us, won't you?"

"I have to be back in Paris tomorrow. But both of you know the script, I'm no longer needed. Erica, call me Tuesday when it's over. Carlos, if there's an emergency you can contact me at my office. But only in an emergency."

Carlos nodded. "And where will my wife be?"

"I'm not sure. Perhaps with my parents for a while. Afterward?" She looked at Mace, who said, "It's best you avoid the public until the press tires of looking for your husband."

"That's logical," Carlos remarked, "and I've been thinking of going to—"

Mace held up a hand to silence him. "We don't want to know where you go—better for us all. And if you find yourself in a small native village, don't throw money around, don't exhibit lordly airs. That could bring police and awkward questions."

"*Por favor,*" Carlos muttered irritably, "credit me with some intelligence. I'll need some kind of identity papers—how can I get them?"

"If I had known you were to be released I could have brought documents from Paris, but it's too late for that. And I have no Geneva contacts. So you'll have to be resourceful."

"What can you suggest?"

"In a big city try printing shops, passport photographers, buy drinks, ask questions—say you have a friend needing a small service."

"Good ideas, thank you. Erica, we need to go over divorce details."

"Yes, we do."

Mace rose from the table. "I'll take a stroll, see you later."

He went out through the kitchen, down steps and past garage, greenhouse, and servants' quarters until he was walking down a gentle slope through knee-high meadow grass. A hundred yards from the château he stone-stepped across a shallow stream that bordered woods whose trees were greening. There were elms and maples, beech, acacias, and stands of silver birch. An ancient towering oak spread branches over all. And as he walked among them a pair of partridges burst from a clump of ferns and thundered away. It was a fine, well-tended estate, he reflected, whose spacious grounds were unusual in a land where every hectare was put to use.

Above, a silver-tailed hawk cruised in lazy circles, peering always below for meadow mice. In the distance white gulls flapped toward the lake. Sun warmed earth through a nearly cloudless sky, and he welcomed the sensation of isolation and tranquility.

When he returned to the château husband and wife were at the backgammon board, playing apparently lightheartedly. Carlos glanced up at his entrance, and said, "All problems resolved. Now we have only to wait."

* * *

263

Evening came. Sunlight left the meadows and soon only the white-capped peaks of the Alps were visible along the far horizon. Because of Carlos's clothing they had dinner at the château: wurst, potato salad, black bread, beer, and wine. Mace started a fire in the sitting room and they played three-handed rummy until, at eleven, Erica smothered a yawn and said she was off to bed.

"Good idea," Mace remarked, "you have a full day tomorrow."

After she left them Carlos poured glasses of cognac and gave one to Mace. "You're a remarkable man," he said, "and now I under-stand why Erica trusts you so completely." He drank and gazed at the firelight. "I don't expect you to like me—we are what we are—but you've befriended me in ways I know about and ways I will never know. So my gratitude is eternal." He sipped again, and con-tinued. "I mind the divorce less because I know Erica's future will be in the best possible hands. I want you to understand that. Am I resentful? Yes, I admit it. Because you are a man I could never be, a man I greatly admire." He paused for what seemed a long time. "I wanted to get that out because it's not likely we'll see each other again."

"Probably not," Mace agreed, "and I have one other matter to mention. Do not for any reason get in touch with any of the young companions you entertained in Paris. A reward will be offered for you—probably a large one—and loyalties can crumble when tested by promised wealth."

Carlos grimaced. "I understand. Already I've learned how rapidly one's friends can vanish. A good point, but my lesson is learned." He finished his cognac, got up, and stretched. "I'm very tired, too. The past twenty-four hours—" He broke off as the entrance doorbell sounded. "Are you expecting someone?

Mace shook his head. "Get out of sight while I see who it is."

When Carlos was concealed in the closet Mace went to the door, listened, and opened it a crack to see the smiling face of Ed Natsos. "Ed, what are you doing here?"

"Heard you were in town, Mace, sorry it's so late but you're a hard man to find. Thought we'd have a drink together—you know, two *amis* in a foreign land." He paused. "Is the hospitality mat out?"

"Not hardly," Mace replied but opened the door wider.

Behind Natsos he saw a second man whose face was bruised where it was not bandaged. A sling supported his left arm, and his right hand held a blue-steel pistol.

twenty-five

The Visitors

Natsos shoved him and Mace backed into the hall. "Quite a little love-nest," Natsos said enviously. "Where's *La Belle Comtesse?*"

"Sleeping—if it's any of your business—and who's your body-guard? Next time, open your parachute, fella." He managed a chuckle and dug an elbow in Natsos's ribs. "Get it, Ed? Looks like he went free-fall. Believe me, it ain't the same."

Natsos swallowed, grated, "This 'bodyguard' is Yuri Chesnikov, as you probably damn well know."

Mace peered at the damaged face whose visible parts were contorted in anger. "His mother wouldn't know him, Ed, why should I?"

"Because, dammit, you set him up."

"I did? How do you figure that?"

"Well, for God's sake, you got that printout from me. You can't deny that."

"Wouldn't try. But there was no photo, right? How would I know what the bastard looks like?" He stared at the Russian and laughed again. "Jesus, what a team."

"You got me to give you the printout so you could embarrass my friend here."

"Me? What's my interest in him? Like I told you, a client wanted a check on Chesnikov. Let's see—" he frowned—"French alias, too."

In French Chesnikov growled. "Who is your client? Name him. I want his name."

Mace moved toward him, noticed only a soft splint on the right arm. "It's confidential. Maybe you don't know about client confidentiality. Tell him, Ed."

Natsos grunted, "He don't give a shit about confidentiality. He came here to get you, man, that's the kind of trouble you're in. So tell him, for Christ's sake, cut the bullshit."

Mace appeared to think it over. "All right," he said slowly, "I'll tell him—but not you." Leaning close to Chesnikov's unbandaged ear he whispered, "A banker—Vartan Chakirian."

Chesnikov snapped erect. *"Chakirian?"* he yelled. "You tell me Chakirian did it?"

"I said he was my client, I don't know what he did, or why." He turned to Natsos. "Ed, get this mook outa here and we'll forget you ever came."

"Careful, Mace, he's killed a lotta people."

"Yeah, bound and kneeling. Bullet behind the ear, Soviet style, real brave. What are you doing with this piece of shit, anyway? Don't tell me, let me guess: You told him about the printout, named me, and hopped the next plane." He shook his head. "Still don't know why."

From his pocket Natsos unfolded a newspaper photo and gave it to Mace. Handing it back, Mace said, "Your friend's been keeping bad company. Looks like the ragheads caught up with him." He grimaced. "Jesus, he looks awful."

Natsos said, "You say Chakirian did this?"

"I didn't say that. What I said was that I provided a report for a client. Yuri, here, was the subject—as you well know—and yes, Chakirian was my client. How does that tie me to a couple of ragheads mugging your friend in a dark alley?"

Uncertainly, Natsos said, "Maybe not. Yuri, Chakirian didn't need Mace, here, to do the job, he's got his own muscle."

Furious, Chesnikov shouted, "He's Chakirian's man, I know it. I've seen him with the secretary."

Mace grunted, "That's proof of—what? Sure, I've dated the secretary, a fine young woman, too, and maybe we've gone to bed, but Chakirian doesn't know that. She warned me he's the jealous type. Okay, I did one job for Chakirian, and Ed, here, knows all about it. Hell, he gave me your file printout. If you're eager to pull a trigger, point the barrel at Ed."

Natsos swallowed. "This has gotten confusing. Maybe we were wrong, shouldn't have come."

"Well, I can understand your role, Ed, you carry Yuri's bags while he packs iron."

Chesnikov snarled. "You talk too much. I'm going to shoot you."

"Do I kneel? That's how you like it." He bent over, and before the gun barrel could lower, whirled, and slammed his hand edge against Chesnikov's sling. The Russian screamed in pain and grabbed at his arm, hand still gripping the gun. Mace grabbed the gun arm and levered it across his chest, but the Russian's body eased away from the pressure until they were face to face. Both hands on Chesnikov's wrist, Mace bent it inward until the barrel dug into the Russian's belly. "Baby-killer," Mace snarled, "pull the trigger now." Chesnikov's unbandaged eye was wide with fear. "Don't—" the Russian begged, but Mace pushed relentlessly trying to snap wrist or trigger finger. He bore hard, twisted, and the pistol went off, sound muffled by the Russian's flesh and clothing. Chesnikov yelled and dropped to his knees as Mace snatched away the pistol. Blood flowered across the Russian's chest.

Hysterically, Natsos cried, "Do something, aren't you going to do something?"

"Do—? Why should I?" He blew a wisp of smoke from the barrel, turned it at Natsos who was shaking uncontrollably. "He came here to kill me and you helped him. Why shouldn't I kill you?"

Chesnikov now lay on his back. He sighed and death rales came from his throat. The sound was like the crushing of dry leaves. The body lifted slightly and went limp. Mace stared at it, muttered, "You'll murder no more," and looked at Natsos who dropped to his knees. "Don't kill me, Mace," he pleaded, "we're old friends." His voice rose. "Don't kill me," he begged. "I won't tell, I'll do anything you say." His shoulders began to shake.

Mace bent over and scooped up the empty cartridge case, slid on the pistol safety. A 9mm Makarov, he noticed. Red Army issue in prime condition. "You've got problems, Ed, no question about it," he said musingly. "I want to kill you and will if you give me the slightest cause." He toed Chesnikov's body. "You came here with him, shouldn't you go back to Paris with him?"

"Oh, God, God no—how could I? What do you mean?"

"Well, if you don't want to fly him back, he stays here. That's your immediate problem. Any suggestions?"

"We could—I mean, couldn't he be buried?" he croaked.

"I'm thinking along those lines. Get up and stop blubbering—you disgust me."

Slowly Natsos got up. There was a stain down his pants leg. He looked at it and a flush spread across his pallid face. With a look of distaste, Mace patted him down for a weapon. "What do you want me to do?" Natsos husked.

"You came by car, give me the keys."

Hand scrabbling in pocket, key ring produced.

"Where is it?"

"Down—just off the road."

"Did you fly under your own name?"

"Alias, I'm not that dumb."

"That limits your exposure. Rental car?"

"Yuri paid cash."

"Convenient, he was thinking ahead. That proves he was going to kill me."

"No, no, the Afghanis stole his wallet, money, cards, driving license." Natsos swallowed. "He had to pay cash."

Mace faced the closet and called, "Hide your face and come out." Carlos appeared, scarf hiding his features. "Stay where you are," he told him, and turned to Natsos. "In case it ever occurs to you to kill me there's a witness to swear you killed Yuri. I know who the witness is, you don't. Bear that in mind, Ed. Forever."

"I will."

He gestured at Carlos, called, "Go to bed," and turned back to Natsos. "Now, one of two things is going to happen. You can drive Yuri up lakeside, crash the car into a tree and make sure it burns. Or, you can dig a grave down in the woods, and bury your friend. Then drive the car back to the airport."

"Dig the grave."

Mace nodded. "After tonight, Ed, I don't want to see you again. You're a disgrace to yourself, the Agency, and the U.S. government. Tomorrow's Monday. Put in for retirement and get the hell out of

Europe. If I see you skulking around, expect a bullet. Do you understand?"

"I—I understand."

"Load him on your back, fireman's carry, and follow me."

Natsos knelt, hoisted the body on his back, and trudged unsteadily behind Mace. Down the entrance steps and around the side toward the greenhouse, Natsos breathing heavily. Inside, Mace found a shovel and carried it across the stream and into the woods.

There was enough light to make out a small clearing fifty feet from the bordering stream. "Here," Mace said, and dropped the shovel, as Natsos dropped the body. "Start now."

Wheezing from effort, Natsos began to dig, the shovel making soft sounds in the loamy soil. "In Nicaragua," Mace observed, "I saw a good many graves dug, helped dig some myself, so I'm in a position to critique your work."

The only response from Natsos was harder shovel strokes. After a while he rested on the shovel handle and said, "How do I know you won't kill me, bury me, too."

"You don't," Mace replied, "but the deeper the grave, the better your chance to survive." He got up, stretched, and looked up at the moon through branches. After a while he said, "The body will rot all summer until the winter freeze sets in. Next spring and summer it rots more, and so on, year after year, worms helping as they can."

"Christ!" Natsos exploded, "you're a cold-blooded bastard!"

"So I've been told." He pointed the Makarov at Natsos. "Keep digging. And keep your mouth shut." He looked down into the grave, saw Natsos's hands tighten around the shovel handle. Stepping back, he said, "If you think you can slam me before a bullet hits you, try it." He moved out of shovel range. "You're too slow, Ed, not making good progress. Put your back into it. You're only two feet down, another two feet to go."

Time passed until finally Mace said, "Get down there."

"You'll kill me!"

"I want to see how deep you've gone—do it."

Natsos stood in the grave. The ground came even with his hips. Mace walked around him. Moonlight bleached his features. Mace shrugged. "Should do it," he said, "so get up here and leave the shovel alone."

Kneeling beside the stiffening corpse, Mace went methodically through each pocket, loosened the waist and found a money belt. It contained a return ticket to Paris and eight hundred French francs. He pocketed the currency and showed Natsos the ticket. "One way to avoid inconvenient questions is to leave this ticket in the airport john. Someone may use it, in which case it will appear that Chesnikov—"

"He traveled as Lanoix," Natsos interrupted.

"That Frederic Lanoix returned to Paris. You follow me?"

"Yes."

"Leave the money belt. If the corpse is ever found they'll wonder what was in it. That's our little secret."

Wordlessly, Natsos took the ticket, looked glumly at his blistered hands.

"I'll help you," Mace said, and dragged the body to grave edge, toppled it in. "You do the rest."

Natsos stared at him briefly before picking up the shovel and starting to fill the grave with earth. When it was finally tamped level Mace told him to scatter leaves and branches over the soil, and carry the shovel back.

After leaving it in the greenhouse Mace walked around to the château entrance, Natsos shuffling behind. Mace halted at the steps and held up the car keys.

"Can I get a drink? Jesus, I've never been so thirsty."

"A friend would give you a drink, but we're not friends. It's two thirty-five. I want you and the car off this property in three minutes or you'll walk to town." He returned the keys. "Get going. Hup, hup, get the lead outa them feet. Hup, hup." He smiled, remembering his DI at Penn State, as Natsos jogged down the drive into darkness. Presently an engine started and the car drove off. Mace listened a while, then went up the steps and locked the entrance door. On the flooring there was drying blood where Chesnikov expired. Mace got a wet cloth from the kitchen and cleaned it up. Then he went to the sitting room, poured a full glass of cognac, and sat facing the fire-

271

place. The coals were mostly ash, only a thread of smoke drifted upward in the still, silent air. He filled his mouth and swallowed, got out the Makarov and extracted the magazine before removing the ready shell from the chamber. He was thumbing it into the magazine when, peripherally, he saw Carlos come in from the hall, naked but for underwear. "What's on your mind?" Mace asked, and Carlos stood by the fireplace. After swallowing, he asked, "What was all that about? Would you tell me?"

"You heard most of it, maybe all of it, so forget whatever you heard, names, gunshot, everything." He drank deeply from his glass. "It had nothing to do with you or Erica, everything to do with me. In simple terms, it involved a client of mine, that's all you need to know."

"It was just a miracle the way you got the upper hand," he said admiringly.

"Training. The man pulled the trigger, shot himself. I wouldn't have killed him. Did Erica wake?"

"The gun going off woke her, that's all she heard." He shivered in the cold room. "She asked me, I told her nothing."

"You're learning discretion," Mace told him and held up the pistol by its barrel. "Ever do any handgun shooting?"

"No. Only *escopetas*—shotguns." He stared at the weapon as though it were a cobra.

"There's no time to teach you—besides, if you're as resourceful as you're going to have to be you won't need a firearm." He replaced the pistol in his pocket. "I'll get rid of it."

Carlos nodded. "Before you go upstairs—now that all of us have full understanding—I wanted to say there is no reason for you to sleep in your room and Erica in hers." He swallowed again. "You understand?"

Mace nodded. "No slinking around. All right. Follow the plan precisely, no variations, and find safe haven for yourself."

"But I must ask this: How will I know when vindication comes?"

"You'll read about it," Mace told him, "wherever you are. Good night."

"Good . . . night." He drifted away silently as a wraith.

For a while Mace reviewed the night's events, and finished his drink. He set the glass on Chesnikov's francs—they would be useful to Carlos along the way.

He was halfway up the stairs when he saw Erica sitting on the top step looking down at him, and he wondered how long she had been there. Drawing her to her feet he kissed her, and together they went quietly down the hallway past Carlos's bedroom and into his own.

Book Four

twenty-six

The Tapes

Before leaving Cointrin airport Mace dumped Chesnikov's pistol in one trash can, its magazine in another, then flew back to Paris. During the flight he had a continental breakfast and dozed until the 737 landed at De Gaulle. From the airport he phoned his office, told Yasmi he was back, and asked if there was any urgent business. "Not really," she told him, "but your British Embassy friend phoned earlier and asked you to call her."

"It's eleven-fifteen now. I have some errands to take care of and won't be in until later this afternoon."

His next call was to Selina. Guardedly he let her know he was back and en route to the safe house. "Delighted," she replied, and hung up.

In the taxi Mace thought that by now Carlos should have acquired new clothing and a bank account. If he followed the plan precisely he should be across the border in less than twelve hours. Tomorrow Erica was to close up the château and fly out before her husband's absence became apparent.

At the safe house he found Selina in bed, naked, and waiting. Hungrily she kissed him and loosened his belt. "All weekend I've been miserable wanting you," she said throatily, "but I suppose you've been enjoying your countess."

"No comment." He got in bed beside her and in a little while they were making love.

While Selina dressed he asked whether Chesnikov was continuing to harass Victor. "No," she shrugged, "and Victor hopes that's the end of it."

"I don't imagine the Russian is popular in certain official quarters—perhaps he's been expelled from France. Did Victor complain to the police?"

"He considered it before realizing Chesnikov could reveal embarrassing things—so he did nothing. But he's still fearful of the Russian."

"I like that." He sat up and glanced at the computer setup. "I better hit it before banks close."

"Sorry you have to do so much." She bussed his cheek and left. Mace locked the door behind her, took a shower, and seated himself at the console.

In less than two hours he managed to transfer six million before bank computers shut down for the day. Carrying his suitcase, he left the safe house and taxied to his office. Told Yasmi to take the rest of the day off and went to bed.

Toward six a call from Jessamyn woke him. "Are you avoiding me, precious luv?"

"I've been out of town a lot, but I'm afraid that's not the whole story."

"You're seeing someone!"

"I am," he admitted, "a very jealous person, so—"

"Beast!" Noisily she broke the connection.

Well, he thought, getting off the bed, *adieu* Jessamyn, *adiós*, and dressed to meet Selina for dinner.

Next morning—it was now Tuesday—Mace lingered at the office expecting a call from Erica. Instead, he answered a call from Albert Boulet, who asked if he was satisfied with photo placement. "Couldn't be better." Mace told him, "and I owe you."

"Forget it. Several reporters have been trying to get a statement from the fellow but can't locate him. Any ideas?"

"Probably gone to ground," Mace replied, pleased with his double entendre.

"Yes, I suppose that's the answer. In his position that's what I would do."

"Hold on—as I recall it he was supposed to have an office in Monte Carlo."

"Sounds like a good lead, I'll pass it along. And thanks again."

"Thank you."

As he rode to the safe house he wondered if something had gone wrong and Erica had been arrested with Carlos. In which case, he mused, all their planning and preparation had gone for naught.

From time to time he phoned Yasmi asking if Erica had called, got the same negative reply. That worried him for it was unlike Erica to ignore a promised contact. So when banking hours ended Mace placed a call to *Maître* Schreiber in Geneva, and asked if he had heard from their client.

"I have. Indeed I have." He cleared his throat. "She telephoned from an unnamed location—long-distance—and asked me to close up the château, not needing it any longer. I am also to pay the servants."

"And you're doing it."

"One of my people is handling details even as we speak."

"Did she indicate where she might relocate?"

"She did not. But I supposed you—"

"There were options, alternatives. Thank you, *Maître*."

"Always glad to be of service, *M'sieu*."

If the price is right, Mace thought as he broke the connection. He should have asked about the Montaners' divorce action, he reminded himself, but decided not to call back.

Working a full day at the computer, Mace sucked twenty-two million from Chakirian accounts, and after totaling all transfers saw that he lacked only fifty-four million for a clean out.

Having brought along Selina's videocassettes, Mace left the safe house and took them to a video specialty shop for duplicating. He waited while the work was done, and when the clerk began wrapping dupes and originals he smirked and said, "Home videos, *hein?*"

"Gifted amateurs," Mace responded, and took the package to his office where he locked all four cassettes in his safe. He was at his desk thinking of ways to spend his wealth enjoyably when he heard

Yasmi answer the telephone. "Mademoiselle Mansour," she said and Mace picked up the receiver. Because Yasmi could overhear him he said, "Hello, how are you? What can I do for you?"

"Mace, I'm calling from a kiosk. It's urgent I see you."

"Oh? When would that be?"

"As soon as you can get there."

"I see. More work for your employer?"

"Tell you when I see you—I'm quite concerned."

"Very well." He glanced at his watch. "Say I'll come now."

She broke the connection, and as Mace replaced the receiver he told Yasmi he would be gone the rest of the day. On a hunch he took the duplicate videos from his safe and brought them to the safe house, where Selina waited. Turning from the printouts, she said, "I don't think we should take anymore."

"Victor's suspicious?"

"I'm afraid so. And I need a drink. It's been a difficult day."

"Cocktail time, anyway." He poured liquor for them and sat beside her on the sofa. "Tell me."

After drinking, she said, "Around eleven Victor told me no one was to disturb him, hold all calls. He locked his office door, and in a few minutes I heard the sound of his printer."

"Hmm. Doing what?"

"I'm convinced he was making interbank transfers and discovered several accounts were empty. Because just when I was leaving for lunch he burst out, wild-eyed, came into my office, and shut the door. He was nearly inarticulate, but told me his bank accounts had been tampered with, asked if I knew anything about it. What could I say? I told him I had no knowledge of his bank accounts." She sipped and looked worriedly at Mace. "Of course I'll deny it to the end but I'm afraid he'll finally focus on me."

"We anticipated that." He pointed at the videocassettes. "First line of defense."

"So far he hasn't threatened me. Tomorrow I expect he'll spend the day checking his accounts. How much is left?"

"About fifty-five million."

"Leave it," she said, "we've got more than enough."

He nodded. "I'll get rid of all equipment and printouts, keep only our own records. He could place holds on all his accounts, have any transfer attempts reported to him." He sipped thoughtfully. "What's done is done and our transfers can't be traced." He gazed at the computer. "From now on I assume they will be."

"What shall I do? Leave Paris?"

"That would only feed his suspicions. No, wait until he threatens you, that would give you motive for leaving."

"That could be very soon."

"Unfortunately. So let's decide how best to protect you. Is there a VCR in your offices?"

She shook her head.

"Then you'll have to get him to your place. Pretending to be furious at his impudence could get him there. He'll be expecting a brutal whipping. Instead, show him a tape and tell him your lawyer has others with instructions to give them to porno houses should you vanish or be harmed. And continue denying any responsibility for his loss—it can never be proved. Offer him the tapes to prove your lawyer has copies."

"Yes, that would convince him." She rose and walked distractedly around the room until she stopped and turned. "The final confrontation between incestuous father and daughter. Mace, the thought thrills me but it chills me, too. Among other things I'll say I'm glad he was robbed—he robbed me of my childhood, years that should have been my happiest. And his cruelty killed my mother." Her eyes glinted in anticipation.

"Should be quite a scene."

"You could be there—watching, protecting me if he gets violent."

He shook his head. "If he sees us together he'll think conspiracy and I have further plans for him that won't involve you."

"You mean—Montaner."

"That's my scene, not yours. Besides, you can protect yourself. Kick him in the balls, slash his face—you know what to do."

"I suppose I do," she sighed. "For years I feared him, but not now, not anymore."

He got up and refilled their glasses. "After dark we'll remove the equipment using my car. Take it across the river, dump it there." He drank. "Someone is going to be awfully lucky tonight."

She smiled. "I feel so much better now that we've talked—as I always do. Will you be leaving Paris?"

"Not for a while."

"From time to time would you travel to meet me?"

He nodded, and her fingers traced his lips. "I confess," she said, "that hearing your voice, seeing your eyes watch me is exciting. I get wet thinking about you." She began undoing her blouse, freeing her breasts. "I want you now."

After dinner they drove his BMW to the safe house and carried down the computer equipment. From there Mace and Selina went to his office where they shredded the banking printouts, and he placed their account records in his safe. In a dark Left Bank alley they unloaded the computer equipment, then returned to the safe house where they checked carefully for any traces of computer work.

They had a nightcap together, while the upstairs couple began a pulsating lovers' serenade.

Later that night, alone in his bed, Mace wondered if the Chakirian project was beginning to fray and come apart. Victor had become aware of account drainage sooner than expected, and he speculated over what the old man might do. Well, time would tell. Mace turned over, closed his eyes and thought about Erica.

Apparently she was lingering in Divonne and it irritated him that he had learned indirectly. She should have phoned in the morning, confirming Carlos's safe passage. Instead, she'd phoned Schreiber about the Château du Cerf. That was reasonable under the circumstances, he told himself, and if the buried body was ever found there were no clues connecting her, Carlos, or himself to the anonymous corpse. Aside from Natsos only Carlos knew what had occurred, and Mace assumed the Spaniard would keep his mouth shut in his travels. Carlos had everything to gain from silence, Bradley Mason being his sole hope of vindication.

He was drifting into sleep when the bedside telephone rang. Answering, he heard Erica's voice. "Did I wake you, darling?"

"Almost. How did things go?"

"Very well, no problems at all."

"Terrific. So why didn't you call me?"

"I didn't earlier because I was simply exhausted from everything that's been happening. And I slept late. Forgive me?"

"Of course—where are you?"

"Home. How long should I stay?"

"Oh, two weeks or so. I've heard nothing about the passage but expect a firestorm when it breaks."

"Yes, the environmentalists are sure to form an opposition."

"Wish you were here."

"So do I."

"Now that I know all's well with you I won't be calling for a while. Enjoy a long rest, dear."

"You, too."

That afternoon Pascal Covici telephoned and said, "I'm just back from a short trip, *amico*, and I want you to know that my principals are well pleased with the—ah, restoral. They are grateful to you."

"Unnecessary—I did the right thing."

"True. And enhanced my position. Also, I have been instructed to be at your disposition for whatever service you may require."

"You've already offered your villa."

"A small gesture. Something more serious."

"I see. Well, that may come sooner than I expected."

"*Amico*, you have only to let me know."

Mace hung up, thinking how useful it could be to have The Brotherhood's vast resources available. He had done for them what they could not do for themselves, placing them under obligation to reciprocate. With their backing, he mused, he could have accomplished more in Nicaragua. Only in Cuba, thirty-five years ago, had they accepted defeat.

That night Mace took Selina to dine at the Rotisserie Normande on Rue Saint-Lazare whose specialty was spit-roasted chicken *aux herbes*. Toward ten they left the restaurant and were walking toward a taxi stand when Mace heard his name called. Halting, he turned and peered at a curbside car, a black late model Mitsubishi. The door

283

opened and he saw retired army colonel Forbes Paxton beckoning. To Selina Mace said, "I'll see what he wants," and walked to the car. "Haven't seen you in a while, Forbes."

"That's so. We need to talk."

"About what?"

"Business."

"Yours or mine?"

"Both." His graying mustache twitched. Mace noticed that his face was flushed as though from drinking. "Call me tomorrow," Mace told him, and turned to gesture at Selina. "Can't keep a lady waiting."

"Afraid you'll have to."

Mace looked back, saw a pistol pointing at him.

twenty-seven

The Ride

Get in," Paxton ordered. "You drive." He moved to the passenger side. Mace looked at Selina and shrugged. "Sorry," he said, and got behind the wheel.

"Now, start the engine," Paxton said in a patronizing tone, "and engage the gears. See—the car moves ahead." As Mace steered from the curb he felt the pistol muzzle in his ribs. "By the way," Paxton said, "are you carrying?"

Mace grunted. "On a dinner date? What's this about, Forbes?"

"Just keep driving."

"Where?"

"Bois de Boulogne. Quiet there. Won't be disturbed."

"Anything you say." He took Friedland to the Etoile, and out Neuilly to the edge of the park.

"Pull over—there." Paxton pointed at a dark stretch of road. Mace slowed and braked. Turned off the engine. "What business is so urgent it couldn't wait?" He faced Paxton's weathered features, thin, set lips.

"You've taken it upon yourself to interfere in my business disruptively—and I want to know why." He edged back against the door, pistol pointing menacingly.

"I don't understand, Forbes. What business? What interference?"

"Before that, let me say, I believe you were responsible for my mugging. Right? Those hoods were looking for you, not me."

"Possibly," Mace replied. "I deal with a lot of strange people, not all have brilliant minds. Can we go now?"

"Not so fast. We'll set aside the mugging and get to the real issue. When did you last see Ed Natsos?"

"Ed? Not sure. Week or two. Why?"

"We had a meeting set for this morning only he didn't show. I called his office and got a mysterious reply."

"Like what?"

"Oh, that he hadn't come in. By day's end he still hadn't appeared. I go to his house and the servants haven't seen him since Saturday."

"So?"

"Saturday morning he called me, said he was flying to Geneva for a chat with you, taking along a friend."

"Maybe he lied."

"I don't think so."

Mace felt his throat getting dry. "Ask the friend where he is."

Paxton shook his head. "Can't. He hasn't shown either. So what I want to know—on pain of death—is where are my partners?"

"Partners?"

"Yeah. Ed and me, we formed a triumvirate with Frederic Lanoix, also known as Yuri Chesnikov. We had business plans, very big, profitable ones. A client of yours was going to put up enough money to buy control of the most corrupt country in the world, a little three-island nation in the Caribbean—Antigua. I spent time there, had everything laid on."

"Yeah? Who's this supposed client of mine?"

"Victor Chakirian."

"Jesus, Forbes, this is way beyond me. Ed gave me a file extract on Lanoix that I passed to Chakirian. One job only. How does that involve you—or me? I don't get it."

Paxton sighed. "I'll put it this way and I'm not going to waste time on you. Chesnikov got it into his head that you had him beaten up—maybe you saw the newspaper photo?"

"Yeah. I figured he was hustling rough trade—but I had no beef with Chesnikov."

"Let's say Chakirian did—after reading your report. Wanted to eliminate a potential partner, save possible embarrassment."

"This is getting pretty speculative, Forbes."

"I deal with the facts as I know them, see where they lead. Our sense was that Chakirian hired you to do a job on Chesnikov, so Chesnikov wanted to—let's say—do you in. That's why they went to Geneva."

"Guess I'm lucky they didn't find me. I wasn't staying at a hotel, Forbes. I spent the weekend at a lakeside château. No way they could locate me. Not even my secretary knew where I was."

"Why not?"

"I'm not accustomed to letting her know my weekend activities, no reason to."

Paxton's free hand rubbed the side of his face. "Who were you staying with?"

"If you must know, the Countess de Montaner, okay? She's a client. The Château du Cerf, far side of the lake, near Vésenaz."

Paxton's expression was troubled. "I'd halfway believe you if I didn't know you as a slippery bastard. You made it all the way to Guat City through a goddamn jungle that would have killed anyone without your balls."

Mace smiled. "I had a gun."

"And so have I." He gestured with it. "So my situation is this: I had two partners ready to develop a really profitable business with Chakirian's backing, and suddenly they're not to be found. Any ideas how that came to be?"

Mace considered the question. "Follow the money is a time-proven rule. Chakirian had the money, according to you, so it's not beyond the bounds of reason your two partners decided to slough you off and make their own deal with Chakirian. Ed was money-hungry, told me so, and that's no secret from you. And while we're characterizing players, Ed was pretty slippery himself, but I can't believe he'd be an accomplice in murder—my murder. He'll show up eventually. My guess is he and Chesnikov are holed up in some Geneva hotel with a couple of Swiss broads, drinking and fucking the time away. Ed would go for that—as long as Yuri paid the bills."

"You're fucking with my mind, Mace, you talk too damn much."

"Hell, Forbes, you asked if I had any ideas." Shrugging, he turned to face the window as a car with dim lights slowly passed. "By now my date must be pretty worried. I don't want her all chilled-out when I get back. That would disrupt *my* plans. Tell you what, Forbes, let's head back and forget the bullshit—I won't hold it against you."

Paxton's eyes narrowed. "If only I believed you were telling the truth . . ."

"Well, parley with Ed, check it all out. I'm not leaving Paris, I'll be around if you're not satisfied. I'd like to help you, I really would, because you did good things for me in Guat City—for a while. I don't forget favors."

For a while silence was unbroken until Paxton said, "Maybe you're not jerking me around, maybe you've told it like it is. I don't know. But you've given me a lot to think about."

"There's something you maybe overlooked: Airline passenger lists would tell you when they got back to Paris."

"Shit, there's twenty airlines flying between here and Geneva."

"So you make twenty phone calls, big deal." He sucked in a deep breath. "Beyond that I can't help you."

"Your restaurant date—Chakirian's secretary, right?"

Mace shrugged. "We stopped by for tofu and grits. So what?"

"That ties you to her boss." The pistol shifted in his hand.

"Negative. We keep it from him, the old guy's madly jealous. He'd have me mugged like Chesnikov if he found out. And she'd lose a damn good job."

Paxton grunted. "With her looks and figure she'd be unemployed fifteen minutes max." He shook his head. "You've got the countess *and* the secretary and you don't look all that special to me. How the hell do you do it?"

"Hypnosis. Now you know my secret let's get outa here."

Paxton shook his head. "Sorry. I've decided I'm not going to get more from you and I've told you too much about our three-way deal. Can't have you blabbering to the embassy, understand? Get out of the car, very easy, and step over there by the trees."

"Whatever you say." He got out, turning away while he pulled the Beretta from its shoulder holster. Watched Paxton get out on the other side, and knelt beside the hood, both hands resting on it, covering Forbes Paxton. "Drop the gun, Forbes," he barked, "and look at mine."

He thought the colonel would do it. Instead, Paxton gave him a startled look, whipped up his pistol, and fired. The bullet grazed the hood and whined off. Mace ducked as Paxton fired again, then snap-shot at the shoulder to bring him down. Paxton staggered back, fling-ing his arms in the air. The pistol spun upward and Paxton fell on his back, one hand clawing at his throat. Mace went quickly to him, saw blood pumping out between his fingers, and knelt by his head. The eyes moved to focus on Mace, became dull. The blood flow stopped. Mace pulled aside the bloody hand and saw a small hole in the throat. He pressed the neck carotid and felt nothing. Retired Colonel Forbes Paxton, USA, was dead.

Shakily, Mace stood up, holstered the Beretta and opened the car door to turn on the dimmers. He found his ejected cartridge case, pocketed it, and turned off the lights. Then he dragged Paxton's body far into the trees and laid the colonel's pistol nearby.

He drove out of the Bois, mind groping for a durable solution. When it came to him he turned south and crossed the river, taking the sequential boulevards that girdled the city. When he reached Charenton railway yards he steered the Mitsubishi into a parking lot used by night workers, wiped his prints from steering wheel, gearshift and keys, and laid the keys on the front seat. He closed the unlocked door and walked away, hoping the car would be stripped by morning.

He walked a quarter of a mile through the dark industrial section to the Daumesnil Métro station. From there a train took him to the Concorde station, where he emerged on the Champs-Elysées. He stopped at a brasserie for a *fine café* with an extra shot of cognac. Feel-ing calmer, braced, he phoned Selina's apartment. She answered on the second ring, breathed in relief when she heard his voice. "Par-don the interruption," Mace said cheerfully. "I—"

"But that man—why did you go with him?"

"There was a misunderstanding, cleared up now. Sorry I left you there—at least it wasn't raining."

"No." She managed a strained laugh. "It wasn't. So I waited a few minutes and found a taxi. Very worried about you."

"I can understand why." He looked at the wall clock. "Not yet midnight."

"I was undressing for bed but I'd love to see you, reassure my-self . . . Can you come?"

"Glad you asked."

She met him at the door, champagne glasses in hand, and kissed him. "Let's drink to your safe return. *Mon amour,* I was truly worried." Their glasses touched and she sipped. "Did it have anything to do with Victor? Me?" She was wearing a long black silk robe gathered above her full hips with a silver cord.

He shook his head. "Concerned another client. I straightened him out, and here I am."

"I didn't like the tone of his voice—did I catch sight of a gun?"

"Cigarette lighter. What's under the robe?"

"Me." She parted it briefly exposing thighs and dark delta. "Am I overdressed?"

"I'd say so." He got out of his jacket, draped it over the back of a chair. Drew off his shoulder holster and laid it on the seat.

"Do you feel naked without it?"

"No."

"How do you feel then?"

"Disarmed." He unknotted his tie, unbuttoned his shirt. She leaned over and kissed his nipples. Her lips sent a thrill through his body. He took her in his arms and kissed her deeply, felt himself entering safe refuge after the trauma of death.

As she moved against him he undid the silver cord and loosened the robe from her body until it lay in a dark pool at their feet. He clasped her body and lowered it to the carpet where she waited until he was naked, too.

Later, as they lay side by side, she murmured, "There was more to it than you told me, wasn't there?"

"More to what?" he parried.

"That man—the 'misunderstanding'."

When he said nothing she persisted. "Wasn't there?"

Finally, he said, "Very little."

"But you knew the man—he called your name."

Wearily he said, "I met him in Nicaragua a long time ago. Tonight had nothing to do with you." He turned and kissed her breast. "He recognized you, so he must have called on Victor, looking for business."

"What kind of business?"

"Anything he could scrape together." Rising, he drew her to her feet, led her to the bedroom. In the dark he held her hand and said, "There's an old story you may have heard. It tells of a man who prayed to the Lord to give him land. The Lord said he could have all the land he could run around in one day between dawn and sunset. So the man began running, east, south, west, north, and as the sun set he reached the place where he began. There he collapsed and died."

"So?"

"All the land he needed was a plot six feet by two—for his grave."

She was silent for a while, then, "It has something to do with us?"

"With me. I don't need half of eight hundred million, *chérie*, don't even want it. Oh, I'll keep enough to do a few things I want to do, but the rest . . . don't need it."

She kissed his cheek gently. "You've thought that all along, haven't you? So why did you—?"

"Chakirian is evil, you know that. And Carlos de Montaner is suffering for Victor's crime. That's very wrong. What I've wanted was to cripple Chakirian, expose him, and set Carlos free." Slowly he stroked her flank. "You get revenge."

"Yes," she replied, "but for you it isn't over."

"Not yet."

She kissed his cheek tenderly. "I'll help you any way I can." Lying back, she gazed at the dark ceiling. "Today Victor acted really crazy, shouting and stomping around his office. I think it's dawned on him how much he's lost."

"Accuse you again?"

"I could see it in his face, his eyes. But he said nothing."

"Bad sign," Mace told her, "so the next move must be yours."

"Using the tapes—how soon?"

"What time is it?"

She shrugged. "One—two . . ."

"Tonight."

Mid-morning, Mace took a call from Peke Parmalee, who asked, "Mace, what can you tell me about Ed Natsos?"

"Ed? Oh, sort of an average fellow, mentally not too savvy—but, hell, Peke, I hardly know the guy. He works for you."

"Yeah," he said sourly, "or did. I asked the wrong question. What I mean is: Can you tell me where he is?"

"Must be two, three weeks since he stopped by. No, Peke, can't help you." He paused. "Is Ed, ah—missing?"

"Uh-huh. Left a letter of resignation and apparently just took off."

"His wife ought to know."

"Separated over a year, lives in Canton, Ohio."

"I see. Not likely she'd know. What about Ed's house?"

"We checked—Monday he paid the housekeeper. Period."

"Very strange. Well, if I see or hear of him I'll let you know."

"Appreciate it," the Paris COS replied. "Oh—one other thing—remember Colonel Paxton—Forbes Paxton?"

"How could I forget him? He helped me in Guatemala City a bunch of years ago. Forbes came by the office a while back—it was never clear why he came. Ah—don't tell me he's missing, too."

"Not anymore. Body found in the Bois. Apparently he fired his pistol and took a bullet in return. The defense attaché is trying to keep it out of the papers."

"Poor Forbes—robbery?"

"Looks like it. Car can't be found."

"Jesus, our little town is sounding more and more like Miami."

"Ain't it the truth? Thanks for your time, Mace, but I'm checking all bases."

"Anytime, Peke." He broke the connection and sat back in his chair. So Ed was gone, and Forbes was found; the equation balanced. But someone in the embassy could theorize a connection between Paxton's murder and Ed's disappearance, only to find it couldn't be proved. Anyway, Natsos was probably back in Amarillo, where he came from, Mace mused, and pushed thoughts of both men from his mind.

Lunching alone, Mace thought of Erica and hoped their separation would not be prolonged. Meanwhile, she was at her parents' home, safe from surveillance and insulated from the assorted threats that had become the dark side of her life in Paris. All that would end when Carlos's innocence was established and Chakirian's guilt revealed. By now Carlos should be thousands of miles from his Geneva prison, making his way unaided for the first time in his life. As for Chakirian *(Daddy, Have You Humped Your Kid Today?)* tonight at the hands of his ravished daughter he would suffer the beginning of retribution.

When Selina came to the safe house at six Mace found her nervous and uneasy until, after drinks, he said, "Look, if you're concerned about confronting Victor I'll be there, out of sight, listening. In case he—"

"No, I'm not afraid of him, but I've never stood up to him before. It's—it's going to be strange." She walked around the sofa and came back. Drank deeply. "If I were afraid, I'd want you there. But I really want to do it alone, have that satisfaction."

He nodded and took her hand. "When's he coming?"

"At ten. I wanted it to be earlier but he said he had to attend a meeting."

Not with Chesnikov, Mace thought; not tonight, not ever, and said, "I'll be at my place expecting your call."

"From now on we won't need to hide ourselves. Let's start tonight, dine where *tout Paris* can see us."

That meant the Eiffel Tower restaurant high above the city where they could view the lights of all Paris far below.

* * *

293

Mace left Selina at her apartment building and taxied to his own. Entering his office door, he noticed that the time was slightly after nine. He got his bank account record sheets from his safe and began going over them to review how much he had on deposit and where. As he made rough notes he realized that he felt no sense of power or exaltation. So far the figures were only that. It was going to take a while before the reality sank in that he commanded a multimillion dollar fortune. Meanwhile, the question tugging at his mind was: what to do with it?

At ten-thirty his desk phone rang and he picked it up, mind still flooded with figures and only remotely aware that it could be Selina's call. Her voice was husky, breathing labored, and Mace felt a chill grip his body. "He fought me," she gasped, "hurt me, please come."

"Yes, yes, but where is he?"

"Here—God, please hurry." The line went dead.

Through light traffic he managed to reach her building in under ten minutes, Beretta in his belt. He unlocked her apartment door, stepped in and locked it. Then he looked around.

Her television set lay smashed on the floor, the broken VCR surrounded by yards of pulled-out videocassette tape. Chakirian had not taken entrapment lightly. Mace drew his pistol and crossed the white carpeting toward her bedroom and bath.

Under dim light he saw Selina lying on the bed. There were spots of blood on the coverlet and on the tourniquet around her left arm. As he hurried to her he saw more blood on her blouse. Seeing him, she began to sob convulsively. Suddenly there was pounding on the bathroom door. "There—" she pointed—"he's in there."

"Let me out," Chakirian's voice yelled. *"Damn you, let me out!"* Mace went to the door, turned the bolt, and jerked open the door. Knife in hand, Chakirian lunged at him until Mace fired one shot above the enraged man. When Chakirian froze, Mace knocked the knife from his hand and kicked it toward the bed.

"You," Chakirian gasped, "so it was *you!*" There were red stripes on his face from Selina's fingernails. One hand touched them. "She blackmailed me," he cried, "but I wouldn't have it. Let me out of here!"

Mace shoved the pistol in his belly. "You don't give orders here. Down on your knees."

Slowly, Chakirian sank to the floor, bowed his head submissively. Mace slammed the barrel against his skull and the man fell forward with a grunt and a sigh. His white blouse was marked with blood. Mace locked the door again and went back to Selina, turned on bright lights, and tore the dress from her shoulders.

Just below her left breast bright blood marked a slanting gash, and there was a nick in her throat. She had torn a sheet for the arm tourniquet and he tore more strips from it and loosened the tourniquet. The knife slash was about three inches long. He fashioned a fresh tourniquet and tightened it around her arm, then folded a pad and pressed it against the rib cut to staunch bleeding. He kissed her lips and felt them almost chill, realized she was close to shock.

From the bar he brought a raki bottle and filled a glass. "Drink it," he ordered, "all of it," and ripped more strips from the sheet.

When he opened the bathroom door Chakirian's position had shifted. Mace pulled both arms behind his back and tied his wrists together, then bound his slippered feet at the ankles. Leaving the door open so he could watch Chakirian, he returned to Selina and propped her upright with pillows. Slowly she finished the last of her glass. He went to the bar again and half-filled it, poured vodka into another, and gulped it down. While Selina sipped he said, "You're going to be fine—a few stitches, and—"

"But Victor," she interrupted, "what about him?"

"He won't hurt anyone for a while."

"Then I want to tell you what hap—"

"Later," he said sternly. "Loosen the tourniquet for thirty seconds and tighten it again. Now listen to me." He breathed deeply. "That man in there is more dangerous than ever before. Something has to be done with him, and—"

"*Kill him!*" she shrilled.

"I'm not ready for that, and I need him alive." He glanced at the night table phone and nodded thoughtfully, then picked up the receiver, searching his mind for Covici's telephone number. He dialed. The phone rang three times before the manservant answered. Mace gave his name and said, "It's urgent I speak with *Signor* Covici."

"The *Signor* has retired," the servant said stiffly.

"Wake him or he'll cut off your balls—or I will. Now, do it."

While waiting, he tightened Selina's arm tourniquet, then heard Covici's voice. "Mace, this is unexpected. Is there something I can do for you?"

"I need a doctor—a person of confidence—help from two of your men, and your plane."

"Of course. Where are you?" His voice was calm, unhurried. Mace gave him Selina's address and said, "We need the doctor first, there's some bleeding . . ."

"I understand. Leave everything to me."

After hanging up, Mace turned to Selina, who said, "Pascal Covici?"

He nodded. "He's going to return our favor."

She wet her lips. "You mean—the five million?"

"Exactly. So far it's our best investment. How are you feeling?"

She smiled wanly. "Better because you're here—much better. But I feel weak, trembly."

"Pain?"

"The raki helps."

Chakirian rolled over on his back and began shouting for help. Mace tore off a length of sheet, folded it into a wad and forced it between Chakirian's teeth. Then he wound a strip around his head to keep it in place. Bending close to Chakirian's ear he said, "There's a chance you can live if you behave yourself." He looked at his watch, hoping the doctor would arrive before the others. Then he sat beside Selina, loosened her tourniquet and held her hand. She said, "When he saw us on the TV screen he went crazy—you saw what he did—then he got out a knife and began slashing at me." Her eyes closed and she shuddered. "I got him in the bathroom for bandages and locked him there." She swallowed. "What would I do without you?"

"We'll have time to talk about it," he told her, as the doorbell sounded.

Carrying his Beretta, Mace went to the door and unlocked it, let in a short man with a thin black mustache and swarthy skin. No shirt, a pajama top tucked into his waist, under a jacket. He carried a black physician's bag. "Where is the patient?"

Mace led him into the bedroom, closed the bathroom door on Chakirian whose eyes were wild with rage and fear.

With economy of motion the physician got to work cleansing the wounds. He had Mace hold Salina's left hand while he stitched the slash in her upper arm. She winced and closed her eyes, shivering from needle pain, then the doctor examined the cut under her breast. He closed it with butterfly clips and attended to the nick in her throat. "Close," he said in a low voice, "very close," and dusted all wounds with antibiotic powder before bandaging them neatly. Sitting back, he looked up at Mace. "I could use a drink," he said, and Mace brought him iced vodka, had one himself. "What the patient needs," said the physician, "is rest." He stood up. "No charge. Compliments of our friend."

"Thank you. There's one other thing, doctor. The man who did the knifing is in there." He gestured at the bathroom door. "I'd like you to check his heart and blood pressure—after I've blindfolded him."

"Of course. The examination will only be superficial, you understand."

Mace nodded. "I want to know if he's strong enough to travel tonight. The man is excitable and noisy, so we'll all be more comfortable if he's asleep."

"First, the examination." He waited while Mace blindfolded Chakirian with a strip of sheet, then went in and knelt to apply the inflatable cuff and stethoscope. After a while, he deflated the cuff, rolled and returned it to his bag, left the bathroom with Mace.

"His heart is borderline," the physician said when they were in Selina's bedroom again, "and his pressure is abnormally high. Of course, part of that may well be attributable to being bound and apprehensive." He opened his bag, got out a hypodermic syringe and a small vial of clear liquid. After knocking off the end he filled the syringe partway and eyed Mace. "If the man were my father I would not risk it, so I'll compromise. The injection will keep him sedated for perhaps three hours. Is that sufficient?"

"Better than nothing," Mace replied. "Jab him."

When the physician returned he said, "Done," and asked, "Anything else, *M'sieu?*"

"Pain pills for Madame."

From his bag he took out a small bottle and poured half a dozen pills into an envelope. "Two now, two every three hours—but no alcohol." He bent over Selina and, for the first time, smiled. "Madame, do not be concerned about scars. Any competent cosmetic surgeon can restore you as you were."

"Thank you, doctor. I'm grateful for everything you've done," she said politely.

"I am happy for the opportunity to be of service to so beautiful a woman," he said gallantly, and walked with Mace to the door. "I'm grateful, too," Mace told him as they shook hands.

"Then if you are satisfied with my actions, you might care to tell our—ah—mutual friend."

"Gladly." Mace let him out and relocked the door. At the bar he poured a glass of Evian and took it to Selina, who swallowed two pills and lay back. "You spoke of travel, Mace. Tonight? Where are we going?"

"You'll know when we get there." He looked at his watch. Where were Covici's men?

"What about Victor?"

"Oh, he goes with us. Can't leave him in Paris just now. When he's more receptive I'll reason with him, discuss his future—and ours. Now, while we have a few moments, did he accuse you of robbing his accounts?"

"No, as I told you he saw a few feet of the tape and went insane. He accused me of trying to blackmail him, suck his blood, like my mother—" She broke off, lips trembling, and looked away. Finally she gathered enough composure to say, "It was dreadful, frightful—it really was—seeing him come apart like that. His face—it looked a thousand years old. The hate-filled face of a maniac . . . the knife in his hand . . . I was terrified."

After a while she said, "If I'm to travel I want to get a few things together, change to another dress. So help me off the bed."

A brave woman, he thought, who took life as it came, and watched her pack a cosmetic kit and a small overnight bag. He helped her into a dark, two-piece pants suit, and fitted a change of shoes on her feet. "There," she smiled, "that's better, much better. If we're waiting, let's wait in the living room." He helped her to the sofa and was making her comfortable when the doorbell sounded.

Pistol in hand, Mace opened the door, saw two well-dressed men in their mid-thirties. The fair-skinned one asked, "A removal problem, *M'sieu?*"

"In the bathroom." Mace led them to where Chakirian lay unconscious. "He's alive," Mace told them, "but very sleepy. I like him better that way."

With Selina beside him Mace carried her bags to the elevator and held open the door, while Covici's men carried Chakirian inside. Then he went back to lock the apartment door before riding to the street where he saw Covici's waiting limousine. The driver opened the trunk and helped fit Chakirian into it, then closed the trunk and got behind the wheel. Both men sat on the front seat beside him and the limo pulled away.

Selina's head lay against his shoulder and he felt her body relax. "Where are we going?" she asked, and Mace repeated her quiet question to the driver. "Orly," he said, and she nodded, satisfied, saying, "The service is marvelous, don't you think?"

"Shows what a few million can do—in the right hands."

The driver turned south and crossed the river into the Latin Quarter, picking up the Route Nationale at Villejuif, with its signs pointing toward Orly. Presently Mace realized that Selina was sleeping, exhausted from fear and tension, soothed by the doctor's pills.

The driver entered the airport by the General Aviation gate and drove onto the tarmac, toward a gleaming white Hawker 125 executive jet. Its interior lights were on, showing pilot and copilot in the cockpit, and the clam-shell stair-door was down to receive them. When the limousine braked a man got out and hurried into the jet. Presently he reappeared, followed by Pascal Covici. Mace got out and went to where he was waiting. "The doctor did a fine job on Selina and we thank you."

"Selina?"

"Selina Mansour."

"I see. I thought you might have been shot." He gestured at the plane. "Where do you want to go?"

"Punta di Volpe, if that's convenient."

"Entirely. As you know, my place is at your disposition."

"The man who knifed Selina is in the trunk. He'll come with us so I can converse with him in tranquil surroundings. The doctor was accommodating enough to give him a pacifying injection."

Covici nodded. "Excellent idea. May I ask his name?"

"He's one of your fellow directors, Varti Chakirian."

Covici glanced at the limousine. "Chakirian, eh? He would be the one who—?"

"The guilty party. Stole IFT funds and framed Count Carlos de Montaner. You may have some questions to put to him—I won't mind."

"Questions, yes. So if it is agreeable to you we will all go together. In any case I had thought to accompany you to make sure you were comfortable at the villa. Will Mademoiselle Mansour require a physician?"

"She will."

"Then when we are airborne I will radio ahead to have everything in readiness for our arrival." He looked at Mace and there was a faint smile on his lips. "Chakirian—I should have known, but it took you to expose him." He beckoned to the waiting man and presently the trunk opened and Chakirian's limp frame was lifted out and carried into the plane. That done, Mace woke Selina and helped her from her seat. She stood groggily beside him while she reoriented herself, and Covici approached. "Mademoiselle, my extreme regret for what befell you. I am Pascal Covici, at your service." He lifted her hand briefly to his lips.

"Thank you," Selina smiled. "The service has been of extraordinary quality." She looked around. "Victor?"

"On board," Mace told her, and with Covici at her other side they helped Selina up the stairs and into the cabin.

The interior was lavishly fitted, with galley, table, and a pair of pull-down bunk beds. Selina chose a reclining chair and settled into it, while Mace and Covici buckled in nearby.

Machinery hummed, the clam-shell door rose and closed, and a jacketed steward secured it from inside. One jet engine whined into life, then the second. Presently the plane pivoted and turned toward the flight line.

Covici said, "May I offer you a drink? Something to eat?" He looked at Selina, who shook her head. "Not just now," she said sleepily, yawned, and closed her eyes. Mace said, "I'll drink with you," and as the plane moved into takeoff position the steward took drink orders.

The Hawker gathered speed down the runway and lifted off smoothly. Mace glanced out at the receding lights of Paris and raised his glass to Covici's. After a sip of strega the Sard said, "Depending on night winds, we should be able to see Mont Blanc in an hour. Another hour will bring us to my island." He sipped again. "So now, my friend, perhaps you will tell me what all this is about?"

twenty-nine

The Villa

The plane flew southeast above cottony clouds bleached by moonlight, and by the time it entered Lyon flight control Mace had summarized for Covici how his work for the Montaners had positioned him against Chakirian. While Selina slept nearby, Mace told the Sard as much as he thought would satisfy him, withholding Selina's incestuous relationship to Chakirian, and how Selina and he had drained Victor's secret accounts.

"A remarkable story," Covici remarked, and asked the steward for coffee. "What remains for you is clearing the count."

"For that I need Victor's cooperation," Mace replied.

"Doubtless you have the means in mind."

"I do."

The steward set their demitasses on the table, and Mace noticed that the coffee surface showed hardly any vibration. Covici said, "We're in luck." He pointed to windows along the left side of the cabin and Mace saw the distant peak of Mont Blanc rising through a layer of clouds, coldly pure in the moonlight. As the plane bore on Covici said, "At the risk of impropriety I am going to pose an intimate question."

Mace sipped from his cup and set it down. "Go ahead."

"Do you and the Countess de Montaner have—I put this as delicately as possible—an understanding?"

"I believe so."

"You and Selina?" He glanced at her sleeping face.

"Companions—more than friends. I care for her, I believe she cares for me." He looked through the windows but Mont Blanc was no longer to be seen. "That answer you?"

"It does. Where is the countess?"

"With her parents in Denmark."

"And the count?"

Mace shrugged. "I don't know where he might be."

"But probably not in Switzerland."

"Probably not," Mace agreed, adding, "A divorce is under way."

Covici smiled. "Then I wish you much happiness. I myself am an advocate of marriage. For five years I have been a widower—my wife died in a speedboat explosion off Nice. I thought then and now that my death was intended, not hers. A heavy burden to carry."

Mace nodded understandingly and for a while they were silent. The steward collected cups and saucers and told Covici that they were leaving the coast of France. "Presently," Covici remarked, "we will begin descending over the Mediterranean to land at Olbia." He looked at his gold Rolex wristwatch. "Very soon."

Selina stirred, opened her eyes briefly, and closed them again. Covici said, "A very handsome woman who I suspect is as intelligent as she is beautiful. You have not told me why Chakirian attacked her."

"I'm not entirely sure myself," Mace lied. "Perhaps she will tell you—but I don't think we should make things difficult for her. She's gone through a frightening time. Doubtless she would prefer putting it from her mind."

"My natural curiosity," Covici said mildly, "which I will now suppress."

Mace felt the plane begin descending over the dark sea. It would be an instrument landing, he reflected, and at the airstrip Chakirian could be transferred from the aircraft without being seen. Despite all his power and money, Mace thought, the old villain was helpless at last.

Just before landing Mace woke Selina who rubbed her eyes and looked around as the wheels touched lightly down. Covici said, "Welcome to Sardinia, Mademoiselle. Everything will be done to heal you and make you comfortable while you are here."

"Thank you for everything, *Signor*. And please call me by name— Selina."

"Pascal," he said. The aircraft stopped and the clam-shell door wound out and down. "Permit me to help you."

"That would be very kind.

Just under the left wingtip there was a waiting limousine, clone of its Paris mate. Covici helped Selina onto the rear seat and got in beside the driver. Mace sat beside Selina and held her hand. He heard the trunk open for Chakirian's body, it closed, and the limousine accelerated away.

Over rough, unlighted roads the trip to Punta di Volpe took twenty minutes during which Mace heard Chakirian moaning and kicking inside the trunk. Selina heard, too, and smiled wordlessly.

The limousine pulled up in front of a rock face into which steps had been cut. They led to an immense three-story sandstone villa whose interior lights blazed. Below, waves crashed on huge boulders that marked the beach. Mace steadied Selina up the steps to the villa entrance, where Covici joined them. Four uniformed servants waited inside, bowing in greeting as the party moved farther into the foyer. "It's been lonely here," Covici told them, "so I'm glad to have interesting company. Let me show you to your rooms and then I recommend we all sleep. Selina, a noted cosmetic surgeon is on his way from Ajaccio to examine your wounds—I expect he will waken you for that."

"I'll be very glad to see him," she said as they took a winding staircase to the second floor.

"In that case," said Mace, "separate rooms are preferable."

"As you wish," Covici replied. "Meanwhile, Chakirian is lodged below. Do you intend to begin questioning him today?"

"Later," Mace said, "after he's had time to ponder his situation."

"Exactly," Covici responded, and opened a bedroom door. "You will be here, Mace, Selina in the room adjoining." He paused. "It was my wife's. Now, I bid you both good night. You can breakfast in your rooms or on the patio." He left them, and Mace walked Selina to her bedroom. As Covici implied, the room held feminine touches—vanity table, gauzy curtains, a four-poster, canopied bed whose pink coverlet was of silk and lace. Mace helped Selina undress, saw no blood on her bandages, and kissed her good night, turning out lights as he left.

His own room was masculine, with leather furniture and a conventional, thick-mattressed bed. In the large bathroom he rinsed his face at a marble basin, and saw shaving gear, toothbrush and paste laid out on the marble counter. For a moment he contemplated showering, but fatigue surged, and he undressed quickly and got into bed. In the moments before sleep captured his mind he thought of all that had happened since their dinner on the Eiffel Tower, and decided that a few hours working on Chakirian ought to be enough.

What then? he asked himself. After that what do I do with Chakirian? But before his mind could generate any answers a dark cloud enveloped and smothered his thoughts.

He woke gradually to an unfamiliar sound, presently recognizing it as the wash of waves along the beach below. His eyes opened to a dark gray void that he studied before realizing that curtains were depriving his room of light. He felt drugged, groggy, as he made his way to the bathroom; there was a dull, moldy taste in his mouth. He showered, letting steaming water cleanse his mouth and body, and then he shaved, rinsing in cold water.

Almost fully awake, he found his shirt washed and ironed, his suit pressed, and shoes shined. His watch showed the time as close to noon.

Laughter rose from below. He opened the blinds and looked down on the patio. There, beside a buffet table, Covici and Selina were eating. She was wearing a long-sleeved kimono and straw sandals, their host in beach togs. Mace made his way down to them, kissed Selina companionably and filled his plate at the buffet, while a servant poured coffee into his cup. Seated with them, he said, "That was quite a night. Everyone okay?"

"Quite," Covici nodded, and Selina said, "Doctor Alfonsini examined me earlier and feels he should operate before the wounds heal."

"Well, that's good news," Mace said, cutting into a sausage. "How soon?"

"The plan," said Covici, "is to fly to Ajaccio this evening, settle

Selina in his hospital, and operate in the morning. Alfonsini says she can return here the following day to recuperate. He's spending the afternoon with a friend at the Hotel Cala di Volpe."

Mace noticed bright magnolias with deep green leaves along the sandstone walls. Terra-cotta jars of tropical plants decorated the patio's ornate balcony. Below, white foam washed the sand. He drank true espresso and studied the black volcanic boulders that bounded the beach. He felt an atmosphere of relaxed expectancy among Selina, their host, and himself. Offshore a red-and-white speedboat plowed the blue water, arching a white tail astern. Covici asked, "How are you feeling?"

"Better. Rested. The doctor is optimistic?"

"Very," Selina replied. Breeze lifted the hem of her kimono, exposing one molded thigh. The vista, Mace noticed, was not lost on Covici. "It's heavenly here," she continued, "so very unlike the dust and noise of Paris."

"And you may have it all to yourselves," Covici told them. "Business calls me to Paris tomorrow."

"So soon?" Selina exclaimed.

"Actually I can postpone it until you're back from the hospital—if you prefer."

She looked at Mace. "What are your plans?"

"A séance with your—" 'father,' he was going to say, but caught himself and said—'employer.' "As we discussed, Pascal, I'll need a videocam."

"There are two here at the villa. Anything else?"

"One or two men, if you can spare them."

"Easily."

From pines on the hillside around the villa the smoky smell of resin wafted across the patio. Mace inhaled pleasurably, drank more espresso, and decided not to eat more of the food on his plate.

As though anticipating Mace's question, Covici said, "Our other guest has been given food and water. He seems disoriented but aware of his hopeless situation. Repeatedly asks what is happening to him."

"I'll read his palm," Mace said thinly, "tell him what his future holds."

Covici chuckled. "You have a certain way with words."

"He does," Selina concurred, "and means every one of them."

Mace accepted a warm moist cloth from a servant and cleansed hands and lips. "I'd like Chakirian shaved and wearing a clean shirt. Meanwhile I'll check out a videocam and write the old thief's script." He got up and reached for Selina's hand. "You're needed, too," he told her, and they left the table.

Covici produced a Sony videocam from a cabinet, along with a pair of fresh cassettes. Mace sat at a desk and began writing on lined paper, while Selina read over his shoulder. Presently she said, "He'll never speak those lines—he'd rather die."

"You said that before last night but you were wrong. Maybe this time you'll be right." He finished writing, drew a line at the bottom and printed: VARTAN CHAKIRIAN.

As he read what he had written, Mace thought of Carlos de Montaner and wondered where he was, how the pampered count was getting along in the real world. To Selina he said, "This should do it," and got up, turning to Covici who had been watching interestedly. "As soon as Victor is presentable I want him strung up—the way you found me."

"I remember very well. You'll employ the *bastinado*?"

"Don't want his face marked more than it is." He glanced at Selina's long fingernails. Covici left to make preparations and Selina said, "After this, what will happen to Victor?"

"Our host is a man of great experience in these matters. Undoubtedly he will find a way to neutralize your father and insulate us from harm." He touched her arm. "Much pain?"

She shook her head. "The pills make a big difference."

"You have confidence in the surgeon, Alfonsini?"

"He seemed very knowledgeable and efficient. Yes, I'm satisfied he'll do as well as anyone." She smiled wanly. "At least my face isn't damaged."

It must have been a wild scene, Mace mused; father chasing daughter around the apartment, slashing at her, yelling, screaming . . . Well, it was over now; denouement was at hand. He asked, "What's your impression of our host?"

"I'm impressed—seems to be a gentleman, and he's an exceptional host." She looked around. "Imagine having a place like this."

"You can have a dozen like it, twenty, fifty, anywhere in the world."

"I suppose I can," she sighed, "but nothing seems very real."

"I'm glad you'll be staying to recuperate."

"You'll stay, too, won't you?"

"I plan to," he replied and heard Covici approach. He beckoned to them and Mace picked up videocam and cassettes. Selina carried the writing paper and they followed their host down a curving stair-case into the coolness of a wine cellar. Covici opened a heavy door and through the opening they saw Vartan Chakirian suspended by bound wrists from a rafter, body turning slowly. Covici said, "My man will stay if you want him."

"For a while," Mace said and picked up two lengths of split bam-boo from a chair. He had the impression that the chamber had been used before for torture. "Then," said Covici, "I will leave you to deal with the thief."

As Chakirian's body turned he saw Mace and screamed. Covici closed the door, and the blue-shirted man who had attended to Chakirian stepped toward Mace. "How shall it be?" he asked.

"Hold his feet," Mace ordered, and when—despite Chakirian's struggling—the soles were nakedly exposed, Mace struck with the bamboo. Chakirian screamed again. Grimly Mace said, "You ain't felt nothin' yet," and struck repeatedly.

When Chakirian was sobbing convulsively Mace laid down the bamboo and told the man he could leave. Chakirian's body turned slowly in the air. Mace locked the door and lowered Chakirian, sat him in the chair.

While Chakirian watched, fear in his eyes, Mace undid Selina's kimono and let it drop to the packed earth floor. She started to cover her breasts but he pulled away her hands so that she stood naked before them. Mace pointed to the bandages on her body. "These are your doing," he rasped. "Years ago you raped your own daughter, made her life a living hell. Made her your concubine like her mother, tried to kill her. You don't deserve to live."

Chakirian's gaze was fixed on his daughter, whose hips moved slightly, sinuously. Her hands began caressing her breasts. "You don't deserve to live," Mace repeated. "Do you?"

"No."

"Say it."

Hoarsely, fixated on what Selina was doing, Chakirian gasped, "I don't deserve to live."

"But you want to."

"Yes." He licked his lips lustfully.

"Say it."

"I want to live."

Mace turned to Selina, whose hands were stroking her loins. "He accused you of robbing him. Ask him why."

Shoulders moving, Selina murmured, "Why did you accuse me, father?"

"I—I—because I thought no one else could."

"But you were wrong," Mace suggested.

"I was wrong." Cords in his neck stood out. He stared hungrily at Selina's writhing body.

"And you tried to kill her with a knife."

"She tried to blackmail me," he whined.

"By that standard she would have been justified to kill you for raping her."

"Yes," he gasped, "it would have been right."

Mace moved closer to him. "If you leave here alive you are not to harm your daughter, do you understand?"

Chakirian swallowed. "I will never try to harm my daughter."

Selina came around Mace and went to her father. She bent forward, let her swollen nipples brush his face. When he tried to lick them she drew back. "Naughty," she taunted. "I should beat you for that."

Mace pulled her away. "You stole from the International Financial Trust and framed Carlos de Montaner," he said harshly. "Admit it."

Closing his eyes, Chakirian gave out a long sigh. "I stole from the International Financial Trust and framed Count Carlos de Montaner."

Mace laid the written sheet on his bound hands and said, "This is your confession." He picked up the videocam and focused it on Chakirian. "Read it aloud," he ordered, "and look at me."

Slowly Chakirian opened his mouth and began: "I am Vartan Chakirian, a director of the International Financial Trust. I stole nearly eight hundred million dollars from the Trust by electronic means and concealed my theft the same way." He paused, seemed to listen to the camera's low hum, then continued: "To conceal my guilt I diverted fourteen million dollars to Madrid bank accounts of Count de Montaner. Then I arranged to have charges of embezzlement brought against him." He swallowed again, licked his lips. All traces of lust had vanished from his face. Again he read: "As a result of my crime, Count Carlos de Montaner was imprisoned in Geneva, Switzerland. Having made this confession of my own free will, I urge that Count Carlos de Montaner be freed and all charges against him dropped. I will do all in my power to make restitution of the stolen funds. When charged with my crimes I will admit them in open court."

Mace let the camera run a few moments before turning it off. He handed Chakirian a ballpoint pen and said, "Sign."

Chakirian scrawled his signature and Mace took back paper and pen. A vein stood out in the old man's forehead like a blue worm. Mace could see it throb, pulsing with blood; he was breathing heavily. Selina sidled to him and straddled his legs, shoved her breasts lewdly against his face. Whimpering sounds came from her father's throat. She rocked back and forth on his thighs, and Mace knew that he had never seen anything as evilly erotic as the obscene act grotesquely unfolding before him. He felt unwillingly excited, saw from her quickening movements that Selina was excited, too. Absently, he wondered if she was going to climax.

He heard harsh animal sounds tearing from her father's throat; Chakirian leaned back, freeing his face of Selina's smothering breasts, and gasped for breath. But Selina clutched his head and buried it in her breasts. Her face was flushed, taut, intense, her eyes glittered in arousal. Then, from Chakirian's throat came a long, drawn-out squawking sound. His body went limp. Selina cried out and got off him. She backed away and Mace saw Chakirian's glazed eyes. Quickly he felt the man's neck artery, then his heart, shook his head.

"Is—is he—dead?"

He turned to her. "It's what you wanted, why you excited him."

"And you got what you wanted." She picked up the kimono.

He nodded slowly. "We both got what we wanted. So let's leave him in peace."

"Fuck me," she demanded. "Fuck me now!"

"With a corpse nearby?" He shook his head. "I can do a lot of things, Selina, but not that. You killed him for reasons of your own and I don't say it was wrong. I won't judge you because I can't. You have your revenge, cherish it."

"I will," she said hotly. "I will for the rest of my life."

"Enjoy," he told her, went to the corpse and untied the bound wrists. The damp trousers gave off the sharp odor of urine.

Behind him the door opened and he heard Selina walk away.

After a while he touched the damp, white, forehead, said, "You sick bastard!" and went slowly up the stairway to find Covici.

thirty

The Plant

Before an early dinner, while Dr. Alfonsini drank and watched sunset from the patio, Pascal Covici asked Mace and Selina into his study. "While we dine," he said, "the body will be taken from the cold room—where game is hung—and placed in the car trunk. We drive to Olbia airport and the body is put on the plane. Selina, you and the doctor leave us at Ajaccio, while Mace and I fly on to Paris."

Selina looked at Mace. "You're not staying?"

"I have urgent business to attend to."

"But you'll come back?"

He nodded. "Pascal, what happens in Paris?"

"My men will meet us at Orly, take Chakirian's body to his estate at Passy. I've been there, seen the woods surrounding the house. They'll find a convenient place to leave the body. When it's found the theory will be that Chakirian took a stroll in his woods, suffered a heart attack and died there. Autopsy will confirm the cause of death from natural causes." He shrugged. "How does it sound to you?"

"Excellent," Mace replied, and Selina said, "Perfect."

Covici smiled thinly. "I'm not going to pretend remorse for his death, he had a weak heart, and my principals would probably have had him killed, had he survived. Theft of that magnitude requires the strongest reprisal, you understand."

Selina nodded.

Covici asked, "Did he say where the money was hidden?"

"I was going to ask him," Mace said, "but he died before I could."

"Then the IFT shareholders will not be reimbursed." He stroked the point of his chin. "And the only beneficiaries will be the banks where the money is hidden, and Carlos de Montaner."

"So it seems," Mace said indifferently, and glanced at Selina's placid face.

"Well," said Covici, "I wanted to go over these things privately. No need to include the doctor." He looked at his Rolex. "Now let us have dinner."

For the benefit of his Paris guests Covici identified Sardinian dishes as they were served: arugula and tomato salad in olive oil; trout baked in coarse sea salt; brown suckling pig; tubular pasta with gamberoni, and for dessert ricotta and lemon curd with blueberry liqueur. Still gripped by the basement scene, Mace sampled each dish but ate little. Selina, however, ate hungrily, exclaiming over the rich cuisine.

Dr. Alfonsini, a thin, brown-skinned man in his late thirties with dark eyes and hooked nose, seemed absorbed in thought. After coffee they left the table and descended to the waiting limousine.

Already the sea was dark, only a few stars speckled the horizon, the moon had not yet risen.

From Olbia airport they flew the few minutes to Ajaccio, where Selina and the doctor left the plane. She and Mace exchanged brief kisses then Covici confirmed that the plane would return for her in two days. Selina hugged him and entered the doctor's car.

Airborne again, Mace and Covici drank at the table until roused before landing at Orly.

After Chakirian's body had been transferred to the waiting limousine Covici said, "You'll ride with me?"

"Out of your way, I'll take a taxi."

"Very well." He hesitated before saying, "I sense that you do not intend to be at the villa while Selina recovers."

"There's some friction between us. I think she'll be more contented under your care. Selina won't need me, but the countess will."

"It's up to you." Covici told him, "but I must say in all honesty that I find myself strongly attracted to Selina—you understand?"

"What will be, will be." Mace thanked the Sard again and rode with him as far as the airport taxi stand.

Half an hour later he entered his office and went up the stairs, found Su-Su sleeping on his bed. She yawned sleepily, but jumped down when she heard him open a can of food. While the Siamese ate, Mace opened his safe, got out Chesnikov's wallet cards, and shredded them. He placed the videocassette with Chakirian's confession in the safe, intending to duplicate it in the morning. Then he half-filled a glass with cognac and drank as he undressed for bed.

For a while his mind filled with images of all that had occurred over the past forty-eight hours, reprised Chakirian's death scene, and felt repelled by Selina's lascivious urgings. To purge his mind Mace stood at the window gazing out at the lights illuminating the Arc de Triomphe through veils of night mist. He thought of Erica, and dialed her parents' Viborg number, only to hear from her sleepy, irritated mother that her daughter had gone to Paris.

He considered calling Erica's apartment, but decided against waking her. Morning would be soon enough, he thought, went back to bed and sleep.

He woke at eight, took the cassette from his safe and went out for breakfast. When the video store opened at nine Mace handed over the tape for duplication. That done, he taxied up the Champs to the offices of Samuelson Frères, where he was admitted to Jules's office.

The lawyer blinked in surprise as Mace placed a cassette on his desk with Chakirian's signed confession. The lawyer read it and looked up. "So?"

"Vindication for Carlos. It was Chakirian all along."

"Where have you been? I've tried to reach you."

"Out of the country," he replied, and gave Jules the duplicate tape. "For *Maître* Schreiber. Please send it to him."

Jules's finger tapped the desk top. "I'm afraid it's too late to do any good."

"Why?"

"Evidently you haven't heard—Carlos is dead."

"*Dead?*" Shocked, Mace stepped back, found a chair to sit in. "When? How?"

Jules breathed deeply. "It's very sad, tragic, really. It seems Carlos left Geneva sometime last Monday and fled Swiss jurisdiction into France." He looked away. "He got as far as Lyon, took a room under an assumed name—which is why his body was identified only yesterday." He shook his head sorrowfully.

"But—how did he die? When?"

Jules shrugged expressively. "Wednesday afternoon a maid found his body in the bathtub. An electric razor was submerged beside him. Either it fell into the bathwater or Carlos unwisely attempted to shave while bathing." His hands opened and spread. "Accidental death," he said somberly, "just when he was poised to enjoy the fruits of freedom." He touched Chakirian's confession, the videocassette. "I judge you went to a great deal of trouble to secure this for Carlos. Alas, it comes too late. Though it will clear his name postmortem."

Still stunned by Jules's revelations, Mace stared at him silently. Finally he asked, "And Erica?"

"Arrived in Paris yesterday."

"How did she take the news?"

"As women will, she cried. Blames herself for getting him out of prison. Very emotional yesterday. Perhaps today will be different." He looked at his desk clock. "She will be here at eleven to go over various legal matters. Will you stay?"

Mace breathed deeply. "I think not, Jules. I'd rather see her in less formal surroundings."

"As you wish." He picked up the confession. "May I show her this?"

"Yes—it may help her morale."

The lawyer nodded agreement. "In time I'm sure she will appreciate your labors. Tell me—is M'sieu Chakirian likely to recant his confession?"

"I don't think so," Mace replied and left the office. For a while he walked aimlessly, trying to sort things out, stopped at a brasserie for a *fine café*. It seemed atypical of Carlos to use an electric razor, but he could have bought it last Monday when he shopped for clothes. Or Erica pressed it on him . . .

After paying the bartender Mace took a taxi to Schoffman's Banque Suisse-Allemagne, where he withdrew three hundred thousand dollars in bank drafts for fifty and two hundred fifty thousand, the larger in his daughter's name. Schoffman cashed the smaller draft for dollars and Swiss francs as Mace requested. Fingering the larger draft he said, "I want to set up a fund for my daughter's education and expenses, but I don't know how to go about it. Do you have a correspondent bank in the States?"

"In Washington, San Francisco, and New York."

"I want Jeanette to enjoy a life of advantage but I don't want her mother or stepfather to have access to the money."

"Any of our branches can take care of that by means of a trustee-ship," Schoffman told him. "Where is your daughter now?"

"On the East Coast as far as I know. Washington would be nearest."

Schoffman nodded. "The bank trustee will examine payment requests, and if they are reasonable and appear legitimate, payment will be authorized."

"She'll want a horse and riding instructions, ballet lessons, a private school, vacation travel . . ." A lump swelled in his throat. "A good life."

"I will make the necessary arrangements—and I thank you for your trust and confidence."

"You've earned it," Mace said, and left the banker.

On returning to his office, he found Yasmi and Jean-Paul having coffee at the conference table. Yasmi jumped up, exclaiming, "Where have you been? We've been terribly worried. It's not like you to be out of touch so long."

"Various matters," he said vaguely. "You two okay?"

She smiled. "Going over marriage plans."

"Wonderful." He kissed her cheek. "When?"

"July. During *la grande vacance*. Will you come?"

"If humanly possible." He gripped her fiancé's hand warmly. "The very best to you both."

"Thank you, Chief." She paused. "I suppose you'll be getting married, too." When he did not react, she continued: "I mean now that the count is dead and Erica is a widow . . ."

"We haven't discussed it—too early. In fact I haven't even seen her to offer condolences."

"Umm. Following office routine, I should eliminate the Montaner file."

"Just make it 'Inactive,' " he told her, "there could be some loose ends. But, frankly, I'm getting tired of Paris. It can be warm and beautiful, but there's been too much action for too little pay."

"The Secours bank account is very healthy," she observed.

"Good. Yasmi, you handle everything so well, know all the ins and outs of the business that it's occurred to me you might like to be in charge. I'm not fully decided, but I want to leave Paris for a while, perhaps a long while—maybe forever. I don't yet know. But before reaching a decision I'd appreciate your thinking." He paused. "Yours and Jean-Paul's, I meant to say."

She looked at her fiancé before saying, "It would be a wonderful opportunity for us. You mean—we buy you out?"

"I mean take over, no charge." Her face lightened, but before she spoke he said, "Or I could ask Henri Troyat if he's interested in acquiring Secours, with the provision that you, Jean-Paul and Raoul work for Montpelier. But you don't have to decide today, tomorrow will be soon enough."

"Chief—we'll talk it over, of course, and ask Raoul. But I'm sure we'd like to manage Secours. And if you ever decide to come back—"

"If I leave I won't come back. But I want to know your decision before I make my own."

"You are most generous M'sieu," Jean-Paul said. "And where are you thinking of going if I may ask?"

"Someplace the natives are friendly," he replied, and went toward the stairs. Turning, he said, "Part of the deal is caring for Su-Su until I send for her."

"Of course, Chief, she's part of the Secours family."

Mace smiled as he went upstairs.

By now, he thought, as he unknotted his tie, Selina should be out of the operating room, attended by Alfonsini. Tomorrow she was to be flown back to Covici's villa for what, Mace suspected, would be a prolonged recuperation. He pulled off his shirt and stripped to shower.

Although it was only midday Mace lay on the bed and closed his

317

eyes reviewing matters to resolve before he left Paris. He would have Jules's office draw up the papers for a legal transfer of Secours, then leave sufficient capital with Yasmi so she could hire and expand if she cared to. His parting gift to the newlyweds.

The account printouts were in his safe, his and Selina's. He would take them with him for he was unwilling to have her go on a spending spree that could bring official inquiries. Later, perhaps, when both could see things more clearly. Then he reversed himself and decided to cache the printouts with Samuelson Frères, where they would be entirely secure. He had ample travel money, and could draw on his account with Schoffman, as needed.

As yet he had not decided where to go. Maybe Mexico or Canada, look into buying a ranch. Possibly visit the widowed Alaya al-Jamal in Montana, see how young Rashid was getting along.

A thousand possibilities.

First, though, he needed to see the newly widowed Erica Hanson de Montaner. Her husband's death was providential, he reflected, eliminating divorce and clearing her way to all of Carlos's holdings, not just the agreed 40 percent. Under the circumstances the Swiss court might refund the posted two million-dollar bail, enriching her further. Plus the half-million Carlos never had a chance to use.

All in all, Erica would make out like a bandit.

Opening his eyes, he reached for the bedside phone and dialed Erica's apartment. The *femme de ménage* answered, recognized Mace's voice, and told him *La Comtesse* was resting. "When she wakes, tell her I'll come by at six and we'll dine out."

"Very well, *M'sieu*."

He hung up, wondering why Erica had not called him, and got off the bed. For a while he watched a TV production of the Bolshoi Ballet, then switched to a news channel. The third item reported the death of international financier Vartan Chakirian, who had been missing for several days. The body was discovered in a wooded area on his estate by servants. Chakirian had been a director of the International Financial Trust, whose failure closed many banks and ruined numerous shareholders. The late financier was never suspected of embezzlement, which was charged to Spanish Count Carlos de Montaner, whose death occurred earlier in the week at a Lyon hotel. Accidental electrocution while bathing was given as the cause by Lyonnais authorities. The death of Vartan Chakirian was attributed to heart failure.

Turning to results of the Monte Carlo regatta—

Mace switched off the picture, relieved that Covici's men had set the death scene so crediby. And there was no urgent need to clear Carlos's name. With the confession tape Erica could rehabilitate her late husband when convenient.

He opened his safe and slid the account sheets into a large envelope, sealed it, and wrote across the face: *Property of Bradley Mason.* He asked Jean-Paul to take it to Jules Samuelson for safekeeping. That done, he dressed and went out to a florist shop, where he ordered a large arrangement delivered to Erica.

At six he parked in front of Erica's building and went up to her apartment. She met him at the door in a black silk dress, black satin shoes, and a necklace of black pearls. "Mace! How wonderful to see you," she exclaimed, and flowed into his arms. He kissed her, careful not to smudge her lipstick, and as she drew him inside he noticed suitcases by the door. "You're leaving."

"Yes," she sighed, "for Madrid. Carlos's funeral services are day after tomorrow."

"I should have thought of that. But even in widow's weeds you look terrific. Ah—no veil?"

She smiled. "Not until I leave the plane. Dear, I'm afraid we won't have time to dine tonight."

He frowned. "You could have called, told me."

"I know, I know, but I've been so tied up in so many things, countless calls from Montaners, *Maître* Schreiber, Jules . . . Oh, I haven't seen the tape you left for me, but Jules told me about it. Imagine— Carlos dies and Chakirian confesses—or was it the other way around?"

"Who knows? Anyway, it's yours to do with as you choose."

"And I'm grateful, the Montaners will be, too. Since we can't dine let's at least have a drink together. There's only champagne, I'm afraid."

He took a bottle of Bollinger Brut from the fridge while Erica found glasses. Mace popped the cork and poured. "What shall we drink to?"

"Oh, I don't know," she said carelessly, "you say it."

"Then, here's to crime." He touched her glass with his, but she shook her head. "That's not awfully appropriate, dear, can't you come up with something better?"

"Continued success," he said, and they sipped together.

"Much better," she pronounced, and they sat together on the sofa. Looking around, Mace said, "I have this sense of being abandoned—just when all our dreams are coming true."

"But I'm *not* abandoning you, don't even think it," she protested. "We'll be together sooner than we thought, not having to wait for my divorce."

"Good point." He sipped thoughtfully. "Where've you been since Geneva?"

"Viborg—you know that. I even called you from there."

But were you there? he wondered. "Then your mother said you'd come to Paris."

"I did—but you were nowhere to be found. Your secretary was very unhelpful and even Jules didn't know your whereabouts. So, where were you?"

"Out of the country on business."

"I assumed that, but we were out of touch for, oh, such a long time." She glanced at her platinum wristwatch.

"Obviously everything went well with Carlos's escape to France."

"Just as you planned it, dear. No one saw him leave Geneva or enter France. At Divonne I distracted the driver while Carlos got out of the trunk." She sipped again. "Perfect timing."

He nodded. "One thing surprised me—Carlos using an electric shaver. He doesn't—didn't—seem the type."

"Well, he thought it was easier than carrying razor and shaving cream as he moved around God knows where. So we bought the razor while we were shopping for his clothes."

"Foresighted," Mace observed. "Police ask you any questions?"

"No, why should they?"

"Never know about police. They tend to make much of little."

"But there's nothing to be made of anything, dear, can't you see that?"

"Oh, call me a worrier. I suppose you've talked with *Maître* Schreiber about recovering the bail."

She nodded. "Two million dollars isn't something I want to leave lying around."

"Or the half-million maintenance money."

"Actually, I reduced that by half."

"A substantial saving," he remarked. "But you'll never have to concern yourself with such trifles."

"That's true. Once I have the full inheritance."

"I worried more about you than I did about Carlos," he told her, "and now I realize I shouldn't have. Nothing went wrong, you did everything right." He drained his glass. "Think the Montaners will put up a fight over your inheritance?"

"Possibly. But, what could they do?"

"I've been thinking about that. Wondering if they'll hire investigators to track Carlos from Geneva to Lyon, question the bus drivers, the hotel clerk, room maid . . . Little people often have long memories that can be refreshed when money is passed around."

He watched her frown. "But would Marisol and the others *do* that?"

"Put yourself in their place, Erica, watching all Carlos's holdings pass out of the family into the hands of a foreigner. You'd fight that, so would I." He got up and brought back the Bollinger, refilled their glasses. "Here I looked forward to a night of scarves and switches, find you're leaving, and now we're talking of unpleasant possibilities." He shook his head. "I don't think you'll recover that bail money if the Swiss suspect you aided and abetted Carlos's escape."

"But only you know that."

"Schreiber must have his suspicions, although his lips are sealed—like mine."

She squeezed his hand. "You're wonderful."

"You're pretty wonderful yourself—amazing even."

"Amazing?"

"Uh-huh. The way you managed everything, planned it all out, and never let me suspect what you had in mind. Congratulations are definitely in order." He sipped from his glass, avoiding eye contact. Finally she said, "But Mace, you're not suggesting I—"

"Erica, c'mon, I'm not stupid. I'm just concerned that smart investigators could put together a credible scenario with you as the star." He smiled disarmingly.

"I— I don't understand."

He shrugged. "So much will depend on how really careful you were. Hell, I can visualize you, the supportive wife, riding that bus to Lyon with Carlos, picking that small hotel and not registering at the desk with him. Going up the back way to his room, drawing a hot, relaxing bath for him, then dropping in the shaver. Waiting until he stopped convulsing to make sure—before sneaking out the way you came." He nodded in feigned admiration. "Taking a bus back to Divonne, being careful not to be seen entering the hotel and your room when it was already daylight and the casino long closed . . ." He looked at her eyes; her face was frozen. The Ice Princess again. "That's what investigators could surmise, and for details they'd look for witnesses—anyone who saw you where you weren't supposed to be. They'll check to find out whether Carlos's face was clean shaven—"

"Why?"

"If he'd already shaved would he take the shaver to his bath? Questions like that, dear, so remember it's to the Montaners' advantage to raise the premise that you killed Carlos. You had motive: money and divorce—the investigators' job is to establish opportunity."

"Mace, please, you're frightening me."

"Sorry. I just wanted to lay it all out the way a professional will look at it. Of course, the Montaners may never make a move, passively accepting their loss." He paused. "But that's not the way rich families stay rich." Her body was rigid, a look of desperation in her eyes. "Even if nothing could be proved they could create a lot of difficulties for you, postpone your inheriting for years." He sighed. "Why didn't you ask for my help?"

She swallowed, moistened dry lips. "I hinted at it soon after we met, but—"

"I remember. I said I wasn't in the murder business. Well, maybe it will all work out to your advantage." He drained his glass and got up. "You've done marvelously well so far." He looked at his watch. "Flying on Iberia?"

"Yes—but we have a few minutes. Please tell me what I ought to do."

"It's pretty simple: play the sorrowing widow to the hilt, ask the Montaners for advice, make them believe you couldn't possibly have zapped their pride and joy, and by all means placate them at every opportunity. And don't be stingy."

She looked up at him. "Stingy?"

"Let them keep a castle, a favorite townhouse, land, a ranch, you'll make instant allies. And you'll need them. It's their turf, Erica, not yours. If necessary, be subservient—after all, you're a commoner in their eyes, and a foreigner at that." He drew in a deep breath. "Finally, stay out of France, French jurisdiction until you're very sure there's no possible danger of prosecution. Travel, spend time in Denmark while the Montaners forget you . . ."

"But, dear, that could be a long time. What about us? Everything we planned?"

"Life doesn't always work out as we'd like it to. We can't foresee every contingency—like a death in the family. Adjustments have to be made, like it or not."

Her eyes narrowed. "I don't like what I'm hearing."

"I liked you best while I was convinced you were doing everything possible to free Carlos primarily for his sake. The way things happened I think you wanted him free to carry out your plan. In prison his life was safe. Once out . . ." He spread his hands. "Carlos told me you wanted him dead, warned me about you. Even now I don't know what you really think of me—lover or useful fool? Carlos had his failings and he married you under false pretenses, but he didn't deserve to be murdered. Knowing what you did, how you used me, I wonder what you'd do if you tired of me or decided I was getting out of line, and I don't think I'd sleep very well."

"But, darling, I love you, I could never harm you."

"Maybe not, but it's something to think about."

"You mean—?"

"We need a breather, Erica, space between us while we decide what's best for each of us."

"You may be right," she said tightly.

"After the funeral you'll be involved with estate lawyers for weeks—maybe months—and having me around in Madrid would complicate everything unnecessarily."

"And while I'm doing all those things that have to be done, what will you be doing, love? Where will you be?"

"I'm giving up Secours."

"You are? Oh, I'm so glad." He wondered if she was going to clap hands childishly, but she said, "Then there'll be nothing to hold you to Paris."

"Only memories."

"But you'll have me, dear, and wherever we are we'll make ourselves new memories, wonderful ones to replace ugly ghosts." Her face was almost glowing.

"And the deceit," he said in a strained voice. "Unknowingly I've been your accomplice, and that will be hard to forget." He swallowed. "I don't know where we'll meet again, or when. I must have loved you because I find it so hard to say good-bye."

"I love you," she said simply. "Don't make it all in vain."

"For me the hardest part is this: I'll always remember you as you were the day Jules brought you to my office. And I'll try to forget this mourner's black—it clashes with other memories."

"Don't be a hypocrite, you've killed."

"Never to enrich myself." He turned away.

"I'll call you from Spain."

"Perhaps," he said, and left.

Below, her Bentley had pulled up behind his car. Recognizing him, the chauffeur touched his cap. *"Bon soir, M'sieu."*

"Bon soir, Charles. The countess is ready to go."

"Merci." He touched his cap again and walked off to bring out her bags. Mace started the engine and looked up at her apartment windows. When lights went off he drove away.

Almost unseeingly, he steered up the Champs-Elysées, rounded the Etoile, and headed over into the Left Bank. For a while he drank in the Jazz Caveau, thinking he might encounter Monique Denoize again. But he didn't see the little slut in the crowd and decided that she was gone, too, like Erica and the others. Gone beyond recall.

Slowly, unsteadily, he drove home, managed to enter without setting off the alarm, and went to bed. His last conscious vision was of Erica, enjoying wine in the first-class compartment as the plane carried her ever closer to Madrid.

thirty-one

The Clients

Two weeks after the discovery of Vartan Chakirian's body French fiscal authorities entered his office and broke open the hidden safe. Mace was surprised and pleased by their prompt response to his anonymous, phoned tip, and in banking circles expectations were high that IFT's embezzled millions would be recovered. But a week later the public learned that only 6 percent of the stolen hoard remained for distribution—barely enough to cover lawyers' fees. The far greater portion was assumed to be lost forever.

At a table outside Rond Point brasserie, Mace relaxed in the late spring warmth, watched pedestrians pass by, and heard the hum of cars along the Champs as he sipped his second *fine* and fingered the color postcard that had reached him an hour ago. Mailed in Rome, it showed an aerial view of St. Peter's Square. On the other side Selina had written:

> My Dearest Friend: The surgeon completely
> restored me, and Pascal and I have been
> traveling for a week. Next month we will be
> married at Punta di Volpe and count on your
> presence and your blessing.
>   Your ever-grateful, always-loving
>
> Selina

For her, he thought moodily, the end of a long, twisted road. Freed of her father's cruel shadow, she was emerging into a world of light and happiness. He wouldn't be at the wedding to distract them from each other, but he would send a million of her father's stolen dollars to secure her independence should things not work out as a mafioso's wife.

All the rest of their sequestered millions he had decided to return to IFT's conservators; Jules and Bernard Samuelson could arrange discreet, anonymous transfer. Less the four million in his Banque Suisse-Allemagne account he was keeping as a finder's fee.

Mace tucked the postcard in a pocket, drained his cup, and idly watched two expensively dressed women walking toward the café. One was in her early forties, with dark hair and a voluptuously mature figure. Her companion was slender and much younger, with a turned-up nose and coppery hair that crowned her shoulders in a free fall. She was wearing a salmon-colored blouse and designer jeans so tightly fitted as to accent the cleft of her crotch. Their faces resembled each other's, and both were unusually attractive. Reaching the sidewalk tables, the women stopped and looked around as though orienting themselves, finally gazing at Mace and hesitantly approaching.

After glancing at each other the elder spoke.

"Pardon me, are you Bradley Mason?"

"I am." He stood up.

"Your secretary said we might find you here." She paused. "I'm Barbara Bellinger and this is my daughter, Sandy."

"Please sit down." He drew back chairs and sat as they did. "If you were thinking of hiring me, my secretary should have told you I've given up Secours." The daughter's eyes were chestnut brown, her mother's a startling gray-blue.

"She told us that, but I persisted. You see, Mr. Mason, we have a rather difficult problem—"

"No," Sandy interrupted, "it's *my* problem, I want that understood."

Her mother covered her hand with *hers*. "Dear, we do things together, face things together." To Mace she said, "An old friend gave me your name, and—"

"Who was that?"

"Alaya al-Jamal—you remember her—and her son?"

"Very well," he admitted. "How are they?"

"Just fine—now that she's a widow. And she asked me to convey her regards and continuing appreciation. She told me that but for you she wouldn't have Rashid with her."

Mace shrugged. "Probably an exaggeration—but I'm not working anymore. I can give you the name of a reliable agency—"

"Wouldn't be the same," Barbara Bellinger said firmly, as Mace felt her knee brush his. Her daughter's hand rested casually on his thigh and he saw her lips form a smile. "Not at all," Sandy murmured. "The way Alaya praised you we know we really need you."

Both of you? he wondered, then Barbara said, "Won't you at least hear what the problem is?"

He nodded. "I owe that much to Alaya."

"It's blackmail," Barbara said. "Sandy came to Europe after her father's death, and—"

"Met this gorgeous Italian stud in Monte Carlo," her daughter finished. "I took him everywhere, bought him jewelry, clothes, a Ferrari—paid his casino losses, and that wasn't enough," she said bitterly. "The bastard took pictures of us while were in—ah, intimate positions." She paused. "Like, me with my bare butt in the air while I'm chomping on—"

"Please, Sandy," her mother interrupted, "I'm sure Mister Mason can visualize the scene without such graphic description." She looked at Mace, who said, "I can. And now he wants to sell the photos, right?"

"Right," Sandy echoed. "Obviously you've heard this story before—or others like it."

"Blackmail is alive and flourishing in Paris and the Côte d'Azur. How much does he want?"

"Two hundred thousand dollars," Barbara replied.

"Can you afford it?"

"Easily." Sandy turned to her mother. "But I refuse to pay. He'd make more prints and sell them, too. Paolo turned out to be a real shit."

"He did," Barbara agreed," and I won't have my daughter's nudity shown all over Montana to titillate every damn rancher we know." Her knee pressure increased and her face seemed slightly flushed.

"My attitude exactly," said Sandy, moving her hand over Mace's thigh. "Would you be willing to persuade the prick to return those photos—and negatives?"

Mace touched his chin. "Possibly. Why don't you ladies have coffee and give me some details?"

Barbara said, "I have a better idea, Mister Mason. We're at the Crillon. Let's lunch in the suite and discuss it in a relaxed atmosphere. If you're free, that is."

"I am—if you'll call me Mace."

"And I'm Bobbie." She turned to her daughter. "Hon, I just had a brilliant idea. Wouldn't it be wonderful to have Mace visit us in Montana? Alaya would love to see him, and we'd be as hospitable as we possibly could." She touched Mace's hand possessively. "We'd make you really comfortable, give you that down-home feeling we all need." She paused as her daughter nodded agreement. "Since you're leaving Paris anyway."

So Yasmi had told them. He sighed. "I couldn't decline so generous an invitation without a lot of thought."

"Then you'll really consider it?" Sandy asked, and Mace nodded.

Riding between them as they taxied down the Champs, Mace reflected that neutralizing the blackmailing stud wasn't an overwhelming problem. He could take care of it himself, or set Covici on him. In the event he decided to help the Bellinger ladies . . .

He felt the seductive warmth of their bodies as they wedged together on the narrow seat, and he thought that although Bobbie and Sandy might be his last clients they could also become the most stimulating ones he had ever known.